COLD ANGEL

P J PEACOCK

Other works by this author

The Call of Echoes

Towers of London

A Serpent in Amber

For

S

Prologue

LONDON 1943

The old man raised his face to the corrugated roof of the A.R.P. shelter in Harmsworth Park and listened to the air raid siren as it moaned out a warning across Lambeth.

'Blimey. Don't them buggers ever sleep?'

Across the upturned beer crate that served as a table, the playing cards that were fanned out in the young boy's hand began to shake.

'Now never you mind about that, young William,' said a second old man to the boy, a veteran of the Great War just like the first. He passed William a mug of tea, taking the cards from the boy's hand. 'Now, let's see what you've got – fifteen two, fifteen four, and one for his knob.' He broke another matchstick in half and studied the holes in the cribbage board. He looked up. ''Ere, the young 'un's getting the hang of this good an' proper.'

'Need to play a good hand of cards if yer going to follow that dad of yours into the army,' said the old man. ''Ave yer ruddy boot laces off yer if yer can't.'

The veteran counted up William's score and glanced over at him.

'Still waiting for those call up papers, son?'

William nodded.

'Blimey, boy,' grumbled the old man. 'What they waiting for, ruddy Christmas? It'll all be over by the time they gets you into khaki.'

'Good job if it is,' came back the veteran. 'You don't want to do no soldiering unless yer can 'elp it son, take my word for it.'

'Ain't nothing wrong in doing service.' protested the old man. 'First in our street to volunteer in 1914, I was. In the front line when the first shot was fired.'

5

'Yeah and back home by the time they fired the second.' The veteran chuckled with a wink at the boy.

Suddenly William's ears pricked to a noise outside. A bicycle was being pedalled towards the shelter across the grass. A second later he heard it drop to the ground. He saw a hand come around the blackout curtain.

'Cor, I reckon you Bobbies must be able to smell tea a mile off,' the old man moaned, seeing the visiting policeman.

'Well, I won't say no if you're offering. It's brass monkeys out there tonight.' The policeman slipped off his bicycle clips and rubbed the warmth back into his hands. 'By the way, I thought I saw a light showing on me way over. Oswin Street it was. Newington Mansions.

The old man passed the policeman a mug of tea.

'Newington Mansions? That old lodging house?'

'Yeah. Top floor it was.'

After a moment the old man gave a sigh, then began to pull on his helmet. 'Oh well, no peace for the wicked.' He lifted his eyes at William. 'Come on young fella-me-lad, we'd best take a look.'

*

'Getting another contact, sir, bearing south, south east.'

Major Charles Armstrong clicked his fingers impatiently in the back of the radio detection truck.

'Map, corporal!'

Armstrong was known as the "rat-catcher". He was on the trail of three I.R.A. quislings: Two men and a red haired girl. They had been a thorn in his side ever since the outbreak of war. Now he was closing in.

With the map laid across the vehicle's bench, Armstrong's eyes flicked across it. 'Distance?' he barked.

The radio operator cupped his hand to his headphones. His voice was excited.

'No more than a mile, sir.'

Armstrong was already pulling open his dividers across the map. Swinging them in an arc over the lower half of Lambeth, he shouted to the man behind the wheel. 'All right, driver. St. George's Circus, and fast.'

*

'Blimey, would you Adam and Eve it,' said the old man. 'I'll 'ave their guts for garters.' He and William were standing in the middle of Oswin Street, looking up at Newington Mansions. A bright light was showing through a rent in the curtains at the top floor window. William took his eyes from it and turned them to the night sky; he'd heard the faint drone of aircraft. 'Can you see 'em yet, son?' the old man asked.

'Not yet,' replied William, his eyes searching the darkness.

'Well, it'll only take two ticks to sort this light out. And then we can get ourselves off to the shelter down at the Elephant.'

The boy felt the old man's hand in the middle of his back. He was hurriedly steered towards the house.

After mounting the front steps, William watched the old man tap on the front door, but there was no reply. The old man knocked again, then tried the door. It was unlocked. He pushed it open. They both went inside.

*

'We're right on top of their signal, sir. Clear as a bell. Can't be more than a few streets away.'

As the truck screeched to a halt just past Harmsworth Park, Major Armstrong drew another circle on the map. He stabbed at the centre.

'All right, sergeant. Get onto H.Q., will you. I need some more men down here. I want a cordon around the whole place.'

'Sir!'

Armstrong pulled back the canvas flap at the rear of the truck. He jumped down with his men.

He found the street deserted, the road shining as if it had been polished, the drizzle turning to ice upon its surface. Overhead the pulsating throb of aircraft engines was getting nearer. A couple of searchlights snapped into life down on the Embankment and shot two cones of light up into the inky sky. The beams flicked back and forth as they battled to pierce the darkness, but they were blunted by impenetrable cloud.

7

From the North Bank of the Thames there came the boom of anti aircraft guns as they blazed away at their unseen enemy. It was followed almost immediately by the *crump, crump, crump* of exploding bombs, their detonations punctuating the night with red orange balls of flame.

Armstrong motioned to his men and they started walking, though they had moved no more than a few paces when behind them came the whistle of a bomb that sent them diving for cover. The ensuing detonation ripped through a house opposite, blowing off the roof and raining debris down onto the road, the sharp roof tiles shattering as they landed, skimming through the air like tiny scimitars, a handful of which Armstrong caught full in the face.

Then there was a rumble like thunder beneath their feet and a build up of pressure before an ear-piercing shriek. The tarmac in front of them unfurled as a gas main exploded, sending up chunks of concrete, earth and rubble. Out of the crater there came a giant blue column of fire that looked deceptively cold, though they were cowered by its heat. Armstrong looked across at his men who were lying on their stomachs taking cover.

'Get those men up, Sergeant Morris,' ordered Armstrong, undaunted by the raid and the blood that was streaming down his cheeks.

As the men rose they were instantly rocked by another explosion and were pinned down once more. Armstrong felt a sudden pressure on his chest and the breath was knocked out of him. He stumbled to the ground, his head thick with the blast. After a moment he looked up through the dust and debris and saw that Sergeant Morris was shouting at him, but Armstrong could not hear him above the ringing in his ears. Then Morris began pointing and Armstrong followed his gaze. Yes, he could see it – a suspicious light at the top floor of a building across the street: Newington Mansions.

*

William was making his way up the stairs behind the old man, the pair of them clinging for support to the banister rail as the whole house shook in the teeth of the raid. Downstairs they had checked the rooms and had found no one, all having gone to the shelter. As they made their way up the stairwell, the old man called to anyone who might still be there, but his words were lost in the thunderous noise from the falling bombs.

As they neared the top landing, William suddenly cried: *'Look!'*

His keen eyes had spotted a sliver of light that was seeping from the bottom of a door.

The old man went across to investigate. He knocked on the door and called, but his voice was yet again muffled as the house shuddered from another explosion. He put his hand to the door handle and turning it, pushed it open.

From where he stood out on the landing, looking into the room, William could see a young red haired woman inside. She was sitting at a dressing table with her back to him, her left elbow resting on the table's edge. For a moment William thought that she was listening to the radio that was directly in front of her, until she turned. It was then he saw the Morse key.

William went to shout a warning, but the old man had already taken one pace into the room. There an arm came from behind the door, jerking back the man's head. It tightened around his neck, and William looked on in horror as he saw a flash of steel, a thin blade finding its way between the old man's ribs.

For a moment William stood on the landing disabled with fear, until a second man appeared in the doorway. He was holding a revolver.

William began to back away, his eyes wide with terror. Then finding his feet he fled back across the landing and bolted down the stairs. Behind him the man with the revolver walked calmly to the top step where he took careful aim. Firing at the boy's retreating figure a round thudded into William's back. The force sent him tumbling to the landing below.

As William squirmed, the man took aim once more. The revolver kicked again.

The young red haired woman who had been at the transmitter, rushed out across the landing. She stood at the top of the stairs and looked down, her hands to her face. The man raised his revolver and ordered her back into the room. She returned and resumed her position at the transmitter, building back up to speed on the Morse key. Hurriedly she finished her transmission. She wound in the aerial.

*

Major Armstrong was taking the stairs two at a time, bounding up them towards the top floor. It took the body on the lower landing to slow him.

The boy was laying face down, his helmet askew and tipped backwards. Armstrong knelt down. Cautiously he put a hand to the dead boy's shoulder. He turned him over.

Armstrong stepped back, a sickness to his stomach. He grabbed the banister for support. Then he straightened, turning to the final flight of stairs as he raced up them, his revolver cocked and drawn.

Crossing the landing to the door, Armstrong barely checked his stride as he put his boot to it. The door shuddered on its hinges and swung open. An old man's body lay to one side. The remainder of the room was empty.

*

Outside it was quieter now. The air raid was over, the sound of bombs replaced by the crackle of burning buildings and the distant, but frantic clang of a fire engine's bell.

Sergeant Morris was breathless as he came into the room.

'They got away, sir . . . slipped out the back . . . . escaped over the gardens.' Morris went to the old man's body and knelt down beside it. He felt for a pulse. 'This one's had it, sir. The boy out there too.'

Armstrong did not speak. He was in a state of shock. He stared down at the oddments that had been left on the dressing table: an empty purse, a cracked hand mirror, a woman's hair brush with a long strand of red hair snagged across the bristles – the only clues to the death of his son, the young boy who lay murdered on the stairs.

10

Part One

Winter 1944

<u>1</u>

From the train, Kathleen O'Callaghan gazed out at the bleak English countryside. It must be nearly Christmas she thought, Christmas back home in Dublin with hot food on the table, a fire blazing in her father's grate, snow outside and candles flickering in the window of the little church across the street. Had it really been three years now? Three years of *this*?

Wearily she turned, unable to gaze upon the image of herself reflected in the window. She looked across at her brothers.

Eamonn was sleeping. His muscular arms were folded across his mighty chest. His broad shoulders rose and fell as he snored – a bull of a man.

Then there was Michael. Clever cunning Michael. Didn't he ever sleep? No. Even now she could see those intelligent brown eyes of his were trained on a soldier who was sitting opposite. The man had been there most of the journey, staring up at her suitcase.

'When are we due in at Cambridge?' the soldier had asked when the door to the compartment had slid open and a ticket inspector had appeared. The inspector had consulted his fob-watch.

'About half an hour.'

It was closer to forty minutes later when Kathleen noticed they were nearing the town, her view of the countryside replaced by houses – English houses with their backyards, their tarnished air raid shelters, lines of washing, rabbit hutches, their "Dig for Victory" vegetable patches. Yes, it was a British victory now – at least theirs

11

for the taking. Not that she cared.

She felt the train quiver and begin to slow, then it came into the station where it lurched to a halt with a heavy belch of dirty steam. Carriage doors began to crash open. Michael shook Eamonn awake. Kathleen began to rise from her seat. Reaching up to the rack to retrieve her suitcase, the soldier got there first.

'Here luv. I'll take that.'

Michael was there in a flash.

'The lady can manage.'

'All right chum. Just offering.'

A cold gust of air greeted Kathleen as she stepped down from the train. It hit her squarely as it howled down the station. Pinching the collar of her thin summer raincoat she began to trudge forwards. She lugged the heavy case at her side.

Going down the wet platform the sleety hail peppered her face. The wind blasted her eyes. The rain soaked in through the holes in her worn out shoes. Struggling on she noticed a poster. *"Is your journey really necessary?"*

She would have laughed. But she'd forgotten how.

'Will yer come on!' Michael bellowed at her after they had left the railway station, Kathleen falling behind with the heavy suitcase as they headed for the town.

'Yes, Michael. I'm coming.'

'Well see that yer do. Or you'll be getting me boot up yer arse.'

She knew that Michael did not want her out of his sight – not after a time in Coventry.

'You'll not tell Da about Coventry will yer, Michael? Nor McManus. Promise me – promise!'

When they reached the town they found it practically deserted, empty but for groups of servicemen who walked like muffled ghosts about the streets and alleyways. The light was failing now. And although the blackout regulations had been relaxed, force of habit still prevailed: curtains were being drawn. Blinds were being pulled. Before long, Kathleen and her brothers were swallowed up in the gloom, stumbling on as they searched for a lodging house.

Eventually they found one that would take them. It was opposite a large building where cloaked figures shuffled back and forth in the darkness. *A convent?*

Kathleen bumped into one of the cloaked figures, assuming her to be a nun.

'Oh I beg your pardon, Sister.'

The cloaked figure passed her by, her face unseen, all but for the glowing end of a cigarette.

'That's all right, ducks.'

Kathleen turned. She crossed the road to the lodging house.

It was another place like so many she'd seen before, her room the same as hundreds of others – rooms she'd inhabited before slipping into the night, leaving behind her nothing but the haunting click of Morse. There was a chair, a dressing table, a single bed, the pillow which was Brylcreem stained. There was an unlit gas fire coupled to a meter, a drawn blackout curtain at the window. Snapping open the catches of her suitcase, she lifted the lid.

The transmitter looked innocent enough, she thought, nestling amongst her raggedy clothes, concealed as it was within the casing of an ordinary looking wireless. She had been schooled in her trade by a German called Kreuz, brought in off the west coast of Ireland by arrangement with her father. The man had taught her Morse in her father's back room, drumming the alphabet into her by rote. Not that she minded back then. In fact she had been flattered, proud to have been "chosen". Pulling the radio out of the suitcase she stood it on the side of the dresser. Strangely it gave the place a homely feel.

The room she'd been given in the lodging house was at the front. Her brothers had taken one on the floor above. They were nice clean room according to the landlady – soldiers' rooms – soldiers who'd been billeted on her and who'd gone on leave. Kathleen recalled Michael's face at the mention of the word "soldiers". Once again she'd seen the caution in his eyes.

'Soldiers, yer say missus?'

'Yes – infantry – nice bunch.'

Then they had followed the *clap, clap, clap* of the landlady's carpet slippers across the hallway and up the stairs. 'You boys not in the forces yourselves then?'

'No, missus. We're conscript exempt. Just here looking for work – you know – for the war effort.'

The landlady said that that was good of them – patriotic. Then she had showed them down a dingy hallway to one of the rooms, telling them there was a dugout at the bottom of the garden. 'In case you need to shelter from any stray doodlebugs.'

Michael cast his eyes around the flea-bitten room. Kathleen heard him mumble

'Doodlebugs? Bedbugs more like.'

*

At 8 o'clock that night, Michael and Eamonn came to Kathleen's room. There they lit cigarettes. They draped themselves over the furniture.

'McManus is paying us a visit tomorrow,' announced Michael, exhaling a lazy stream of cigarette smoke as he lay on her bed. Kathleen shuddered. Sean McManus was their quartermaster, their enforcer.

'Is it about the money?' Eamonn inquired. 'Are yer going ter ask him for it, Mikey?'

'That's his job isn't it?' spat Michael. 'We've had nothin' in our pockets since Coventry. Not since she . . . . '

Kathleen saw Michael look across at her. She could see the disgust in his eyes. 'I hope yer got yer story straight for him,' Michael added. 'Yer know what McManus thinks of people who do that sort'o thing. And he's a terrible man when he's gets the drink inside him.'

'So that's it, Michael. You told him?' said Kathleen. 'You went and told him about Coventry.'

'Aye. I did that. And Da too.'

'You told Da? But . . . . but what did he say Michael? What did he say?'

'Oh nothin' much. Just that you'll have ta be punished – just like yer poor cousin Mary.'

Kathleen's stomach knotted with fear. She remembered her cousin well – pretty some said – until McManus had thrown the acid.

*

When her brothers had left the room, Kathleen sat fretting about her punishment, about that time in Coventry. She had been working at a factory back then she recalled, in a machine shop making tank parts, earning money for her brothers. They had often put her to work like that, when they had drunk and gambled away what little cash McManus had brought them. But oh, they had always made a point of dragging themselves away from their pleasures come Friday, she remembered: pay day – her wages. Back then they'd left her penniless. She'd had no option.

 Kathleen went to the window and pulled aside the blackout curtain an inch. She looked out into the impenetrable darkness. Maybe the convent across the road would offer her sanctuary, she wondered, that's if she could slip out unnoticed. Though she wagered that Michael had somehow thought of that. Yes, he'd be watching – watching from his room upstairs – watching with those intelligent brown eyes of his. No, she was condemned to her fate, to her quartermaster's will, just like her cousin. Besides, in truth she knew she'd find no sanctuary in God's house. God had abandoned her.

It was icy cold in the room and she went to the bed and drew off the bedspread, dragging it to the unlit fire. Then, after brushing her hair and tidying herself in front of the mirror, she went and settled down on the bedspread on the floor, listening for a moment to the sudden wail of the air raid siren, then the drone of a solitary doodlebug that filled the skies somewhere over the town. The landlady was right: a stray. They were overshooting London, most probably. Or perhaps coming in from the east, across the North Sea. Then again she had heard they were even being dropped by German aircraft now, such was their desperation.

Desperation. She knew it well, laying there as she listened to the doodlebug's drone getting louder and louder, coming nearer and nearer, hearing its engine splutter before finally cutting out, praying in that moment, in that terrible bleak moment, that it would find its target and end things. But, a few seconds later, she heard it land nearby, safely but with the most enormous *crump,* Kathleen feeling the bomb's huge vacuum as the floor rose beneath her body, seeing the ensuing and tremendous flash that for a while lit up the room, its brilliance defying even the thickness of the blackout curtains.

And then all was calm again. And cheated by fate's hand, she slipped her own into her purse. And taking out every sixpence she owned, she loaded them into the gas meter and turned on the tap, laying back down.

Regrets filled her mind. Gas flooded her lungs. All quiet now. All hushed save for the steady hiss from the fire's unlit grille.

*

Kathleen had always known the start of it: that freezing winter's day before the war, that time when the men had come to her father's house. He was a powerful figure was her Da, the Dublin Commander of the Irish Republican Army. Yes, he was a big man. Everyone knew Patrick O'Callaghan. Feared him too.

She had been but a child back then when the men had called, a child happily skipping without a care, shoeless in the grimy backyard. She remember that Eamonn had been there too, sitting looking up at her, his chubby knees stung red raw by the cold. Sweet Jesus it had been bitter that day. Only Ma had been truly warm, sweating in the washhouse at the end of the yard, bent over her boiling tubs.

Da was in the house in his usual chair, receiving the men as they began to assemble, the ageing band of Republican Nationalists filing in. Young Michael was already there, at Da's feet. Then she and Eamonn were summoned in from the yard. The next thing Kathleen remembered was being in the parlour, then watching Da pull the cork from a full bottle of Jameson's whiskey, then throwing the stopper irretrievably into the fire. She recalled the men's faces at the gesture; it was to be the full story, the one she'd heard so many times before: six glorious days in 1916 when the air had crackled with gunfire: the Easter rising.

'I remember it as if it was yesterday,' Da had begun to the

16

assembled crowd, taking a swig at the bottle and passing it around. 'Surrounded and out-numbered we were – British lead flying everywhere. And me with me own dear brother, Billy, lying dead in me arms.'

Heads had nodded sombrely.

'If only we'd had more rifles,' someone had spoken. 'Then we would have given them a beating – ran their ragged British arses right back across the water.'

'Ah, you're right there,' chipped in another. 'We'd not have seen 'em for dust.'

She'd watched Da as he'd leaned back in his chair. She'd heard him sigh.

'Ah, it would all be different if I could have me time again,' he'd said.

One of the men had shaken his head.

'Our time's over, Pat. It's the turn of the youngsters now. Have yer not read the papers? They say there's gonna be a war.'

Another man had leaned forward. She'd seen him nod at Michael who was listening wide eyed.

'Would yer send him, Pat? Would yer send young Michael to fight the British if it all blew up?'

'Now there's a silly question,' Da had said, ruffling Michael's hair. 'Of course I'd send him. He's my best boy.'

Kathleen watched the same man point his finger at Eamonn.

'And what about young Eamonn there Pat, would yer send Eamonn too?'

'Of course. He's an O'Callaghan, isn't he?'

The man had then turned his eyes on her, so Kathleen recalled. She saw him tip the whiskey bottle at her.

'And what about young Kathleen? Now surely yer wouldn't be sending the likes of *her*?'

She'd seen her Da wink at her – always remembered what he'd said.

'Kathleen? Ah, she'd be me first choice, so she would. She's me jewel in the crown.'

His jewel in his crown. Yes. *And* more, especially on those nights when he'd come home drunk from Cahill's bar.

*

There came the sound of tapping. Kathleen could not make it out. A code? A cipher? Morse? It did not make sense.

Tap, tap, tap – it came again. This time it woke her.

She came round suddenly. With a gasp she filled her lungs. She opened her eyes.

It was morning – that much she knew. For she could hear the busy chirping of birds outside. Dizzily she turned. She looked across the room.

Yes, she could make it out now – the tapping was coming from the door – the insistent rap of knuckles – the landlady? The next moment she could hear the woman's voice calling from out on the landing: 'Coo-ie dear. Are you awake? I've something for you.'

Slowly Kathleen pulled herself together. She rose to her feet. She went across and pulled the door open. The landlady was standing there, proffering a cup of tea.

'Morning dear. Thought you might like this.'

Kathleen forced a smile.

'What? . . . . oh yes . . . . that's kind.'

The landlady told her not to mention it. She passed her the cup.

'Now drink it while it's hot. You look like you could do with it. What, didn't you sleep – that bomb I expect. Close wasn't it? What a noise! Never mind. We're all in one piece.'

The woman turned to walk down the landing, telling Kathleen that she was going to fetch some coal for the fires and the kitchen range. 'Breakfast in about half an hour, that all right?'

Kathleen muttered a reply. She closed the door.

In her room she slowly collected herself. Her head still throbbed from the gas, though obviously it had not done its work. Something had gone wrong. Horribly wrong. It had just left her feeling sick and groggy. She went over to the window. She let in some air.

Looking out she could see that a heavy fall of snow had settled overnight, forming a thick white carpet over everything: the

18

pavement, the street, the rooftops, the convent across the road. No, wait! It wasn't a convent at all. She had been mistaken – mistaken too, she guessed about the nun she had seen in the darkness the previous night. For clearly the woman had been a nurse in cap and gown, and the building was nothing more than a hospital.

*

It was mid afternoon when McManus came – closing time, the stink of whiskey on his breath, the stench of the alehouse on his clothes. Michael and Eamonn had come to Kathleen's room to wait for him, Eamonn by the window, picking at his nails with his lock-knife, Michael lying on her bed, his brown eyes scanning the newspaper. Kathleen felt bound up with nerves as she sat at her dressing table, her index finger tapping out a tense and habitual flurry of Morse.

'Fer Christ sakes, will yer shut that up!' Michael screwed up his newspaper as he rolled off the bed.

Kathleen knew he was edgy too, wary of McManus. It was the acid in Cousin Mary's face that kept him so. The attack had been carried out on her Da's orders, so Kathleen had heard; punishment for a similar offence to her own. The vitriol had burned right down to Mary's jawbone. And all while McManus had just stood there. Yes, thought Kathleen as she sat waiting, justice came swift and brutal from their quartermaster.

But the next moment she heard a thump on the door downstairs. McManus!

It was Michael who greeted him at Kathleen's door. Kathleen watched as the quartermaster shook his hand, the pair of them sharing words before McManus stepped inside. His eyes were piercingly blue. His hair wiry, the colour of rusty nails. He shook hands with Eamonn too, then Michael said. 'Have yer brought the money with yer, Sean?' His voice was insistent.

McManus told him not to start with the "belly-aching", and "have I not just walked through the door?" Then producing a bottle of Jameson's from his coat pocket he said. 'Can a man not have a civilised drink first?'

Eamonn was first in line as the bottle was opened, grinning as

19

Kathleen watched him proffer her tooth mug. Michael had found a tea cup and had shot the dregs to the floor. After McManus had filled the cups, Michael asked again about the money. 'Yer realise that we're flat broke, don't yer?'

McManus nodded.

'I know, Michael. But it won't be long now – six months at the most and the war'll be over.'

'And what are we meant to do in the mean time? You know there's soldiers billeted in this house?'

'Then find somewhere better, why don't yer.'

'With what? I told yer – we're flat broke. And what about the transmitter? It's time we got rid.'

'*I'll* tell yer when it's time to get rid, Michael. Now have another drink . . . .'

Kathleen saw McManus refill Michael's cup, then she saw McManus look across at her. She looked away, but he started to come over. He stopped beside her and sat down on the edge of the dressing table. A moment later Kathleen felt the rough tip of his finger slide beneath her chin. Slowly his hand turned her face towards his own. 'And what's this I've been hearing, Kathleen? Michael's been telling me things.'

Kathleen looked up into his eyes. She knew he meant Coventry.

'I'm sorry, Sean. It won't happen again. I promise it won't.'

McManus gave her a thin smile, Kathleen glimpsing the glint of a gold tooth somewhere between his barely parted lips.

'Ah, but promises are easily broken, Kathleen. Sometimes we need a reminder. Yer see me ears are telling me one thing, but me heart is telling me another. Yes, it's a reminder is what we need.'

As he spoke, Kathleen saw McManus reach into his coat. She became petrified as she saw the glint of a small bottle from his pocket. But just then Michael's voice broke in: 'Okay Sean, we keep the transmitter. We could use it to get help – persuade the Germans into sending a ship – *anything*. But in the meantime what about the money? We *must* have that money.'

McManus rounded on Michael instead. He went over and stared

menacingly at him.

'Hasn't the penny dropped yet, Michael? Are yer stupid, is that what yer are? I *have* no money for yer, don't yer understand?'

Michael came straight back.

'That's a lie,' he stormed. 'Da's agreement was money for information. And we've given plenty – risked our lives.' Michael levelled his finger. 'Yer know I wouldn't be surprised if you and Da were not lining yer own pockets an' ... '

'That's enough, Michael!' barked McManus. 'Now just hold yer tongue and remember who yer talking to.'

McManus stared Michael down, then snatched up his whiskey bottle. He took a generous gulp then pulled a hand across his mouth. 'Yer know you've been away from Ireland too long. You've no idea what's going on back home. Sure there's money, but it's being spent elsewhere – yer Da's buying arms, explosives – making sure that when our time comes next . . . . *that's* why I've got no money for yer. *That's* why you've got to bide yer time – bide yer time 'til the war's end and a ship back home.'

Michael shrugged his shoulders. His mouth was set in a grim line.

'And until then, Sean? How are we meant to live?'

McManus' voice softened. 'Why, do what you've always done, Michael.' He flicked his eyes at Kathleen. 'Put the girl to work.'

For a moment neither man spoke. McManus simply moved across to the window where he leaned his bulk against the frame and took another swig of whiskey. Then Michael lifted his chin at him and said.

'Work is it? And where's the girl gonna find work in a place like this?'

McManus shrugged as he looked out the window.

'Ah there's always work if yer look for it, Michael.' He gestured with his whiskey bottle. 'Is that not a hospital over there? Could she not get some work scrubbing or cleaning or somethin'?'

Michael cast his eyes at the snow capped building.

'And if she gets up to her tricks like she did in Coventry?'

Kathleen saw McManus look across at her. She saw his hand go to his pocket, then the glint of the small bottle again. 'Just let her try, Michael. Just let her try!'

*

Not long after McManus' suggestion of work, Kathleen found herself cast outside the boarding house, trudging through the snow across the road to the hospital. It was bitter cold as she reached the entrance, and pausing she blew some warmth into her hands, looking up at a recruitment poster: *"Women! Now our men need you more than ever – be a nurse."*

Suddenly there was a voice at her side.

'Thinking of joining us?'

Kathleen looked across. A nursing sister had come down the hospital steps.

'No, but I *am* looking for work. I can cook and sew and wash and clean.'

The sister smiled.

'That's as maybe, but like the poster says – it's nurses we need.'

Kathleen shook her head.

'Oh I'm not clever like that. Besides, it takes years to become a nurse, doesn't it?'

The sister laughed.

'Yes, a fully qualified one. I'm not suggesting that! I'm talking about the nursing reserve. Training only takes a few days and then you'll be on the ward before you know it.' The sister nodded at her. 'Go on. Give it a try. The pay's not bad and then of course there's the uniform.'

Kathleen hesitated. A *uniform?* She looked back up at the poster. She looked down at her worn out shoes.

*

It was dark when Kathleen returned to the boarding house. Thankfully McManus had gone, though her brothers were still in her room, drunk on his whiskey. Eamonn was sat on her chair that he had turned back to front; his bristled jaw resting on his huge forearms. Michael was lying on her bed, smoking.

'Well? Did yer find work over in that hospital?' He blew smoke

22

towards the ceiling.

'I did that,' said Kathleen, clearing her throat before making her announcement. 'As a matter of fact I'm going to become a nurse.'

Michael looked at her. He burst out laughing.

'A nurse is it?' he roared. He looked across at his drunken brother. He jerked a thumb. 'Have yer heard this, Ea? The girl's going to become a nurse. And there's the likes o' her passing out whenever she sees blood!'

'I know,' laughed Eamonn. 'A nurse! Why, she'll shat her drawers!'

The two men continued goading her before Eamonn began to quieten. Kathleen could see he was thinking; there was a look like jealousy on his face. 'Nah, you're not doing it, Kathleen. I won't have it – all those . . . . *men!*'

'Is that so?'

'It is that. Besides, that's a military hospital over there,' he added, 'full of gobshite British soldiers. It'll be too dangerous.'

Michael, his handsome face fixed with a drunken grin, dragged himself up on the bed. Kathleen could clearly see he had thought of something; he'd started to laugh again.

'No, Eamonn. Do you not see?' he said, trying to get his words out. 'Why it's not dangerous at all. It's perfect – the perfect cover. I mean who'd suspect one of those innocent white robed angels?'

Her brothers collapsed once more into whiskey fuelled mirth, and Kathleen just stood there. But the next morning, while the boys were still hung over, she rose early and washed and dressed. Then crossed the road for her first day at the hospital.

2

On the morning of her fourth day at the hospital, Kathleen found herself standing with several other girls in their newly issued uniforms, gathered around the hospital's notice board. With three days initial training completed, they were anxious to see the wards to which they had been assigned. Before Kathleen could read the list, she heard two girls talking –

'So who's got the Livingstone Ward?'

'Oh, that redheaded girl.'

'Oh bad luck – suppose someone had to get the short straw.'

The short straw?

Five minutes later, when the others had hurried off to take up their new positions, Kathleen found herself at the foot of the main staircase, a sign pointing up. And although there was a lift that was used for transporting patients, she knew it to be out of bounds, so she began to climb, working her way up flight after flight, step upon step, counting as she rose. 'Seventy one, seventy two, seventy three, seventy four.' Nearing the top she heard a voice – a Londoner's voice.

'A hundred and twenty five if you're wondering. I know. I've climbed every one a million bleeding times.'

As Kathleen arrived on the upper most landing, she saw a girl – a blonde haired nurse. She was leaning over the banister smoking a cigarette. Kathleen told her she was one of the new intake.

'As if I didn't know. It's the rustle of that new uniform – the starch. It's a give-away.' The nurse proffered a hand. 'Joy's the name. Joy Deakin.'

Kathleen gave the name she always used – the one on her false papers: Kathleen Cassidy.

The nurse looked her up and down. 'Irish is it? Well, we've all sorts here. You'll fit right in.' She crushed out her cigarette. She turned towards the ward doors. 'Come on. I'll show you the ropes.'

Entering the ward, Kathleen saw exactly what the two girls downstairs had meant. For it was a grim and dreadful place, an attic of sorts, and under a pitched roof she could see metal beds placed either side of a central aisle, the floor covered in red linoleum. In the beds she could see the patients – British servicemen, lying sick and pale. The stench of antiseptic and death was overpowering.

In the absence of the ward sister, Nurse Deakin took her over to an occupied bed which they proceeded to remake, stripping back the covers on a serviceman who was no more than skin and bone.

'This man's my special,' the nurse announced, sounding proud as she tugged at the man's sheets.

Kathleen gazed down at the gaunt face. The patient's skin was sallow, his eyes closed to the world.

'Your *"special?"*.'

'Singled out for special attention – by sister when they get real poorly. I mean that's when you have to watch them. They can pick up all sorts when they're like that – respiratory illnesses, infections – you name it. Not that it makes much difference in the end.'

'What do you mean?'

'Work it out for yourself, Irish. Oh, and by the way, yer don't have to keep whispering.' She nodded down at the man in the bed. 'He won't hear yer.' She lifted her eyes to the others. 'None of 'em will.'

Kathleen stopped abruptly. And looking around, she noticed for the first time that each man on the Livingstone ward was sick to the point of unconsciousness.

*

Later that day, when Kathleen was busy working on the ward, the air raid siren suddenly wailed. But when she began moving the beds, employing the evacuation methods in which she had been trained, she heard Nurse Deakin call over.

'No, we don't do that on this ward, Irish. Just leave 'em be – leave 'em and get yourself down to the shelter.'

Ten minutes later, Kathleen was deep within the freezing bowels of the hospital, sitting next to Nurse Deakin on a bench in the basement. Around her were all the patients in beds and on trolleys, the walking wounded in their dressing gowns. As she sat there she began to think about something the nurse had mentioned earlier.

'When you said, *"Not that it makes much difference,"* you meant that whatever you do for those boys up there on the ward, they end up dying anyway. Isn't that so?'

'You catch on fast,' the nurse replied. 'Why do yer think they're left up there, while we're sitting pretty here?'

'You mean they're expendable?'

'If yer want to call it that.'

'Well what else would you call it?'

'Oh I don't know – practical, I suppose. I mean there *is* a war on. And well, you have to be a bit practical in wartime, don't yer?'

'Yes, the war. It's terrible.'

'Yeah and so is running out of fags. You got any?'

'Sorry. I don't.'

'What, skint, eh? Maybe you should wise up.'

'Wise up?'

'Like me. Like the hospital – get practical. So where are yer staying Irish. You got lodgings – a room somewhere?'

'Yes, across the road.'

Kathleen saw the nurse grimace, as if she knew it well.

'Oh, yeah – stayed there once meself – a flea pit – backs onto the railway line and the gasworks. 'Ere, you're a lucky girl.'

'For finding lodgings in a flea-pit?'

'No, I didn't mean like that. I meant lucky the other night – that doodlebug that came down, landed right at the back of you, didn't it?' Don't say yer didn't hear it!'

'Oh, I heard it,' said Kathleen. 'I saw the flash too.'

'I'm not surprised – that was the gas works going up.'

'What?'

'Yeah. Didn't you know? It landed on the gasworks – blew a ruddy great hole in the gasometer – cut off all the gas.'

Kathleen fell quiet. The siren wailed.

*

26

That evening, when Kathleen returned to her lodgings from her shift at the hospital, she saw a kit bag lying in the hall. It belonged to the soldier whose room she had taken. He was back from leave. And as such the landlady wanted her out.

'You do understand, don't you?' the landlady had said.

Kathleen understood completely; she had seen enough of English ways to know that the Irish were rarely welcome, and hardly for long in a boarding house. But on this occasion she looked upon that bias as a blessing. For earlier, at the hospital, Nurse Deakin had put a proposition to her.

'Well Kath? What do yer think – interested?'

Indeed she was. Puzzled too, mainly by the nurse's change in mood – so she was "Kath" now was she! "Kath", instead of just plain "Irish"! No, there was something going on. Not that it mattered, she thought. For Michael would never sanction the idea; it was too soon after what had happened in Coventry for that. But in view of the soldier's return, she knew it was worth a try.

'So yer say it's a nice quiet place, this flat that you've been offered,' said Michael after she had gone to his room to explain.

'Yes,' said Kathleen. 'I'll be sharing with a girl from the hospital.'

'But you'd have your own room, wouldn't yer?'

'I think so.'

'Yer *think* so?'

'Well that's what she said.'

Michael appeared to consider the proposal for a moment. Then much to Kathleen's surprise, she heard him say: 'All right – go pack yer things.'

Kathleen hurried to her room. She took down her case from the top of the wardrobe and began to pack. But such was her delight at Michael's decision that at first she did not see him enter, did not notice him come up behind her as she was folding her meagre belongings into her case. It was only then, as he pushed her to one side, lifting the radio off the dresser and into her open case, that Kathleen realised his motive: she knew exactly what he planned.

27

*

That night, Kathleen walked through the blackout to the nurse's flat. Michael and Eamonn came with her, naturally. The flat was hard to find in the darkness. It was over a butcher's shop, and the only way of gaining access was to go around the back, through a brick tunnelled passageway and up a wrought iron staircase that led to a rear door above. After Kathleen had knocked upon it, the door had quickly opened.

'Oh, it's you, Kath.'

Nurse Deakin was standing there in the doorway. She looked like she was expecting someone else, thought Kathleen. She was wearing make up and a red dressing gown embroidered with Chinese dragons. To Kathleen's eyes the gown looked like pure silk. 'Oh and I see you've brought company!' Kathleen saw the nurse smile, as her attention switched to her brothers. Kathleen introduced them. They went inside.

After being led down a hallway, the nurse took them to look over the room. Then she went to make tea. Kathleen gazed about her.

The first thing Kathleen noticed was how well it was furnished, though she could plainly see that Michael's thoughts were elsewhere. For he was over at the door, checking the lock, turning the key, making sure it was secure.

'This'll do just fine,' Kathleen heard Michael say, more to himself than anyone else. Then he reached into his coat pocket and handed over Kathleen's identity card and ration book. Kathleen put them in her raincoat pocket, then Michael said: 'As soon as that floozy gives yer a key, let me have it. I'll get a spare cut.'

Then she saw Michael nod at Eamonn, and to her relief they walked back into the hallway and out the door, Kathleen hearing their boots clanking down the iron steps at the rear.

When the nurse returned with the tea, Kathleen apologised for her brothers' abrupt exit.

'Oh, don't bother about that,' Joy Deakin told her. 'I know what men are like – never there when yer need them – always there when yer don't.' Joy laughed. 'Tea?'

28

She began to pour and Kathleen told her the room was "very nice", then asked what had happened to the girl who had occupied it last.

'Oh, she went away,' Joy said with a dismissive wave, 'to the country I think . . . .' Just then there came a knock on the front door: *Rat ta tat tat.* Joy got up. She went across to the hall. 'Just a tick.'

A moment later, she was back. 'That was just Kenny,' she said. 'A batman in the R.A.F. He's always coming round. A nuisance really.' She looked down at the cups. 'Now, where were we? Oh yes – *tea!*' She sat down and began to pour again. 'So how d'yer like it?'

'With sugar if you've some?'

Joy laughed. 'I meant the room silly – so you'll take it?'

Kathleen nodded. 'Oh yes. It's a grand room. Just *grand.*' She looked around her at the other fine furnishings: a standard lamp with a tasselled fringe. An upright piano against the wall. A gramophone. Pictures and ornaments. 'In fact you've some very nice things.'

'Well, a girl's got to have nice things around her, especially in wartime. Did you see my bathroom?' The nurse jerked a thumb across the hall. 'I've a brand new Ascot in there – hot water on tap. "Ere, you can have a bath later if yer want.'

Kathleen almost swooned at the thought. *A bath!*

'Yes, I'd like that.'

'And then we could go out.'

'Out?'

'Yeah. If you're keen there's this nice pub I go to – the Eagle. Yer get a lot of R.A.F. in most nights. And not just the likes of Kenny – pilots I mean!'

Kathleen's mind suddenly threw up a picture of her father, those nights when he'd come home after drinking in Cahill's Bar. Would any decent man want her after that?

'No, I think I'll just stay,' she said. 'Stay and have that bath.'

Joy just shrugged. 'Well, please yourself.' She got up. But not before adding that she was "going to the Eagle anyway." Then she gave a sly smile. 'Can't miss out on a chance of bagging one of those lovely pilots!'

Later, after Joy had gone out, Kathleen went into the bathroom to take her bath. As she undressed she looked about her, noticing that the room was every bit as grand as the rest of the flat. For there was the famous Ascot water heater in all its glory, over the bath. So too a pair of Joy's stockings, hanging on a line. Kathleen ran her fingers over the stockings. Pure silk again, just like Joy's robe.

She drew her bath, then stepping in she lay back. Why, Holy Mary, did not the very water feel like pure silk too! Such luxury. Such luxury with the flat, the furniture, the dressing gown with the Chinese embroidered dragons – and all on hospital pay?

But more than the luxury, it was the freedom which cheered her; to have obtained a little distance from her brothers felt like living again. And a far cry from last time. For that time had been Coventry.

It had been one Friday as she recalled, at the tank factory gates. She had been waiting for her brothers to arrive, to give them their "wages". But they had been late in coming. And taking full advantage, she had taken to her heels.

It had been a spur of the moment affair, spontaneous, with neither thought of capture nor the consequences; she had just headed for the railway station as fast as her legs could carry her. But, as if Michael had read her mind, he had found her there and had taken her back. Desertion, Michael had called it. And he and Eamonn had beaten her, then had threatened her with McManus. It had been the misery of it all that had weighed upon her that first night she had arrived, driving her to that terrible act of despair.

She ran more hot water into the bath, laying there as she heard the Ascot water heater gurgle, looking at the blue gas flame as it began to dance, thinking back to that night the bomb had fallen with such timely intervention. But had it really been a timely intervention she began to wonder? What if it had been a *Godly* intervention? What did it all mean?

3

Kathleen could remember the exact time and place when she first laid eyes upon the English airman, Flight-Lieutenant David Asher. It was a week before Christmas and he was coming out of the hospital's lift. Though as he did so she felt strangely unsettled, as if his appearance held some kind of significance, one that she could not explain. It was an odd feeling, she thought, though she knew for a fact that the airman could shed no light upon the matter. For upon his arrival on the Livingstone Ward that day, he appeared little different to any of the other patients: pale, sallow, deep within a coma.

Kathleen watched as the hospital porters pushed his trolley out of the lift and onto the ward, then, when he had been transferred to his bed, she had stepped closer.

The airman looked near to death, she thought, as she had gazed at his gaunt and hollow features, his skin almost translucent in the shaft of daylight that shone down from a skylight above, his body little more than skin and bone, almost like some handsome cadaver.

And then there was his hair, black but in places prematurely grey, turned white as if by some dreadful experience. But then, when she was helping to change his dressings, she noticed the reason.

The man had been tortured; there were terrible wounds to his body. Though beyond those fresh dressings, she knew there was little that anyone could do. And as such, she went about her duties, changing sheets, making beds, generally busying herself in the sluice room. But after she had done so, and despite the sheer futility, she felt drawn back to the airman's bedside, where she stood, feeling something, something strange inside.

'Is he going to die?' Kathleen asked a passing sister, staring down. 'Only I've heard – '

The Sister gave her a scolding look, then said in a solemn but ominous tone: 'Get on with your work, girl. We'll face that time when it comes.'

*

That night in her room, Kathleen could not get the airman out of her mind. And it had not taken her long to grasp the reason. For seeing him like that, lying there, lying there sick and wounded, had reminded her of all that was decent and courageous in the Englishman's world, while all was cowardly and despicable in her own.

And there were the nurses too, she thought, all those women at the hospital who had been working towards victory, while she had been working against. It was as if seeing those things, first hand, close up, had brought it all home. And not for the first time. For she'd felt something similar one night in London. Then she'd felt sick – sick and mean and wretched. But something else too: she had felt ashamed.

But then came a knock at the door, a knock that was both secretive but familiar. And snapped from her thoughts she went down the hall.

Pulling the door open, she saw the bright red buttons of Michael and Eamonn's cigarettes, glowing in the darkness.

'Are yer alone?' Michael asked.

It seemed an innocent question, but Kathleen knew its truer meaning. She nodded. She let them in.

Once in the hallway they made straight for her bedroom, Michael turning when they were all inside and locking the door behind him. Then lifting his chin towards the radio, he said:

'Get it set up. I've something to send.'

With that Kathleen saw Michael take a grubby piece of paper from his pocket. He handed it over. Kathleen glanced at the scribbled details. It looked like a plea for help, she thought, a request for money, the possibility of a ship.

'Just do it,' he said when Kathleen looked up at him questioningly. Then with slow reluctance she began to make a move, setting up the radio on the dressing table, unscrewing the back plate, removing the transmitter inside. Then, when that was done, she began to make it ready, drawing out the antenna, switching on,

32

carefully arranging the Morse key to her right hand side. A moment later, Eamonn whispered from the door.

'Mikey! I think I heard something.'

Michael shot him a glance.

'What?'

'Shhh! Can yer not hear it?'

They all stopped. And in the silence, Kathleen looked at Michael. His handsome face was creased with concentration, listening. A moment later there came a noise: *Rat ta tat tat.*

'It's the door,' Eamonn said urgently. 'Someone's at the door.'

No sooner had his words left his lips than it came again. Louder:

Rat ta tat tat!

Kathleen saw the panic in Michael's eyes. They flashed at her, seeking explanation.

'The floozy?'

Kathleen shook her head.

'No. Joy would use her key.'

'Then who?'

Kathleen did not reply and Michael gestured at his brother.

'Eamonn – go see.'

Eamonn nodded and Kathleen saw him take out his lock knife. As he flicked out the blade, Kathleen began to panic.

'No, wait,' she whispered. 'It's just someone for Joy – one of her men friends.'

'Eh?'

'A "gentlemen caller"'

'You mean – ?'

'I don't know, Michael. I think. Maybe . . . just wait – wait 'til they get tired and go.'

The three of them waited. Then a moment later, just as Kathleen had foreseen, they heard the faint clanking of retreating footsteps down the wrought iron steps at the back.

Kathleen breathed a sigh of relief.

'There. I told you. He's gone.'

Michael nodded, and Eamonn folded his knife back into his

pocket.

Back on top of the dressing table, the transmitter was waiting; the Morse key lay silent and ready. Michael gestured Kathleen back to the table that she had vacated and she came across and sat down.

With Michael standing behind her, Kathleen's hand trembled on the Morse key; she felt unnerved by the caller at the door. In fact she wondered if Michael had ever been aware of the pressure she'd been under, the strain of which had caused her to make mistakes within her messages. No, she hoped he did not realise. For she had been making "mistakes" for a long time now, ever since that night in London, that terrible night when her brothers had murdered the old man and the boy.

4

A few days later, while Kathleen was up a stepladder, stringing up Christmas decorations upon the ward, the air raid siren wailed again.

'Right c'mon, Kath,' ordered Joy. 'It's straight down to the shelter for us.'

For a moment Kathleen hesitated. 'Oh yes, but this won't take a minute. Besides, it's probably just a false alarm.'

Just then there came the most tremendous roar – an explosion rattled the hospital's windows.

Kathleen saw Joy look up at her.

'You were saying?'

Hurrying down the red linoleum they both went towards the stairs. The other staff had already gone, but they had only taken half a dozen steps down towards the first landing when another explosion came behind them. Looking back, Kathleen saw the ward doors batter back and forth, then saw an ominous red-orange glow. The ward! It was on fire!

Without hesitation Kathleen began to run back up.

'Where yer going?' Joy called, stopping her.

'Back of course.'

'What? C'mon, Kath. You know the rules.'

Kathleen stared up at the red-orange blaze.

'I don't care,' she said, suddenly turning again and running up as fast as she could. 'I'm going back inside.'

Re-entering the ward she found out exactly what had happened – a piece of hot shrapnel had smashed its way through one of the skylight windows, upsetting a bottle of surgical spirit near to one of the beds – the airman's bed. It was surrounded by flames!

Rushing over she tried to stamp them out, but was beaten back. Then, discovering a fire bucket filled with sand, she grabbed it then quickly shot the contents across the burning lino. Then whipping the smouldering blankets off the airman's bed she began to beat at the flames. A moment later, to her relief, she saw that the flames were dying back. When they were completely out, she went straight to the airman's side.

'Thank God,' she murmured, seeing he was unharmed. 'Thank God,' she almost wept.

But at that moment, as she fussed around him, Kathleen was aware of someone standing over by the ward doors. At first she thought it was Joy. But no.

It was the ward sister.

*

The next morning on her way to the hospital, Kathleen felt sick with nerves. For she had been thinking back to that time when the bomb had cut off the gas, that "Godly intervention". She was positive it had been a sign. Not just proof that *He* had not deserted her, but more – that *He* was giving her one last chance to redeem herself, perhaps to run.

Yes, in fact in her heart she knew there was no better time. For it was Christmas Eve, and being so she guessed that Michael and Eamonn would be drunk most probably, in some alehouse, completely off guard. And as such she had decided to wait until her shift was over, then go to the hospital's pay office and collect what was owed to her, then, in the darkness, she would slip out the back entrance, go to the flat, collect her things, then catch a bus to the railway station. Once there she would buy a ticket to London. And Michael and Eamonn? Why, she would be gone before they realised.

Yes, London. It would be the perfect place to start again, she thought. And she wagered that Michael and Eamonn would never dare follow her *there*, not after what happened with the old man and the boy.

She walked on towards the hospital, still sick with nerves, though it was not until she had reached the hospital, going up the stairs and onto the ward that she felt that sickness become worse still. For the airman's bed was missing, and all she could see for a moment was the charred area where it had been, the broken skylight above, boarded over. Then with some relief she noticed he had been moved beneath another. But her sense of foreboding still prevailed.

'He's not so good today,' said Joy calling over after Kathleen had reached the airman's bedside. And looking down at him, Kathleen could see that the nurse was right. For his breathing was ragged, uneven.

'What's wrong?' she asked.

'Pneumonia – got took bad in the night. Came over with a temperature. Shame. I suppose his time has come.'

Kathleen looked down at the airman again. It did not seem right. For he had obviously survived so much, she thought, not just the fire on the ward but other things too – unimaginable things. And for what – to die like *this?*

It seemed neither just nor fair, though as she worked that last shift on that Christmas Eve, seeing the airman's condition worsen by the hour, slowly nudging towards its end while all the other nurses wished each other well, bidding one another a "Merry Christmas" and putting on their coats to leave, Kathleen was just putting on hers too, when –

'Oh, before you go, nurse. A word please.'

It was the ward sister; she was beckoning her to her office. It was obviously concerning the fire, she thought, a reprimand for disobeying hospital rules.

And going over to sister's office, it appeared that her suspicions were right. For the sister began by saying: 'Come in. I want to talk to you about yesterday. It's about the fire.'

Yes, it was just as she had thought, and Kathleen began to apologise.

'I'm sorry, sister. I know I did wrong. I should have gone straight to the shelter with the others. It's just – '

'I know,' the sister replied. 'Actually I saw what happened – what you did. I thought it commendable.'

For a moment Kathleen was lost for words. *Praise? From sister!*

The woman gestured her to a chair and told her to sit down. Kathleen did as she was asked, though was mindful that time was ticking by; she was losing her advantage – she would miss her train if she did not hurry. And being Christmas Eve there was only one train to London; she had checked. But sister appeared to be in no hurry.

'Now,' she began. 'You know the patient whom you help save? You're aware he's gravely ill, of course?'

'The airman, sister? Yes.'

'And you know he has pneumonia and it's only a matter of time, don't you?'

'So I believe, sister.'

'Well I've spoken with one of the doctors and we're both in agreement.'

'In agreement, sister? In agreement with what?'

'With my decision – I'm going to give the airman to you as a "Special". You understand what that means?'

Kathleen was stunned. *No. No you can't, sister. You can't!*

'Now I know what you're going to say,' sister began. 'You're going to tell me you haven't been with us long, but don't worry. I'm not asking you to do anything difficult. I just want someone to sit by him through the night, so he won't be alone when he passes. Do you feel able to do that for him?'

Kathleen lowered her gaze. Finally she spoke. 'Yes, sister. Of course, sister.'

The sister rose from her desk. 'Good. Then that's settled,' she said. 'Now what I suggest is that you take an hour off and go and get washed and changed – get yourself something to eat. It may be a long night.'

Two minutes later, Kathleen found herself back on the ward. It was quieter now, most of the staff having left. And in that prevailing silence, punctuated only by the slow and laboured breaths of the dying airman, she looked down at him.

His brow was sweat beaded, his sick but handsome face wan, his black/grey hair slicked back with moisture. The poor man was fighting for his life, struggling to pull what little air he could into his feeble lungs. At that moment Kathleen knew – knew exactly what she had to do.

And reaching down she gently held his hand, trying to explain, albeit silently the reasons why she could not stay. For it was *God's* wish, she told him, *God's* wish that she should leave – to distance herself from her past – her final chance to start again. Gently she held the airman's hand one last time, hoping he would understand. And somehow she knew he would. For even though he was an Englishman, she knew he was a good man at that, decent and kind. But then she was threading her arm through her coat, then walking away, then pushing through the ward doors at the end of the red linoleum aisle. There she looked back, one last time, one last time before quietly then quickly disappearing down the stairs.

Hurry – that's what she told herself when she came out of the pay office on the ground floor. And clutching her money she walked at a pace through the long hospital corridors, emerging into the night.

Click click click went her heels on the pavement as she nervously looked behind, but she saw no one – no one in the shadows save for the imagined figures of her brothers waiting to stop her, or maybe McManus stepping out to splash her with acid. But no one did. And arriving at the flat she quickly packed her things, throwing the radio transmitter into her case, her intention being to hurl it from the train lest is be discovered. Then she hurried out, closing the door behind her.

Clank clank clank, went her feet as she made her way down the wrought iron steps at the rear of the flat, echoing along the brick passageway to the road. There she saw a bus at the stop. She ran and jumped aboard.

Sitting there she looked out the window, her stomach churning with tension as her eyes flicked at the passing buildings, expecting to see her brothers come reeling out of some roadside ale house and spot her, their eyes full of whiskey fuelled vengeance. But they did not, and before long she felt the bus slow and come to a halt at the railway station. Her plan was going to work. It was really going to work.

A Salvation Army band were playing outside the station, and the sound of Christmas carols wafted through the entrance where she found herself queuing at the windowed cubby hole of the ticket office.

'Where to miss?'

'London, please. Is that the train over there?' She gestured to a waiting locomotive that was shrouded in a cloud of dirty steam. The ticket clerk nodded.

'Better look sharp, miss. Return or single?'

Kathleen asked for a single, then began to fumble in her purse for change. As she did so she felt a hand on her shoulder. It spun her round.

She was confronted by an angry face.

'Oh do hurry up *please*,' said the impatient man. 'There's others waiting to catch that train!'

Kathleen felt the relief course through her, then paying for her ticket she hurriedly moved onto the platform. There she jumped aboard the train. She slammed the door behind her.

As she waited in the carriage, listening for the shrill of the whistle, the jolt and pull of the engine, Kathleen's thoughts began to drift back to the hospital. She felt sick at leaving the airman, guilty for letting him down. But she was sure that God had spared her for *this*, for her new life, far away from her past.

Though as the engine began to move, gradually picking up speed, something else occurred to her. What if God had spared her for another reason, perhaps to *stay* – to *stay!*

Thoughts tumbled helter-skelter into her mind. Yes, it was possible. What if she had been spared to try and save the airman's life? Yes that was it – this wasn't about *her* at all, it was about the *airman* – the *airman!*

But the train was moving quicker now, gathering pace as it began to pull out of the station. Though before it did so, Kathleen grabbed the door. She threw it open, jumping down with a scrape and stutter of her heels.

There on the platform she collected herself, gathering her breath. Finally she straightened.

And as the train went off down the tracks without her, evaporating in a ball of swirling steam, Kathleen slowly turned. Then she began walking back down to the station's exit, back towards the hospital, back to the airman's side where she knew she belonged.

Part Two

Spring 1945

<u>1</u>

It felt like morning, though he could not be sure. All he knew was that it seemed to be the start of something rather than the end of it. And as if in answer, as he opened his eyes, he could see the first slivers of daylight coming from the edges of a curtained-off skylight window above his head. But where had he been? On a journey? To another land? Another world?

It had been a dark world that was for sure – dark like a forest where by day the sun had never penetrated the thick canopy above him, and where by night he had sometimes heard strange and unexplained activity, echoing unseen. Then somewhere in the back of his mind he remembered a voice. A sweet voice. It had spoken to him often. *'I'm here,'* it had said. *'I'm here . . . . '*

Yes it was odd, he thought, but then again there was much of his strange land that he did not understand, like the time when he had been really deep in that forest, completely lost in that terrible darkness, lost but for the sudden and unexpected striking of his old college bell, thin and tinny as the chime announced itself, bringing back a memory of Cambridge, a vision of spires and buildings and universities, the lazy river winding like a ribbon through green patchwork fields – fields that were once familiar.

'Yes, you're home . . . . you're safe', the sweet voice had said to him then. And at the same time he could have sworn he had felt a hand being slipped into his own, one which had almost physically pulled him back, a hand that somehow had begged to be

acknowledged, affirmed with a squeeze. And somehow, with a mighty effort, he had managed to do so.

'Yes, that's it,' the sweet voice had encouraged. 'You must fight. You must fight, David!'

David? But who was David?

Of course it was he – Flight-Lieutenant David Asher. Pilot. Seconded into wartime intelligence – that much he knew as he finally opened his eyes on that spring morning – that and the realisation that a hand, maybe even the same hand, was gently lifting him towards something, directing his mouth to what looked like a vessel. Instinctively his dry lips connected with it, then he felt a cooling liquid splash into the fiery furnace of his throat. He almost whimpered at the pleasure. *Fruit juice!*

Eagerly he drank. He examined his surroundings.

It was some kind of attic, as far as he could tell. For there was nothing above him save for that skylight and the roof, and beyond that, he presumed, the kingdom of heaven, a place where he guessed most of the other poor souls around him were bound. For he realised he was in a hospital. A God awful place.

Though strangely, as he lay there, he felt very much alive – alive at least to waves of pain that rampaged through his body, nagging at his every sinew, gnawing at his very soul. Though mercifully it did not extend to his legs. In fact, he could not feel his legs at all.

But what had happened? Yes, he had been on a mission in occupied France – he remembered that much. Then he had been captured. Something had failed; he'd been betrayed?

Suddenly the vessel from which he had drunk had gone, and he could feel the hand easing his head back down to his pillow. Then the hand came and dabbed away the dribbled fruit juice from the corners of his mouth. He felt the same hand apply something to his dry cracked lips, sensing the gentle pressure of fingertips as a soothing salve was spread upon them.

'God bless you,' he quietly said. 'God bless you.'

Then he looked up.

She was rather beautiful he thought, young, in her early twenties, he guessed. She had green eyes that were flecked with hazel. Auburn hair the colour of burnished copper. Her skin was milk white save for her cheeks which had the glow of the country about them; the look of a fresh-faced Irish girl, he thought.

He tried to utter something else, but she put her finger to her lips. 'Shhh. Rest now. Don't speak.'

'No, I must,' he murmured. 'There's something I need from you.'

'Anything,' she said.

He tried to lift himself up. He whispered to her softly. 'I need you to help me remember.'

*

That day, after Kathleen had left the hospital, before walking her now familiar path back home to her room at Joy Deakin's flat, she called in as usual to a nearby Catholic church. As she climbed the steps, going towards the great oak doors, she felt a certain weariness in her bones. It had been there since Christmas, she noted, since a change to the night shift to care for the airman, building in a wave that had often swept over her on those long and gruelling hours spent at his bedside. But somehow none of that mattered anymore. Not that morning. That morning nothing mattered.

Going inside she said her prayers, giving thanks to God for his miracle, His mercies, asking little for herself save for an end to the war. And praise be to God it *was* coming to an end, grinding to a close, gradually petering out. And praise too, because of it, she had seen less of her brothers. For they were lying low now, hiding out with all work for the cause suspended, skulking like the rats they were. Of course they had surfaced on occasions, seeking to check on her at the flat. But any other time they were simply too frightened to appear, or maybe too drunk, she wagered, waiting as they were for their passage home – the vain and silly hope of their *ship*. And as for McManus, no one had seen him in an age.

'Perhaps he's deserted,' she had once dared to suggest to her brothers, unwisely as it occurred. For Eamonn had slapped her – thrown her to the floor – raised his boot. But Michael had pulled him away. Yes, clever cunning Michael; he knew not to kill the golden goose. For the rats would always surface from their holes come pay day, to collect their "wages". But there would be little or nothing for them now, she decided. Not with the airman to care for.

She left the church feeling better, less drained and ready for the fight ahead. For her work with the airman had only just begun, she realised. He would need building up. Feeding up. And not with hospital rations either. He would need nutritious things like fruit and meat and eggs, scarce things too like oranges that she could only get on the black market. Yes, that would all cost. And all on her hospital pay?

Of course it was all right for some – Joy. *She* could well afford such things. But then again Kathleen had seen the R.A.F. caps on the hat stand, noticed the kit bags in the hallway at the flat, heard the cries of passion through the wall as Joy "entertained" the troops.

'Well, you have to be a bit practical in wartime, don't you?'

Not that it mattered. For she considered herself little better, worse in fact with all she had done, becoming her father's weapon of war, the way she had let him rally her to the cause. It was times such as those that she tried to blank out, longing to put her past from her mind. Strange, she thought, that while she yearned to forget, the airman was desperate to remember.

*

It was getting dark when David Asher woke next – dark but for a large harvest moon that he could see shining down upon him. It was pale in colour and not unlike a balloon, tethered or so it seemed, fastened should it fall from its place in the heavens into his very arms.

Yes, it appeared that close. And in its glow which spread shadows across the ward, he could just make out the oblong shapes of those hospital beds and the patients within them, prostrate, each one like some brave knight upon a tomb, the ward deathly silent like a church, hushed but for the slow laboured breathing of men quietly dying.

'What yer looking at?' said a voice at his side.

Asher slowly turned his head. It was a blonde haired nurse. Not the Irish girl. A Londoner, by the accent. She was squeezing a cloth into a bowl. Asher heard the squeak of the cloth as it was wrung out, then felt the sheer bliss of it upon his temple, cool and wet.

'I was gazing at the moon,' he said

He saw the nurse look up to the blacked out skylight window above his bed.

'What? Oh yeah – pretty.'

Asher smiled wearily. He knew she hadn't seen it; he was just being humoured.

'No, you don't understand. The moon!' he told her. 'The moon!'

She wrung out the cloth again.

'No, I understand all right. You're poorly, that's what you are – have been for some time – still are. Just rest now. Kath'll be along soon.'

'Kath? The Irish girl?'

'Kathleen. You're her special you are.'

'Special?'

'Never you mind. Just you sleep now.'

*

That evening in her room, Kathleen's alarm clock rattled her awake. Wearily she rubbed the sleep from her eyes. As she gradually came round, her first thoughts were of *him,* and suddenly she seemed less tired.

Rising from her bed she went about her routine: she washed, she dressed, she went into the kitchen where she made some tea. Then after eating two slices of tasteless war time bread, she put on her coat. She left for work.

As she walked, stepping out beneath the canopy of trees above the pavement, budding as they were with the first blossoms of spring, she cast her mind back to darker days, a time when she had been briefly switched to the day shift, and he had been more poorly than ever; it seemed he might die. But she had willed him back, calling upon God. For He had saved her from taking her own life for that one purpose: to look after him. It had been her promise, her pact. But some, like Joy, had misunderstood –

'I reckon you must be falling for that boy,' Joy had once said. 'What with all that attention.'

'Him? No. I'm just doing my job.'

Joy had laughed. But what did she know of such things? With Joy and men it was purely commerce.

Arriving at the hospital, Kathleen went up the stairs to begin her shift, passing as she did so those nurses who had completed theirs, the bleary eyed band of angels who were coming down, dead on their feet with fatigue. Joy was one of the last. Kathleen bumped into her on the top landing. She was just throwing on her coat.

'How is he today?' Kathleen asked.

'Your boy? Not so good.'

'What do you mean?'

'He's running a temperature.'

'Again? Is it bad?'

'Bad enough – he reckons he can see the moon. The moon!'

'Perhaps he can – through the skylight?'

'No, the blackouts drawn. Anyway, he's sleeping now. Best thing really. See you in the morning.'

When Kathleen got to the airman's side, she found that Joy was right; he was sleeping. Though a while later she noticed that he began to stir. Then he called out. His voice was no more than a whisper.

'Is that you Kathleen?'

'Yes. I'm here.'

'I thought it was you. It's your time – the night time?'

She smiled, but then she told him that being the night time it was all the more reason for him to sleep. But he did not want to sleep, she heard him say. He wanted to remember. 'You said you'd help me?'

'I will,' she soothed, 'but first you need to be well again, then you'll remember. Then things will come easier. You'll see.'

'But I see things now – things I don't understand.'

'That's because you have a temperature,' she explained. 'When that's gone you'll – '

'No, I see the moon,' he said. 'Do you see it too, Kathleen? I can see it. And it's full. It's always full at this time.'

For a moment Kathleen felt perplexed. It was just as Joy had told her; he was seeing things. For when she looked up at the skylight, she clearly saw the blind had been pulled. But then, as she followed the airman's gaze –

'Oh yes,' she said. 'So it is! The moon! So it is!'

Her eyes were drawn to a pale moonlike glow – it was one of the ward's globe lights that hung down from the ceiling near his bed. Kathleen looked at him. She smiled. He smiled back; a weak smile of acknowledgement; they both understood one another.

'Doesn't look a quarter of a million miles away,' he even managed to joke. 'It's so close.'

'Yes, so close you could almost reach out and touch it.'

'Bright as well.'

'Too bright?' she asked. 'Is the light troubling you?'

'Yes, it is.'

'Then I'll do something about it.' She got up from the chair at his bedside. 'I'll have it put out.'

She saw him feebly try to raise his hand to stop her.

'No. I didn't mean like that. I mean it troubles me for another reason.'

'Oh?'

'It reminds me of something – a *real* moon – a full moon and a field – a French field. There's an aeroplane – people shouting – soldiers, I think.'

He began to cough and Kathleen cradled him up. She gave him a little rose hip syrup, then his coughing ceased. She eased him back down.

'German solders?' she asked.

'Yes, I think. But there's a name – a name I can't remember, but I must. I must – '

'Shhh,' she soothed. 'That's enough now. Try and rest. The name will come back to you in time.'

'You think it will?' he asked

'Of course. You remembered *my* name didn't you.'

48

She saw him smile weakly again before closing his eyes. As he did so she thought she heard him whisper something – *"As if I could forget."*

Or at least that's what she hoped.

*

The next morning, when Flight-Lieutenant David Asher came round again, he did so to the distant sounds that filtered up to him: the noises of the hospital as it began to wake – the clatter of a trolley in a far off corridor, the chink of milk bottles in their crates, the gentle banging of double doors, the soft whistling and singing of a hospital porter on one of the floors below . . . *"We'll met again, don't know where, don't know when . . . ."*

At the blacked out skylight window above him, he could see a sliver of light. He called out.

'Kathleen?'

He heard her answer. 'Yes, I'm here.'

'Something's different!'

'It's the morning,' he heard her say.

'No. I mean I *feel* different.'

'That's because your temperature's down. Here – a sip of water.'

He felt her hand at the back of his head, gently lifting him up. As he drank he looked up at her. He had not been mistaken. Her face was really quite beautiful, he thought, though he detected something in those green eyes of hers. It was not the flecks of hazel within, but rather a hint of sadness. Or perhaps he was wrong. Switching his attention to the skylight he looked up and asked: 'That window . . . do you think – ?'

'The blind? You'd like me to take it down?'

'If you could?'

As she went to remove it, Asher watched as she leaned over him, reaching up. Her body was slim – war-time slim, ration slim, but graceful too; her back was arched as she stretched for the blind. The light poured down, playing across her auburn hair beneath her cap.

'That's better,' he smiled, looking up at the crimson and blue streaked oblong: daybreak. 'I just wanted to see out – the sky. You understand?'

'I think so. You've not seen it in a while. You've missed it?'

'Does that sound foolish?'

'It does not – not for a pilot. Why it's where they live isn't it? Up in the clouds?'

He smiled weakly again, then joked that only the good ones usually stayed there. To which he heard her say: 'Oh I bet you're a grand pilot. Grand.'

He told her: "Perhaps". Though in all honesty he could not exactly remember.

'Then what *do* you remember?' she asked him. 'Do you remember last night – what you said?'

'Last night?'

'Yes, you said something about the moon – a moonlit field in France – an aeroplane – the sounds of people shouting – soldiers, I think.'

He tried to recall. Yes, she was right. He remembered now.

'Yes, it was the night I was captured,' he said. 'A moonlit night.'

'When your plane was shot down?'

'No. It didn't happen like that.'

'What do you mean?'

'I mean I wasn't shot down at all. I was already there.'

'In France? What were you doing?'

'I can't say – just sent to do a job.'

'But something went wrong?'

'Yes – when the job was over – when I was due to fly back.'

'Then the plane you mentioned – it was coming to pick you up?'

'As far as I recall.'

'And it landed in the field?'

'Landed? Yes, I'm certain.'

'But something happened?'

'It must have.'

'You were betrayed perhaps?'

'Why do you say that?'

'Nothing really. It's just that last night you mentioned about a

50

name.'

'A name?'

'Yes, but you couldn't remember.'

'Damned if I can now.'

'But you will, I'm sure. You just need time. Besides, I must be going now.'

He saw her get up to leave. He looked back at the light flooding in from the skylight and said: 'Yes, of course. It's the morning, isn't it. You must be tired – working all night while all I've done is sleep.'

'No, sleep is what you need,' she told him. 'It will help you remember. So sleep now and I'll be back this evening.'

David Asher flicked his eyes towards the ceiling and to the globe light that hung near his bed.

'Back when the moon is full?' he asked.

'Yes,' she smiled. 'When the moon is full.'

*

When Kathleen left the hospital that morning, she did not go straight home. She went to another address, a place which, on occasions, the other nurses had cause to frequent. Though it was odd, she thought, that whenever the subject of the place had cropped up, it had been spoken of in whispered tones, as if those nurses who had need of the services on offer there were somehow ashamed. But Kathleen felt no such shame. It was just a case of being "practical", as Joy was fond of saying.

The house in question was not far from the hospital, near a place called Parker's Piece, an expanse of grass not unlike a park, quite close to the Catholic Church in which she had prayed so hard for the airman's life. And passing the church it made her think of the forces chaplain at the hospital, a man called the Reverend Summerbee, and that time back in those dark days of the winter when she had found herself switched to the day shift, the time when the airman had been close to death, the forces chaplain at his bedside . . . .

'I'm afraid it's up to God now,' the chaplain had said, turning to her. 'You or I can do no more.'

'No, there must be something,' Kathleen had protested. 'There's always *something*.'

'Prayers,' said Summerbee.

Kathleen had shaken her head.

'No, not just prayers – something we haven't thought of. If only his mother and father were here.'

'Both passed on, I'm afraid.'

'A wife, perhaps?'

'No. He's a single man.'

'How do you know these things?'

'The Red Cross. They were the ones who found him.'

'Found him where?'

'I suppose there's no harm in telling you. They think he escaped from a German prison camp and tried to walk his way across the Pyrenees. That's where they found him, barely alive before he fell into a coma. Quite extraordinary really. He's been listed missing in action for two years.'

'Two years?'

'Yes, poor soul. He's been away all that time – away from Cambridge.'

'He's from the town?'

'He grew up here – attended one of the colleges. I expect that's why they brought him to the hospital – compassionate reasons, so that at least he would know he had made it home at last.'

Kathleen had thought for a moment. Then she had said: 'That's if he *realises* he's home. Will you excuse me a moment.'

Kathleen had gone straight to Joy. The blonde haired nurse had looked mystified at her request.

'You want me to do what?' she'd asked

'I want you to help me move Lieutenant Asher's bed out onto the balcony on the floor below.'

'Whatever for?'

'I haven't time to explain.'

'And what about sister?'

'Joy, the boy's dying! *I'll* deal with sister.'

Five minutes later they were both pushing the airman's bed out of the lift on the floor below, trundling it down the corridor. A cold blast of wintry air hit them as they pushed through the doors onto the hospital's front balcony.

'What's this, some sort of kill or cure?' asked Joy.

'Just wait,' said Kathleen. 'I know what I'm doing.'

Taking his pillows she propped the airman up in bed. She took his hand and began to slap it. She gathered up the loose skin on the back of his hand and pinched it hard: a trick she had seen other nurses perform. 'David. David, listen to me,' she had whispered. 'Do you know where you are? Yes, you're home my love. You're safe. It's England.'

'Oh it's no good, Kath,' said Joy after a while. 'Whatever you told him he can't hear. He can't hear nothing.'

But as Joy spoke the bell from one of the colleges sounded far off in the distance. Kathleen shook her head.

'No, he *did* hear. He *did!* Didn't you see?'

'See what?

'He squeezed my hand. He squeezed my hand . . . . .'

The sun was beginning to shine by the time Kathleen neared the address she was looking for, and she could see that the house in question was just one of many houses in an ordinary brick terrace. Though on closer inspection she saw that it seemed more prosperous than those which flanked it, a fact which became apparent as she drew closer. For she could see thick velvet drapes at the window, and beyond, through the diamond taped glass, a nice carpet across the floor. As she went to slam down the knocker, she looked at the house number: Number Ten. Yes, this was the address all right, the place the girls at the hospital would talk of in their hushed tones.

"Go to number ten," they would say. "Number ten will sort you out."

And so it was that Kathleen found herself checking the money in her purse, waiting for the door to be opened.

*

David Asher was lying awake. He was thinking back to the time of

53

his capture, the night they had sent the aeroplane to pick him up. Yes, he had been betrayed all right, of that he was sure. But by whom – the man whose name he was so desperate to recall?

That seemed evident, though there was another possibility, one that was quite the reverse, the prospect that the name meant nothing whatsoever; it was simply due to the turmoil of his mind. For ever since he had surfaced into the waking world, he had found himself beset with confusion, plagued with restlessness and dreams. One dream in particular had come to haunt him. It had been a man's face that he had seen, or rather that of a monster, a figure with leathery skin and prominent eyes. It was the strangest dream ever. It did not make sense. Then again, what did?

But there had been other dreams too. Dreams of a more agreeable nature. For example the voice he'd heard calling to him in his coma, the "sweet voice" that had stayed with him all along.

'Yes, you're home . . . . you're safe. It's England.' And did not that same sweet voice call him "my love?" *'You're home . . . . my love?'*

Yes, that voice had been his only comfort all right, his lifeline, his rock. And now, as he thought back, there was little doubt in his mind to whom that voice belonged. For suddenly, as he lay there, it was all perfectly clear to him – it was her. The one girl he thought he would never forget: Evelyn.

*

That morning when Kathleen arrived back at the flat, Joy was in the kitchen. It was her day off and she was late in rising, still in her red silk dressing gown with the embroidered dragons, still wearing her make up from the night before. She was filling the kettle at the sink.

'Just in time . . . . tea?'

'Please,' smiled Kathleen. 'I'm tired out.'

'Late too. Where yer been?'

'Oh no place special. Just something I had to do.'

'Well you've missed your brothers.'

Kathleen felt a ripple of unease.

'They were here? What did they want?'

Joy laughed. 'What do they always want. Especially that Eamonn. It was kind of awkward.'

Joy began to lay out the tea cups. Kathleen noticed there were three.

'Awkward? You mean your friend Kenny's here?'

Joy pulled a face. 'Kenny? Goodness no. I'm moving up in the world from Kenny.' Joy flicked her eyes at her bedroom down the hallway. 'A wing commander no less.'

As Joy spoke the bedroom door suddenly opened and a man appeared. He was dark haired. Tall. Very good looking. He proceeded to tuck his shirt into his trousers, then he strode into the kitchen. Kathleen watched him throw a knot in his tie before he slipped on his R.A.F. tunic.

'Right. I've got to be going,' he announced, seeming in a hurry as he looked at his watch, Kathleen noticing at the same time the ring on the finger of his left hand. Joy replied with something like "what about your tea, your breakfast?", but the man did not seem interested; he was already half way down the hallway. Kathleen saw Joy go after him in a swirl of red silk, then she heard the door slam and a moment later Joy was coming back on her own, despondent, into the kitchen. She sat down.

'Well? What do yer think?' Joy flicked a glance at the hallway. 'Handsome devil isn't he.'

Kathleen could only agree. 'He is that,' she smiled. 'But a handsome *married* devil too.' Kathleen pointed to her finger. 'Was that not a ring?'

Joy batted the air with her hand, as if to say "it didn't matter". 'Besides,' she said. 'His wife is seeing someone else.'

'And you're seeing him?'

'I aim to – that's if I can get me hooks into him.'

'So where did you meet?'

'Down the Eagle last night. Oh it was a riot, Kath. You should have come. Why don't yer ever come? Don't yer get fed up with just working at the hospital?'

'Oh no. I *like* the hospital.'

She saw Joy give her a quizzical look, as if she was mad, then laugh.

'Yeah, and I've a fair idea why – it's that special of yours isn't it. You've got sweet on him.'

'Oh Joy, I'm not *sweet* on him. I've told you before. I'm just doing my job.'

'Yeah, and I'm the Queen of Sheba. Yer know he's probably got a girl somewhere don't yer?'

'No, you're wrong.'

'What? Not a sweetheart? A wife?

'Not a soul. I mean the poor man's had no visitors in all the time he's been with us, has he?'

Joy appeared to think back. 'No. You're right.'

'I know I'm right. Besides, the hospital chaplain told me. David's got no one – that's why I feel so sorry for him.'

Joy laughed again. 'So! It's *David* now is it!' She got up and went to the whistling kettle. Then she said: 'Well yer certainly feel something for him, I'll give you that, but I doubt it's anything to do with *sorrow* – *love* more like.'

It was Kathleen's turn to laugh and she said. 'I'm telling you, Joy, it's not like that . . . . not like you think. It's more . . . . more of a promise I made – to care for him, I mean.'

Joy brought the tea over to the table. She sighed. 'Well you've certainly got your work cut out there girl. Has anyone told him about his legs yet?'

Kathleen shook her head. 'No. It's too soon, according to sister. The ward doctor's going to speak to him in a few days time.'

'Well God help him when he does. He'll need all the love you can give him then.'

'Joy, I told you. It's not like that . . . . not . . . . *love*.'

'Isn't it? Then look me in the eye, Kath. Look me in the eye and tell me you don't love him.'

Kathleen told her she would do no such thing and "not to be so silly". Then she stirred her tea. Her gaze never left her cup.

2

David Asher was staring up at the skylight. His eyes had seldom left the window all day, laying there motionless, recalling glimpses of his past as he watched thin clouds drift slowly by, the occasional aeroplane crossing the blue filled oblong. At least it was going to be a beautiful night, he thought. A starlit night. And as the blackout restrictions had been relaxed, he had thought to ask if the blind could not remain open. For the heavens were a fascination to him, the stars a passion. He had but a few. One was Evelyn.

It had been a night such as this, he remembered, some two years ago, just before he had left for France, when he had seen her for the last time. They had dined that evening at the home of the Risdale family: Wroughton Hall. It had been a party of sorts and they had danced on the great terrace. Evelyn had looked wonderful, he recalled, her dark hair shimmering in the moonlight, her eyes sparkling like the stars themselves. She had spoken that night in that ridiculously seductive way of hers, he recalled, playful, as if every word contained some hidden meaning, a coded message that he had to break down, examine for its true value. It was like picking at flowers, he thought. Or the verbal equivalent. *She loves me. She loves me not. She loves me. She loves me not.* But did she really love him at all? Sometimes he wondered. For she loved a good time even better. And everything was just a game. . . . .

'You know my spies tell me you may be leaving us,' she had said as they'd danced.

'Your spies? No don't tell me – young Athos over there?'

'Oh I never divulge my sources, David. But on this occasion – '

'Ah I thought so – infernal blabber mouth.'

'*Rich* blabber mouth, don't you mean?'

'Oh they're the worst kind – the rich ones. Intolerable.'

'Well, intolerably handsome maybe.'

'Why Eve, I do believe you're trying to make me jealous. What did he say to you anyway?'

'Oh don't worry, David. He didn't actually *tell* me where you're off to exactly – he's not that indiscreet. But I can hazard a guess.'

'Yes, and I can hazard a guess too – he volunteered to look after you in my absence, am I correct?'

'I do recall something along those lines.'

'To which you said?'

'Oh naturally I turned him down.'

'Well I'm impressed, Eve – you turning down flat a man like Athos.'

'Oh I didn't say I turned him down *flat*, David. I did have to think about it.'

'Really? For how long?'

'Oh for all of second.'

'Ah, a second eh? My powers over you must be weakening. I can see I'll have to slip something into your glass.'

'Yes, poison if it's true, David. Tell me it's not. You're not really going away are you? '

'Sorry Eve. I must.'

'So Athos was right. You *are* leaving – heartless beast. And what am I expected to do without you?'

'Well, it's just a thought but you could always make yourself useful – join the W.A.A.F.'s or something?'

'Oh David, you know I'd be hopeless at that. No, I'd rather just sit and pine.'

'You pine? Little chance of that, Eve, with Athos around.'

'Athos? Oh, believe me David. I'd rather throw myself off a cliff!'

'And ruin your nails?'

'Oh don't tease me darling, I'm trying to be serious. Honestly, what am I going to do when you've gone? Why, I don't even see *why* you have to go.'

'Eve. I was studying languages before this whole ruddy balloon went up. Do I have to explain?'

'Of course not darling. I *do* understand – you're *needed*. But I

58

need you too. I mean really! How am I meant to amuse myself? Would you really have me join the W.A.A.F.'s.?'

'It's an idea, but there is something else you could try.'

'What's that?'

'You could marry me.'

'What?'

'I said you could marry me.'

'Oh now you're just being silly.'

'No, I've never been more serious in my life. We could get married. That's if you want.'

'Well of course I *want*. But when?'

'As soon as I get back.'

'Oh David, why not before?'

'Because there's no time – I'm due to fly out.'

'I might have guessed there was a catch.'

'Yes, sorry, Eve. But I'm afraid there's another catch too – I may be gone a while. Maybe a couple of months. Do you think you can manage to wait that long?

'Oh I expect so. At least for you David, I can try.'

'Bless you Eve. I know patience isn't your strongest suit.'

'Why David, how little you know me. It's a well known fact that I've the patience of a saint.'

'Oh now you are stretching things, Eve. You a saint! Look, just promise me you'll be here waiting when I get back.'

'Darling, I'll be waiting with a bottle of the finest champagne.'

*

That evening, as the globe lights came on across the hospital, Kathleen made her way up the stairs to the Livingstone Ward to begin her shift. She was feeling excited. For she had a present for him: a surprise. Though after pushing through the double doors and walking down the red linoleum aisle to where he lay, she saw he was asleep. Instead she placed the present on his bedside cabinet. And as she did so, he began to stir, though not in a gentle way, but violent and disturbed.

'Shhh,' she soothed. 'Shhh . . . . it's all right . . . . it's all right.'

Eventually, as he woke, she saw him begin to calm. And taking a cloth she dabbed at the beaded sheen of sweat on his forehead. He had been dreaming, or so he explained, a dream of a leather skinned man.

'That's not a dream,' Kathleen had remarked. 'That's more a nightmare. What does he do this man – chase you?'

'No. It's the others who are doing the chasing.'

'Others?'

'Soldiers – that's my dream – nightmare – call it what you will. It's the night I was captured.'

She slipped a hand behind his head and gently eased him up. She gave him water. After he had sipped a little he told her that he'd had the dream many times. 'And it's always the same,' he remarked. 'I'm in the field – a clearing near a wood, waiting for the aeroplane to pick me up. The resistance had lit flares – a makeshift runway.'

'And the soldiers? They spotted you?'

'They must have. Or someone tipped them off.'

'Then the man in your dream – he's the one who betrayed you?'

'I don't know. I can't remember. And I can't see his face either. At least not all of it. It's just – '

'Just what?'

'Those eyes of his – large, inhuman eyes.'

'What about them David?'

'I know them. I damn well know them. It's just – '

'*Shhh*. Enough now,' she soothed. 'Here – a little more water.'

Kathleen let him sip again. As he did so he must have noticed the present that she had placed on his bedside table. For she saw him stare at it for a long moment, almost in disbelief. Then she saw a smile come across his face. 'My God, is that what I think it is?' he said.

Kathleen smiled back. 'I was saving it for later.'

'Saving it for who?'

'For you of course. You'd like it now?'

He nodded, then Kathleen reached over and took it in her hand. She felt him watch her as she proceeded to dig her nails into the objects luscious outer flesh, slowly paring away the peel in one long spiral.

'You know I haven't seen an orange in years,' he said. 'I didn't even know that hospitals had such things.'

'Oh it's not from the hospital,' said Kathleen. 'I bought it myself.'

She took a segment, explaining how she had purchased it from the black-marketeer at "Number ten". Then she brought it dripping to his lips. But he would not eat.

'You disapprove?' she asked, referring to the black-market.

'No. Only of eating it by myself,' he smiled. 'Won't you have some?'

She smiled back and thanked him. Then popped a segment into her mouth. They both began to eat. The taste felt heavenly, thought Kathleen as the succulent juice jetted to the back of her throat. Then the pair of them swallowed with pleasurable greed. They both laughed.

'You know that's the first time I've seen you laugh,' said Kathleen, whereby his laugher died.

'I suppose I haven't had much cause to do so,' he said, looking away sombrely.

'More cause than some,' replied Kathleen, flicking her eyes across the ward at the other men, silent and unconscious in their beds. Kathleen saw him nod, as if he understood.

'Yes, but sometimes it's hard to think like that,' he replied 'Especially like this.' Kathleen saw him look down at his blankets. And in turn she knew he meant his legs.

'There's a doctor – Doctor Langdon. He's going to speak to you tomorrow,' she told him. 'He's going to explain.'

'Nice of him,' said Asher, a touch sarcastically. 'Nice of him to finally get around to it.'

'I suppose he didn't want to tell you,' replied Kathleen, suddenly realising what she had said. 'I mean – '

She went to look away, but Asher fixed her with a gaze.

'Didn't want to tell me what?'

There was a silence between them. It lasted a long moment before

61

Kathleen decided to explain – explain as best she could that he'd had a thrombosis in both his legs. 'But there's every hope,' she added, trying her best to sound positive. 'I mean it's going to take time.'

Asher turned his head away.

'Time? I haven't got time.' His voice was stubborn. 'You see I have to get out of here.'

Kathleen thought she understood – he was just being impatient – wanting to get back at the man who had betrayed him, the figure who he had seen in his dream; he was desperate to find him and take his revenge. But when Kathleen put that theory to him, he'd shaken his head, and she was rocked by his reply. 'No,' he'd said. 'It's not just that. You see there's a girl – Evelyn. We were going to be married.'

*

At 3 a.m. that night on the Livingstone Ward, Kathleen was busy going about her duties, all of which had become second nature to her – there was the sluice room to clean, dressings to change, buckets to empty. But more importantly she was still thinking about David, or rather how Doctor Langdon would explain his condition come the morning.

'*Better face up to it old chap. There's a very good reason why you can't feel your legs. It's because they're useless.*'

Yes, he would be frank to the point of brutality. But that was just the way with doctors. Though at least she had softened the blow in telling him beforehand, making him prepared. At least more prepared than she, when he had told her of Evelyn.

So he *had* a girl after all. But why had she not been to the hospital to see him?'

'Because she's forgotten all about me,' he'd said earlier when she had asked him, his voice slightly wistful, though without much trace of self pity.

'No, that can't be true,' she'd replied, trying to give him hope. 'Most probably she hasn't been to visit because she doesn't know you're here.'

'Oh she knows I'm here all right,' he firmly countered. 'The Red Cross have told her. But she just hasn't bothered. That's what's happened. And in a way I can't blame her. Two years I was away – two years in France when I said two months. That's a long time to wait.'

'Not for someone you love,' said Kathleen. 'I mean . . . . I mean you said you were to be married, didn't you?'

'Married?' He had laughed, hollowly she thought. 'I don't think Evelyn was really the marrying kind.'

'But isn't that every girl's dream?' she said, somewhat taken back. 'To be married?'

'Maybe, but you don't know Evelyn. She's more independent than most – spirited – used to having fun – a party girl.'

'Is that where you met,' she asked. 'At a party?'

He nodded. 'Yes, a place called Wroughton Hall. It's owned by the Risdale family. I was up at Cambridge with their son. Strange fellow – Athos, the Bursar used to call him.'

'I've heard that name.'

'It's from the Three Musketeers. The other two were myself and a chap called Handley – Rex Handley. We were all friends you see – inseparable – did everything together. Even joined the R.A.F. when war broke out – became pilots. But then there was Evelyn.'

'And she came between you?'

'Not between me and Handley. Rex would never do that. He's a good fellow – a fighter ace – got thirty six kills to his name. Besides, he's happily married – has been since the start of the war. No, it was Risdale. He couldn't stand to see Evelyn and myself together. He was madly in love with her himself, you see. And he wanted her for his own. He's the type, if you know what I mean – rich, set to inherit a fortune. Selfish too – always gets what he wants.'

'But she chose you.'

Kathleen saw him stare up at the skylight. He looked sad she thought – sad and hurt.

'So I thought,' he said. 'I must have been wrong.'

*

That morning, soon after Kathleen had completed her shift and had collected her weekly wage, she was just passing through the hospital gates when –

'Michael! You gave me a fright!'

'I'll give yer more than that if you don't dig deep.'

Michael was looking dishevelled, she thought. Eamonn too. They had not shaved in a while and their clothes looked rumpled and dirty. She almost felt sorry for them. Almost.

She took her purse from her bag and began to rummage through; hoping Michael would not see the small brown pay packet envelope with which she had just been issued. Instead she brought out some change.

She watched Michael's handsome face as his brown eyes swept over the coins.

'Five lousy bob?' He snatched at her purse. 'Give me that!'

He began to rifle through it, then his eyes spied the envelope. He slipped it readily into his pocket. 'You try that again and there'll be trouble.' Then he turned to Eamonn who was holding the morning's newspaper. He snatched it from his hand. 'Here,' he said to Kathleen, thrusting the crumpled paper at her. 'You seen this?' She flattened it out and read the headline: **Russian Troops Enter Berlin – Victory Near**.

'Then it's almost over,' she said.

Michael had lit a cigarette. He took a good hard pull. He looked up and down the street.

'It is that. We're going back home.'

'What?'

'McManus has been in touch. There's a ship coming. I'll let yer know when we get the word.'

The thought of returning to Ireland had caught her off guard; she did not know what to say. Then, almost as if her heart was controlling her head, the words leaped from her mouth.

'I'm not going home, Michael. I'm taking my chances here.'

For a moment Michael said nothing. Eamonn was quicker to act. He grabbed Kathleen's arm in his enormous hands. Kathleen winced as he wrenched it behind her back.

'You'll do as you're told,' Eamonn sneered, Kathleen smelling his breath on her cheek. 'Or do yer want us to tell McManus what yer said?'

'No. No, I'll go. I'll go,' she said. 'If that's what you want.'

Michael was more controlled. She saw him step closer. 'It's not a case of what we want, Kathleen. It's just it's too dangerous to leave anyone behind. Do yer understand?'

Kathleen nodded meekly, though she did not truly understand at all, not even when Michael went on to explain the meaning of that danger – a British Army Officer who they called the rat-catcher.

3

So that was it, his life was over, thought David Asher later that morning after Doctor Langdon had made his rounds, finally giving him the news:

'Better face up to it, old boy, you're going to be in a wheelchair for the rest of your life. Sorry old chap.'

The words still rang in his ears. Yes, that was it all right. His life was over – over at just twenty six. Done and finished. Small wonder that Evelyn had not come to visit him – she had got word of it – couldn't bear to face him. For he was an embarrassment to her now, a cripple, no more use than the poor souls in the beds around him, those silent men who lay like beached freighters washed up on some forgotten shore, left to rot, left to rot and die. Yes, he was a distant memory to Evelyn now. In fact he wagered she had not even given him a single thought.

Even so, he had never stopped thinking of *her* – *her* in another man's arms, in another man's bed – Risdale's bed! And he could guess their conversation:

'Guy, darling, you'll never guess who's back – David Asher.'

'David who?'

'Yes exactly! I had a telegram from the Red Cross. Apparently he turned up in Spain – Spain of all places.'

'Just like the bad penny?'

'Bad Peseta don't you mean?'

'Oh yes. Very good, darling. Anyway, they've brought him here to Cambridge. He's in the Military Hospital.'

'And will you be going to see him?'

'And why would I wish to do that?'

'Well, because you and he were close once, weren't you?'

'Oh that was ages ago. Besides, it was David who was the serious one. Why he even proposed to me once.'

'Proposed? Why of all the nerve! You know he hasn't a penny to

his name, don't you? Why, I've a good mind to go to that hospital and – '

'Oh forget him darling. I know I have.'

Yes, that would be the truth of it, he thought. That would be Evelyn – Evelyn the party girl – the good time girl – the girl who could not even be bothered to wait for him – had not loved him enough to do so. But he would have waited for her – waited until the world's end – loved her until the world's end too – why, he *still* loved her now in fact. He had even confessed as much to Kathleen –

'Oh yes. I don't think you just stop loving someone like Evelyn. That's impossible,' he had said, recalling Kathleen's face at his remark, seeing a strange look in her eyes. as if he had wounded her in some way. 'But it's over now – finished.'

For he truly believed that was so.

*

Kathleen could not sleep when she came home from her night shift at the hospital. It was hard enough trying to do so in the day time at the flat, though it had little to do with the light which spilled in from the window, or even the rumble of traffic which filtered in from the road outside. For one thing she was thinking of David, or rather what might become of him if Michael forced her to return home. Then again why *should* she return home, she wondered? For David would need her more than ever now wouldn't he, especially as Doctor Langdon had no doubt told him about his legs.

Yes, he would be eaten up with misery at the news. And he deserved better. For even though he was an Englishman, (who, according to her father should never be trusted), he did not merit Doctor Langdon's cruel prognosis.

But what did that doctor really know, she thought? For Langdon had been wrong before – *he'd* been the doctor that time on Christmas Eve when David had had pneumonia, when sister had asked her to sit by him – sit by him because they all thought he was going to die. But he had lived. He had *lived!* And in doing so she had proved them wrong. And if then, why not now? Why should she not get him walking again?

Unable to sleep, Kathleen threw back the covers. She pulled on some clothes and went into the kitchen to make tea. As she waited for the kettle she went to her bag. From the bag she pulled out a book.

Yes, she had seen this day coming, a day when she would need to take things into her own hands. And as such, one time when it had been quiet on the nightshift, she had crept downstairs to Doctor Langdon's office on the ground floor. There, checking that no one was in his room, she had borrowed the key to the hospital library from his desk drawer, then had crept up two flights of stairs to the wood panelled library door that was marked: *Doctors and Senior Hospital Staff only*. Then unlocking the door she had sneaked in, locking it behind her.

For a while she had wandered about the maze of dusty shelves, wide eyed at all the books. She had never seen so many, only perhaps on those times she had gone to the great library in Dublin. But these were not ordinary books, not by anyone's standards. And finding one that caught her eye, she slipped it from the shelf into her apron, after which she unlocked the door, creeping back out onto the landing once again, before hurrying downstairs to Doctor Langdon's office where she replaced the key in his drawer.

Yes, she had seen this day coming all right. And after the kettle had boiled she made her tea and brought it over to the table, opening the book on the title page: *The Mechanics of Paralysis by Professor T.W. Meyer*.

Quietly she began to read.

*

How quickly his thoughts of love had turned to hate – *that's* what David Asher lay there thinking, long after the light had faded from the skylight window above him, replaced by a blanket of stars. Not his hatred for Evelyn. For despite the way she had treated him, he could find no such malice in his heart. *That* was just Evelyn, *who* she was: a girl whose love had simply "cooled", slowly dissolving into nothing over those two long years following his capture. No, his hate was reserved for the resistance worker who had *caused* that capture, the swine who had betrayed him.

But it was of little use just hating the man, he thought. He needed to remember *who* the man was. He had *always* needed to remember, right from the outset. He needed to *know* this person, this cruel fiend who had caused him such pain, this monster who had figured so greatly in his dreams. Yes, that was the answer, right from that first moment he had woken from his coma and had asked Kathleen to help. He needed to remember the man's name. But already an idea had come to him, a dangerous idea at that, one which he had already put to Kathleen, one which, in turn, she had swiftly rejected –

'No, David. I can't. I just can't!'

'But it's the only way. Don't you see?'

'No. No I just can't!'

Of course he understood her refusal implicitly. For not only was it dangerous, it clearly violated everything the girl held dear. For obviously it had been her task to make him well again, not to put his health at risk like that. He knew that for a fact. For that day she had clearly been thinking about him, knowing the gloomy prognosis which the doctor had given him.

'The thing is David,' she had begun. 'I don't believe any of it. Why *shouldn't* you be able to walk again?'

'But Langdon said – '

'Oh I know, David. I know what he said. But he's been wrong before. Besides, I've heard he's just an old fashioned country doctor, not an expert. You see, I found this book – '

Asher had felt his heart sink. *'A book?'*

'Yes. And I'll ask you not to look at me like that. You see it's by a very eminent professor, a specialist. He has this theory called *Muscle Memory* – the ability for the body to find its way back even after long periods of inactivity. He says that with time and intensive treatment – '

'But I haven't *got* time, Kathy. I need to find the man who did this to me right now – find him and – '

'I know, David. I know. And I'm sure you *will* find the man. But first we have to get you mobile, or at least try. Don't you see?'

Asher thought long and hard. He had wanted to believe it would work. Oh *how* he wanted to believe. And after a moment he had looked up at her, into her young and innocent eyes.

'Do you really think it's possible, Kathy? – to get me walking again? Really possible?'

'I don't see why not. I mean you have everything on your side – you're young. *And* you're getting stronger every day. The only thing is – '

He saw her enthusiasm dim a little. He noticed that she lowered her gaze.

'Yes, Kathy? What is it?'

'Nothing. It's just that left leg of yours. It's quite bad. I mean it might never . . . . well, you know . . . . you might always need a stick or something.'

He had almost laughed. A stick! A *stick!* Why, if he could even shuffle along he knew he would settle for that!

'Do you think I'd be bothered about a stick,' he had said. 'When do we start?'

'Soon, David,' she had said. 'Soon.'

*

Later that night on the ward, after Kathleen had performed all her usual duties to the satisfaction of the night sister in charge, she went downstairs to the nursing staff canteen. She sat at a table with a cup of tea. There she began to think about David and the man who had betrayed him.

It was quite shocking she thought, this proposition of David's, this idea of his to free the man's name from his mind. It was thoroughly dangerous too. For what if David died in the process? How would she feel then, knowing that she had killed him? Or what if his mind was altered in some way – damaged? How would she live with herself, knowing she was to blame? No, she could not go through with it. It was just too awful, too awful to contemplate – a stupid dangerous exercise. But then again, what if it worked?

Yes, what if she went through with it and it worked, and the identity of the man who had betrayed him was suddenly revealed?

70

What would happen then? The answer was very little, she thought. For he could hardly move, let alone pursue a course of action and go to France and hunt the culprit down.

Kathleen sipped her tea, thinking deeper still. But was she not missing some vital point, she began to wonder? For if David *did* recall the man's name would it not give him the strength he would need for the greater struggle ahead, that long hard road to regain his mobility and walk again? Yes, it could work to his advantage that man's name. It could provide a kind of motivation. For there was nothing like the thirst for revenge to drive a man forwards. In fact she could almost picture it, David taking those first few steps with herself willing him on –

*'Yes, that's it David. You can do it! Just think of the man who did this to you. Come on. Don't let him beat you. Don't let him **win!**'*

Yes, she could see it might work. But only if she could get hold of what David needed to free his mind. For until he had mentioned it, she had never heard of the drug Scopolamine.

*

In his bed, David Asher lay like a prisoner. For that's how he saw himself now: captive, confined to a living hell. Hell? Why, he was already acquainted with the place. It was on the Avenue Foch in Paris: Gestapo Headquarters. The memory haunted him still – the things he had endured. But what information had he volunteered under that terrible duress? What had he divulged? As far as he could remember, absolutely nothing.

Yes, he had told them nothing, and certainly not any of the names of whom he had worked. But then they had tried something different: Scopolamine.

They had shot him full of the stuff. And his mind had suddenly become an open door, an unguarded gateway. Names had poured out. *Names, names, names.* All completely useless. For they had been the names of the already dead, those he had once seen on gravestones whilst hiding out in a French cemetery. But they had been names nevertheless. Names which he'd had no right to remember. But he *had* remembered. And if it had worked back then . . . . well, why not again?

Yes, it was worth a try. And he even wagered there must be stocks of the drug somewhere within the hospital. For he recalled it was kept in small measures for ophthalmic use. There must be a vial on a shelf somewhere? But he also knew that Kathleen had refused to help. And in a way, he understood her reasons.

*

Later than night, when Kathleen returned to the ward from her break in the canteen downstairs, she found David gazing up with fascination at the inky firmament that was captured in the small rectangular window above his bed.

'Looking at something?'

'The stars,' he replied. 'I'm afraid I've something of a weakness for them. Did you know for instance there's more stars in all the heavens than grains of sand on all the beaches and deserts in all the world? It's true. Don't you think they look wonderful. '

Kathleen sat down on the chair next to his bed, gazing up alongside him.

'Yes. And especially tonight,' she said, noticing their brightness and the effect they appeared to have on him, seeing a child-like look of wonderment in his blue-grey eyes. 'Like jewels.'

He nodded in agreement.

'If they *were* I'd grab a handful for you,' he joked.

She laughed.

'That's kind, but I don't think I'm deserving of jewels.'

'Why do you say that? Because of what I asked you to do for me – because you refused?'

'Well I did refuse, didn't I.'

'Well yes, but you think I'm going to hold it against you after all you've done? You saved my life for goodness sake.'

'No, David. Not just me. I can't take the credit for that alone.'

'Then who? The other nurses?'

'No. I meant God.'

Kathleen saw him smile – smile gently, almost mockingly, but not quite. Then his face became serious, his voice respectful.

'Oh yes, of course. *God*,' she heard him say. 'Of course *He* had a hand in it, but it was you who did the work, Kathy – you who nursed me – you who brought me back from the brink.'

Kathleen shook her head.

'No it wasn't, David. You see I made a pact with Him.'

'A pact with God? What sort of pact?'

'A pact for forgiveness.'

He laughed softly. 'And whatever does someone like you need forgiveness for?'

'For my sins,' she said.

She heard him laugh again – laugh at the very notion.

'Sins! Well I can't imagine what those must be! Unless you're telling me you've been knocking back sister's surgical spirit!'

This time Kathleen laughed – laughed weakly.

'Why the thought! As if I'd ever!'

'Then don't be so foolish,' he told her. 'You've no reason to reproach yourself. You're simply a good Catholic girl with too much of a conscience. Am I right? Why you're an angel, that's what you are. An angel! No one could have looked after me the way you have. I simply couldn't have asked for more.'

'But you have,' she reminded him. 'You *have* asked for more. And I told you *no*.'

He seemed to understand immediately what she meant – the scopolamine.

'But I realise *why* you've said no, Kathy, and I've told you you're not to blame. You're just being . . . . *ethical*.'

'No I'm not, David. I'm just being . . . well . . . . *afraid* – afraid of what might happen to you.'

'Then don't be, Kathy. Because all that's going to happen is that I'll remember that man's name – the swine who did *this*.'

She saw him flick his gaze to his blankets and his useless legs beneath.

'It means everything to you doesn't it – to remember.'

'What else have I got left?'

'I know, David. That's why I've been thinking – '

'What – you mean you've changed your mind? You're going to help?'

Kathleen nodded. 'If I can. If I can lay my hands on what you need.'

'Then bless you for that,' he said. 'But it may be difficult. You'll probably need to get your hands on some keys – no doubt wherever it's kept it will be locked away.'

'No, I can do that – I know where the keys are.'

'Then we'll go ahead and do it shall we?'

Kathleen nodded.

'Yes, God help us, we shall.'

4

The next morning when he woke, David Asher had a strange feeling it was going to be a day unlike any other, a monumental day perhaps, or at least a day that might bring with it some good cheer. Though as he opened his eyes, the only positive thing he could see was from a headline of a newspaper lying on his bed: *"Top fighter ace wins D.F.C."*

It was an article about his old friend Rex Handley, and he smiled.

'Well you blighter. Good for you, Rex. Good for you!'

Yes it was nothing less than Handley deserved, he thought as his bleary eyes focused upon the print. For not only was Rex a damn fine pilot, he was a thoroughly decent man, honourable and kind. Moreover, in addition to being strictly teetotal, he was just about the most smartly turned out person he had ever known, fastidious in the way he dressed almost to the point of obsession. Why once, when he and Handley had shared a room at university, he had even caught him ironing his shoe laces. Good old Rex!

Yes, they were happier days back then, he mused – Handley, Risdale and himself, those three musketeers before the war. Though as Asher lay there quietly reminiscing, he suddenly heard a commotion coming from the stairwell. Someone was shouting, running up the stairs; he could hear the heavy slap of their footfalls on the stone treads. Asher turned his head towards the double doors just as a man battered through them – a hospital porter.

'It's over,' he announced breathlessly, bent double with effort. 'Have you heard? It's over!'

'What do you mean you clot?' Asher heard one of the nurses say – the blond haired Londoner who was called Joy. 'What's over?'

'The war,' he replied. 'It's over!'

Asher smiled weakly at the news, looking on as the handful of day shift nurses began to cheer, some throwing their linen caps in the air, whooping with jubilation. Then he saw Joy make her way towards him. She smiled and hugged and kissed him. 'Well done ducks,' he heard her whisper. 'Well done.'

As they celebrated, he thought how well they deserved their victory – these nurses. For he knew that none had earned it more – none more than these handful of angels, these selfless girls who had worked so tirelessly about him. And then there was Kathy, surely the most gentle angel of them all. For earlier that morning, in those small hours before he had been properly awake, something of a revelation had occurred to him – the voice he'd heard in his coma, his "sweet voice" – it hadn't been Evelyn's voice at all. Of course not. It had been hers. *Kathy's!*

Yes, he knew that now. For in those waking moments, like something from a dream, he had half remembered a hospital balcony, felt a cold winter's chill upon his face, sensed himself being lifted up in his bed, lifted up to see a vista of Cambridge, to hear the striking of his old college bell.

'Yes, you're home my love. You're Safe. It's England.'

Yes, it had been Kathy's voice. Kathy! And with such intuitive reasoning that almost belied her years, he knew that she alone had thought to present that familiar vista to him, to give him hope, to give him strength, to show him he was *home*. But what of *her* home he suddenly thought? Would there be any longing in her heart to return where *she* had once lived, back to Ireland, now that the war was over?

He lay there thinking of the possibility. It was almost too painful to bear.

*

Kathleen had sleep fitfully that day. For news of the war's end had spread and the people in the street outside her bedroom window were noisy with excitement. "Isn't it marvellous," she'd heard them say. And "Wonderful news! Wonderful news!"

Indeed it was, but what did the war's end hold for her now, she wondered?

But after she had risen, washing and dressing and walking to the hospital to begin her night's work, none of that seemed to matter as she thought about David and the promise she'd made him. For on her previous shift, at around 3 a.m., she had quietly slipped out of the ward and had gone downstairs, finding the keys to the dispensary in Doctor Langdon's drawer. Then, once inside the dispensary, she had wandered amongst the rows of glass fronted cabinets where the pills and drugs and serums were kept, rifling through the vials and boxes. By the time she reached the last cabinet she had found what she had been looking for.

The fat glass ampoules were packed six to a box, and taking two from the carton she had popped them into her apron pocket for safety. Then she had hunted through the cabinets again for the syringe, finding one in a long blue box. She placed that too in her apron, before setting off to return the keys, then back up the stairs to the ward where she had slipped the things she had taken into her coat pocket.

She could feel those very objects nestling in her pocket as she walked, nearing the gates to the hospital where flags and victory bunting had already been draped from the balconies, fluttering in the cool evening breeze. Though as she passed through those gates, that coolness suddenly turned to a chill, for she could see McManus. He was waiting for her by the steps. So Michael had told him after all? – told him of her momentary display of defiance, those words which had somehow found their way from her heart and onto her lips.

'I'm not going home, Michael. I'm taking my chances here.'

Yes, McManus had been sent to "persuade" her? That was it. Well, she would not have it. And as McManus had clearly not seen *her*, hidden as she was by the tide of other nurses who were making their way towards the hospital's entrance, she slipped down a path to the side of the building instead, passing quietly through a door at the back.

Once inside, the outgoing day shift looked tired but happy, she thought, still full of cheer at the joyful news. On their exit they kissed and wished her well. Then she went onto the ward and straight to David.

'It's over then,' he said to her, giving her a weary smile.

77

'Yes, it's over,' she repeated. 'Isn't it fine?'

Then she saw him beckon her.

'Well, won't you kiss me?' he asked. 'Everyone else has. Oh come on, Kathy.' He nodded at the night sister. 'Oh don't worry about her – *she* won't mind.'

For a moment Kathleen was hesitant. Then she moved nearer. Slowly she leaned down to him, closing her eyes as she felt his hands reaching up, gently taking her and pulling her down onto his lips. He did not smell or taste like her father, she thought. There was no whiskey breath or rasping stubble. He smelled only of hospital soap with which she had bathed and shaved him.

And so she kissed him for as long as she thought was decent, lingering perhaps too long. Then she drew back, seeing as she did so that he was looking straight at her, looking at her with concern. But then she saw his face break into a smile again as he asked: 'Now you wouldn't do anything silly like leave me, would you? I mean now that the war's over?'

Kathleen thought briefly of McManus outside. Then, after a moment she simply smiled back. She shook her head.

'Of all the things,' she said. 'Of all the things!'

*

That night, after Kathleen had attended to the other patients, she had taken a chair next to David's bed where they had sat and talked again, Kathleen telling him that she had let herself into the dispensary with Doctor Langdon's keys, and had taken what they both needed.

'So do you still want to go through with it?' she asked.

He nodded grimly. 'Yes . . . . that's unless – '

'No . . . . no I made you a promise.'

'Then?'

'Then we'll do it later – when sister goes for her break – around 2 a.m.'

'2 a.m. it is – plenty of time yet.'

'Time to change your mind?'

'No,' he said. 'It's made up. It's the only way'

And so they had waited, neither saying much as the hours ticked by. Then, sometime in the night a mighty storm had come and they had both watched it together, lashing down on the skylight window above their heads, beating down through the darkness onto the glass. They heard it cascade off the roof, spilling out of the gutters, splashing down into the streets as it washed the roads clean in preparation for the great day ahead: V.E. Day.

Then, when all was quiet again, Kathleen said.

'Are you ready?'

David Asher had given a nod. 'Yes. Let's get it done.' . . . . . .

. . . . he could not remember the spike of the needle. In fact even sometime after Kathleen had administered the solution, discharging it deep into his veins, David Asher could not recall much at all, and certainly not the name of the resistance worker who had betrayed him.

'Perhaps it would help if you went over it again,' Kathleen suggested to him. 'Tell me about that night – recount what happened.'

He nodded and lay back.

'Okay. As best as I can. Well, I was in that field as you'll remember. It was dark – dark but for the flare path set out by the resistance.'

'And you were waiting for the aeroplane – the one to fly you back to England?'

'Yes. And I remember flashing a torch.'

The scene began to come alive in David Asher's mind, becoming clearer, more distinct. It was working! It was working! 'Yes, that's it,' he began. 'I can see it now. I can hear the plane – a Lysander. I'd know that engine anywhere.'

'And what do you see now, David? It's coming into land?'

'Yes. I mean I see it but no, it's not landing. It's circling. It keeps circling – come on you fool, land why don't you – land!'

'Perhaps the pilot's spotted something – something on the ground?'

'Attracted something, more like.'

'What do you mean?'

'A convoy of soldiers. They're coming. Their lorries are coming along the road at the top of the field. I can see their headlights through the trees. Now they're stopping. Getting out. I can hear the slamming of doors, the clatter of tailgates.'

'And the aeroplane, David? Where's the aeroplane?'

'I don't know . . . . yes. I see it now. It's landing. It's landing at last! God it's going to be close.'

'The soldiers, David? They're coming for you?'

'Yes, down through the field. Dogs too. I'm trying to out run them.'

'Towards the aeroplane?'

'Yes as hard as I can – across the field.'

'And the other men – the resistance?'

'They're giving me covering fire. Buying me time. But I'm getting closer now – closer to the Lysander. Just twenty yards. . . . . No! No, what are you doing you idiot. Don't! *don't!*'

'What's happening, David? What's happening?'

'He's taking off. The pilot's taking off without me.'

'Why, David? Because there's no time?'

'No. There's time! There's time! But he's leaving. He's just leaving me there. But not before – '

'Before what, David?'

'Before I notice something. . . . it's him Kathy. It's him – the figure I saw in my dream – the leather skinned man!'

'Yes it's the pilot, David, the pilot! – it's not one of the resistance at all. Now look at the man who's wearing that leather flying jacket. Look at his face, David. Do you see his face?'

'I'm trying, but his face is obscured – the collar of his flying jacket's turned up – he's wearing goggles.'

'Then look behind the goggles, David. Look at his eyes. You know those eyes don't you? And you know his name.'

'By God, Kathy yes – it's Guy Risdale.'

5

V.E. Night

Guy Risdale was brandishing a pistol, waving it in the Eagle's smoke filled air. Throwing back his head he gave a drunken howl, then loosed off a shot towards the ceiling. A slab of nicotine stained plaster fell to the bar room floor.

For a moment the bar was silent; the customers who were gathered around the piano in the corner stopped their rendition of "Roll out the Barrel" and moved back a pace, out of harm's way. It was the second time Risdale had performed his "party trick", and behind the bar the landlord folded his arms and raised an indignant eye to his damaged ceiling.

'Now I told you what would happen if you fired that thing again, Mr. Risdale. 'I *did* warn you – I'll call a constable. This is a public house, not a blessed shooting gallery.'

Rex Handley got up from his table and pushed his way through to where Risdale was standing. On his way he stopped to pick up the lump of dislodged plaster. The fragment was covered with writing – the scrawled signatures of pilots: a bar room tradition.

Rex Handley's face was apologetic as he laid the lump of plaster on the bar in front of the landlord.

'Sorry about that, Harry. He's drunk, that's all. I'll see he doesn't do it again.' Handley turned to Risdale. He held out his hand for the pistol: a German Luger. He said. 'For Christ's sake, Guy give me that ruddy Jerry pea-shooter before you do some real damage.'

Risdale wouldn't hand it over; he held it out of Handley's reach.

'Not until you've had a drink,' he said to his teetotaller friend. 'And I mean a *real* drink. Why, you've been sat at that table looking glum all night. What's the matter? Don't you know that the war's over? Cheer up for God's sake – cheer up and have a *real* drink.'

Handley looked at him for a moment, then let out a sigh. 'All right. I'll have your bloody drink! Just give me the gun.'

Risdale handed it over. He seemed pleased at last.

'That's the spirit, old boy!'

The landlord duly poured the beer and the two men went back to Handley's table, Risdale only pausing to pat the backside of a young blonde W.A.A.F. girl whom he knew more than well! 'Lovely little filly that one,' he grinned, 'What do you think?'

'I think if Evelyn ever caught the two of you, there'd be trouble.'

'Evelyn? Oh don't mention that bitch to me! You know I wouldn't be surprised if she's not doing something similar, now that America Colonel's out of her life.'

'And are you surprised? I mean the way you treat her!'

'Well it's no more than she deserves. You know what she's like. Oh, and she's started to drink too. I mean yes, she's always liked a good time has Evelyn, but now! I can't understand her.' Risdale shook his head. 'I mean she's *got* everything she needs – she wants for nothing. And she throws it all back in my face. For two pins I'd . . . . Rex? Rex? Are you listening? Oh for God's sake man, what's the matter with you tonight. Snap out of it!'

But Handley felt he could not "snap out of it". For written across the rough yellow plaster of the ceiling he had spotted something: the signatures of a night bomber crew, all of them dead now. And one name stood out from the rest. It was his younger brother, Leslie.

*

At the flat, Kathleen was sitting on her bed. She was rolling on a pair of silk stockings that Joy had loaned her for the evening. For being V.E. day, she had been excused her night shift at the hospital, accepting instead an invitation from Joy to attend a party at the Eagle, a party to which she did not want to go –

'No, you must,' David had insisted when they had talked earlier. 'Go and enjoy yourself.'

'What? While you lay here thinking about your friend and what he did to you? He left you there didn't he – left you in that field to be captured, to be taken by the enemy? Why?'

'Isn't that obvious?'

'You mean – ?'

'Yes, of course. He just wanted me out of the way – to have Evelyn to himself – to get me out of the picture.'

Kathleen shook her head in disbelief. 'To think a man could do that. And to get away with it. Why it's almost like – '

'Murder? You think that hasn't crossed my mind? Or what I'd do back to him if we ever met?'

'Would you, David? Would you go that far?'

He shook his head. 'I don't know. But it's purely academic now, unless – '

She saw him look down at his blankets, at the faint rise of his useless legs beneath. In that moment she sensed his desperation, his need to walk again. *And you will my love. I promise you – you will!*

In her room, Kathleen finished rolling on the stockings then slipped into a cornflower blue dress, borrowed again from Joy. Joy herself was wearing a pencil thin skirt together with a tight fitting sweater.

'Just like Betty Grable,' Joy had laughed, as she had turned sideways, kicking up a heel.

Then, as they had both finished getting ready, there came a knock on the door – a knock which Kathleen recognised: *Rat ta tat tat.*

'That's Kenny, isn't it,' she said. 'Shall I let him in?'

'Oh, don't bother,' replied Joy. She was primping her hair in the mirror. 'Let him wait.'

'On the step?'

'Oh he'll be happy enough. Besides, I'm trying to get rid – don't want him spoiling my chances with my new wing co.'

Kathleen recalled the good looking pilot whom she had once seen with Joy.

'You're seeing him tonight?'

Joy nodded as she put on lipstick, smacking her lips. 'Hmm, meeting up with him at the Eagle – that's if Kenny doesn't ruin it.'

Kathleen saw Joy glance across at her. 'Look, I don't suppose you and Kenny . . . . I mean?' After a moment Joy sighed then turned back to the mirror. She gave a shrug. 'No, I don't suppose you would. Silly question really. I know you've only got eyes for "David".'

'Oh Joy. Not *that* again!'

'I only see what I see, Kath.'

'Joy, you've seen *nothing*. How could you? We've been on opposite shifts most of the time.'

'Until this evening,' Joy reminded her. 'I'm starting on nights.'

'Yes and I'm changing back to days.'

'Ah, there you are! I did say you're hiding something, didn't I.'

'Oh it's a silly girl you are. Don't you see? It's for David's sake – so I can begin his treatment – get him walking again. I can hardly do that on the night shift when he's sleeping, can I?'

Joy finished preening herself. She sighed. 'Get him walking again? Ha! Well I'll say one thing for yer Kath – you're not afraid of a fight.' Finally Joy turned from the mirror, making a pose. 'Well, what do you think? Every serviceman's dream?'

'Oh it's grand you look. Grand,' said Kathleen. 'But shouldn't we be going? I wouldn't want your handsome wing commander kept waiting, like Kenny out there.'

Joy laughed as she clipped her purse shut.

'My wing co? Slim chance. My boy waits for no one.'

*

From his table at the Eagle, Risdale was watching the door. He was waiting for *her* to come in – not the silly bitch of a nurse he occasionally saw, the girl all his men referred to as "The Serviceman's Groundsheet". No, he was waiting for Evelyn.

When she finally arrived, he saw she was on her own – wise move, he thought, given the punishment he would have doled out to her if it had been otherwise. But instead he just watched her in the doorway as she took off her silk head scarf, shaking loose her dark hair, smoothing her hands over her hips in her expensive "off the ration" dress which he had bought her, her almond shaped eyes doing all they could to avoid his gaze. So! She wanted to play it like that did she? She wanted to make out that he was invisible, like he was nothing to her, as if he wasn't remotely aware of the American Colonel of whom she'd been so fond, nor any of the other indiscretions he'd had to tolerate. Well, he thought, two could play at that game. Then in walked the "Groundsheet."

*

At the flat, Kathleen was on her own. She had decided not to go to the Eagle, changing her mind at the last minute as she and Joy had made to leave by the back door. 'Oh, looks like rain,' she had said. 'You and Kenny go on ahead. I'll fetch my coat and catch you up.'

But on closing the door she had done no such thing. In fact she had bolted the door shut. Then, hurrying over to the window, she had watched as both Joy and Kenny had left, clanking down the iron steps, going towards the brick tunnelled passageway where, seconds earlier, she had spotted a man in the shadows.

It was McManus again, she was sure. Yes, she had only seen a wisp of cigarette smoke, only half glimpsed his hat, his face, his shape within the tunnel's entrance, but she knew it was him. He was out there – out there waiting – like at the hospital – waiting to do her harm. Yes, he would not merely try and talk some sense into her, she thought – *beat* some sense into her more like. Or maybe worse. Maybe the acid.

She went into her bedroom and sat down, feeling trapped – trapped in her own home. For the place had become just that to her now. And not just the flat either – the hospital – England – *everything!* It was her life now. Her *new* life. And *she* had made it so, without Michael or Eamonn or McManus himself – their lives were just bitter ones, filled with hate and destruction. It was as if they had drunk from some terrible poisoned chalice, she thought, but in doing so had made her drink from it too. But since starting at the hospital, since her very first day in fact when she had seen the patients lying there sick and wounded, like her crimes made flesh, something wonderful had happened – that poison had slowly drained away, leaving her a changed person, someone better, someone useful.

Could she really give that up so readily, she wondered? After all, what was it Joy had said that very night: *'Well I'll say one thing for yer Kath – you're not afraid of a fight.'*

Slowly Kathleen got up. She went down the hallway to the door where she paused, looking up at the bolt. Her hand went to it, but not to check that it was secure, but rather to slide it back. Then collecting her coat she walked out and went down the clanking iron steps towards the passageway. For this was a night of victory, she thought, and if needs must, she would strike one of her own.

*

Risdale wasted no time in humiliating Evelyn for the way she and the American had humiliated him. Yes, later he would exact a harsher kind of revenge, he thought, though for now the blond haired nurse would do just fine. For after coming through the door he saw that the "Groundsheet" was now standing with a group of men over by the piano, swaying to the music, her voice occasionally soaring with vulgar pride: *'We'll meet again. Don't know where, don't know when. But I know we'll meet again some sunny dahhhy . . . .'*

Yes, she was crude all right – crude but ideal, he thought – just the right sort of woman with which to deliver Evelyn the perfect insult – not unattractive, but common as hell!

. . . . and then he was outside with her. In fact it had only taken a few whispered words, a couple of pink gins, the latter bought with a ten shilling note he'd borrowed off Handley –

'Oh come on old boy. Be a sport. It's only ten bob. I'll pay you back tomorrow.'

'Oh take it all if you want – see if I care.'

'For God's sake Rex. What's wrong with you tonight?'

Yes, there was something bothering Handley – the death of his brother most probably. But he couldn't care about that now. For he found himself in the ever darkening alleyway with the "Groundsheet" at the rear of the pub, by the wall, his hands under her slim-fitting sweater, fondling her breasts that jutted with an almost comical fullness.

'Oh, Guy,' he heard her whisper as he pushed up her sweater, unfastening her brassiere, the next minute his tongue licking and probing. 'Oh Guy. You *do* love me don't you?'

'I'm here aren't I?'

'Oh you are . . . you *are!*'

'Then what?'

'Then nothing lover boy, but just hurry up – I'm working tonight.'

'I thought you already were.'

'I was talking about the hospital! I'm a nurse, remember? Don't you ever listen to anything I say?'

He just grunted and said he did – it was the Cambridge Military Hospital – he remembered that – the Livingstone Ward. Then with her a little happier he proceeded to push his blue-grey serge trousers to his knees. The next moment there was a flap of white shirt-tail. Then a clumsy fumble. Then . . . .

'Oh, Guy. You do love me, don't you – just a little?'

He said nothing. He just stared blankly at the brickwork, his mind filling with the image of Evelyn and the American, the very thought making him quicken his stroke as he thrust the "Groundsheet" ever harder against the wall.

*

At the back of the flat, night was being to fall as Kathleen cautiously approached the gloomy entrance to the tunnelled passageway. At first she saw no one, then, as if in way of a warning, she saw the red button of someone's lighted cigarette. Then she saw a face.

'Well, well, well,' she heard McManus say, smiling as he came out of the shadows. 'Now aren't *we* a sight for sore eyes. Going somewhere?'

Kathleen stood her ground.

'Yes, if you'll let me pass.'

'Sure – once we've got things straight. Michael tells me you're being difficult.'

'Difficult?'

'Don't play games. I haven't time.'

'All I said was that I wanted to stay – take my chances here.'

'And did Michael not explain? You've no choice. You either go or . . . . '

Kathleen saw him draw on his cigarette. He picked tobacco from his lip. He spat to the ground. 'Let me ask yer something,' he went on. 'Have yer ever heard of a man they call the "rat-catcher?"'

She nodded. 'Yes, Michael spoke of him.'

'And did Michael ever tell yer who he is – he's a gobshite English Army Major by the name of Armstrong. And he's out for our blood.'

She had never heard of him. And saw no reason why she should. 'Out for our blood? – why? The war's over.'

'Not *his* war,' said McManus. 'Did Michael not say?'

'Say what?'

'It was Armstrong's son yer killed – remember?'

Kathleen was struck cold. The *boy*, she thought. The **boy!**

'But that wasn't me,' she protested, feeling sick and cowardly. 'That was Michael and Eamonn.'

'And yer think Armstrong would argue the difference? Why, he'd hang yer soon as look at yer. But not before you'd given him names – our names.'

'But I'd tell him nothing, I swear.'

'Sure, that's because it's not going to happen.' Kathleen felt him grab her arm. 'You're coming with me, bitch.'

He began to drag her into the darkness of the tunnel, but Kathleen resisted, her feet scraping upon the ground. She tried to grasp for a handhold upon the rough brickwork, but when she could not find purchase, she turned on McManus instead. Before she knew it she had swung her free hand at him, smacking him in the face.

The blow echoed like a pistol shot in the confines of the passageway, and for a moment McManus stopped. He looked stunned, thought Kathleen, if not by the blow then by what happened next. For a trickle of blood appeared from the man's nose. Kathleen watched it almost spellbound as she saw it track down from his nostril in a straight red line. She had hit McManus! She had hit McManus and had drawn blood! The man wiped it away with the back of his hand, staring for a moment at the crimson stain. Then in the darkness, Kathleen saw his eyes flare.

'Why, you – '

He reached into his pocket, for what Kathleen wasn't sure. All she knew was that for a split second she felt his grip relax upon her arm and she was free. Immediately she took to her heels.

Within moments she was running – running hard, coming out of the passageway where she rushed straight across the street, dashing along the pavement before veering down a side road, then down another passageway between some houses. Some way behind her, in the darkness, she heard the clatter of rolling dustbins; McManus was behind her, following in clumsy pursuit.

Then, moments later she found herself on some waste ground, a bombsite where houses had once stood, now reduced to a mountain of rubble. She began scrambling up the vast bank, the brick dust choking her as she clawed her way to the top. There she paused, recovering her breath, the blood pounding in her ears, the ridiculous sound of people cheering from a street party someway off, then the "plink plonk" of a tuneless piano dragged from parlour to pavement. *'Ran rabbit run rabbit run, run, run . . . .'*

Then she heard something else: McManus! He was scrambling up the rubble mountain behind her. Instinctively she grabbed a brick and hurled it at him. McManus ducked. The brick bounced harmlessly past with a *clunka, clunka, clunk.*

Taking to her heels again she stumbled down the rubble at the other side, spotting a bombed out house a small distance away, jutting up three stories, in defiance of gravity. Finding a door she rushed inside.

The banister wobbled precariously as she shot up the stairs, working her way up. Then getting to the top she began trying the doors off the landing, but they were all either locked or stuck in their frames. With nowhere else to go, she turned, then realised her mistake. For entering the building, McManus had followed her up; he was there on the landing. He came straight toward her.

Kathleen's initial instinct was to back away, but instead she came forwards, trying to slip past him. But McManus caught her by the hair and flung her back. She landed heavily in the corner, crashing to

89

the floor.

For a moment McManus stood before her, no more than a few paces away. But then as he moved forward, the house gave out a monumental groan. The next second there was a sickening crack as the staircase began to give way, then the sound of snapping timbers and the rush of falling masonry. Ripped from the side wall, the staircase began to swing out. It stopped abruptly in the centre of the house, the sudden jolt sweeping McManus off his feet. He tumbled towards the wooden banister rail, crashing straight through.

Kathleen was clinging onto the staircase's opposite edge. She gathered herself before working her way across the tilted landing. As she did so she caught sight of McManus. He was still there; she could see his bunched up knuckles on the lip of the staircase. He had not fallen after all. He was hanging over the void.

'Help me! Help me!' she heard him cry.

Kathleen stared across. The staircase creaked and groaned. Everything told her to climb down while she could, but she shuffled her way across the tilted landing and reached out a hand.

'Here. Take hold,' she called. And she saw McManus release his right hand, as if to grab hers, though he did not. He reached downwards instead, sinking his hand into his coat pocket. Kathleen saw him take something out: a bottle. Then smashing off the neck, he threw some liquid up into Kathleen's face.

The liquid came within inches of her before gravity took it back down. And it landed in McManus' face instead. The man gave out a scream as it burned his flesh. He let go and fell to the hallway below. His body landed with a *thud*.

A few moments later, after carefully descending what was left of the unsecured stairs, Kathleen picked her way through the rubble on the ground floor, going over to where McManus lay. Cautiously she took hold of his wrist. She checked for a pulse. There was none to be found.

*

He was drunk. Rex Handley the non drinker was drunk, though nowhere near drunk enough, not for his liking, nor sufficiently numb either for that matter.

He had been sitting at the same table at the Eagle all night, quietly imbibing one pint after another, silently brooding over the death of his brother. He had even seen off Guy, his friend, collapsing drunk to the floor, muttering something about Evelyn as usual, upon which he'd had the presence of mind to place the man in a cab back to the airdrome.

'Why does she do it to me, Rex old man?' he'd slurred as he'd bundled him into the cab's back seat. 'She's meant to love me . . . but she just loves herself . . . *bitch* . . . . always has . . . . always will. Well damn her, I say . . . damn her to *hell!*'

Then, as the cab had pulled away, Guy had pulled down the window and had called out. 'But you're still my friend aren't you Rex . . . . despite everything . . . . despite all that's happened . . . . despite Leslie? It wasn't my fault, old man – what happened to your brother . . . . it wasn't my fault!'

Getting up from the table he decided he'd had enough – enough of the beer which he did not like, enough of the celebrations which he thought he did not deserve. And going outside he walked to his car nearby, a red M.G. It was late now and he just wanted some peace. Climbing behind the wheel he drove away, knowing exactly where he would find some.

But before long the car began to falter, the engine misfiring, his speed dropping as he began to slow in a country lane. It was the number one plug again, he thought: a loose cap. It was always giving trouble, but now? Now of all times? It was nonsensical to stop and fix it, he knew, but it irritated him, spoiling his sense of perfection – always perfection. Eventually he pulled over. He stopped.

It was nearly midnight now, and he needed a torch to see what he was doing. He retrieved one from the car's boot along with some blue overalls, which he slipped on over his uniform. Lifting the bonnet he fixed the plug; a simple job. Then driving off again he did not stop until he had reached the millpond in the village of Grantchester.

After he had parked, he switched off the engine. He took out an envelope from the pocket of his uniform. Unfolding a half finished letter inside, he positioned his torch over it and began to write. Then, when he was done, he folded the paper back into the envelope, tucking it neatly into the top pocket of his overalls.

Getting out the car, he went and stood by the deep swirling waters of the millpond, then realising that he was still wearing his overalls, he took them off, returning them to the boot of his car before going back to the quiet spot that he had found at the water's edge.

A stiff breeze was coming in off the dank meadows behind him and it brought with it the scent of victory bonfires. It made the tall reeds around the millpond's perimeter tremble and sway, though he did not feel its chill. He was numb, dead to all but his crushing remorse.

Somewhere he heard a church clock faintly chiming midnight. He began to count the soft dull tolls in his head. *Two, three, four.* He could smell the scent of freshly cut grass, sweet and moist. It reminded him of every single airfield from which he had ever flown. *Five.* Those blessed English meadows where he had defended a nation from the avarice of others. *Six.* He turned his face to the sky, the space where he had been at peace with his thoughts. *Seven.* That wonderful domain of solitude, which he had sullied with his own hands. *Eight.* Now he was going back there, free from guilt. Returning home to that blue celestial heaven. *Nine.* In the distance he could see the glow of Cambridge, lit up after the long dark years of the blackout. *Ten.* Burning not with the murderous white heat of incendiaries, but with the soft benign luminescence of electricity. *Eleven.* It gladdened him. Life had returned and he had played his part. He reached into this tunic pocket, pulled out Risdale's pistol, and raising it to his head he pulled the trigger on the last stroke of midnight.

*

After she had left the bombed out house, Kathleen did not return immediately to the flat. Instead she walked the darkened streets in a daze, with neither purpose nor direction. So McManus was dead. He was dead and she was responsible, or at least partly so, just like the night in London when they had killed the old man and the boy – Armstrong's boy! Oh what misery they had caused. What misery *she* had caused!

Feeling desolate and wretched she suddenly found herself in the street near the flat and decided to go inside. Joy was still at the Eagle, she presumed, for going through the door she found the place empty. Then she remembered that Joy was working a late shift at the hospital which was just as well, as she found herself in a mess. For glancing in the hallway mirror she noticed that her face was grubby, her stockings ruined. The blue dress that Joy had loaned her was grubby too, grimy with brick dust. She slipped it off and went with it to the bathroom, filling the bath with some water from the Ascot with which to wash it.

Taking up a bar of soap and a nailbrush she began to scrub frantically at the material, working away with almost a hysterically zeal. And soon, without forethought or realisation, Kathleen had turned the brush upon herself, rubbing her fingers raw, desperately trying to scour the memory of everything from her dirty filthy hands.

*

There was a vacant bed next to David Asher's. The occupant had died around midnight. Though the bed had not stayed vacant for long. For soon after that time another patient had been admitted to replace him, Asher noting his arrival as the hum of the lift had woken him, then the clatter of the lift door being pulled back. As far as he could tell another poor soul was being wheeled onto the ward by a hospital porter, escorted down the red linoleum aisle by a lone nurse, the one he knew as Joy. Under the soft glow of the ward's "harvest moon" lights, he could see that the man was in bad shape, lying ill and unconscious, his head swathed in bandages, seeping blood.

Asher looked on as Joy and the porter had transferred the man to the adjacent bed, the nurse making him comfortable as the porter made his exit, retreating back down the aisle with his wheeled trolley towards the lift. Then the lift door had closed again with its usual clatter, sinking once more with its familiar electric hum. Then the ward had fallen silent again, Asher seeing Joy leave too.

93

After she had done so, he had casually glanced over. The new patient had made an attempt to take his own life by all accounts, or at least that's what he had gathered from an overheard conversation between the nurse and the porter, the porter having spoken to the ambulance driver, who in turn had spoken to a man who had discovered the poor chap whilst walking his dog. Asher was saddened. He could hardly comprehend anything more tragic than a suicide on such a night, anything more desperate with all its celebrations of victory and its merrymaking. Then he looked closer.

*

Guy Risdale was amazed how quickly he had become sober, astonished at the speed with which he had come around.

After stumbling out of the taxi at the airdrome, he had gone straight into the officer's mess where he had promptly fallen asleep. At 2 a.m. he'd felt a hand on his shoulder.

'Sir – the telephone. The police.'

It had been the word "police" that had pulled him so rapidly to his senses, then the short and worrying conversation that had taken place once he had lifted the receiver –

'Yes. . . . speaking . . . . well of course I know Squadron Leader Handley; he's one of my men . . . . oh . . . oh I see . . . . right . . . . right . . . . yes . . . . and where have they taken him . . . the Military Hospital you say, ... the Livingstone Ward . . . . no, I'll inform his wife. . . . . and thank you. . . . thank you very much for informing me.'

As he had put the receiver down, his brain had swiftly clicked into gear. Within a second his drunken haze had gone. He was thinking fast. *You bloody fool, Rex. You bloody fool. And all because of Leslie!* But what if Handley had left a suicide note? Yes, that would be difficult, a catastrophe in fact – doubly so if it fell into the wrong hands – the police for instance. God, it would mean ruination, the finish of him if the truth about Leslie ever came out. *Damn* Handley and his precious conscience. He had to find that letter. Find it and destroy it!

He began his search by going straight to Rex's office. He began to rummage through the paperwork on the man's desk. Then he tried the man's quarters, picking through the chest of drawers in his room and then the pockets of his spare uniform that he found hanging in his wardrobe. *Nothing! Nothing!* Risdale sat down on the bed. Damn Handley. Damn him to hell! What had he done with it?

He rubbed at his temple and began to consider things. Maybe there wasn't a letter at all, he thought, but he doubted that very much; Handley wasn't the type. He was the sort of man who planned things. His attention to detail was almost an obsession, everybody knew that. No, Rex would not have exited this world without an explanation. Of course there was a note.

Naturally though there was a possibility that the police had it already, he pondered, though if they did not then he wagered it was still in Handley's possession, in one of his pockets? He would call the hospital and get someone to check.

Then he had a brainwave – the *Groundsheet!* Yes, *she* worked at the military hospital, didn't she. And on that very ward – the Livingstone Ward.

He picked up the phone again and asked the operator to connect him. When he heard the Groundsheet's voice, he told her what to do.

'Oh I can't do that,' she replied. 'It's too late.'

'What do you mean, it's too late?'

'His clothes were burned when he came in, at least most of them.'

'Burned?'

'Yes, they were dirty – soiled. They went into the hospital's incinerator. I'm sorry Guy. We've still got his effects though. But I don't remember no letter . . . . . Guy? . . . . Guy . . . ?

Risdale had already slammed the phone down. Quickly he went back to the officers' mess where he put on his cap. Yes, maybe the letter was with his effects – that stupid girl had missed it. He would drive over to the military hospital and find it. And if he drew a blank, then he'd wring the truth out of Handley himself.

*

3 a.m. on the Livingstone Ward and David Asher was lying watching the double doors at the end of the ward, listening for signs of activity

on the stairwell. For he knew a visitor was coming. A very special visitor.

He had overheard the news some forty minutes ago now, when, after being called to the telephone, Nurse Deakin had reappeared on the ward with a smile on her face.

'What are you looking so happy about?' Asher had heard one of the other nurses say to her. 'Don't tell me you're glad to be working nights again?'

'Only the ones where my new pilot boy comes in. He's on his way right now – be here in about half an hour – coming to see that new patient we had in – Guy and him are pals.'

. . . . well that half an hour was up now, Asher decided. And if that man was who he suspected, then Asher knew he was going to give him one hell of a surprise. Risdale? It *had* to be. For those thirty minutes had lapsed into forty now and was that not typical of the man to be late, he thought – late like the night he had waited for him in that foreign field – late to land – late to pick him up – *late, late, late!*

But oh, Risdale had been quite the opposite with his departure, hadn't he. Yes, he'd been quick enough in taking off, quick to abandon him to his fate, quick to leave him there and make a clear pathway between himself and Evelyn.

But then suddenly his ears pricked to a noise from the end of the ward. Asher listened. Footsteps on the stairs? No, it was the sound of the lift; he could hear the faint electrical hum that signalled that someone was coming. Yes, and that was typical of Risdale too – lazy, lackadaisical – never stand when you can sit – never sit when you can lie – never exert yourself unless absolutely necessary.

But none of that mattered now. What mattered was that in a few minutes time, Risdale would be there – there after two long years. David Asher swallowed deeply with a kind of nervous expectation, listening to the lift as it rose gradually within its shaft, rattling its way to the top, getting steadily louder under the tug of its cables, bringing the man ever closer, closer, closer, the lift indicator slowly moving around – *first floor, second floor, third floor, fourth.*

And then with a jolt the lift was there, Asher hearing the soft metallic *clunk* as it stopped, then the clatter of the lattice door as someone pushed it back. Momentarily his pulse began to race. *Two years. Two long years!*

And then he saw him. Yes, it *was* Risdale – Risdale after all this time. But still slim and dark and impossibly handsome, a wing commander now he noted. For he could plainly see the rings on the sleeves of the man's uniform. Yes he had obviously "got on" – gained promotion – and no doubt at the expense of others, he wagered. But that did not matter either. For in a strange and peculiar way, it seemed that fate had delivered the man to him: Athos, this third musketeer. And as Asher lay there quietly watching, he saw the man walk slowly down the red linoleum aisle between the beds, seeing Risdale's eyes flicking from one hollow cheeked patient to the next, obviously searching for Handley. And then, finding him, Asher saw him go over, then rifle though the man's bedside locker for something. Then he turned his attention to Handley himself, slapping the young pilots pallid face.

'Rex . . . . Rex! Come on old man. What have you done with that damned letter? Speak to me. Speak!'

But the next man to speak was Asher himself.

'It's no good, Risdale. He can't hear you.'

Risdale turned sharply. For a moment he saw that the man was caught off guard, disorientated, hesitant, disbelieving perhaps. Then his expression changed. He smiled thinly.

'Well, well, well. As I live and breathe – David Asher!'

'What's the matter Risdale, you look surprised.'

'Only surprised in a good way, old boy. I mean I knew you were back. I'm just glad to see it's true – you're alive.'

'Oh I'm alive all right, but with no thanks to you.'

'What are you talking about?'

'I'm talking about two years ago or have you forgotten? Because I haven't. I remember every single moment.'

Risdale appeared to feign a look of innocence.

'Hold on old chap. If you're talking about that night in France, I had no choice. It was nip and tuck old boy. Nip and tuck.'

'What do you mean?

'I mean if I hadn't taken off when I did . . . . well, the Germans would have had the pair of us. There wasn't time. I thought you realised?'

'The only thing I've come to realise is that you left me there – *chose* to leave me there.'

'But that's ridiculous. Why would I do a thing like that?'

'We both know why, Risdale – have you seen her? Have you seen Evelyn?'

'Evelyn? But what's Evelyn's got to do with it . . . . why, you don't think . . . . why that's preposterous! You're just ill old boy, that's all – must be to think like that. Just wait until you're better. You'll start thinking straighter then – then you'll see it differently. You'll see I'm right.'

'I'll see you dead before that.'

'And you'll achieve that how exactly?'

'Oh I'll find a way Risdale. Just keep looking over your shoulder.'

'Oh I never look back, old boy. But something tells me you'll be doing plenty – look at you. Why, you're halfway to the grave by the looks. How Evelyn would laugh.'

Risdale turned. He went to walk away.

Asher called after him. 'Then you *have* seen her?' His tone was pleading, his voice almost pitiful. 'You *have* seen Evelyn?'

Risdale had only taken a few paces down the red linoleum aisle when he stopped. He smiled.

'Seen her? Of course I've seen her. Evelyn's my wife.'

6

The next morning, when she woke, Kathleen's thoughts were of the night before. She'd not intended for McManus to lose his life; it had just happened. But as she left for the hospital, thinking what a terrible man he'd been anyway, what little sympathy she'd harboured for him began to ebb away, her thoughts slowly turning to his body. For how long would it take for someone to find him, she wondered? Quite a while, she guessed, being half hidden under the rubble of that bombed-out house. And quite a time hopefully before reports of it reached the newspapers and the suspicious minds of her brothers.

She tried to forget the issue as she arrived at the hospital gates, bumping into Joy who was just leaving. She looked weary and spent thought Kathleen as she gave Joy an apology for her absence at the Eagle, lying that she had "come over sick".

'Talking of which,' said Joy. 'We had a new boy in last night – head wound. Keep an eye on him will yer Kath? Oh, and you'd best keep an eye on your David too.

'David? Why? He's not sick too is he?'

'No, he's doing well. It's just . . . . well, he seems *unsettled* – he didn't get much sleep last night – like there's something bothering him.'

Minutes later she was at David's bedside. She soon found out the reason – the new patient was his friend Rex Handley.

'They said he tried to kill himself, Kathy. Can you believe that? A man like Rex? Is there anything you can do for him?'

Kathleen went over, though she could do little more than make the man comfortable.

'I'm sorry, David. I'm afraid he's terribly sick. Small wonder you're upset.'

'It's not just that, Kathy. It's Risdale – he was here last night.'

'He came onto the ward?'

He nodded. 'Yes, he came to see Rex, but he ran into me instead.

You should have seen his face. He looked like he'd seen a ghost.'

'Perhaps he had, David. I mean maybe he thought you were dead – killed that night he deserted you.'

'No, he knew I was back all right – he said so. Besides, Evelyn must have told him – I had her down to be informed by the Red Cross – Risdale must have seen the telegram. You see they're married now.'

'Married? So you were right. Risdale just wanted you out of the way, to have Evelyn to himself?'

'Of course he did. And I told him as much.'

'And what did he say?'

'Oh he denied it, naturally – said if he hadn't have taken off when he did, then the Germans would have had the both of us.'

'But disproving it will be hard, David.'

'I know. And getting even will be harder still. That's why we've got to get these things working again.'

She saw him gesture to his blankets and his useless legs beneath.

'I told you David. I've a plan.'

'Oh yes, a *book* I believe you said.'

'Yes, and I'll kindly ask you to keep your sarcasm to yourself – you'll be eating your words in a few minutes time.'

'Why, what's happening?'

'It's the start of your treatment – I've sister's permission to use the rehabilitation facility in the basement.'

She saw him raise a smile.

'Sorry, I didn't mean to be rude just then. It's just – '

She smiled back. 'I know. But I had to make a switch to the day shift first. Now we can get busy at last, busy working wonders on those leg muscles.'

She saw him look over at Handley. His expression became serious again.

'If only you could work one of your miracles on poor old Rex,' he said with a sigh.

She shook her head.

'Only God can work miracles, David. But we could say a prayer.

He might at least hear one of our voices.'

Kathleen saw him turn his face back to hers.

'Your *"sweet"* voice perhaps?'

'What?'

He was looking at her differently, she thought, lovingly perhaps; there was something in his gaze.

'It doesn't matter,' he said, smiling again. 'Just me being foolish.'

*

At midday, Kathleen had her lunch in the hospital canteen after returning David to the ward. His first session of rehabilitation in the basement had not gone well. For one thing she'd had to summon a hospital orderly to help him from his bed. Then, once in his wheelchair, he had been physically sick, and she'd had to return him immediately.

Then later, when he'd sufficiently recovered, and she had tried once more, something else had happened. For after they'd gone down in the lift, upon her wheeling him out into the basement room –

'No. I want to go back!' he had almost shouted. 'Take me back will you!'

It had confused her. Then, when she'd asked if he was feeling sick again, he'd replied: "No, it's not that – ", which had confused her still. It was odd. Really odd. Had he lost his nerve? No. He was not like that – not a cowardly man. Quite the opposite.

She began to eat her lunch again amid the canteen's busy chaos. Perhaps he knew himself to be too weak, was *that* it? – too undernourished for the rigours ahead? But she was spending all she could to supplement his diet and could spend no more. Not that it had made much difference. For he had seemed so terribly frail when she had helped him from his bed into that wheelchair, looked so terribly thin, seemed so fragile when, draped in a blanket around his shoulders, they had descended to that basement to begin their work. He had been quiet too, she had noticed, pensive, obviously concerned over his friend Handley and his encounter with Risdale. Perhaps the appearance of those two men had lost him his focus? Though earlier, when she had been absent from the ward, busily fetching the

101

wheelchair, she had returned to find yet another distraction: an attractive blonde who was sitting at Handley's bedside.

'I think she's Rex's wife – Joan.' David had told her as they had descended in the lift. 'I know *of* her, but we've never met.'

'The poor woman,' said Kathleen. 'The news must have come as a shock.'

David had nodded in agreement. 'And to everyone who knew him I expect.' Then Kathleen saw him shake his head in disbelief. 'What makes a person do something like that Kathy, a wonderful chap like Rex – to put a gun to his head? And on V.E. night?'

Kathleen's mind began to reel back, dwelling on all she had done.

'It's the war, David. Sometimes it drives people to do bad things.'

'What, to end their own life? A good person like Rex?'

'Especially a person like Rex.'

'But you're a good person too Kathy, but I'm willing to bet you've never contemplated anything so foolish.'

'I wouldn't say that.'

'What do you mean?'

'That I'm a good person.'

'Well of course you are. Why, I wouldn't even *be* here if it wasn't for you – you saved my life.'

'I told you David, that wasn't me.'

'Oh yes. I forgot – this *pact* you had with "God".'

'You don't have to say *His* name with such disbelief, David. It's true.'

'That's as maybe, but I know this much – when I was close to death it wasn't God who came to me. It was you.'

'What do you mean?'

'Oh, come on Kathy. We've no secrets between us. It was you. I know it was.'

Before she could say otherwise, he told her about the voice he'd heard in his head, his *sweet voice* he'd called it. Then the faint recollection of being taken onto one of the hospital's balconies where he'd heard that same voice again – *her* voice.

'So you've remembered?' she asked, finally giving in. 'You've remembered that time?'

'I remember it was cold,' he said

'You were dying,' she confessed. 'I had to think of something – anything.'

'Like pinching the back of my hand?'

She smiled. 'That was just to bring you round. But I held your hand too. Do you remember that?'

'Yes, and something else. You called me "my love".'

Kathleen felt herself blush.

'Oh did I? I can't recall.'

'Well you did. So are you saying that you didn't mean it?'

'I didn't say that. It's just – '

'Oh yes, I know. It's just an expression isn't it.'

'I didn't say that either.'

'Then you mean – ?'

But as Kathleen was about to confess, her courage deserted her. Then the next moment the lift had ground to a halt at the basement where David's courage seemed to desert him as well, asking to be returned to the ward.

*

Kathleen could not get to sleep that night; there had been too many of Joy's "gentlemen callers". Perhaps more than usual, she thought. Or perhaps it was just that she was more aware of them, changing as she had to the day shift, and being home in the night-time. Whatever the reason they had been a nuisance, getting her out of bed as they'd hammered on the door. They had been servicemen in the main, mostly drunk, usually in pairs.

The first had been an army corporal and a private, one short, the other tall. The men had grinned and leered at her, leaning on each other as they had drunkenly stood askew in the doorway, giving her the "hungry eye".

'She's not here,' she'd explained. 'She's at the hospital.'

'Why, what's wrong with her?' quipped one.

'Got a bun in the oven, has she?' quipped the other

Then they had dissolved into mirth, a terrible hacking wheezing laugh which had quickly developed into a cigarette induced coughing fit, whereby one of the men had fallen to the ground, knocking over some empty milk bottles which, in turn, had duly rolled then smashed upon the iron steps.

The next caller had been the boy Kenny, Joy's R.A.F. batman. He had stood at the door sober but forlorn as the spring rain had pelted down upon him, soaking into his blue serge uniform. Kathleen had invited him in, putting the kettle on and laying out cups. Then later, while she had poured out the tea, Kenny had poured out his heart.

'Of course I know she doesn't love me,' he had confessed drearily as Kathleen sat there and listened to his woes. 'In fact I don't think she really loves anyone, except perhaps herself. Or maybe Wing Commander Risdale.'

The name had brought Kathleen up sharp. *Wing Commander Risdale? The tall good looking pilot who she had once seen at the flat?*

'Risdale you say?'

Kenny had nodded sombrely. 'Oh yeah. She's mad about him.'

Then, after the realisation about Risdale had sunk in, and after Kenny had gone, the door knocker had slammed down one last time.

It had been a Canadian on that occasion, another serviceman, smart in his uniform as he had stood there with a bouquet of flowers in one hand and a box of "candy" in the other. He had been different from the others, thought Kathleen, initially respectful; he had removed his cap, giving her a snow white smile. He had called her "Ma'am".

Moreover he had looked clean and wholesome, and initially had acted unfailingly polite. For when she had explained Joy's absence by informing him about her change to the night shift, he had simply smiled again, saying. "Gee. That's too bad."

Then, at that point, his mood and manners had changed. For she had seen him give her the same "hungry eye" as the others. Then he had produced a money clip from his pocket, one that she saw was stuffed with large English white five pound notes. "Then how much for you, then honey?"

Kathleen stared at the clip of five pound notes. The things she could buy David on the black market with *that*, she thought, all the things she needed to build him up. And the image of David came back to her, frail and fragile in his wheelchair, weak and undernourished on the hospital ration. And in that moment of weakness, another image came to her too. It was one of herself, standing there at the door wearing something of Joy's, something she had found discarded in the hallway and had thrown on out of convenience. And in doing so it explained the serviceman's mistake. *And* her own. For she was wearing Joy's red silk dressing gown, the one with the Chinese embroidered dragons.

*

Later than night, when it was dark, David Asher was laying thinking about the basement and the way he'd reacted when Kathleen had taken him there earlier that day. He had been stupid. Stupid and fearful. What a coward she must think of him, he pondered, and he cursed himself for being so. For as soon as those lift doors had opened he'd begun to crumble, his courage swept from under him the moment he had lain eyes on that basement room. And why? He had not even dared tell her, sparing her the filthy details.

Then again he wondered if she had already guessed? For did she not know every inch of him? But what did he know of her? Absolutely nothing – nothing save for the way she made him feel, like the times when she would smile at him. Or when he would notice the curve of her hips when she would lean over him. Or the way the light would sometimes catch that auburn hair of hers from the skylight window. Yes, perhaps he knew little of her but those few wonderful things. But one thing he *did* know was this: he was falling in love with her. And he hoped that she felt the same.

Then, as if by magic, when he opened his eyes, she was there at his bedside. What's more he saw that her arms were laden with many things. And she was busily placing them in his bedside locker – chocolate, fruit, tinned goods – things he had not seen in an age.

'Kathy? What are you doing here?'

'Oh I couldn't sleep. Besides, I've got this for you.'

'I can see that. But so much! Where did it all come from?'

'Oh just a man.'

'And I thought you only had eyes for me,' he joked. 'The black market again?'

'Shhh,' she whispered, joking back. 'Careless talk costs lives!'

'But where did you get the money?

'Oh never mind about that.'

He watched as she knelt at his locker, placing the things inside. There was more, or so she told him – much more set aside for him downstairs in the hospital's kitchen. But as she spoke, he saw a white five pound note fall from her coat pocket onto the red linoleum floor. She looked furtive and embarrassed, he thought, as he watched her pick it up.

'There,' she said, closing the locker door. 'That should do for a while. We can't have you going hungry with all that work ahead. Have you managed to get any sleep?'

'A little,' he said. 'I'm afraid I've been too preoccupied.

'Thinking?'

He nodded to the skylight. 'Watching.'

He saw her look up, seeing the night sky captured in the small rectangle. 'Oh yes, the stars. You've a weakness for them.'

'Amongst other things,' he smiled, meaning her. He patted the bed. 'Here – come and sit. I'll show you.'

He watched as Kathleen sat down beside him. Then together they gazed up at the inky firmament. 'Did you know you've a star named after you,' he asked.

'I'm flattered. Which one?'

He pointed to a tiny pinpoint of light. 'There,' he said. 'It's called the Angel star – a binary, a physical double in fact – two stars so close that they appear as one. You see they circle each another on an orbit that takes them millions of miles apart, but they always return to be together again at the end of their passage. It's called the Journey of Separation.'

He saw her gaze up at the vast blanket. She said it was romantic, the notion that stars had names and lives that seem to mirror their earthbound counterparts.

'And those?' she asked, pointing innocently to a group of stars, inquiring if they had names too. And as he looked up, for some reason David Asher felt a chill run through him. For he realised she was pointing at the constellation of Orion: The Hunter.

7

The army dispatch rider was riding hard across the Fens, his motorcycle blasting a path down a dead straight road to the bleak army camp on the northern edge of Cambridge. Stopping at the candy-striped barrier he reached into his belted mackintosh and showed the sentry his papers. The sentry looked at them briefly, then pointed to a huddle of dilapidated wooden buildings.

'That's where you'll find him chum – the rat-catcher.'

Inside his hut, Major Charles Armstrong was at his desk. His office was a makeshift affair, little more than a shack raised off the ground on concrete blocks, ringed by whitewashed stones. And when the wind blew in from the Fens it brought with it the strange scent of the countryside, reminding the major just how far his pursuit had taken him: Birmingham, Manchester, Coventry. And now to East Anglia. But it was London he would never forget. London where . . . . no, he could still hardly bear to think of it, young William lying there. He just wanted to think of *them*, the dogs responsible, the Irish Republican unit who had perpetrated that heinous crime – the two men and the girl. Yes, the *girl!*

He had a strand of her hair still – her red hair, salvaged from a hairbrush on that fateful night. And sometimes he would just look at it, twisting it around his fingers. He would muse on what he would do to her, on what the *hangman* would do to her. It gave him satisfaction – picturing that girl's neck stretched by the rope.

And that day was getting nearer, he thought. For he had been working flat out, going over every scrap of information, scouring every single document, every single file that the intelligence services could forward to him. More of the same had just arrived. And Armstrong's right hand man, Sergeant Morris was just walking in with the latest files he had just received from the dispatch rider. Armstrong did not bother to look up. His face, pitted with shrapnel scars from that night in London, was bent over a magnifying glass, his tired eyes scanning a photograph of a group of men gathered around an Irish flag.

'Where would you like them, sir?' Sergeant Morris asked him. 'On the pile with the others?

At that moment they were interrupted by the telephone. Major Armstrong reached over and picked up the receiver. It was an Air Vice Marshal – Sir Arthur Mawsbury-Browne.

As the sergeant waited for him to finish his conversation, hovering the files over the ones in the tray, he looked down briefly at the tray and the file on top. It was marked O'Callaghan. After a moment, Morris shrugged, then dropped the new files on top.

When he put the telephone down, Major Armstrong got out of his chair and put on his cap. He went over to the hut wall where there was a map of Cambridge, a district he and his men had been searching for weeks following a tip off.

'Where to today, sir? asked Morris.

Armstrong ran a finger vertically down the map, then tracked horizontally into the corresponding square.

'Area 13,' said Armstrong. 'Trumpington Street to Lensfield Road taking in the military hospital.'

'13?' replied Sergeant Morris. 'Unlucky for some.'

*

It was mid morning on the Livingstone Ward and David Asher was leaning back in his bed. His sheets had been drawn back and his hands were behind him. His fingers were curled around the iron rails of his bed head for support. He braced himself once more, his body trembling with exertion as he tried to move his right leg.

A moment later he collapsed with defeat.

'This is impossible!' he snapped.

'No, try again, David,' said Kathleen. 'Again.'

He gave her a doubtful glance, then exhaled wearily. Then concentrating all his efforts on his withered limb, his gaunt frame stiffened. He tried once more.

But there was no movement at all, just the creak and squeak of his iron bedstead as it flexed under the effort of his body. He sighed.

'It's no good, Kathy, I can't. I can't do it!'

'Yes, you can, David. Keep trying. Don't give up.'

He tried one last time. But then . . . . slowly –

'It's moving, Kathy. It's *moving!*'

To his amazement his injured limb had moved an inch or more off the bed sheet. He held it there for all of a second before he slumped back to his pillow, grey with exhaustion. 'Did you see it, Kathy, did you see it? It moved didn't it, just like you said.'

He reached out a hand and felt her take it in her own. Then their eyes met with a shared jubilation and their faces beamed with triumph. It lasted but a moment. For suddenly out of the corner of his eye, David Asher saw they had company; a number of soldiers had come onto the ward.

Immediately he saw the day sister go across to confront them. She began remonstrating with the man who appeared to be in charge: a tough looking army major with a scarred and pitted face. He was searching the area, or so Asher could just about make out, searching the area to check on identity cards.

'Well you can't do it here,' Asher heard the sister reply. 'This is a hospital ward, not a barrack room.'

'Then you've somewhere else – private? An office perhaps?'

Eventually Asher saw the sister give a conciliatory nod, then gesture to her room. Then, all but for a burly looking sergeant, he heard the major dismiss the remainder of his men and make a request that the sister begin to assemble her staff. It was at that moment that Asher glanced up at Kathleen. The colour had drained from her face.

*

It was a good day for flying, thought Guy Risdale as he took off from the aerodrome, banking the long mullet head of his Spitfire south as he prepared himself for the short flight to Farnborough. He had been summoned there by Air Vice Marshal Sir Arthur Mawsbury-Browne, a family friend who'd selected him to serve on an R.A.F. air accident board that the old man had put together. As he recalled, Mawsbury-Browne had an uncanny knack of getting to the truth. How ironic, he thought, that in this instance, the board's main purpose was the suppression of it.

The case under discussion that day, he remembered, was the demise of a Lancaster bomber which had crashed en-route to County Antrim, Northern Ireland, coming down some sixty miles from its destination on a hillside on the Isle of Man. And not just any Lancaster either. It had been piloted by Rex's brother, Leslie. Yes, it was going to be a difficult task, the cover up, one which most probably involved going to the island itself, to the crash site. After all, they had at least to make some sort of pretence to an investigation, didn't they? But how long would he be away? Days? Weeks? Months? Away from Evelyn all that time?

Oh it was all right for the other members of the board who would be going – Saxby, Stoddard and Fox-Williams – their wives could be *trusted*, left back at home amusing themselves with their card games and their sherry parties. But Evelyn? No, he dare not leave Evelyn, not with the possibility that she might find someone like the American Colonel again. Yes, that man had proved to be quite a problem, he thought. The trouble he'd had in getting rid! But then again the American had stubbornly refused to remove himself from Evelyn's life, until he had lost his own. Ha! How he'd laughed! To die like that! Yes, to die like that in that fashion! Oh, and then to be handed the task of hushing the whole thing up. It was so ironical. So utterly priceless!

'I'll let you handle things once we're out on the island,' Mawsbury-Browne had said to him on a previous occasion when they had talked informally about the crash, gifting him the opportunity. 'Just make sure that no one finds out the truth old chap, there's a good fellow.'

Yes, the air had been thick with irony of late, he pondered, climbing the Spitfire ever higher. David Asher for one – seeing him in the hospital like that had proved to be of great amusement – Asher, a shadow of man, while he himself had come through the war unscathed. And then hearing the man beg for word of Evelyn. *Beg!*

'Have you seen her? Have you seen Evelyn?'

'Seen her? Of course I've seen her. Evelyn's my wife.'

Oh how exulted he had felt at giving Asher the news. To the victor the spoils! – the spoils of war! But how had the man survived, he wondered, that was the question? That time in France he had left him for dead. Dead! And then, over two years later to see that Red Cross telegram to say he was alive. He could hardly believe it!

Risdale levelled the Spitfire off at 10,000 feet, still thinking. Yes, he certainly had to give Asher credit; it had been a neat trick, to survive like that and get back home. But what now? Would Asher present a problem with Evelyn? A threat? No, he had *done* for the man. He was but a shadow of himself. Gone! ***Gone!***

And feeling invincible he banked the Spitfire hard, then began to dive, passing down through layers of strato-cumulus cloud, laughing into his mask as he thought of Asher lying helpless in his bed. He dived through 7,000 – 5,000 – 3,000 feet, his altimeter spinning as the big Merlin engine screamed. He went down through 2,500, then 1,000, plunging towards a patchwork of green hedgerows and fields. He dived and scattered the figures of small and insignificant people by a farmhouse, scaring a horse which bolted in terror with wide saucer eyes. He dived and drove them into the dun brown earth. Just because he damn well could.

*

These four walls were not so bad, thought Kathleen as she looked about her. Yes, windowless and a touch airless, but not so bad. There was certainly no reason to be afraid.

Afraid; she knew the feeling well – she had experienced it that very morning when she had come face to face with Armstrong, the "rat-catcher". And a more appropriate name she could not imagine.

He was looking for an Irish girl, or so he'd explained, once she had come before him inside sister's office. And all while outside on the ward, the man's burly sergeant had been relating the story to David . . . .

'Yes, that's it, sir. Five foot seven. Early twenties. Red hair. Slim build. Much like the girl who's in there with the major right now.'

Asher had laughed. 'Yes, and much the same as thousands of other Irish girls I shouldn't wonder. I expect half of them are working right here in this hospital!'

'Girls like her, sir?'

'Oh believe me sergeant. There's not another like her.'

. . . . . she blessed David for his defence of her in front of that sergeant; David had told her all about it himself, when later, after the pitted faced major had finished with her, the man being "reasonably" satisfied with her identity card, she had returned shakily to David's bedside. There, with the relief still coursing through her, she and David had watched as Armstrong and his sergeant had taken their leave, exiting through the ward doors, the soldiers going back down the stairs, driving away from the hospital.

After they had done so, she truly believed it was over. But then, with the sergeant's talk of fifth columnists obviously at the forefront of his mind, David had suddenly turned to her. Then, with his eyes filled with hurt and suspicion he had said:

'So, you think you've got away with it, do you?'

'What do you mean?'

'Oh come on Kathy. You can't fool me. Why, I've known it right from the start – those hooded eyes of yours, the hawkish nose, that long thin scar that you carry down the side of your cheek. Why, you're Lord Haw-Haw himself – a spy!'

There was a moment of silence before David had burst out laughing. She had laughed too. Then she had rushed away to be sick. Deceiving Armstrong had been one thing, but David?

She looked around the room to which she had fled – the basement room, filled as it was with its grim paraphernalia of crutches and walking sticks and callipers: all the things she needed to restore him to his former self. Yes, she would make it up to him here, she thought, make good her promise, build on the work she had already begun on the ward – get him mobile again. But why had he shown such an aversion to this place, she wondered? It was just a room like any other. Just those four walls. And four walls did not a prison make.

And with that, she suddenly had her answer.

8

It was just after lunchtime on the ward and David Asher was finishing his meal. A feast in fact – all the good things which Kathleen had bought for him: two real eggs (not powdered), spinach, carrots, peas, and apricot charlotte.

'But Kathy, where *did* you get the money?'

'Ask no questions – get told no lies!'

He cleared his plate and put his tray to one side, hearing as he did so the ward doors come open. He looked up. She was here again – Mrs. Handley.

She always came as regular as clockwork, he noted, every afternoon just after lunch. He had not spoken to her as such; he had merely been on nodding terms with the woman, purely to let her grieve in peace. But now, as he watched her take her seat next to her husband's bed, his longing for company got the better of him.

'I think he's looking a little better today,' he ventured.

It was a clumsy introduction and a monumental lie, though he could think of little else. The woman had smiled weakly back.

'Yes, a little more colour I think . . . . mister – ?'

'Asher. David Asher.'

The woman got up. She came over and extended a hand, introducing herself as "Joan" – Rex's wife, just as he'd presumed. He smiled, noting the immaculate way in which the woman was dressed, the attractive but quizzical look she gave him. 'Asher? You know I've a feeling I've heard your name before.'

'From Rex perhaps – he and I were at university together.'

The woman appeared to remember. 'Yes, of course . . . . David – David Asher! He spoke of you often – you both joined the R.A.F. together, didn't you. You must have known my husband well.'

He nodded. 'Well enough to know what a damn fine pilot he turned out to be – received the D.F.C. recently, didn't he?'

Mrs. Handley shook her head.

'He never really mentioned it. Rex wasn't a boastful man. Quite the opposite.'

'Yes – that's just how I remember him. You must be very proud.'

He saw Joan Handley's shoulders begin to heave at his comment. Tears came into her eyes.

'Proud? How can I be proud with these awful rumours.' She looked up at him. 'You know what they're saying, don't you – he tried to take his own life.'

He passed the woman his handkerchief. He told her he was sorry, watching her as she dabbed her eyes. In truth, *he* was just as confused; he could not make sense of it either.

'It's just the war, I suppose,' he said after a moment's consideration, more in sympathy than anything else. 'The filthy war.' Then: 'Look. Tell me to mind my own business, but sometimes it helps to talk about these things.'

The woman looked across at him. And through the tears he could see something like trust in her eyes. Then she began telling him that she believed her husband's actions had nothing whatsoever to do with the "filthy war" as he had put it, but rather a single incident: the death of his brother whose aircraft had crashed upon a lonely, fog enshrouded hillside.

'An accident, you mean?' he said.

'No,' she replied. 'No accident at all.'

*

The next morning, at his own request, David Asher found himself back in the lift, descending to the rehabilitation room in the basement. For it was clearly ridiculous, he thought, to let his fears rule him like that. After all, they were beneath the British Military Hospital in Cambridge, not under the German Headquarters on the Avenue Foch.

The lift bumped to a halt and jolted him from his thoughts. Though as the doors opened with a metallic clang, his eyes panning around the cold dungeon-like walls, the similarity struck him all the same. He shivered with the same uncomfortable chill. But then he felt Kathleen's hand upon his shoulder, and suddenly he was more at ease. For he was certain she knew the truth. She had figured it out, somehow, clever girl.

Once inside the room, he watched from his wheelchair as Kathleen went to fetch something from a tangled heap over in the corner. It was a pair of callipers, one of which she proceeded to strap to his weaker left leg.

'Don't worry. This is just to help until your leg gains strength,' she said, seeming to read his thoughts. 'Now tell me if this is too tight . . . .'

He felt the cold metal through the warm flannelette of his pyjamas, feeling the bite of the buckles as she fastened the straps around his leg. Then he watched as she slipped his bare foot into the ugly oversized shoe. She stood up, hands on her hips. 'Well, are you ready?' He nodded, then feeling her arms go about his waist, he felt her lift him from his wheelchair.

Pushing himself up with his stronger right leg, he tried to help. And no more than a moment and a short struggle later, he found himself between the walkway of some parallel bars, his forearms acting as support upon the two rails, the wood worn smooth by the hands of those who had gone before. He saw Kathleen walk to the bar's end, a distance of no more than ten feet away. She turned.

'Come on then, David. Now walk to me.'

For a moment he stood immobile, trapped by unfamiliarity; he had never needed to *think* to walk before. Then he heard Kathleen say: 'From the hip, David. From the hip.' And firmly gripping the rails, he did as she bade, bracing himself before he swung himself forwards, his leg dragging after him, in the approximation of a step.

'Good, David. Good. Now again – the other leg.'

He reaffirmed his grip and repeated the motion. It was a little easier this time, he noted, better with his stronger right leg. And gathering momentum he began to hit a slow rhythm, half swinging, half walking, grunting and sweating as he inched his way along the rails. He felt like a clumsy child as he worked his way towards her, stumbling as he dug heavily into his reserves. He wondered why she was even bothering with him, this girl, this woman, this angel who

116

had already done so much. Unless? Unless it was the same for her?

Her loud encouragement snapped him around.

'Come on, David. You're doing it! You're nearly there!'

And looking up he found she was right – he *was* doing it. He was closing the distance between them, getting nearer – four foot – three foot – two foot.

But then, with just one stride left, he tripped and fell, Kathleen catching him in her arms. The pair of them collapsed to the floor.

Lying there side by side, the two of them began to laugh, thrilled by success. Then, eventually they fell silent, becoming serious.

'I suppose you know what's happened between us, don't you,' he asked,

She quietly nodded. 'I know. I just didn't want to admit it. '

'Then it's the same for you?'

'It is David – for a long time now – since that very first day I saw you. It's just – '

'Just what, my darling?'

'It's just I wanted to be sure – sure that *you* were sure.'

He knew exactly what she was talking about.

'Evelyn, you mean?' he said. 'You're wondering if I still have feelings for her?'

'It was just something you said, David – a while back. You said you thought you'd never stop loving her, remember?'

He nodded.

'Yes, I know. But I said a lot of things back then. But I wasn't myself. I was sick. I didn't know what I was saying.'

'But you know what you're saying now.'

'Yes. And it's the truth.'

'Then say it, David,' she begged him. 'Say it.'

And then he did so. And as God was his witness, he meant it.

*

Later that same day, on her break, Kathleen found herself checking her purse and removing the rest of the English white five pound notes that she had yet to spend, should Michael discover them and take them for himself. As she stared down at them, she thought back.

To acquire money like that, in that terrible fashion, why, it had nearly made her sick.

She tried to ease her conscience by telling herself that she had done such a terrible thing for David. And, in fact, even though it was of little comfort to her, it was true. But that was back then, before she had bought the black market food – the chocolate, the fruit and the tinned goods, the fresh eggs and the apricots and everything else, before she realised that David's fear of that basement room had little to do with his physical condition.

Nevertheless, that terrible thing she'd done was over now. All to be forgotten. All except by Joy. For one time, when Kathleen had opened her purse, Joy had glimpsed the five pound notes inside and had said:

'Well, ain't you a dark horse.'

'What do you mean?'

'Oh come on, Kath. Don't kid me – that money. You've wised up ain't yer? I knew you would sooner or later.'

'Joy. I've no idea what you're talking about . . . . oh *this* – ! What? No! No this money is nothing to do with *that*. Why, I'm surprised you could even *think* such a thing!' She covered her tracks quickly. 'No, as a matter of fact I was given it – given it by Eamonn. He won it on a bet.'

'Oh a bet was it! Pull the other one, Kath. That dim brother of yours couldn't win a bet in a one horse race.'

'Well Michael, then.'

'Oh now yer are clutching at straws – your Michael wouldn't give yer the time o' day, let alone cash. No, yer don't have to play coy with me. There's no shame in it. You've just seen sense at last, haven't yer? You've come round.'

Kathleen said she had done no such thing, and told her not to be so disgusting. But Joy kept on, telling her that it was "ok", and she didn't mind in the least. In fact she had planned it that way right from the start, getting her to share the flat in the first place, because a nice looking girl was always good for "business". And besides, there was always plenty of "mugs" to go round – plenty for both of them.

Kathleen told her that the only "mug", as she had put it, was Joy herself, for letting men make use of her like that.

'Oh, so I'm a mug now am I?' countered Joy. 'A mug for letting men make use of me? Ha, that's a good one coming from you – you're being made a mug of every single day. And yer don't even know it!'

Kathleen asked her what she had meant by that and Joy had retorted. 'Why you and your precious "David" of course – the way you fuss about him, bringing him this and that, working on his legs for hours on end, getting him special grub. I mean if that's not a good example of letting a man make use of yer then I don't know what is.'

'Joy, he's just a patient. And I'm just doing my job.'

'Oh don't give me that old chestnut again, Kath. It won't wash. Not this time.' Joy had looked across at her. 'Don't yer think I don't know what's going on? Why, he's just getting what he can from yer, that's all, toying with yer, giving yer the old flannel. They all do it. Believe me. I've been a nurse a long time now.' Joy turned away. Kathleen had noted a war weary type of smile on her face. Then Joy said: 'Has he told yer yet?'

'Has he told me what?'

'That he loves yer?'

Kathleen's expression must have betrayed her. For still smiling, Joy said: 'He has, hasn't he. Yeah, I thought so. And a lot more besides – how wonderful yer are, how you're the only girl for him. Oh, I know what they're like. But they're not the same as you and me, Kath. They're from a different class, a different background. You'll never be able to hang onto a boy like David for long. Oh it's not that I've anything against him, nor his kind. I mean in a way I don't even blame the poor sods – starved of women one moment, then in hospital the next, suddenly surrounded by plenty who're at their beck and call. But before long he'll be taking advantage, telling yer all sorts. Then he'll be talking marriage. And it's all false promises, Kath. Just words – words!

But she told Joy that she was wrong. David was good and kind.

'Yeah, the kind who leaves you in the lurch at the first

opportunity. 'You'll see,' said Joy. 'You'll see.'

*

When Kathleen returned to the flat that evening, going into the kitchen, she found Michael and Eamonn there.

'We've been waiting for yer,' said Michael, pulling heavily on a cigarette as he sat at the kitchen table. 'There's trouble.'

Kathleen went and filled the kettle at the tap. She put it on the stove. One look at Michael's face told her it was something bad. Perhaps he knew about Armstrong being in the area, she thought. Perhaps he knew he'd been to the hospital.

But it wasn't that at all.

'It's McManus,' said Michael, a moment later. 'He's gone missing.'

A ripple of panic ran through Kathleen as she stood there. She tried to keep calm. Michael knew nothing. How could he?

A thick silence prevailed that was broken only by Eamonn; he had found Joy's gramophone over in the corner. He was winding the handle in his enormous hand. The next second the scratchy blare of "Stardust" wafted across the room.

'Well?' Michael quizzed her after a moment. 'So what have yer got to say?'

'Me?' asked Kathleen. 'Why should I know anything about McManus?'

She saw him look at her accusingly. 'Because I sent him to see yer, V.E. night.'

Kathleen shrugged. She went over to make the tea. 'Well, he didn't show.'

'What do yer mean he didn't show?'

'I would have known – I was here at the flat all evening, was I not?'

'And who said anything about the flat?'

Kathleen hesitated. 'Well . . . . that's what you meant, didn't you?'

She saw Eamonn dart his brother a glance from the gramophone. 'See, Mikey!' Eamonn's voice was excited. 'It's just like you said.

You were right.' He looked at Kathleen. 'Why, the little gob-shite!'

Michael pulled on his cigarette. Slowly he got up from his chair. Kathleen watched as he came towards her.

Eamonn, after turning up the volume on the gramophone, moved towards her too. As he did so, Kathleen backed away.

'Why, the little gob-shite,' Eamonn spat again. 'The little gob-shite!'

'He is that,' nodded Michael, meaning McManus. 'The filthy coward's deserted!'

*

The next afternoon, when David Asher had just finished another agreeable meal, all courtesy of *her*, he looked up expectantly at the clock. Mrs Handley was late today, and it was most unusual.

As he waited, he began to wonder if she was even coming at all. For in all honesty, looking across at his friend Rex in the next bed, he could hardly see the point. The poor man's condition was unchanged for one thing, and likely to remain so; there was scant hope, or so he'd heard. And, as the clock ticked by, and his boredom set in once more, he began to give up hope of her company. It was a shame, he thought; they had been getting along so well . . . .

'Call me Joan,' she had told him on a visit the previous week.

'And you must call me David,' he'd replied.

He noted that she had taken the habit of sitting *between* the beds, not on the other side, near to her husband. It had made their conversation easier.

'So have you been a patient here long, David?'

'Quite long. About six months or so.'

'Goodness. Poor you! But you're getting better now of course?'

'Slowly. It's just my legs really. But I'm making progress – giant strides, you might say.'

They had both laughed, quietly. Then Joan had said that he reminded her of Rex.

'He was always making light of serious things too,' she said, Asher seeing her look sadly across at her husband. 'That is until – '

He nodded, knowing she was talking about Rex's attempt to take his own life, and his sudden change in temperament that had driven him to do so.

'You say it had something to do with the death of his brother?'

'Yes, his younger brother, Leslie. His aircraft was on a routine flight when it happened – bound for Ireland – hit a mountain in the fog.

'Yes I remember you saying. But you said you believed it was no accident?'

'I think that's what Rex believed.'

'He told you as much?'

'Not in as many words – just a feeling of sorts.'

'Intuition you mean? No more than that?'

'David, I know my husband. He was troubled by something. And that something was Leslie's death. Or rather the manner of it.'

. . . . David Asher looked up at the clock again. Yes, there was little hope of Mrs Handley's company today, he thought. Though a moment later he saw the ward doors open.

At last! She had come. But not alone.

The taller of the two men was heavily built. Rotund, was the word that came to Asher's mind. The man looked like he'd had a "good war", he thought, with his well fed appearance, his expensive looking suit and his cigar which jutted from his moon-like face.

The smaller man, on the other hand, appeared less prosperous, he noted, though Asher's impression was, like that of his larger counterpart, of a man who had neither graced a serviceman's uniform or had been of any great assistance to his country. For he had a pious look about him, almost like a priest. In fact Asher could even see that the man carried himself in the same manner – hands clasped together, like some self styled preacher.

They were Victor and Clifford Handley, he found out a moment later, after Joan had introduced them, her husband's older brothers.

'I wasn't aware he *had* any brothers, other than Leslie,' he remarked later, when, after the briefest of visits, the two men had made their excuses and had left the ward.

'Actually they're his half brothers, from the other side of the family,' Joan explained. 'Rex was never particularly close to them. You see Leslie and Rex were both pilots, whereas Victor and Clifford – '

He listened to Joan's explanation, though it was hardly necessary; he knew vultures when he saw them. And he guessed they had already begun to circle.

*

She was in the clear. Sean McManus lay dead not ten minutes away, and her brothers were of the opinion that he had run.

'Why, the little gob-shite.' 'The filthy coward's deserted.'

Odd she thought, considering that she had once dared, albeit jokingly, to suggest the same. And on that occasion she recalled she had received a good hard slap around the face for her troubles. But this time, well, they had almost embraced that very notion as if it were their own! Desertion? Well of course. It all fitted into place. And it all became clearer still once they had calmed down, she recalled, the two of them lighting yet more cigarettes, drinking the tea she had made them as they'd bemoaned their situation. For she'd heard Michael say that with their double crossing quartermaster gone, so too were their chances of getting home. For McManus held the details of their ship back to Ireland, its name, its date of departure, the port from which it was expected to sail. Yes, McManus had done for them all right, or so Michael had said. But what seemed to gall him most was not that the man had ruined their chances of escape, but had run off with the money which would have made it possible.

'Ah, the money, Mikey,' Kathleen recalled Eamonn as saying, somewhat wistfully to his brother. 'Yer saw him with it, didn't yer?'

'I did that,' said Michael. 'A great bundle of it – English white five pound notes.'

*

The next afternoon, after a fine lunch, when David Asher was sitting up in bed waiting for Joan to arrive, a letter arrived for him instead. Opening it, he read it once, then once again at length. Well, he'd not seen *that* coming. He'd not seen that coming at all. It had the

123

potential to change everything, he thought, especially between himself and Kathy. He needed to talk to her and give her the news – give her the news as soon as his courage would allow. For there was no point in prolonging the poor girl's misery. He owed her more than that.

*

That same afternoon, when Kathleen went to David's bedside to collect his lunch tray, she saw a worried look on his face. She also saw a letter. It was folded up in the top pocket of his pyjama jacket. Thinking little of it she placed his tray upon her trolley. She began to wheel it away.

As she did so she looked down at his plate. It was licked clean. Well, at least he was eating heartily, she thought, enjoying the delicious things she had bought him. And, in turn, she was enjoying the delicious irony – that the money intended to aid three soldiers of the cause in their bid for freedom, was now being spent on the well being of a British officer. Oh what a delight! If only Michael had known – known also that the very next day after McManus' death she had returned to his body, concealing it more thoroughly with yet more bricks and rubble. And in doing so had come across the English white five pound notes. She thought back. The gorge still rose in her throat. For to obtain money like that, in that fashion, why yes, it had almost made her sick. For there were few things more vile in the world than the robbing of the dead.

But it was all done with now. All done and Michael was none the wiser. In fact she began to wonder, in view of the way she had cleverly outsmarted him, whether Michael was indeed clever at all. Yes, she had always believed so, with those intelligent brown eyes of his, but what was behind those eyes? Little much at all? For he'd had little schooling so she remembered, no proper education as such, and certainly not in comparison with anyone she had met, someone like David for instance. But then again, David was from a different background, a different class.

She paused as she took the lunch tray from the trolley. Hadn't she heard those words before?

'*Oh, I know what they're like. They're not the same as you and me, Kath. They're from a different class, a different background. You'll never be able to hang onto a boy like David for long.*'

Her argument with Joy came swiftly back. A friendly warning? Jealousy? Either way, their argument had deepened . . . .

'Oh is that so?' Kathleen had later snapped back. 'And what about your boy – your precious wing commander? I suppose Guy's the exception, is he not? And the two of you will be gaily skipping off, happy ever after?'

Joy had laughed again, in that knowing war weary way. 'Well, if we do skip off it'll probably be in different directions. No, Kath. I don't kid myself. But I'll tell yer what. I'll bleed him dry before he does.' Joy had paused, looking pensive before she'd added. 'Yer know I might pull the old pregnant routine on him – that's always good for a few quid, especially with someone like that – he's a very wealthy man, yer know.'

'Yes, and a deeply unpleasant one, so I've been told.'

'Unpleasant? From who?'

'From David. They were friends once. But that was before – '

'Before what? They fell out, you mean? Over a woman, I'll bet.'

Kathleen nodded. 'It was that. In fact he told me he loved her once.'

'And what? Now he says he loves you instead? Oh, Kath, you poor little fool. Like I've been telling yer – they say a lot of things. But it's all just words – words . . . .'

Words. Just words. Yes, and she wagered there would be plenty in that letter David had received – words of love most probably – from Evelyn – Evelyn or some other woman he'd failed to mentioned. Or maybe even Mrs Handley. Yes, *she* was his "type", his "background", his "class". And was it just a coincidence that he had put that letter in his top pocket, right next to his heart. A heart? Why, the man did not possess one! "Never trust and Englishman" – that's what her Da had told her.

She calmed herself down. No. David wasn't like that; she knew him well enough. It wasn't "him". Though when she returned after

125

clearing away his lunch things, she noticed he still carried that letter in his pyjama pocket, and that worried look too upon his face. But when he spoke, she became more worried still. For he said to her: 'I need to talk to you, Kathy – urgently. But not here. Someplace we can be alone.'

Putting him into his dressing gown, she went and fetched a wheelchair, wheeling him into the lift but only travelling as far as the floor below where she took him along the corridor and out onto one of the balconies. It was the same balcony where she had taken him when his life had neared its end. And as she stood there, in the sunshine of that late spring day, she sensed another such ending in sight.

'Do you remember the last time we were here?' she heard him say, wistfully.

'Yes – seems an age ago now.'

'The winter?' He shook his head slowly. 'I swear I thought I'd never see another.' She saw him look up at her. 'You know I would never have made it without you, don't you.'

She sensed the ending was nudging closer. It was coming – *coming!*

'And is that why you've brought me here, David,' she said quite sharply, hardly concealing her hurt, 'to buy me off with a simple "thank you" – to show me how "grateful" you are?'

'Look, don't be angry,' he said sounding remorseful. 'At least not until you've read this –.' Suddenly she saw him reach into his pyjama pocket. He brought out the letter. 'It's rather bad news I'm afraid. I mean for you and I.'

He handed it over. She unfolded it, knowing exactly what to expect – Evelyn. *Evelyn!*

And yet –

'But this . . . .' Her eyes scudded the page. 'But this is from the Ministry of Pensions!'

'Yes, isn't it terrible,' he sighed. 'I've been demobilised, Kathy – pensioned-off from the service. And all on just ninety five pounds ten shillings and sixpence per annum. I mean it may be all right once

I get walking properly again and find a job, but how do they expect the two of us to live on that?'

'The two of us, David? What are you saying?'

'Well we're going to be married, aren't we? I thought that was understood.'

Kathleen laughed. And then she wept. Oh how she wept.

9

Summer

It was the hottest day of the year so far, but despite the stifling heat, David Asher was grimily shuffling up and down the Livingstone Ward on a pair of crutches. As he moved determinedly back and forth along the red linoleum aisle, he stopped for a while at the foot of Rex Handley's bed. It was at that moment, as he paused for breath, that he realised the man was dead.

A few hours later, after Joan had received the news, he saw her come through the ward doors. And as was the custom in such matters, he saw her go into sister's office where she collected her husband's effects.

When she came out, he saw her come over. He offered her his condolences. She offered her hand.

'Well goodbye, David. And good luck.' He saw her force out a weak smile. 'I don't suppose we'll ever meet again.'

'No, I don't suppose we shall,' he said. 'Well goodbye Joan. Goodbye.'

He felt her hand on his shoulder, then her lips on his cheek. Then he saw her smile one last time, then she was gone.

It was Kathleen who came to him next; he'd noticed she'd been watching from across the ward.

'The poor woman,' he heard Kathleen say to him, looking toward the ward doors that had just swung shut. 'You liked her didn't you.'

He saw her take a cloth from her apron. Immediately he felt her wipe away Joan's lipstick from his cheek.

'Well I must admit, she *was* good company. God knows what I shall do now.' He sighed, then looked around the grim ward, gazing on the silent patients who for no fault of their own were poor company. Then he asked: 'Kathy? Do you think you could get me moved from here?'

'Moved?'

'Yes, onto one of the other wards. I don't care *where* – anyplace really, just to relieve this bloody awful boredom.'

'You're bored?'

'Oh not with you, my love. I didn't mean! It's just – '

'Oh I know, David. But it won't be long now – a few months at the most, then we'll have the rest of our lives together. That's if you still – ?'

'Well of course . . . . that's unless – '

'Now, there's a silly question.' She patted the bed. 'Enough now! Let's get you off those crutches and back in here. Or I might change my mind!'

He told her that if she ever *did* change her mind about marriage it would certainly solve one thing – that he would not have to convert to her faith. 'I mean isn't that what's expected when you marry a Catholic? You have to become a Catholic yourself?'

'Huh!' she huffed, falsely mocking him. 'As if the Catholic church would even take you! – the heathen that you are!'

'Oh, a heathen, am I? No, you've got me all wrong, Kathy. I mean I *do* believe in something.'

'Yes, and like most men we know what!'

They both laughed and he told her to be serious. And that he *did* believe in God, though not as devoutly as she. Then in turn, she said she would have to work on that side of him, but for the time being it was his body which needed her attention. Then throwing back the covers, she began to massage his legs. While she did so, he spotted a local newspaper on the bed.

'Would you mind if – ?'

She offered no objection and he picked it up.

'Anything interesting?' she asked, seeing him flick through the pages.

'Oh, the usual riveting things.' His voice was somewhat sarcastic; he was more bored than ever. 'Burrows the outfitters have a sale. Five shillings off their range of Macintoshes. Oh, and umbrellas are down to half price in the high street.'

129

'Just the thing for the hottest day of the year,' she joked. 'An umbrella!'

'Well you could always use one as a parasol,' he quipped. They both laughed again, then he spotted something else. 'Hello. This is more like it – a robbery – a robbery at the Rialto picture house.'

'Probably someone wanting their money back. The films are something terrible at that place – I went there once on my day off.'

'On your own, I hope.'

'Oh you'd be surprised, David. You see there was this tall dark stranger.'

'Yes – most probably answering to the name of Ronald Coleman!'

'Actually I'll have you know it was Stewart Granger. And the projector broke down halfway through. Now get on with your newspaper you terrible man. So what does it say about the robbery?

He read on. 'Oh not much. It's only made the stop press – just says the cashier was held up and money was taken . . . . oh wait a minute . . . no, it's a little more serious than that . . . . it says the cashier was shot.'

'Shot? Shot by who?'

'It doesn't say. Just by two men . . . Oh, and something else – '

'What's that?'

'They both had Irish accents.'

*

The next morning, when David Asher was working off his boredom by shuffling back and forth upon his crutches once again, the ward doors suddenly opened. It was Joan. He was surprised. More surprising still was her proposition:

'I'll give you every penny my husband left me if you can find out why he took his own life.'

For a moment he was silenced – stunned by her plain speaking, her manner, her abrupt return. He sat down on his bed. He asked if she had a cigarette. From her bag, he saw her take out a packet and a gold Ronson lighter. She passed them over. He said: 'You know I don't use these things as a rule, but – '

'Yes, I'm sorry, David. I know I've rather sprung this on you, but I'm at my wit's end. I can't stop myself thinking that Leslie's accident was some kind of foul play. He was too good a pilot to simply crash like that.'

Asher flicked up the lighter. He lit the cigarette. He smiled weakly. 'A *good* pilot, Joan? Let me tell you something about "good" pilots – I've never come across one yet who regarded himself as otherwise. In fact the graveyards are full of them.'

'That's as maybe,' Joan countered, 'but it doesn't explain why Rex was never quite the same after he received news of Leslie's death.'

'Well, they *were* brothers,' he said, pointing out the obvious. 'Maybe Rex just felt guilty – guilty he survived the war while Leslie didn't.'

He saw Joan shake her head. 'No, it was something deeper than that, David.' He saw her reach into her bag. 'Here. Let me show you this.'

A moment later, Joan had brought out some papers. It was her husband's Last Will and Testament and she pointed out a paragraph. It was a request from her husband that his body be cremated, and that his ashes be scattered on the hillside into which his brother's aircraft had flown.

'And you think this is odd in some way?' He passed the document back.

'Well yes, when you consider that Rex never wanted to be cremated. He wanted to be buried. You see he was trapped in a burning aircraft once. He always hated fire after that. He was fearful of it.' He saw Joan narrow her eyes. 'This request . . . . it's . . . . I mean it's almost as if – '

'As if he's trying to atone for something?'

Joan looked up sharply.

'Yes, that's it, David. It's as if Rex is still trying to punish himself, even after his own death. That's why I think the answer is somewhere out on that hillside.' Joan placed the document back in her bag and clipped the bag shut. He saw her look across at him.

'Well, my offer still stands. I'm leaving for Liverpool the day after tomorrow, then crossing to the island. I'm begging you – if you are well enough, will you come?'

Well enough? *Was* he well enough, he wondered? He thought about it for a split second, then dismissed it out of hand.

'No, I'm sorry, Joan. Nothing would give me greater pleasure, but – '

He saw Joan raise a gloved hand.

'No, I understand, David. And it's *I* who should apologise. You're nowhere near recovered yet. I should never have asked – never have come.'

She went to walk away, but he stopped her.

'No, it's not that Joan – not my legs. It's just – .' It was then he told her about finding the love of his life in Kathleen, and how they were going to be married, and in the circumstances it would be difficult. 'You do understand?'

Joan seemed taken aback, but he saw her smile all the same.

'Yes, of course,' she beamed. 'Completely. And may I wish you both every happiness.'

Joan proffered her hand and he took it with a pang of guilt. She turned to walk away.

She had only taken a few paces when –

'No. Wait!'

Swinging himself over on his crutches, he looked at her for a moment, then held out his hand.

'You nearly forgot this.'

He saw Joan gaze down at the gold Ronson cigarette lighter in his palm. She smiled up at him.

'It belonged to Rex,' she said, her voice sounding wistful. Then when Asher went to hand it over – 'No. Keep it. Call it a wedding present.' He thanked her and she smiled at him once again and she slipped a hand into her bag, bringing out a card. 'I shall be staying here until the day after tomorrow, at the Royal Cambridge Hotel. I leave at 10 a.m. Please telephone me if you have any more thoughts over my husband's death.'

Then she turned once more and he watched her walk down the red linoleum aisle towards the doors.

As he did so, gazing at the back of her neatly bobbed hair, the arrow straight seams of her shapely silk stockinged legs, David Asher could not help but think that a wonderful opportunity had slipped from his grasp. For after all, he was a man. And a bored man at that.

*

She had not bargained for this. She had not bargained that her brothers would do something so foolish – the picture house? It had to be them. And they were meant to be lying low!

If further proof was needed that it was her brothers' work, it came that same evening when Kathleen arrived back at the flat, finding her brothers there, drunk on newly bought whiskey, heady with success.

'Ah, 'bout time,' said Michael from a chair. She saw money on the table. Blood on his sleeve.

'Yeah. We need grub,' demanded Eamonn. He banged a huge fist. **'Grub!'**

She asked them if their appetite came from their stupid bloodlust robbery at the picture house, but turning drunkenly though swiftly in his chair, Michael told her to shut her mouth. And how did she know anyway?

'It's all over the evening paper,' she said. 'Have you not seen?'

'Ah the papers,' Michael growled. 'They know nothin' – nobody knows nothin'. Why, that stinking flea pit – it was easy – *easy!*'

'Then why's there blood on your coat?' Kathleen asked

Michael turned and glowered once again. 'Did I not just tell yer to shut yer trap?'

'You want me to do it for yer, Mikey?' Eamonn volunteered, scraping back his chair.

'No, you've done enough,' Michael said to him. 'And the next time I give yer the gun to hold, fer Christ's sake just hold it.'

'Okay, Mikey.'

'Then it was him?' Kathleen asked, nodding across.

'Him. Me. What's the difference. What matters is we've got what we wanted.'

'Yes, and the police out looking for us.'

She thought for sure that Michael was going to hit her after *that*, but he just batted a hand at the air and said. 'The cops? Ha! Not for long. It's all arranged. We're finally getting outta here.'

Somehow – somehow she did not know or even care to know how, but Michael then told her he had been in contact with their Da and . . . . no, she still could not believe it. Even with McManus out of the picture, Michael had still managed to find a way – the money – the ship. The *ship!*

'It'll be sailing from Liverpool – the docks,' he said. 'All yer have to do is get there. Then you'll be met by a contact. Give him the money and do everything he says. He'll get yer safely aboard. You'll be back home before yer know it.'

Kathleen was still numb with shock. *Home?* Then she realised that Michael had been talking in the singular.

'Will the two of you not be coming?' she asked.

'No, you're to go ahead – Da's orders. But just in case yer get any ideas – '

Kathleen saw Michael nod to Eamonn who suddenly got up. He came over to her and the next thing she felt was a flurry of slaps and punches as he beat her to the floor. When it was over, Michael got up to leave and stood there looking down. '*That's* so there'll be no misunderstanding, okay? We'll see yer next at the railway station.'

'When?' she asked, looking up. 'When?'

'The day after tomorrow,' he said. 'The 10.40 morning train. Be there. Or we'll come looking.'

*

That next morning, when he woke, David Asher was possessed of a single notion – he had to get out. He'd had enough of the place, this hospital with its crushing routine, its pulverising boredom, the ward with its tight and narrow walls which seemed to be shrinking before his eyes. He was being choked – choked by his life of nothingness, by the grinding, relentless suffocation. Enough. ***Enough!***

He looked around the ward for Kathleen, but she had yet to arrive.

So he hailed another young nurse instead. 'Clothes,' he called. 'Will you bring me my clothes?'

She looked at him for a moment, bewildered, then he saw her run off. She returned a minute later, though she did not bring him clothes, but rather the ward sister. He repeated his request to her, then the sister also left, bringing back a doctor.

'Now what's the trouble old chap? What's all this nonsense? Something about wanting your clothes?'

'Yes,' he said, feeling as if he was asking for the world. 'My clothes. I'm leaving.'

The doctor laughed softly. He shook his head.

'Out of the question, I'm afraid. You're just not ready to leave us yet – nowhere near ready.'

'Well ready or not I'm going. Even if it's just as far as the street. So *will* you fetch me my clothes?'

'And if we do, what about the stairs, hmm?'

'Well I'll take the porter's lift, of course. I'll be fine on my crutches.'

'And once you're outside the hospital – the steps? What about those? You know it won't be like stumping up and down the ward on the flat like you've been used to. You'll become tired. You'll see.'

'Then *let* me see,' he insisted. 'Just let me see how far I can get. Just give me my damn clothes!'

After a few moments, when it appeared that the depth of his resolve had reached the man, he heard the doctor sigh, then with a look of resignation the man turned. 'Oh well sister, better see what you can find him. It looks like his mind's made up.'

Immediately, and in place of his own clothes which had long since been destroyed, the sister despatched the nurse to find something suitable instead. Duly he saw the nurse return. She had a hotchpotch of hand-me-downs by the look of things – clothes from patients who had no more need of them: an old khaki army shirt, some grey flannel trousers, a pair of worn out boots. She laid them on the bed while the doctor gave him a final examination.

'Like I said,' he heard the doctor say. 'You'll tire easily. You'll feel weak. Occasionally dizzy. It'll be hard, old chap. Just you wait and see. Oh and another thing – '

But David Asher wasn't listening. His eyes were focused on the peerless blue rectangle framed within the skylight window above his bed, his mind already fixed on the waiting world outside.

*

That same morning, when Kathleen walked to the hospital beneath that same peerless blue sky, she may as well have been walking beneath a dark cloud. She had underestimated Michael. Yes, he was often drunk, spiteful and cruel, but in the same breath he was also resourceful, determined and organised. Tomorrow? She had until then to organise herself! She needed to think. *Think!*

Of course she could always allow Michael and Eamonn to put her on that morning train and simply get off at the next stop. But then what? She would need to return because of David. And what if her brothers were still there? And if they were not, would they come looking? It was a possibility. No, a *probability*. For had Michael not already explained – they could not leave a living soul behind.

She walked on, going through the hospital gates, that same dark cloud seeming to follow her up the many stairs to the ward. On arrival, that cloud grew darker still. For she could see that David was dressed like some kind of terrible ragamuffin, hanging there pale and lean between his crutches, pitiable like a beggar or street seller, she thought, like a veteran of the previous war, reduced to selling boot laces or the like. But it wasn't *how* he was dressed that gave her cause to panic. It was that he was dressed at all.

'David, what do you think you're doing!'

'Isn't that obvious? I'm leaving.'

'Yes, but . . . . but you can't! You're just not well enough – nowhere near well enough.'

'Yes, so I've been told. But I'm going anyway'

'But why? I mean why take the risk?'

'Because I *have* to, Kathy. Don't you see? Haven't I told you enough times? It's *this* place. And if I don't get out I'll . . . . I'll go mad!'

She told him he would be madder still if he did not stay.

'Then perhaps I've gone mad already,' he said. 'But I'm leaving all the same.'

'But if you *do* leave, where will you go? Where will you stay?'

'I really don't know – or care. I suppose it all depends how far I get. I think there's a hotel just on the corner, isn't there? And if not – '

'But all the hotels have been taken, David – requisitioned by the services.'

'No not all, Kathy. Just some.'

'But what if the remaining ones are full. What then?'

'Then I'll find a boarding house or something. Look, what's the matter, Kathy? There's something wrong, isn't there.'

'Oh, nothing, David. It's just – '

'Just what?'

'It's just that I couldn't help but overhear something yesterday, when Mrs. Handley came in. She gave you some sort of proposal, didn't she?'

'Ah, so *that's* it! You think I'd . . . . with that woman?'

'Oh no. It's not like that, David. I know you'd never. I mean – '

'Well I should hope not. And after all the things I've said – all this time together.' He seemed hurt, she thought, and perhaps rightly so. But then she saw that look in his eyes that told her he could hold nothing against her. And then, with a playful look about his face he said. 'Besides, if you'd taken the trouble to listen to that conversation properly, you'd have heard me turn that proposal down, because of a better one.'

'What was that?'

'Why, the proposal of marriage to you, you sweet lovely fool!'

They both smiled then laughed. Then she told him to wait. 'I've an idea,' she said.

Quickly she began to rummage through her bag. The key! The key to the flat! Why, of course. Joy wouldn't mind. Besides, she had not seen her in days anyway. And as for her brothers? Had they not said they would see her next at the railway station?

She took out the key and scribbled the address on a scrap of paper, telling him he must take a cab. Then she handed both the key and the address to him and saw him smile as he placed them in his pocket.

'Right. Then I'll see you this evening,' he said, Kathleen seeing his eyes turn towards the ward doors, a look of slight apprehension on his face. 'A kiss for luck?'

Gladly she did as he asked, then she offered to take him down to the foyer. But he was too proud, she thought, for he declined, saying only: 'No. I'll be all right. But there *is* something you *can* do for me.' She saw that same playful look about his face again as he gestured to his clothes. The shirt was too big. The trousers too short. The boots too clumsy. 'You might point me in the direction of a good tailor!'

*

He had been fool. A stupid, stubborn, idiotic fool!

'It'll be hard, old chap. Just you see.'

He had only managed to reach the top of the steps outside the hospital, but already he was gasping, pausing for breath, leaning his meagre weight against a pillar at the entrance for support. People were heading toward him in a great wave, pushing past him as they came up the steps, coming and going. This was not the place he remembered, this realm of bustling chaos, this town which he had once known so well, this old friend that now seemed so noisy and dangerous and monstrously large. This was not the place at all.

Like a frightened animal he moved nervously from the pillar, urging himself on, edging himself out on unsteady legs. The first thing to hit him was the light. It was searing and painful, blinding in fact. And he narrowed his eyes, his hand in front of his face. But there was a delicious warmth there too – the sun. The sun! It streamed down upon him, and for a moment he let it wash over his pale skin. Then, with his spirits lifted, he tentatively made his way out, using all his strength upon his crutches as he exited through the hospital gates, heading for where, he did not know.

Across the road, and not too far along it, he found himself in the grounds of his old college and headed down towards the "Backs" as

138

it was known – the river, where he lay upon the grassy bank, humbled by exhaustion and the shocking pace of things. There he rested, sleeping for a while before he woke, slightly refreshed, finding enough strength to reach the shops on King's Parade. Once there, and using the money that the Ministry of Pensions had forwarded to him, he slipped into a jewellery shop and bought Kathleen a ring. Then next door he found a tailor's shop, where he bought a hat and a suit of blue serge.

Then some twenty minutes later, after suffering the indignity of having to ask the tailor for a chair on which to sit, a glass of water to drink, and even, for some ridiculous reason, allowing himself to be pressed into buying a dinner jacket – a dinner jacket of all things! 'Oh, every young man should have one, sir!', he found himself back outside the tailors, in need of a cigarette. And as he flicked up Rex Handley's gold Ronson lighter, he caught sight of his reflection in the shop window.

He barely recognised the man who stared back, the gaunt stranger who leant on crutches for support, this fellow who gazed hawk-like from beneath the turned down brim of a newly bought trilby. But at least that man was alive. Yes, by God, Risdale had failed in that respect. And now he was to be wed – married to the angel who'd remade him, the girl who'd taken the hate from him, replacing it with something good. Dare he ask for more?

He managed to return to the river bank, immediately falling asleep upon the warm grassy slope again, losing himself in a deep slumber for a good many hours. For when he woke, he realised it was getting late, and he decided he must try and find the flat. He took Kathleen's advice and hailed a cab, a wise decision as, out of sheer vanity, he had recklessly discarded his crutches, relying on the strength of his stronger right leg and a cane which he'd purchased from a tobacconist's shop. He'd made slower progress because of it, though what he lacked in speed, he gained in dignity.

He found the address with some difficulty; it was over a butcher's shop and he reached it by means of a tunnelled alleyway which led around the back. There he found some wrought iron steps. He made the ascent with a number of stops, his lungs hunting for breath as he made his way to the door at the top. Pausing, he searched his pockets for the key. Finding it he slipped it into the lock.

Walking into the hallway he was careful with his movements; Kathleen had told him that Joy had not been at the flat for a while, but if she had returned she would most probably be asleep, so quietly he found Kathleen's room and slipped inside.

It was a neat and homely place, he thought, smelling of fresh soap and furniture polish. And for the next few moments he wandered, casting his eyes about him with innocent curiosity. Some items were familiar: Kathleen's hair slide, a cheap brooch he had once seen her wear, a few odds and ends. Though he was surprised not to find more. A photograph maybe, something which spoke of who she was and where she came from? But as she had rarely mentioned herself, he gave it no more thought, and crushed by fatigue he slumped down in a chair, drifting off to sleep again.

When he woke some time later, it was to the sound of a barrel organ in a distant street. It was playing, "Let the great big world keep turning", and he smiled to himself. For he had been starved of music over those passing months in hospital. And even though the organ's rendition was crude, it was still a tonic to him as he sat there, thinking of *her*.

Let the great big world keep turning.
Never mind if I've got you.
For I only know that I want you so.
And as no one else will do.

But then, before long, the music began to fade, then disappear. And as it did so he found himself alone once again, in the thick silence of the room, bereft of music once more, save for the hope or possibility of a wireless. He looked around. Then spotting one, he dragged himself to his feet.

It was a battered old radio which appeared to have seen better days. And reaching for the knob and turning it on, he was not surprised in the least to find that it did not work. Even so, he tried again, twisting the knob back and forth several times and tapping his

140

hand against the side of the cabinet. But it was dead. Then again, he prided himself on the fact there was little he could not fix.

Quietly going into the kitchen, he found a knife that he could use as a screwdriver, then going back to the bedroom he took the wireless and turned it around, then began to unscrew the blanking plate on the back. He worked clockwise, collecting each screw in turn, noting that they already appeared a little loose, almost as if they had recently been withdrawn.

And, as the last screw snaked to the end of its thread, the back plate became looser still. Then suddenly it fell away into his waiting hands.

*

That evening on her way home, before going back to the flat, Kathleen slipped into the Catholic Church near the hospital. It was the same church that, over those passing months, she had visited to pray for David's life. Now she prayed for their life together.

And it was to be a married life at that. All she'd ever wanted. And all by the grace of God. For she felt *He* had forgiven her at last. And in doing so had delivered David into her care, to love and to cherish. She clasped her hands tightly and gave blessed thanks. Indeed the Lord was wondrous, the most gracious God of all.

When she finally arrived at the flat, she went to look under the mat for the key that Joy was in the habit of leaving when she went out. It was still laying beneath, and realising she had yet to return, Kathleen picked it up, and with a certain eagerness, unlocked the door and pushed it open.

'*Da-vid,*' she called, in a cheerful sing-song voice.

But there was no reply.

Walking down the hallway to her room, she pushed open the door.

David was sitting there in a chair, smoking a cigarette. He looked impossibly handsome, if a little pale in his brand new suit.

'I called. Didn't you hear?'

But he did not answer, nor would he even look at her. He just drew heavily on his cigarette, his face turned to the window.

He was tired, she thought. He was tired and exhausted – worn out and overcome by the effort of that first day on his own. Why, she suspected that it had even made him sick. For there was the faint smell of it in the air, evidence too in the kitchen where she found both mop and bucket, rinsed cleaned, David's handkerchief lying washed and drying to one side. Yes, it was only natural, she thought. He needed rest – rest and a little food to re-line his stomach. She went and fed the gas meter with coins and then found two pieces of salt fish that were soaking in a bowl. She threw them into a pan.

A moment later, she saw David limp into the kitchen. He leaned against the doorframe and she felt his eyes upon her as she prepared to cook the meal. Even then he did not speak. And when he did so she thought his manner strange. And then she found out why.

He was drunk. He was drunk on half a bottle of Jameson's whiskey he had found, obviously left by her brothers. Yes, he was drunk, though not blindly so, but neither "happily drunk" either. In fact she could see a strange belligerence in his eyes – belligerence and perhaps a look of sadness.

'So, the angel's back at last,' he slurred. 'Back in the fold. So what kept you?'

'Nothing, David. I just stepped into the church on my way home, that's all – went in to say a prayer.'

'Oh yes. The church . . . the *church!* To say a prayer for your sins no doubt.'

She looked up at him from the boiling fish pan. 'No, not for my sins, David. I went to pray for *us* – for our future.'

'Our future! Ha!' He laughed. 'Well hurrah and hallelujah for that!' She saw him throw a glass of the Jameson's to the back of his throat. She felt confused over his behaviour, his mood, the whiskey. And then he must have seen her give him a disapproving look, to which he said: 'Just drinking to our future my angel, that's all.'

She saw him turn away and go back in the other room, but he soon returned, staggering back on some cane that he must have bought.

'So,' he began. 'So tell me . . . . what made you come here . . . . to

England, I mean . . . . to the hospital.'

'Why, I was sent here David. Didn't I tell you?'

'Maybe . . . . I can't recall . . . . then again you've said a lot of things . . . . then again, nothing. So you were sent here, were you . . . . sent by whom?'

'By God of course – to look after you.'

She heard him make a sound, almost a snort. 'Yes, *"God",*' he said, sounding almost scornful. 'I remember it now . . . . some sort of pact, wasn't it? Well hurrah and hallelujah once again!'

She did not answer that. If indeed it needed an answer. She just supposed again that he was tired, drunk, angry – angry with himself perhaps or the world in general, or maybe even with God Himself. For she knew he had good cause, but then again she knew he did not share her faith, her belief. And duly she tried to explain – it was the Catholic way.

'Oh yes of course,' he went on again. 'And you're a good Catholic, aren't you . . . . from the south . . . . southern Ireland . . . . the Republic. You know I'd really like to meet your father . . . . see what sort of man he is . . . . and I expect I shall, shan't I, to ask for his daughter's hand.'

She told him no, she did not want him to meet her father – *ever!*

'And why's that?' he asked.

'Because he's not a good man,' she said.

'In what sense? he replied. 'You mean he's not of good stock? Why, what does he do for a living?'

'If you must know he cuts turf – peat for peoples' fires.'

'Oh, you don't say . . . . and your mother?'

'She takes in laundry.'

She saw him grin, drunken and lopsidedly. 'Well,' he said. 'What a pretty wedding picture that will make . . . . a bog cutter and a washer woman!'

She told him not to be like that.

'Like what?' he asked.

'Like a snob,' she said. 'It's not *you*, David. You're not like that. I know you. It's the drink talking. Please. Please David. Can we just - '

She was going to say: "Can't we just be nice to each other and have our food in peace?" But he was already turning away again, turning with an expression like that of disgust, an overreaction she suspected to her lowly background, limping back with his cane into the other room, heaving himself into a chair.

A short time later, when the meal was ready, she fought to save the situation by finding two candle stubs which she duly lit, placing them on the table with the hope of changing his mood. For she wanted their first night together to be special, romantic even. Though when the meal was served it was eaten in a stony silence. Then, when it was over, she saw he had really not touched a thing. And she took his plate to the bin and scraped it off. As she did so, she finally realised she could take no more.

'So what is it, David?' she asked, turning on him. 'What's wrong? Is it something I've said? Something I've done? *What?*'

But he told her just to "leave it".

'But I won't leave it,' she snapped. 'You've hardly said a word, at least not a civil one. And you've hardly eaten a thing.'

'That's because I've lost my appetite,' he said. 'You've more drink in the house?'

Reluctantly she went to look. And in one of the cupboards she found some more whiskey that belonged to Joy. More reluctantly she poured him a measure into his tumbler. She saw him drink the whiskey, then take the bottle.

And as the night wore on, and the whiskey was consumed, for the life of her, she could not figure him out. All she knew was that he was slipping away from her. And, when the candles had burned down, and she could see he was numb with drink, she tried one last time, going over to kiss him. But his lips were cold – cold as ice. And his eyes were cold too, the warmth she had once seen in them gone. *Gone!*

But still she would not believe it. And after trying to hug the love back into him, she thought to take his hand, leading him into the bedroom.

There, in the pale moonlight from the window, she began to

undress him, aware that he had turned his face away from hers yet again, his drunken gaze focused on something in the night sky. Then turning also, she saw it too – the star he had once pointed out to her at the hospital – the Angel star.

But the star was fading now, she noted, fading as it slipped from its physical partner, just as he had predicted, pulling away on its journey of separation. And as she watched, a cold chill went down her spine. For turning her gaze from the window again, she saw that tears had come into his eyes. And she felt cleaved in two by his sadness, her heart pierced by that which he seemed unable to explain. And then she began to cry too – cry for all her broken dreams. For this was not their new beginning, she realised: this was just their bitter end.

*

At 6.30 a.m. the next morning, Major Armstrong was at his desk. He was busy studying his files. A headache pounded at a place just behind his eyes. Drawing another blank he tossed the file he'd been reading into his "Out" tray. He went to the window for air.

Standing at the open window, he looked out. He rubbed at his temple. He was all in – exhausted. But he knew why he pushed himself so.

A second later he was back at his desk, reaching to his "In" tray – the next file.

Tugging at the red ribbon, he opened it, almost groaning inwardly. It was the same as thousands of others that had passed through his hands: a man with a history of sedition. This one was called Patrick O'Callaghan.

He was a staunch Sinn Feiner. One of the old school. Armstrong glanced at the details: arrested in the 1916 rising. Two years in Kilmainham jail. Gunrunner, insurrectionist, political agitator. Armstrong leaned back on his chair and drew a hand across his pitted face. O'Callaghan had been quite a handful in his day, but now? No, the man was a spent force. Too old. Too old!

He sighed as he went to close the man's file, but as he did so he came across two photographs that were tucked into the file pocket at the back. One was a standard prison photograph taken in the man's youth, the other a more recent picture taken from the *Irish Times.* Armstrong opened his desk drawer. He pulled out a magnifying glass.

The photograph was of some kind of political rally; a demonstration on the steps of the Four Courts in Dublin. Armstrong skimmed the glass across it, finding a crowd of men, women and children – people drawn by the unexpected; a gathering of the bored and the curious. It was taken around 1939, at the beginning of the war. Armstrong paused. The pain in his head had worsened. He rubbed at his eyes again, then shut them, pinching the bridge of his nose as he fought to maintain concentration. He opened his eyes again.

As he did so he found O'Callaghan in the foreground. The man was standing with his hand raised, his finger stabbing the air. There were some children alongside him, a strikingly good-looking girl of about fifteen. Suddenly a shiver ran through him. Hadn't he seen that girl before? Recently? But where? A dance. A restaurant? Had he passed her in the street? He cursed his failing memory. Come on man, *think!*

*

An hour and a half later that morning, Kathleen was just waking in her room. Reaching a hand across the bed, she noticed the other side was empty.

'David?'

She pulled herself up, tugging the sheets around her. No, he was still there, over by the window, getting dressed, pulling on his new suit of clothes. She smiled at him warmly, but her smile was not returned. And as the cold light of day began to break across the room, she realised that the passing night had meant nothing to him. For he was clearly sober now. And clearer still was this: he was getting ready to leave.

It took a second before Kathleen was struck by the same idea. For in less than three hours, she realised, her brothers would be waiting for her, along with the 10.40 train. The thought chilled her and she

146

decided to throw the dice a final time. For if she had been mistaken, she wanted to hear it from David's lips. If he really loved her, would he go away with her, there and then, that very morning?

'We could go to London,' she heard herself say that next moment, her voice filled with a terrible kind of desperation. 'We could work things out – we could be happy. I know we could.'

For all the world she expected him to refuse. But to her surprise, as she watched him flick a knot into his tie, he simply shrugged.

'If that's what you want.'

She was still unsure whether to believe him or not, but the risk of losing him was greater. Hurriedly she washed and dressed and ran a brush through her hair. She packed a suitcase. She just needed an hour, she told him, to go to the hospital.

'I've some money due and we'll need every penny,' she said, pausing only to glance at her watch. 'I'll meet you in about an hour – nine o'clock on the corner of Parkside and East Road. You know the place?'

She saw him give a weak nod. 'If that's what you want,' he said again.

She looked at his sad handsome face. Then she said: 'All I want is for you to love me the way I love you.' But he did not say a thing, nor even look at her.

*

After he'd heard Kathleen's footsteps down the hallway, heard the back door slam shut, heard the faint receding footfalls of her going down the iron steps, he wept. He wept for all the world, for all those times he had heard those same footsteps upon the ward, those times when she had come to him, when she had come when the "moon" had been full, when she had cared for him, nursed him. Then he thought about how she had kept him alive, sitting by his bedside through those long nights, then how she had helped him recall Risdale's name, using the hate he felt for the man to fuel his recovery, and yet showing him the other side of that coin. Yes, he thought about many things. He thought of what might have been:

'We could go to London. We could work things out – we could be

happy. I know we could.'

Yes, he thought of that too. But he knew what he must do instead; his plans were made.

'I'll meet you in about an hour – nine o'clock on the corner of Parkside and East Road. You know the place?'

Yes, he knew the place. And he was sure the police knew it too.

He lit a cigarette and rose slowly from his chair. He slipped on his jacket and picked up his cane, hobbling out into the hallway. There he laid his key down onto the hall table, feeling an unbearable emptiness. Then, far away, in a distant street, he heard the barrel organ again.

Let the great big world keep turning.
Never mind if I've got you.
For I only know that I want you so.
And as no one else will do.

*

'Lend a hand here will you, Sergeant!'

He was on the floor. Major Armstrong was on the floor of his office and had no recollection of how he had come to be there. All he knew was that an army doctor was on his knees beside him, and the doctor and his sergeant were pulling him to his feet. They sat him down in a chair. Then he saw the doctor pull something from his bag and pass it back and forth beneath his nose. *Smelling salts!*

Armstrong began to come round. He rubbed a hand across his pitted face.

'What happened?' he murmured.

'You must have passed out. Your sergeant here fetched me.'

'Passed out? For how long?'

'I've no idea. Long enough. Tell me – have you been sleeping all right?'

'Sleep? I've not had time for sleep.'

'Is this true, sergeant?'

Sergeant Morris nodded. 'Pretty much, sir. He's not had his boots off in days.'

Armstrong flashed him a glance. 'Sergeant.'

'Yes, sir?'

'Consider yourself on a charge.'

'Yes, sir.'

'And you, Major Armstrong,' said the doctor. 'You can consider yourself relieved of duty.' He reached for his bag. 'You're suffering from exhaustion. You need to rest. And I'm sending you to a place where you'll get plenty – the Military Hospital in Cambridge.'

The next second, there followed a moment of exquisite clarity in Armstrong's mind. It punched right through the lingering foggy haze of his blackout.

The hospital! That's where he had seen her before. *The Military Hospital!*

*

At the hospital's pay office, Kathleen had just collected her money. She had already handed in her uniform, saying her goodbyes, telling sister she was leaving.

'Right away – for London,' she said excitedly, escalating her plans in her next breath – 'To get married. Isn't it wonderful?'

She had wanted to tell Joy about leaving to get married too, but she'd heard some terrible news – Joy was in the cottage hospital, recovering after a beating. And she could guess by whom.

'Yer know I might pull the old pregnant routine on him – that's always good for a few quid.'

Yes, she was sure it was him. But despite her sadness for Joy, she could not think about that now. She had to concentrate on David, on their new life in London. For although his enthusiasm had hardly matched her own – ("If that's what you want," he had said), she knew she could make him happy there. She knew she could lift his spirits, mend his mind as she had mended his body. And all because, in truth, she knew he still loved her. Why, he had said it often enough – more than the world, the moon, the stars! Though the next moment she was snapped from her thoughts by something going on out in the corridor. She could hear the heavy ring of footsteps.

Soldiers!

*

149

At the hospital, Captain Armstrong knew exactly where to find his prey. A few minutes later he had thundered through into the room.

'*You,*' he called to one of the staff. 'Where is she? The Irish girl.'

'Kathy? She's not here. She just left.'

'Left for where?'

'For London, I think. Yes, I'm positive.'

'Then how? By bus? By train? By car?'

'I don't know. I don't think she said. She just came in a few minutes ago to say her goodbyes, then went straight down to the pay office.'

The pay office!

Armstrong was back out of the Livingstone Ward in seconds, hurtling down the stairs. He had passed the pay office door on his way in and knew where to find it. A moment later he had burst through. He looked around. *Gone!*

*

Kathleen arrived panic stricken at the place where she'd arranged to meet David: the corner of Parkside and the East Road. It was five minutes to nine and he had yet to arrive. Breathless, she went and stood beneath a large tree, her back against its trunk, semi-concealed by its spreading branches.

It had started to rain now, and amongst the thickening tide of hoisting umbrellas, she watched for him whilst looking out for Armstrong. Nervously her gaze flicked up and down the road, the tarmac soon becoming awash. Cars and buses trundled by, their wheels giving out a viperous hiss. They sprayed her shoes and summer dress. The raindrops splattered down through the leaves and the branches. Then a horse and cart came past, clattering through a forming puddle. She braced herself for another soaking, and momentarily her vision was blurred. When she looked again, her heart sank – an army truck!

She watched as it slowly came alongside, hearing the lorry's brakes damply squeal as it was halted by the thickening traffic. From his window the driver looked at her. For a moment her heart beat rapidly beneath her clinging dress. Then she saw the driver nudge the soldier in the next seat. The pair both looked across. They whispered as they stared. A second later she saw their faces split into wide dirty grins, Kathleen hearing their cab fill with ribald laughter. As the truck sped away, she sighed with relief. She looked at her watch again: 9.35. Where on earth was David?

*

In a telephone box around the corner, David Asher held the receiver to his ear and listened to the pop and crackle of static. There was a long pause as the exchange began to connect his call to the local police station.

As he waited in the damp confines of the telephone box, his conscience became heavy. It weighed upon him as he considered the consequences of his actions: one simple phone call – *his* phone call, would surely mean that Kathleen would hang for her treachery, the girl to whom he owed his life. Who was the traitor now?

Suddenly a voice came on the other end of the line and he was faced with his decision. He brought the black mouthpiece sharply to his lips. In that moment he knew he held her life in his hands, as she had once held his. Slowly he lowered the receiver, putting it back on the hook. His debt to her was paid. They owed each other nothing.

Stepping outside into the driving rain, he reached into his pocket. He pulled out the ring that he had bought for her the previous day, opening the small square box in which it came. In the gloom of that overcast morning, the diamond shone like the Angel star itself, twinkling brightly in its plump little cushion of black velvet. He took the ring out and held it in his fingers.

He tossed it into the flowing gutter.

Hailing a passing cab, he ducked inside. He sat there in a kind of stunned silence. Eventually the cabby spoke.

'Where to, Guv?'

A moment passed before David Asher reached into his pocket and pulled out a card. He looked at his watch. There was still time. He gazed despondently out of the rain-streaked window.

'The Royal Cambridge Hotel.'

*

151

Ten minutes later, David Asher was resting in the foyer, watching the comings and goings of the morning. Amongst the hurly-burly, he saw two porters take a matching set of leather cases through the revolving doors and out to a red M.G. Sports car. A moment later, Joan appeared. She smiled as she came down the hotel's stairs.

'David. How lovely! But I thought – '

'Yes I know. It's just – '

'It's just what? You've had a change of heart?'

'You could say that. So is that offer still open?'

'Why yes. And you're just in time. I've Rex's car outside. And plenty of petrol and coupons if need be.' She gestured to the revolving door and the wetted pavement beyond. 'Shall we?'

They walked through the foyer out into the pouring rain. He coughed – a hacking cough as the dampness blasted into him. He held down the brim of his hat, pinching together the collar of his coat as he limped with his cane towards the waiting car. Joan, wearing a silk headscarf across her waved blonde hair, looked over.

'Are you sure you're well enough for this, David – to travel?'

'No, I'm fine,' he lied; his leg hurt like hell. 'It's just this damn weather.'

'Then allow me to drive.'

'No. I'll not hear of it. Besides, it'll help take my mind off things.'

'Your pain, you mean?'

'Something like that.'

He shuffled around to the driver's side. He threw his cane in the back and manoeuvred himself behind the wheel. Turning the key the engine burst into life, and gingerly he put the car into gear, easing it gently out into the traffic. They roared off down the teeming wet road.

'I trust Rex's service went well?' he said, after they had both settled.

'The cremation? Yes, if "well" is the word one can use for such a dreadful end to one's life. But those were Rex's wishes. God knows why.'

'Well that's for us to find out. When do we cross to the island?'

'Tomorrow morning. I've booked rooms for tonight at the Metropole in Liverpool.

'Rooms?'

'For myself and Rex's brothers – Clifford and Victor. They're making their way up by train from Euston. We're meeting this evening for dinner.'

He saw Joan bring out a compact from her bag. She began to powder her cheeks. She assured him that the Metropole would be able to find him accommodation too, then she turned in her seat, appearing to notice something.

'David. I've just realised. Have you no luggage?'

He told her he had not. But he had been pressed into ordering a dinner jacket from a tailors across town.

'It won't take a moment,' he promised. He slapped at his coat. 'Cigarette?'

'Please.'

He tried to remove them, but it was difficult with his hand on the wheel. He darted her a glance. 'I wonder. Would you mind?' He gestured to his inside pocket.

Obligingly, Joan leaned over and slipped her hand through his unbuttoned coat and across his chest. He drove the small sports car on, slowing as they approached the corner of Parkside and East Road.

*

Beneath the tree, Kathleen was soaked right through, her hair dripping with rain, her eyes moist with tears. It was ten past ten. She had been waiting for David for over an hour. What was keeping him? Then she saw a bright red sports car.

As it came towards her, Kathleen began to see the two people inside, the woman nuzzling up to the man in the driving seat, her hand playful beneath his jacket. They seemed to be absorbed in each other's company, she thought, the very picture of a well heeled English couple, perhaps embarking on some grand tour, their cases tied to the luggage rack. And for all the world that man behind the

153

wheel looked as if he hadn't a care. And for all the world that man looked like he was in love. And for all the world that man looked exactly like – .

Kathleen sobbed. She sobbed at the sight of him. *Him* with *that* woman! And as the rain came down, she gave a long internal scream, an inward cry of torment. Then, still sobbing, she slowly picked up her suitcase, knowing it was over, realising she had been betrayed. And resentful and bitter, and with little option, she turned and headed for the bus to the railway station, to catch the Liverpool bound train.

*

For over an hour, Major Armstrong and his men had been out combing the streets, his truck butting through the driving rain as he searched every inch of the town. His first point of call had been the railway station. He had left one of his men on guard there, and another at the bus station. It was there he returned, causing mayhem at the entrance where he slew his truck across the road, blocking in the outgoing buses.

Armstrong began to search the buses himself. He climbed on board the first, pushing past a bemused looking conductor, looking left and right as he stared at the bewildered faces. He doubled back, then climbed the winding staircase to the top deck.

Going along the aisle, he suddenly saw her. She was in one of the front seats, a suitcase at her side. Armstrong's pulse quickened. He took out his revolver and strode down, grabbing her arm.

At that same moment, Sergeant Morris came charging up the stairs.

'We've just spotted her sir. She ran off across the green – heading towards Hill's Road.'

'Sorry', muttered Armstrong to the innocent startled redhead.

Two minutes later, Armstrong was back in the truck with his men, his driver grinding the gears as they took off in pursuit.

'There she is!' Armstrong cried a moment later, catching sight of her through the rain blasted windscreen. 'Faster, man! Don't lose her now!'

*

Kathleen was running hard. She'd been surprised by the sudden appearance of Armstrong's truck and was dashing along the pavement. Rounding a corner she glanced back. The truck was still following, so she sprinted down an alleyway instead, concealing herself half way along. As she crouched there, gasping for breath, she tasted the tang of soot and coal in her mouth. Then looking up she saw a high wooden fence, and beyond a dirty plume of steam. *The station?*

Flinging her suitcase over the fence, she climbed over, tumbling down an embankment where she found herself in a good's yard. Picking herself up she grabbed her case, and stumbling over the rails she made her way along the line towards a signal box, then up a ramp to the platform beyond.

Once there, she mingled with the waiting passengers. She looked up at the station clock – 10.38. She willed the hands around its dial. Two minutes. Two minutes, that was all!

Then after what seemed an age – the train! It was coming! It was coming down the track, clanking and hissing into the station, grinding to a halt as its doors were flung open. She stood back. And as she did so she felt a hand on her shoulder. It spun her round.

It was Michael. She felt him push her roughly against the wall. Forcefully, she pushed him back. He looked surprised.

'Well, aren't you all full of piss and vinegar!'

Eamonn grabbed her arm. 'You want me to hurt her, Mikey?'

Michael shook his head. 'No, she's a train to catch.' Then reaching into his pocket her gave her some money, her ticket, then the telephone number of her contact in Liverpool which she could see he'd scribbled down on the back of a cigarette packet. Then the waiting locomotive let out a rip of steam. As the sea of people boarded, she saw Michael look at her one last time.

'Yer know what?' he said, smiling thinly. 'I really thought we'd have to drag yer here kicking and screaming today – thought yer were too fond of that no good hospital – those gobshite Englishmen inside.'

Kathleen looked at him hard. Her stare was venomous.

'Then you really don't know me at all, do you Michael?' she said, flicking her gaze at Eamonn too. 'Neither of you. I hate them. I hate them all!'

Then, from somewhere there came the shrill of a whistle, and after warning them there were soldiers out looking, she boarded the train.

And as the locomotive gradually pulled away, Kathleen thought of David and vowed it would be for the last time. For he was dead to her now. **Dead!**

Part Three

1

LIVERPOOL

'We'll be six for dinner,' said Joan Handley.

She was wearing a gown of silver sequins, powdering herself at a dressing table in her suite at the Metropole. Just across from her, David Asher was slumped in a sofa. Reaching into his dinner jacket for his cigarettes he lit one and blew out smoke. *Six?* Somehow he imagined there would be no more than four: Joan, himself, Victor and Clifford.

'Six, you say?'

He watched Joan as she turned from the mirror. 'Yes, a friend of my late husband will be joining us – Wing Commander Risdale.'

The name brought him up sharp. He leaned forward.

'Guy Risdale? He's here at the hotel?'

Joan nodded. 'With the R.A.F. – he's accompanying an Air Vice Marshal and three others out to the island tomorrow. They're conducting some sort of investigation into Leslie's crash. Why? Do you know him?'

Asher could hardly comprehend it – Risdale! Risdale of all people! 'Know him? Oh, I know him all too well I'm afraid, Joan. He and I have some unfinished business.' He drew on his cigarette as he savoured the prospect, then refocused his mind. 'But that can wait. It's that so called "accident" that concerns me now. So the R.A.F are looking into it themselves you say?'

'Yes – you think that's significant?'

'Well it's certainly unusual – an investigation, I mean. I suppose

157

Risdale's told you nothing about it – told you he *can't*, or something – that it's all very "hush-hush"?'

'Oh on the contrary, David. He said it's just routine.'

'Routine? Well I'd take that with a pinch of salt – anything *but* if they're sending out their top brass.'

'So you think he may be lying?'

'Well, it wouldn't be the first time.' He took a pull at his cigarette. 'Tell me. Does Risdale know I'm here with you tonight?'

'No of course not. Why, would you like me to telephone his room and – ?'

'No. No, let's leave it shall we – pity to spoil the surprise.'

They were both about ready to go down to dinner, and standing up from the dressing table, Joan smoothed her hands over her hips. Asher hauled himself from the sofa and leaned on his cane. He felt tired as hell, so weary in fact that he had only just realised that even with the inclusion of Risdale to their party they still numbered only five.

'So who's the sixth?' he asked, as they both walked to the door.

Joan Handley turned.

'Guy's wife. Evelyn.'

*

It did not take long for Risdale's "surprise" to come into effect. For no sooner had they stepped out into the hotel's hallway, than David Asher saw a door open just across from him. But the man did not see him directly, nor did he see Joan who had just stepped back into her suite momentarily to get her bag. Risdale only saw him when, upon locking his door, he turned.

'Well, of all the . . . .!'

His expression was one of complete incredulity Asher noted, but the man was quick to recover. 'So . . . . so Lazarus has risen from his grave has he? My god Asher, I'll give you credit – when I saw you in that military hospital I thought – '

'You thought what, Risdale? That you'd seen the last of me? Oh, think again my friend. Or maybe you should simply try harder next time.'

'Yes, maybe I shall – that's if you give me reason.'

'A threat? Yes, that's about your mark.'

'Oh get out of my way Asher. I've no idea what you're doing here, but be a good fellow – stay the hell away.'

He barged past. He went to walk off.

'And does that include staying away from Evelyn too?' He watched Risdale stop dead in his tracks. 'I know she's here.'

Risdale turned.

'Is that why you've come, Asher – because of her?'

'As a matter of fact, no. But not that's any of your business.'

He watched Risdale walk back to where he stood.

'Well maybe I'm *making* it my business.' He drew closer. 'Listen, Asher' he said. 'Let me put you wise on one or two points about Evelyn, just in case you've come here with any silly ideas – have you ever wondered why she never came to see you in that hospital? Well, I'll tell you – she can't abide you – never could – never will. You see Asher, you bored her. Yes, you *bored* her to tears – bored her with your incessant whining and the way you tried to hound her into marriage.' Risdale sneered at him. He looked him up and down before he went on. 'Marriage! Ha! – to a man like you. As if she would! As if she'd marry a man who's as poor as a beggar! Oh how she used to laugh at the thought. Yes, laugh. But then your attention became less amusing to her – it began to wear her down – make her unhappy – made her drink. And that's when she came to me pleading for help, asking that I do something – *anything* to get rid.'

'Rid? What do you mean?'

'Oh work it out Asher – work it out for yourself.'

*

Downstairs in the Metropole's chrome and mirrored cocktail lounge, wearing a figure hugging black chiffon dress, Evelyn Risdale stood at the bar and flashed her dark almond eyes once more at the barman. As cool as the marble counter itself, she ordered another glass of champagne. It was her fourth of the evening and, with the champagne duly served, she brought the glass to her full and painted lips. Feeling tight with drink, and all the more venomous because of it, she gazed about the room and the men within.

Amongst the crowd, she could see her husband, smart in his uniform, unusually convivial she thought, at least more so she recalled, than that previous night. For now that heavy hand of his was firmly planted in the palm of one the Handley brothers – Victor, to whom she had already been introduced.

The man was smoking a large and expensive cigar, she noted, dressed in a white dinner jacket, most probably handmade, she guessed, together with a black silk cummerbund around his ample waist. His brother on the other hand, the small and pious looking, Clifford, was a mess, swamped in what appeared to be his larger sibling's hand-me-downs. She surveyed the gathering once more, disappointment setting in. No, there was not a decent man amongst them. Or as far as she could see.

She sighed with a kind of drunken ennui, turning to her cigarette case and her Du Maurier's. But as her bad luck would have it, she saw they were all gone, so she caught the eye of a passing cigarette girl and bought a new pack instead. Taking one out and placing it between her lips, she fumbled in her purse for her lighter, but as she did so she was aware of the faint click of another as it was sparked into life beside her.

Without looking up she leaned in towards the flame, placing her long fingers around the Gold Ronson to steady it in the man's hand. It was only then, when she pulled away, did she see his face. And it was only then, when she had done so, that she promptly fainted to the floor.

*

Some twenty minutes later, when she had sufficiently recovered, Evelyn walked into the Metropole's dining room to join the others at their table. She saw that Guy was in the middle of one of his boorish R.A.F. stories; he had his elbows resting on the white tablecloth, his eyes squinting through an imaginary gun sight, his thumb raised, jabbing on a make believe gun-button: 'So there was I – I'd just shot down two M.E. 109's with a third in my sights when something awful happened. I found I was out of ammunition!'

'My goodness,' Evelyn heard Joan Handley say at his side, looking spellbound. 'What on earth did you do?'

'Well what else *could* I do? I had to get the Jerry off your husband's tail somehow, so I flew my kite straight at the basket and cut his aircraft in half with my wing tip!'

As Evelyn sat down, taking her place with the others, she glanced across at David. He looked ten years older now, she thought, rather than the two it had been since their last meeting. He had lost weight too, and his dark hair was dusted silver. And was that not a cane she could see propped against his chair? Yes, it *was* his cane. And she felt like weeping. But she was damned if she would, at least not in public. Besides, she was not given to such things, and certainly not in the habit of fainting either.

But as the meal progressed, she could plainly see that David had changed in other ways besides his physical appearance. For he appeared cool, distant. Why, he had not even given her a single glance across the table, nor had he spoken a single word save for that moment back in the lounge when she had passed out. When that had happened, as he had tried his best to catch her in his arms as she had crumpled to the floor, she vaguely remembered hearing his voice:

'For God's sake, someone get her a brandy.'

Then Guy's voice: 'Brandy? Can't you see the silly bitch has had enough!'

Before long the meal was over and the coffee was served. She heard the conversation swing toward the island.

'So what's it like over there?' she heard Victor Handley ask. The man was leaning back on his chair. His hand was in his cummerbund, loosening it from his fulsome stomach.

'Yes, I've heard it's quite enchanting,' added Joan.

'Enchanting? No, quite the opposite,' Clifford Handley pitched in. 'I've heard it's full of miscreants and sinners.'

'Miscreants and sinners?' inquired Evelyn herself. 'What do you mean?'

'I think what the dear boy means, darling,' she heard Guy say with more than a touch of sarcasm, more than slightly drunk himself, 'is that the island's full of Jerries – one big internment camp.'

'Is that right, David?' asked Joan with surprise. 'The place is full of P.O.W.'s?'

Evelyn saw David give a nod. 'I believe that's the case. Or at least it was – most have been repatriated now.'

'And a damn good job,' she heard Guy say emphatically. 'You know they were billeted in all the finest places along the seafront, don't you?'

'Trust the Germans to get the best hotels,' quipped Victor.

Both men laughed and then the coffee came. As it was duly poured, Evelyn saw Clifford turn to Joan and heard him say: 'I've chosen a reading from the Book of Revelations for Rex's service, Joan, I hope that's all right – "And a war broke out and an Angel fell from heaven".'

She could see that Joan was just about to reply when Guy broke in: 'Actually, Joan, 'I'm afraid there might be a problem there.'

'A problem? Regarding what exactly?'

'With the service – that's if you still insist on holding it up at the crash site.'

'But of course – those were Rex's wishes.'

'Well that's as maybe, but I doubt very much they'll let you up there, at least not for a while at least. You see the whole area's cordoned off.'

'What do you mean?'

'There's a 500 lb bomb lying up on the hillside. It was onboard Handley's aircraft when it crashed. It's still live and yet to be recovered.'

'Oh I see. Then – ?'

'Oh, not for a while yet. We were expecting bomb disposal to have taken care of it last week, but they've been tied up down on the south coast.' Guy Risdale looked down into his coffee cup. 'Of course there's always an alternative.'

'Being?'

'A quiet service somewhere else – a chapel or churchyard perhaps – consecrated ground of course – you know the sort of thing.'

'Yes, and I know my late husband too. And he'd expect nothing less than his last wishes to be observed – to be carried out to the letter.'

Evelyn saw Guy shrug.

'Well there you are, Joan,' he said. 'That's the situation. But I can tell you this – they'll not let any civilians up on that hillside until that U.X.B. has been taken care of, and that's final.'

And with that, Evelyn saw Guy slap the palms of his hands on the table and smile. 'Well gentlemen – brandy and cigars?'

*

He did not have the stomach for Risdale's cigars and cognac. Nor the stomach for the man's company come to that. In fact, he did not have much time for any one of them around that table that night.

As such, and feeling tired beyond words, David Asher had retired early, retreating to his room to lick his wounds, feeling like a hurt animal, beaten and broken, as if seeking out a place to quietly curl up and die. But instead he just went over to the open window and sat by it, lighting a cigarette, looking out and listening to the sounds of the evening: the restless flap of pigeons up in the gutters, a ship's horn down on the banks of the river Mersey, the very stench of that river seeming no better than those "rotten to the core" individuals with whom he had dined. Yes, rotten to the core.

There was Risdale for one: moneyed, clever, but in the same breath cruel – the conveyor of Evelyn's feelings:

'*Marriage! Ha! – to a man like you. As if she would! As if she'd marry a man who's as poor as a beggar! Oh how she used to laugh at the thought. Yes, laugh. But then your attention became less amusing to her – it began to wear her down – make her unhappy – made her drink. And that's when she came to me pleading for help, asking that I do something – anything to get rid.*'

Rid? Oh yes. He'd worked it out now all right. He'd worked it out just fine. For Evelyn's fears were not that he would fail to return from France, but rather that he *would* return – that he'd come back to "hound" her, to suffocate her with his "attention", to "wear her down", and in doing so make her commit to an unhappy marriage.

163

And perhaps the worst sin of all, at least in Evelyn's eyes, that he would return to *"bore"* her.

Yes, he saw it all now, though he could not remember it so; he and Evelyn had always been happy, or as far as he could recall. Nevertheless, he knew Risdale was capable of such things – capable of getting "rid", to leave him in that foreign field. And also he suspected that Evelyn might even be capable of asking him to carry out such a task. By God, they were a pair. They were a pair indeed! Did they not deserve each other.

And then there was Evelyn herself of course: spoilt, wild, beautiful. (Yes, he had to admit to the latter, even though it pained him to do so). But what was she now, he thought? What had become of that party girl he had left some two years before, that lover of good times? Well, it appeared that those good times had all but dried up now, but the drink had surely not. Oh no, *that* still flowed in abundance, as her performance in the cocktail lounge had clearly proven. For she was little more than a gin soak, a sorry drunkard who was in the habit of passing out in hotel bars. But was she happy? No, clearly she was not. And perhaps it was no more than she deserved.

And then of course there were Rex's two brothers, Victor the "businessman", whom he guessed had made some profit from the war: the black-market. And then Clifford, the false prophet, who he guessed had excused himself from it by dint of his "beliefs", choosing to sit the whole thing out – an objector.

And lastly there was Joan, whom he had yet to figure, but who was perhaps the better of the bunch. And yet, and yet, there had been one girl who he'd *thought* to be better still – Kathy, his angel, a cold angel at that.

Exhausted, he sat and stared out the window, feeling lost, utterly lost, thinking of her, wondering if she would ever realise why he had walked out, or if instead she would end up hating him for what he'd done. He felt wretched at the prospect, and continued looking blankly out the window, gazing at the sprinkling of lights that lay across the bombed and shattered city. He thought of her one last time, feeling lost and wretched once more. For she seemed so very far away. And yet strangely, so very near.

*

'Liverpool! Liverpool, Lime Street! All change! All change!'

Kathleen woke to the slamming of carriage doors, the bustle of people, the boom of an echoing Tannoy. Slowly she rose from her seat and collected her case from the luggage rack. Wearily she stepped down from the train.

She found the station to be cavernous, gloomy, shrouded in steam. The acrid smell of soot filled the night air. It filled her lungs. Following the other passengers along the grimy platform she passed through the narrow gate at the end, out into the vast concourse where she gathered herself, reaching into her pocket for the cigarette packet that Michael had given her. Pulling it out she looked at the number he had scribbled upon it. Then she looked for a telephone box.

The telephone did not ring long before a man's voice answered – a man with a soft Irish accent.

"Wait under the clock," he ordered, but she told him: "No". It was too public. Besides, she could see a policeman on patrol.

'Then begin to walk towards the town hall,' he demanded.

'And how do I get there?'

There came a drunken chuckle.

'Just head for the stink of the Mersey – follow yer nose.'

Fifteen minutes later, Kathleen found herself by the dim light of a Liverpool street lamp, standing near the place her contact had instructed. It occurred to her that it was the second time that day she had waited for a man to appear, the second time since that morning back in Cambridge when she had stood in the rain waiting for . . . . no, she could not even bring herself to say his name, let alone break her vow and think of him. He was nothing to her now, just a lying, cheating, Englishman – the enemy with whom she was at war. But first she knew she had to gather her strength, get organised. And above all, get home.

When her contact arrived, Kathleen saw that he was an old man in a belted Macintosh. His hands were thrust deep in his pockets and he came up and eyed her with a watery gaze.

165

'Kathleen?'

She nodded back and the man's face spilt into a tobacco stained smile. A breeze from the Mersey whipped at his thinning hair. He swept it back with a single motion of his hand. 'Ah, I knew it was you the minute I laid eyes upon yer. I said to meself, she's an O'Callaghan or my name's not Desmond O'Riley. Got the money?'

Kathleen nodded again.

'Good. Then I can get you out of here tonight.' He flashed his yellow smile. He jerked a thumb. 'This way.'

They made their way towards Bootle along the cobblestones of the Waterloo Road. It was there, near the wide dark waters of the river, that Kathleen saw the dockyards for the first time. She noticed they were guarded well, and where they were not, there was a wire topped wooden paling fence. Through the gaps she could see a tantalising glimpse of freedom: ships at berth, tied and waiting.

At a dingy public house on the Regent Road, where a bulb glimmered in a glass lantern over the door, O'Riley stopped and Kathleen saw him hold out his hand.

'Now give me the money,' he demanded.

Kathleen hesitated; she was wary.

O'Riley lifted his unshaven chin. 'Or would yer rather I left yer to get across the water by yerself?'

Kathleen considered her options. They were slim. She gave O'Riley what he wanted and the man turned. He pushed open the door.

The place was called "The Weigh Bridge", and once inside, Kathleen was struck by the smell of men and beer. There was sawdust on the floor. Tobacco smoke filled the air. They cut a path through it towards the bar.

At the counter, she saw O'Riley lean over and speak to the landlord. She thought she heard O'Riley mention her name, for the landlord looked across at her, giving her a nod, then jerked a thumb to a curtained doorway behind him.

Going through, she found herself in a small back room. There an old lady in an apron was hunched over a kitchen range. A pot was bubbling: rabbit stew. Kathleen saw the woman splash some into a bowl and bring it over to a table. Without a word the woman gestured her to sit and eat. She did so, spooning the stew hungrily to her mouth. Then, a moment later, she saw a hand come around the curtained doorway.

O'Riley was standing there with another man, a sea captain, she presumed. For he wore a merchant navy type peaked cap that he proceeded to push to the back of his head, revealing a creased and weathered face with stark blue eyes. She felt those eyes upon her as the man appeared to stare at her in contemplation, rubbing a hand across his bristled chin. Then after a moment she saw him nod at O'Riley, and money changed hands.

When the captain had left, O'Riley joined her at the table. He sat down, rolling a cigarette between his nicotine stained fingers. He smiled.

'You're on that skipper's boat,' he said. 'He ran some guns for us before the war. He's a good man right enough.'

'And when does it sail?' she asked.

'Just after midnight, on the tide.'

'Bound for Dublin?'

O'Riley gave her a toothy grin.

'It is that.' He leaned towards her and put his face up close. He patted her hand. 'Ah I don't know how you're ever going to thank me.'

She pulled her hand away. Then asked for the ship's name. But O'Riley just smiled again and checked his watch.

'You'll know soon enough. Come on. Eat up – time we went.'

Outside the Weigh Bridge, all was quiet. The only thing that Kathleen could hear was the distant clanking of rolling stock coming from the shunting yards over in the docks. She crossed the road with O'Riley and they walked down the wetted pavement that ran alongside the wooden paling fence that separated them from the quayside. At an advertising hoarding that was nailed to the fence, O'Riley stopped. She saw him check the road. There was nothing to be seen, no people, no traffic, just the sheen of drizzle that fell against the doleful backdrop of the street lamps. Seizing his chance, she saw O'Riley go to work on the palings. They loosened easily, coming away as if both method and route had been used before.

Slipping through the gap, they climbed up a steep embankment together to the edge of the railway yard. At the brow, O'Riley motioned her to the ground, and she dropped to the wet grass, catching her breath. Beside her, O'Riley was breathless too, wheezing like an old accordion as he gulped in air, then whiskey from a bottle that he took from his raincoat. After he had drunk from it, she saw him get to his feet and motion her to follow. She picked up her suitcase at her side and went after him, stepping over the railway tracks to a warehouse beyond.

On the top floor of the warehouse, she went to a window and looked out through a broken pane. On the quayside below, under a pool of light, a force of dockers were busy loading the ships, craning cargo into their holds. Nearby, she could see a couple of soldiers on patrol. They were standing talking, their rifles slung over their shoulders, their cigarettes glowing in the darkness. A locomotive shunting goods came up on the dockside rails beside them and she saw the soldier move to one side. The engine belched up a cloud of steam as it passed. She looked at her wristwatch. It was just after 11.30. p.m.

A moment later, she heard O'Riley get up from the floor where he'd been sitting. He came across to her. She felt his whiskey breath on her neck as he peered over her shoulder as he looked down at the solders. His hand was resting on her hip.

'Now it would be such a terrible shame if they caught you, so it would,' he said in a lyrical whisper. 'For it's a terrible mess you're in – all those ships down there and you not knowing one from t'other.' She felt his hand move from her hip. It slid around. She felt his fingers, exploring. 'Now if you were to show me a little kindness – '

She moved so quickly it shocked her, her strength surprising her too as she grabbed O'Riley's arm. She twisted it to his back, pushing him up against the window. His head cracked the pane.

'Then supposing you tell me which one it is?' she hissed. 'The name! The *name!*'

She heard O'Riley groan – felt his body arch as she yanked his arm up a notch.

'The Lars Morgansen!' he yelped. 'The Lars Morgansen, pier five.'

Two minutes later, after she'd run down the warehouse stairs and out into the night, Kathleen found herself at the side of the building. Her heart was pounding, beating almost in time to the ring of army boots that she could hear scurrying towards her upon the quayside; they'd heard the window break up in the warehouse. They were coming!

Pulling back into the shadows, she saw them approach, then run into the warehouse to investigate. When she heard the sound of their footsteps on the stairs, she made off, heading for pier five.

At the ship's berth, using the grimy wharf side buildings as cover, she watched from the safety of some grain sacks as the crew of the Lars Morgansen went about their business. She was just in time. For they were untying the ship from the dock, unfastening the ropes, preparing to sail. A group of soldiers were standing nearby, she noted, on the quayside, between herself and the ship. She needed a moment of distraction. It came the next second, in the shape of the dockside locomotive.

It was clanking down the dockside rails towards her, throwing up a convenient cloak of steam. As it rumbled past, she broke cover, making a dash across the quayside. Veiled in the train's vaporous wake, she was soon aboard, unnoticed by all but the man she had seen in the Weigh Bridge. For he was there waiting for her by the gangplank, on the deck, from which she was quickly despatched, taken below and hurried out of sight.

In the bowels of the ship, she was then ushered through a labyrinth of steel and riveted corridors by a crewman. Then she came to a bulkhead door. The crewman opened it, then gestured her to the tiny dark compartment beyond. Reluctantly, she stepped across the threshold. Then giving her nothing but a lighted candle, the man crashed the heavy steel door shut, Kathleen hearing it lock behind her.

In the resulting draft the candle flickered and nearly went out. But cupping a hand around it, she soon settled the flame. She held it up, surveying her new surroundings.

It was not good. The place was damp and cold, and there was the stench of oil and the scurry of rats. A shallow pool of greasy water lay at her feet. The water slopped back and forth with the gently roll of the ship. But then came the deafening clatter of machinery and she looked up. Suddenly she realised the place to which she had been taken.

It was the chain locker, and great links were clanking into a vast pile in front of her. Then, after a moment, when the clanking had stopped, she felt the sensation of movement – the ship was swinging away, leaving its moorings.

Its bow gently dipped as it chugged off down the Mersey Channel, but it was soon bucking wildly as they hit open water. She braced herself as the waves started to come, pounding and crashing, thumping noisily against the ship's hull, jarring the whole vessel as it fought its way through the water.

She was thrown forwards, then backwards, then forwards once again. Then a huge wave, much bigger than the rest struck the bow and she was slammed back against the bulkhead door. She slithered down into the pool of oily sludge. Before long she was rackingly sick.

And as she lay there, wet and ill and cold, she cursed her God in heaven. And just like the Englishman, she damned them both to hell.

2

The next morning, David Asher woke suddenly. He woke suddenly thinking he was back at the hospital. He woke expecting to see the ward, the red linoleum aisle, the skylight window above his head. He woke expecting to see *her*.

After breakfast, and after packing his things, he found himself standing outside the Metropole instead, where he unfastened the hood of Rex Handley's sports car, waiting for Joan. Behind him, at the hotel's entrance, he could see Guy and Evelyn emerging into the sunlight, whereupon they walked down the hotel's front steps to Risdale's waiting Bentley, both climbing inside.

Neither looked particularly happy, he thought. In fact Risdale wore the same look of barely subdued contempt that he had seen on the man's face that previous night went he'd bumped into him in the hotel's hallway. Moreover, that look had multiplied when, shortly after, Risdale had seen him walk into that cocktail lounge with Joan upon his arm, and then yet more still when the man had found himself dining at the same table. His face had been a picture then, his expression odd, as if out of some kind of jealousy concerning himself and Joan. And then it had all fallen into place. Risdale and Joan were having an affair. Of course! But then again it was none of his concern. But he had spotted something that *was*.

It had been the manner of Evelyn's exit from the hotel that he'd found curious, the cautious way she had walked down those steps, the careful, almost painful easing of herself into that car. It had alerted his suspicions. Poor Eve. But then, he thought, perhaps it was no more than she deserved.

Joan soon joined him in the car and they headed off together, going towards the Fleetwood docks from where the ship was due to sail. He had not been driving long however, when Joan turned, and said with a heavy sigh:

'You don't think this trip's going to be a dreadful waste of time, do you David? I mean if they'll not let us up on that hillside – '

Asher thought back to what Risdale had said about the U.X.B.

'Yes, he rather sprang that on us, didn't he. Strange he didn't think to mention it to you before. Then again he's a rather strange sort himself.'

'I gather you don't care for him much, David.'

'What makes you say that?'

'Well, one can't help but notice things. But you strike me as a fair man. I'm sure you've got your reasons.'

'Reasons? Where would you like me to begin? Besides, I'm not very keen on liars, particularly the way he lied to you last night.'

'What do you mean?'

'Over dinner. You recall that story he told of those three M.E. 109's on your husband's tail?'

'Yes, I remember.'

'Well it didn't happen like that. It was Rex who shot down those aircraft, not Risdale. Those 109's were bearing down on Risdale's aircraft at the time. You see, it wasn't *him* who saved your husband's life. It was the other way around.'

Joan sat there for a moment as she appeared to take it in. She shook her head.

'Oh . . . oh I had no idea.'

'Well I suppose you wouldn't. Rex was never one for bragging, was he Joan. Quite the opposite. So what else did you notice?'

'About dinner last night?'

'Yes – you said "one can't help but notice things". So what else struck you?'

'Oh, only what was obvious, David.'

'And what was that?'

'Why Guy and Evelyn of course? Didn't you see? They really can't stand each other. Didn't you notice how blunt he was with her?'

'Oh that. Well, he's that sort of man, like I told you. But I fear he was blunter still with her afterwards.'

'What do you mean?'

'He beat her.'

He saw Joan look across at him. There was shock and doubt in her eyes. He nodded. 'It's true. I've just seen her getting into his car. She was hurting, most definitely – must have taken place in their room after he went up.'

'Guy?' No, I can't believe it. Are you sure? I mean perhaps it happened some other way. What about when she collapsed in the bar?'

'No, I don't think so. Besides, I caught her in time, or as best I could.'

'Then if it wasn't that –?' She shook head. 'Well the poor creature. I'd never have thought it. I mean I've never had much time for her but . . . . then why does she stay with him if he treats her so? And why come on this trip with him and risk more of the same?'

He shook his head too; he was equally puzzled.

'I really don't know,' he said. 'But I can only guess she must have a damned good reason.'

*

On arrival at the Fleetwood docks, David Asher drove onto the quayside where the boat was being readied for the passage across the Irish Sea. He parked the car in reach of the crane's jib for loading, then he and Joan got out. Queuing with the other passengers, they went onboard.

In the ship's saloon, he ordered drinks for Joan and himself, then went outside on deck alone. There the sun was shining with a kind of brilliant optimism, the crew busily pulling in the ropes. And then, with a blast from the ship's horn, they were underway, the vessel slowly edging out from the harbour, pushing through white plumed breakers into the glittering sea.

And as he stood there, leaning on the rail, taking the weight off his aching legs, he watched the mainland quietly recede into the distance, feeling a strange kind of division, as if part of him was slipping away too: his days and nights he had spent at the hospital, the time he'd spent with *her*. And then the loneliness hit him once more, gnawing at his soul.

It was then he saw Evelyn.

She was standing a little further along the deck from him, at the rail. She looked pale and wretched, he thought, ill as she stood there with a handkerchief to her face, a hand on her stomach. Guessing the reason, he hailed a passing ship's steward and ordered another drink. Then, when the drink was duly received into his hand, he went across.

'Here. Drink this,' he said.

Evelyn turned. He saw her look at him, then look coldly at the glass, eyeing it with a kind of apprehension, as if somehow she should not drink at all.

'No, this one's all right,' he said, as if to reassure her. 'Go on. Drink.'

She did as she was bade. Then he asked if she felt better. She nodded back, smiling weakly. Then she asked what type of drink it was.

'Port and brandy,' he told her. 'An old naval remedy for seasickness – that's what's wrong isn't it?'

She nodded and smiled feebly again. Then she told him that he always knew the right thing to do. 'You were always so good at taking care of me,' she said.

He looked at her. It was a strange backhanded compliment, he thought. Nevertheless, he just shrugged.

'That's all I ever wanted to do, Eve – take care of you. I suppose you thought Risdale would make a better job of it – the better man?'

She looked toward the horizon. He saw her shake her head.

'No. I never thought that at all. It's just – '

'Oh, forget it, Eve,' he said. 'As far as I'm concerned I just don't want to think about it. But just tell me this – why couldn't you have simply been straight with me – told me that you didn't want to marry me, instead of – .' He looked incredulously at her, as if such a beautiful creature could ever do such a terrible thing. He shook his head. 'Did I really mean that little to you? That you thought you could just remove me from your life like that – that you could just get rid? Did you, Eve? *Did* you?'

He shook his head once more, then turned and walked away.

'No, wait – *Wait*,' he heard her call after him. But he was all through with waiting. All through with Evelyn.

*

The Isle of Man that summer: a holiday destination that was slowly emerging from its wartime role; the internment of thousands – P.O.W's, detainees, foreign aliens. Beyond that function it was a seaside resort like many others; mothballed for the duration, gradually coming back to life.

Standing on deck, David Asher watched as the island came into view, a rock of a place that swelled before his eyes, growing ever larger as the ship neared.

Upon disembarkation at the harbour, he felt horribly self-conscious as he made his way down the gangplank, hobbling slowly with his cane, aware of those eager though patient souls behind him, waiting dutifully for him to negotiate the steep wooden descent. Though before he'd reached the quayside, he was faintly aware of a hand, then the slight pressure of that same hand as it dipped into his coat pocket. He gave it no more thought, then as he waited on the dockside for the car to be unloaded, he checked his pocket. There he found a note. He knew the handwriting well.

On the return of their vehicles, they went their separate ways – Victor and Clifford by cab to the Grand on the seafront, Guy and Evelyn to a hotel nearby, requisitioned by the R.A.F. Then in the bright red sports car, he and Joan drove along the great sweeping arc of the promenade, looking for their accommodation amongst the white curve of hotels which had served the British army well, pressed into service to incarcerate those who had been imprisoned there. As they drove, from the open top car, he noted the fresh smell of paint; the wire was coming down, the place was being reclaimed, re-colonised.

Though when they found their hotel, it was a disappointment – it was no more than a boarding house. And once shown to their respective rooms, Joan quietly apologised. He told her he did not mind in the least. He had stayed in worse places.

'Courtesy of the Germans,' he said, smiling tongue in cheek, referring to his incarceration.

He saw her smile back, then saw it fade as she looked down at his cane, as if knowing exactly what he meant, maybe guessing at the things he'd endured.

'Yes, you must be dreadfully tired,' she told him, 'what with everything.' He told her he was. And if she didn't mind he'd be off to his room. 'But you'll be coming down for dinner, won't you?' she asked.

He looked at his watch. It was still quite early.

'I'm not sure,' he said. 'Perhaps I'll just turn in – you're sure you don't mind?'

She told him again she did not mind in the least. Then she smiled once more and bade him goodnight.

In his room, after hanging up his things and placing his case upon the wardrobe, David Asher lay restlessly on his bed for a long time. Over in the corner, by the window on the floor, lay a ball of crumpled up paper. It had been thrown there by his own hand. For it had been the note which had been slipped into his coat pocket upon disembarkation from the ship – Evelyn's note: *"David. I'm sorry. Will you meet me on the promenade at 8.30? I must explain. 'E'."*

No, it was too much to ask of him, he thought. He could not do it. He could not allow Evelyn to simply crawl out of the terrible thing she had done – trying to get "rid". Besides, he wagered that she was only sorry for herself, sorry that he'd found her out. No, she could damn well go to hell!

He lay there in his shame. He did not mean that. In fact he felt wretched that his mind was, to a degree, capable of a certain cruelty just like Evelyn's mind. And he did not want to be cruel to her, despite what she had done. For even though he knew that *she* had never loved him, *he* had once loved her. And he knew also that her life with Risdale must be hell enough alone. Yes, she had clearly made a mistake in choosing Risdale. But who was he himself to preside on matters of love? Had he not made a terrible mistake in love too? A mistake in loving a traitor?

176

He lay on his bed a while longer, thinking of Evelyn, feeling quite wretched again as he looked across at her screwed up note on the floor. Then he looked at his watch. It was a quarter to nine. Turning he looked at his suit which he'd hung neatly over the wardrobe door. After a moment he got up and changed into it, then picking up his cigarettes and lighter and cane, he limped out onto the landing. He went downstairs.

In the hallway, a woman he knew to be the landlady was watering a plant by the front door.

'Going somewhere special? she asked.

'Just the promenade,' he said.

*

He found it to be a beautiful evening down on the seafront. The sun was setting languidly over the bay, and the promenade was mellowed by its fading light. He strolled as best he could upon it, looking for Evelyn, but somehow knowing too that she would not be there. For he was roughly an hour late now, and waiting was not her strongest suit.

So he was greatly surprised when he suddenly spotted her. She was by the promenade rail, looking out across the ocean. She was dressed quite beautifully, he noticed, (whenever had he seen her otherwise?) and her thick dark hair was shimmering in the long fingers of sunlight which broke behind her, slatted by the tall hotels along the seafront.

'Evelyn,' he called.

She turned, smiling as she saw him.

'David – I wasn't sure you'd come.'

'I wasn't sure I wanted to,' he said. 'Does Guy know you're here?'

She shook her head. 'He's having dinner with the Air Vice Marshal. He'd kill me if he knew.'

Asher nodded. 'I know about that – him hurting you, I mean. Have you eaten yet?'

She told him 'no', then he suggested supper. They went in search of a restaurant.

They found one of the better ones just back from the seafront. There they had a meal, Evelyn choosing lobster. Asher the lamb. Then he ordered a bottle of wine that Evelyn eschewed in favour of water.

'Water?' he said with feigned and caustic surprise. 'I seem to remember at our last meeting there was a promise of something stronger.'

He wondered if she would pick up on his reference – that evening at Wroughton Hall before he had left for France – the words she had said to him:

'Darling, I'll be waiting with a bottle of the finest champagne.'

But then he saw her look away, almost shamefaced.

'No, we never did have our champagne, did we,' she said sounding strangely sad he thought, obviously recalling that night before they had parted. 'But I promise you David, we will, if you'll only let me.'

But he said quite bluntly 'not to bother'. And anyway he was tired of promises, tired of the whole dreary world quite frankly. And if they got back together for that champagne he would only end up "boring" her again, falling in love with her once more, and "wearing her down" with proposals of marriage. And where would she find herself then, he asked? Having to get "rid" again – "rid" because he wasn't amusing, and moreover because he was not rich, not rich like some he could mention.

He saw that she was clearly taken aback. But in the same breath clearly quite confused. Then she told him she didn't understand. She didn't understand at all. She didn't know what he was talking about.

He made a play of taking a pinch of salt from the side of his plate and sprinkling it upon his food. He noticed she was sharp enough to see his "pinch of salt" gesture though and she rebuffed it at once, saying: 'David. You must believe me. I've never accused you of anything like that in my life. And as for getting "rid" as you call it, why, if you're talking about France, I never even wanted you to go in the first place! Don't you remember – that night at Wroughton Hall just before you were due to fly out? I told you I'd take poison if you left me.'

A fragment of their conversation suddenly found its way back to him.

'Yes, poison if it's true, David. Tell me it's not. You're not really going away are you?'

'Sorry Eve. I must –'

He told her: 'Yes', he *did* recall her saying some such thing, and then she reminded him of more. To which he replied: 'Yes, that's right. You called me a "heartless beast", didn't you. And then you asked what you were meant to do without me.'

'Exactly,' said Evelyn. 'Does that sound like someone who wanted to get "rid"?'

He said it did not. He said it sounded like someone who really cared for him.

'No, not just cared,' she replied, looking across at him with the makings of tears in her eyes. 'Loved.'

*

After leaving the restaurant, and partly because he did not want to take her straight back to her hotel, thus placing her at the mercy of Risdale's temper, and partly because he could think of little else, he took her to a dance hall.

It was just along the seafront. And going inside, they were immediately hit by the cacophony of a big band, greeted by the sight of a tightly packed crowd who were rotating in disciplined chaos around the dance floor. He realised, of course, that it was a mistake from the outset; he was in no condition to dance, neither for that matter, he guessed, was Evelyn. For he had a notion that she was still suffering from Risdale's handiwork, still bruised beneath her lovely dress. Instead they bought drinks and found a table to the side, at which they both sat, both lighting cigarettes, both knowing in a kind of quiet but sorrowful way that *this* could have been "them" – together, happy, contented had it not been for the war and the fact he'd had to go away. It had ruined everything, had France. With Risdale's help.

In fact as he sat there, he wondered what Risdale might say if he were to walk in that very moment with Evelyn sat opposite. And in the next second, as he was struck by the possible unpleasantness of Risdale's untimely appearance, so too was he struck by a hard slap on his shoulder.

'What the devil! . . . . as I live and breathe. As I live and breathe!'

But turning around, he saw it was just an old friend – Peter Letherington, an army captain whom he knew from long ago. And after he and Letherington had talked, and after the man had left, Asher looked at Evelyn and she had looked at him, both somehow aware of the others thoughts: it could easily have been Risdale. And fearing that possibility, they both decided to leave, getting up and walking back along the promenade.

At ten past eleven, they were nearing Evelyn's hotel, and prudently David Asher stopped short of it, lest they were seen. And there, on the seafront, they lit cigarettes one last time, standing in awkward silence.

'Well, thank you for a very pleasant evening,' Evelyn said eventually, her smile white in the dark and intimate shadows.

'No, the pleasure was all mine,' he replied, feeling horribly formal, switching his gaze from hers and looking at the hotel instead, seeing the lit windows which splashed their brilliance down upon the seafront. 'Will Guy still be up . . . . I mean – '

Evelyn seemed to know exactly what he meant.

'I don't know,' she said. 'But if he is . . . . if he . . . . well, whatever he does to me now, he can't take tonight away from us. And who knows, one day, perhaps we'll get to have our champagne.'

'Yes, perhaps we shall,' he replied.

Then she asked if they might kiss, 'For old time's sake,' she said. And he said: 'Yes, for old time sake, why not.'

And then, in the cold moonlight which bathed the long sweeping arc of the seafront, they drew closer and he felt her warm mouth upon his own. Her lips were sweet – cocktail sweet like cherries in vermouth. And then her mouth was at his cheek, her whispered words in his ear. And as she turned and walked away, he almost wept. For in all the world he had wanted to believe those words, but with his heart damaged, wounded by lies, he dare not do so yet.

3

She had been away from Ireland too long – four whole years. Though as Kathleen stepped ashore from the Lars Morgansen, feeling weary and bedraggled as she made her way up from the quayside, through the streets of Dublin, it seemed as if she had never been away. Nothing had changed – only herself.

She crossed the river Liffey, making her way towards her Da's house, walking up towards Phoenix Park and her local church of St. Joseph's, hearing as she did so her old family priest, Father O'Flaherty in the graveyard; she knew that throaty cough of his anywhere – the hack of a man who had spent too much time in the company of the hard drinkers of the Cause. And as she went by, she saw O'Flaherty look up. Then she saw him hurriedly shuffle away, his black round-toed shoes moving like two quick shiny beetles beneath the hem of his robes, heading no doubt, for his telephone. *That's it Father. Go tell them. Go tell them I'm back. And things are going to change.*

Arriving in the alleyway at the rear of her Da's house, she entered through the back gate. Ma was busy in the old tin washhouse, bent over her boiling tubs: women's work. Her once pretty auburn hair was dusted white now, Kathleen noted, and her face looked puffy and bruised: her father's work.

The rising of the latch had alerted the old woman; she had looked up.

'Kathleen! Kathleen!'

She wiped the beaded sweat from her brow. Smiling, the old woman threw her plump and ruddy arms around her. Together they went into the house.

In the tiny back kitchen, the kettle was placed on the range. The best china was taken down. Kathleen began changing out of her dress and Ma helped her off with it, pulling the raggedy garment over her head. 'Now let's take a look at yer.' She stepped back, still smiling, viewing her as she stood there in her slip. Ma shook her head. 'I can hardly believe it. Back – me own little girl. Back at last!'

Kathleen sat down exhaustedly. She looked around. The whitewashed walls were peeling now, and Ma's collection of religious icons had grown across them like an all pervading ivy – poison ivy at that; her Ma's hand sewn tapestries and wooden crosses stretched almost down the hall and into the parlour. Then, as they waited for the kettle to boil, the two of them began to talk, Ma inquiring about her "boys".

'They're grand,' said Kathleen, hiding the loathing she felt for the pair of them. 'Never better. Just grand.'

'Grand,' said her Ma back. 'Yer Da won't rest until they return – he needs them. He's got plans.'

Plans? Yes. And so had she!

'So where is he?' Kathleen asked, meaning her Da.

'Cahill's,' said Ma, meaning her husband's favourite republican watering hole, a bar down on Grafton Street. 'He's holding one of his meetings there tonight, to put his plans before them,'

'Is that a fact,' said Kathleen, looking up at Ma's injured face. 'And I suppose he gave you that before he left?'

Ma looked embarrassed; she turned away and raised a hand to cover her bruising, pulling up her shawl. Then she feigned a kind of surprise. 'This? – oh, just an accident, so it was – the wash house door.' Then appearing to change the subject, she turned again and smiled: 'My, it's good ter have yer back, Kathleen. Why I thought I'd lost yer – lost yer fer good. Oh you'll never know the worry – '

Worry? – that was a fine one, thought Kathleen – Ma had shown precious little of it when she had been younger – those nights when Da would come home drunk.

Just let him try now. Just let him try!

'Well you can put your worries behind you now Ma,' she said reassuringly, getting up, feeling sorry for her poor mother and placing her arm around her shoulder. 'I'm home now. I'm home and there's no need to fret – I'm going to take care of things.'

It was a fact. And the first thing she intended to take care of was

183

that so called "wash house door".

*

Cahill's Bar was jumping that night, ringing with the sound of the fiddle, the penny whistle and the old worn drum. A thin mantle of dust had risen from the floor, hammered up by the dancing feet that deftly kicked and flailed, thumping the bare wooden boards to the beat of the old rebel songs.

Outside, through the window, Kathleen could see it all. She could see her Da as well, holding court in one of the booths, arm wrestling on this occasion with another would-be contender, slamming down the man's defeated limb to noisy applause. Then she heard the men clap and cheer around him, keeping her Da in good humour, should he turn as sour as Cahill's beer.

She turned from the window. Kathleen was wearing one of Ma's dresses, a garment the woman had long since outgrown. Smoothing her hands over the brocaded green silk, she gathered her courage. She went towards the door.

'She's here Pat! She's here!' Went up the cry that next moment as Kathleen stepped inside. And as she did so she heard the scratchy fiddle die, the music fade then gradually slide to a halt. Then through the crowd she saw her Da. He was in the booth. He swivelled around.

'What's that? What's that yer say? Me brave little girl, home at last?'

Kathleen stood her ground as he came over, his large hands quick on the collars of those who blocked his way. Then she saw him come to a halt in front of her, grinning with his thumbs in his belt, looking at her – looking as she stood there in her mother's dress, her flame red hair loose around her shoulders.

'Well, will yer look at that! If it's not me own little darlin' an' all safe an' sound. An' all grown up as well!' The next moment she felt his arms about her as he pulled her into an embrace. Then up went a cheer. Then on again went the drinking, the fiddle, the whistle and the old worn drum.

*

Later that night, in a vault beneath Cahill's Bar, a cellar which had

184

once echoed to the rhetoric of Collins and De Valera, Kathleen took her place around a long candlelit table as her father prepared to bring his meeting to order. It was strange, she thought as she watched him, how quickly he had sobered, how rapidly he seemed to make the transformation from bully to statesman with the mere act of donning his reading glasses. Not that she was in a position to complain; her attendance was only in respect of her homecoming. For under discussion that evening were the affairs of the 1st Dublin Division of the Irish Republican Army. And this again was men's work.

Men's work. Ha! She looked about her at the faces around the table, the withered washed up alcoholics like her Da – veterans of the '16 rising, survivors of the Irish Civil War, old Sinn Feiner's who'd long outlived their usefulness. Yes, if there was one thing that the division needed, she thought, it was an injection of new blood – *and* a new leader.

But where was this new leader to be found? – well, in herself, naturally. But maybe, just maybe, *that* decision had already been taken. For as incredible as it seemed, earlier she'd overheard a rumour circulating in the bar upstairs.

'They're going to appoint the girl. It's true I say. They're going to appoint Kathleen – head of the whole division!'

It was almost too ridiculous to believe; she was expecting more of a fight. Then again why not? She was certainly more practised than her Da. And younger too. But to displace him? Surely not? She looked across the table at him. How she despised him, this "wash house door" of a man. He was busy laying out his plans to the others, and in particular the plan of which she had heard Ma speak. It was to be a fund raising mission, or so she heard him say, which she immediately took to mean a bank. It was to be "across the water" once again. "Easy pickings", her Da had added, though she doubted it was anything of the sort, and certainly not for the likes of Michael and Eamonn on their own, whom he intended to send upon their return.

But she would change all that if those bar room rumours were true. She would change all that. And sure enough, as the meeting finally wound to a close, the candles burning down to their stumps upon the dusty table, she saw her Da take off his reading glasses as he began to announce the news.

It was true. She was going to be appointed head! And then the humiliation – it was head of the Dublin branch of the *Woman's* Army – the Cumann na mBann!

Kathleen felt sick – sick and foolish. So this was her reward? – to be the leader of a band of sock darning subservient females who typed and petitioned and leafleted? No, it was not good enough. Suddenly she kicked back her chair. She rose to her feet.

The faces turned, amazed. But perhaps none more so than herself. For she began to tear into them, telling them she wanted more – deserved it in fact. Why, was she not the most experienced amongst them? Had she not spent four years outwitting the British army, always staying one step ahead of them, even working undercover in a military hospital. And did she not know the enemy better than any one of them – know them for the lying double crossing cheats they were. Sweet Jesus, what did they think she had been doing all this time!

After a moment she calmed. She began speaking softer, though her argument still prevailed. It was active service that she desired, that was all, a chance to hit back again, to strike at the heart of the enemy. Then, at the end of it, she sat back down – sat back down to the astonishment of the silent men.

They did not remain silent long. For a proposal was made, then seconded, then carried unanimously by all: upon Michael and Eamonn's return, she would be allowed to accompany them on the fund raising mission.

Accompany them? She would see about that! She would see about her Da as well.

4

The next morning, after he had risen from his bed, David Asher found himself upon the windblown promenade, searching for a certain boarding house upon the seafront.

'It's called the Mayeville,' his friend Captain Peter Letherington had told him the previous night, when they had bumped into each other at the dance hall. He and Letherington had trained together once in London, but now the man had been seconded to escort duty, he learned, detailed to transport a prisoner of war across to the mainland.

'I thought they'd all been repatriated,' Asher had said to him.

'Not this one. We're holding him back.'

'Whatever for?'

'He's to stand trial for murder – he killed a fellow prisoner out on the hills – an argument, I believe.'

'What was he doing out on the hills?'

'He was there with a working party, clearing debris from a crashed aircraft. I mean you can't keep the blighters locked up all day, David. You've got to give them some sort of exercise. They get terribly belligerent if you don't.'

'Once a German, always a German, eh, Peter?'

Both men laughed and Letherington pulled out his cigarettes. 'No, have one of mine,' said Asher, producing his own.

'Well, that's awfully decent of you, old chap. Are you sure?'

'Yes, of course. But I might have to beg a favour in return.'

'Name it, old man. Anything for a friend.'

He sparked up his gold Ronson and lit Letherington's cigarette, telling the man he simply wanted five minutes alone with his prisoner. But Letherington shook his head. 'Sorry, David. Nothing doing. I'd get damn well cashiered if he comes to harm.'

'No Peter, you don't understand – not like that. I don't want to beat the fellow. I just want to talk to him.'

187

Peter Letherington looked at him bemused. He blew out smoke.

'Talk to him? What about?'

'About that aircraft. It *was* an R.A.F. Lancaster bomber, wasn't it?'

Letherington nodded. He looked bemused yet again.

'Yes, but – '

He smiled. 'Oh, come on, Peter. You did say anything for a friend, didn't you?'

After a moment, Letherington conceded. 'Oh I suppose . . . . but God knows why you're interested. We're holding him in one of the billets along the seafront, a requisitioned boarding house. You can't miss it. It's right next door to the Grand.'

. . . . He found it with little trouble, just as Letherington had said. And he stood there on the pavement looking up, staring through the rain which had just started to pitter-patter down. It was a tall, decrepit sort of place, a far cry he imagined from the neat holiday accommodation it had once offered the holidaymaking guests before the war. Though as for now, his mind was focused on that one particular "guest" who remained.

'His name's Heinrich Korten,' said Letherington after Asher had gone up the front steps, venturing inside to find his friend the captain behind a makeshift desk on the ground floor, in what he supposed was the old dining room. 'He's not a very pleasant chap, I'm afraid – one of those hard-line Nazi fellows, but he does speak decent English.' Letherington nodded to a man in uniform at his side. 'Sergeant. Show Lieutenant Asher up will you.'

They went up stairs, several flights in fact, the sergeant having to wait for him in his slowness to climb them. But once on the top floor, the man unlocked a door and showed him into a room.

The place was bare and stark. And he found Oberstleutnant Heinrich Korten at a table by closed balcony doors, playing solitaire with a pack of well thumbed cards. He was a man in his mid twenties, he guessed, slim and fit and good-looking. He was shirtless, with his braces over the top of a grubby white vest, his trousers grey serge; the bottom half of a German officer's uniform. Blonde hair cascaded over his pale blue eyes. Those eyes followed him, he noted as he walked in, pointing towards the balcony.

'Is it possible to have a window open, Sergeant? It's a little stuffy in here.'

The sergeant shook his head; it was against regulations. Then the man withdrew to the landing outside, Asher hearing the door close and lock behind him.

Still feeling Korten's gaze upon his back, he walked over to the balcony doors and looked through the window at the wet promenade below. The rain was coming down heavier now, and the waves were lashing into the bay. He turned and came and sat down on the edge of Korten's table. He took out his cigarettes and without introducing himself, he offered one to the German. The man accepted, giving a silent nod in way of thanks.

'I suppose you know they'll be taking you across to the mainland to stand trial soon,' he said, lighting Korten's cigarette first and then his own. Korten leaned back on his chair, drinking in the smoke.

'For me I think it will not be soon enough,' he said.

Asher raised an eyebrow. 'Do you really think so?'

Korten waved his cigarette derisively at the four walls. He lifted his chin at the filthy room.

'Your prisons are not better than *this?'*

Asher looked across at him. He reminded him of a man he had met before: his interrogator at Gestapo Headquarters on the Avenue Foch.

'Oh, I don't think you'll be seeing much of prison, old boy,' he said with a degree of satisfaction, feeling a kind of relish at the reversal of roles: captive turned captor. 'Least only 'til they take you out and hang you.'

The man was quick to reply. 'But Herr Letherington – he said I would get maybe two years, then repatriation.'

He could not help but bait the man.

'Well I'm afraid what "Herr Letherington" knows about the judicial system you could put on a postage stamp.'

He saw Korten look at him from beneath his blonde fringe.

189

'Who are you? You are maybe from the Government? The British Home Office?'

The Home Office indeed!

He ignored the man and went to the balcony doors. He looked out through the rain-spattered glass.

'I believe they sent you out onto the hills a couple of months ago, to clear the wreckage of a crashed British aircraft, is that correct?'

Korten said nothing.

Asher turned. 'It's a perfectly simple question. Were you, or were you not up at the crash site?'

Korten finally answered.

'Yes, I was there.'

'And you didn't protest?'

'Protest?'

'Yes, against working in the vicinity of an unexploded bomb. There must be something in the Geneva Convention about prisoners of war working under those conditions.'

He saw Korten narrow his eyes.

'A bomb? There was no bomb.'

'No?'

'No, just wreckage.'

Asher moved to the door.

'Thank you. That's all I wanted to know.' He rapped on the door. *'Sergeant!'*

Korten looked uneasy.

'You really think that I will hang for what I did?'

Asher half turned. He shrugged indifferently.

'Well, you could always try throwing yourself on the mercy of the court, though I wouldn't think it would do you much good. It might have escaped your attention, but you Germans aren't the most popular of people at the moment.' He knocked on the door again. *'Sergeant!'*

There came the sound of heavy boots on the bare wooden treads.

Korten looked panicked, he thought, as if it were his last chance.

'I have money,' he suddenly blurted.

Asher smiled.

'You can't bribe your way out of this with a few German marks, my friend.'

He heard the sergeant on the other side of the door, the sound of the key turning in the lock.

'No, I have English money. Twenty-five thousand pounds.'

*

Five minutes later, he found himself back outside the Mayeville, upon the steps. The weather was foul. Rain was lashing down with a vengeance now, running like a torrent along the gutters, gushing full bore into the drains. Across the seafront road, he could see the incoming tide slamming itself into the sea wall, arching over the balustrade in a thick white comma of foam. The wind was blowing too. And as he stood atop those steps, a blast caught him, rocking him on his unsteady legs. He felt tired. Wearied beyond his years.

Pulling up the collar of his coat he fought his way to the edge of the steps, feeling a slight dizziness as he made to go down. Then, the next thing he knew there came a noise like the snapping of bone. As it did so he felt his legs give way. Then he rolled –tumbling down to the wet pavement below. There he lay sprawled, barely conscious, blacking out but not before he felt the blood begin to flow.

*

Later that night, after their gathering in Cahill's cellar, and after leaving her Da to resume his drinking with his men in the bar, Kathleen lay in her bed thinking of the stir she had caused at the meeting. No doubt they would view her differently now, she figured, now she had spoken out, standing up for herself, refusing to join her sock darning sisters of the Cumann na mBann. Yes, she had shown another side of herself, but it was a side that, hitherto, she had barely recognised.

It was as if a great change had come into being, one that had overtaken her, sweeping away her former self. That person, she realised, had almost vanished now, in retreat since that day she remembered in Cambridge when she had waited in the rain on that street corner under that tree, watching as the two of them had driven past. She bridled at the memory, at the pain. *The pain!* She could feel it still. Oh what she would give now to see *him* in such agony – the airman, perhaps as before, when she had nursed him so in the military hospital. Or better yet to see him dead – *dead* by her own hand, lying in some gutter somewhere where she knew he belonged. Then she would laugh. Oh she would laugh like hell. Laugh in his lying deceitful face!

She turned restlessly in her bed, cursing herself for breaking her vow and even *thinking* of him. Men. Were they not all the same? Her Da for one. Was he not cut from the same cloth, cruel and wicked, out for all he could get? Suddenly there came a crash from down in the yard and she knew it was him – home from Cahill's. For she could hear the scrape of his boots as he wove drunkenly across the cobblestones, then the clatter of tin as he careened into the washhouse before reaching the back door. She steeled herself as he did so, hearing his key in the lock, knowing she was stronger now, not like before. Yes, she had changed. She wagered he had not.

It was the slamming of the door she heard next. A slam which sent a shudder through the house, skewing the pictures on the walls, rattling the windows in their frames. Downstairs she could hear her Da staggering around, mumbling incoherently. Then she heard him groping towards the stairs. He was coming up.

She pulled herself into a sitting position. As she did so her head touched against one of Ma's framed tapestries: "In God we Trust". *God?* Yes, maybe once. Though as her hand went beneath her pillow, she knew her faith lay in cold steel.

Footsteps on the carpet-less treads next, then a stumble halfway up, then on the landing first a kind of growl, then a groan, then the creak of a floorboard outside her door. This was it. This was it! The next moment her door came crashing open – kicked in. He was there – there in the darkness!

'Get out,' she shouted at him. 'Get out! You've no right!'

'I've every right. I'm yer father,' he slurred. 'And I'll go where I please.'

It was then she pulled the knife from beneath her pillow, taken earlier and judiciously from a kitchen drawer. Its blade glinted in the cold moonlight from the window, and she saw it catch her Da's eye. He growled at the sight of it, in caution, perhaps mindful of the forcefulness she had shown at the meeting. For a moment later she saw him step back. Then finally turn, growling once more as he staggered through the doorway again towards the landing, slamming the door behind him.

Victory! It was a victory of sorts. And laying the knife back down, she lay back down herself, feeling a sense of triumph and empowerment. She had shown him! She had shown him at last! – shown him that "other side" to herself. And it had worked. Worked! Though before long, as she quietly began to settle, hearing her racing heartbeat begin to settle too, she began to hear something else. It was coming from her Da's room.

It was the sound of a sharp smack: the blow of an open hand. Then the dull thud of a closed fist, followed by a half muted grunt. Her heart began to race again as she realised what it was: he was beating Ma.

She listened once more. For she could not do otherwise; the walls were paper thin. And as she listened she began to pray that soon her Da would stop and tire – tire in his drunkenness as he used to, then pass out on the floor, the bed – anywhere. But he did not, and the commotion and the beating went on, then on again, then took a dreadful, sickening turn.

It sounded like a whip crack at first, sharp and keen as it cut through the air. The noise took her but a second to identify; her Da had found his leather shaving strap. Quickly she climbed from her bed. She did not even have to think. She had to act.

Bursting into the room, she found him standing with the leather strap still in his hand, Ma before him on the bed, cowering, whimpering. At once Kathleen tried to grab the strap, but somehow it was wound within his grasp. But the action of it pulled him across to her, whereupon they began to scuffle. As they did so, she called for her Ma to run: *'Run!'* she cried, which Ma did immediately, bolting for the bedroom door and the landing and the stairs beyond. Then alone with her Da, she struggled on, but even drunk he was far too powerful. If only she had thought to bring the knife. The knife! Not that she would have dared use it. Or maybe so. For somehow he had spun her around now, bringing the strap about her neck, Kathleen feeling the bite of the leather as her Da pulled it tightly across her throat.

Then she found herself pushed against the window, up against the pane, the dark glass serving like some terrible mirror upon her slow and imminent death. But she could see something else in that mirror too. It was hovering over her Da's shoulder, partly obscured by the misting of her own failing breath. Yes, there it was! She could see it now! It was like a vision, a shape, a cross. A holy cross!

Suddenly it came crashing down upon her Da's head and he fell to the floor. Behind him stood her Ma, a heavy crucifix in her hands.

After a moment, after Kathleen had recovered, regaining her breath on the side of the bed, she went across to her Da and knelt down beside him. He had not moved an inch since the blow had been struck, nor had he shown any inclination. Upon checking his pulse, she found out why. Her Ma's hand went to her face, realising too. The crucifix fell to the floor.

'But . . . but I never meant – '

Kathleen sat there stunned. She had wanted rid of him, but not like this!

Another moment passed, then before long the "other side" of her began to stir.

'Quick. Lend a hand,' she called to Ma, trying to think for both their sakes. 'Help me get him out onto the landing. Come on now. Lend a hand.'

Reluctantly, Ma did as she was bade. And taking an arm a piece, they dragged the body through the doorway, then out across the landing. After they had done so, Kathleen told her to get dressed. 'Then go to your sister's in Rathangan – stay there until you hear word.'

She saw Ma's face fill with concern.

'And you, Kathleen? What's to become of you?'

194

She told her not to worry. She would take care of things.

'Now hurry,' she told her. 'There's something I must do before I call the police.'

Ten minutes later, after Ma had hurried off with her case, Kathleen rolled and dragged her Da's body the rest of the way across the landing. Then, at the top of the stairs, she pushed him down.

He fell at once, tumbling over the bare wooden treads, his arms and legs limp, flailing like some huge marionette whose strings had been cut, finally coming to halt at the bottom in the hall. Kathleen looked down. Yes, there had been a terrible accident, a terrible drunken fall.

And *that's* what she would tell the police some time later. For who in the world could say otherwise.

*

He had died. He had died and gone to heaven, that's what had happened. For there were angels above him now, their heads bent in a circle, their inquisitive faces staring down.

No, he was in the gutter. He was lying in the gutter, he realised, lying there wet through – wet through and wounded; he could feel a bloodied gash just above his left eye. He climbed to his feet. He fell back down. He passed out once again.

The next time David Asher came round he found himself back in the Mayeville, back in Peter Letherington's office. He was lying on the floor this time and his friend Letherington was kneeling beside him. The man had a flask of something in his hand.

'Here you go old boy. Take a sip. Easy now . . . . easy.'

He felt the taste of brandy on his lips. It found the back of his throat and he coughed. 'Easy now,' said Letherington again. 'That's it. You're all right. You'll be all right. Do you think you can sit up old chap?'

He said he could. And both Letherington and his sergeant helped him to a chair.

'There you go sir,' he heard the sergeant say as the man made him comfortable. 'Now you sit there for a while. You know you gave us a proper scare out there. That was quite a tumble.'

He ran a hand through his hair. He sat up as best he could. His mind was unclear.

'A tumble? Is that what happened?'

Letherington nodded. 'Looks like it, old chap – saw it all from my window just now.' The man was busy tending to the cut on his forehead, dabbing away blood. 'You must have blacked out or something – thought you looked a little peaky when you first came in. Want me to send for a doctor? There's a first aid station just down the road. No trouble.'

'No, it's quite all right, Peter,' he protested. 'I just need a minute or two, that's all. Besides, I've rather had my fill of doctors.'

He saw Letherington study him.

'Hmm. I gathered as much – been in hospital, eh?'

Asher gave a gentle nod. Then Letherington muttered: 'Bloody war. It'll be the death of us all. Anyway, I'd take things a bit easier now if I were you – probably been overdoing it.' The man called to his sergeant. 'Sergeant. Have you got Lieutenant Asher's stick there?'

The sergeant brought it over. It was bust in two. 'Sorry sir.'

'Never mind,' said Asher. 'Better that than me. Look, do you think you can help me to my feet?'

The two men obliged and then once again Letherington said: 'Sure you're all right – sure you don't want me to send for that doctor?'

'No, don't trouble yourself, Peter. I'm fine now – perfectly fine.'

An hour later, David Asher was feeling anything but "fine" as he sat at the wheel of Rex Handley's sports car. Upon leaving the Mayeville he had returned to his boarding house whereupon he had changed his clothes and had bathed the cut above his eye. Now, parked along the rain drenched seafront road, he sat and looked in the car's rear view mirror. His face was gaunt and pale. He felt like death.

'I'd take things a bit easier now if I were you.'

Yes, Letherington was right. But how could he rest when clearly there was something going on, something that was gradually

196

revealing itself. For clearer still was the fact that Risdale had lied about the bomb onboard Handley's aircraft; Letherington's prisoner had said as much.

Glancing at his watch he looked along the promenade. He was waiting for Evelyn, parked near the dance hall where he had taken her that first evening. For earlier, after they had met by chance on the promenade, before he had gone to the Mayeville, she had told him the reason why she had come to the island. She had come because of a man, she had told him. And somehow he was not surprised.

'A man?' he'd answered, somewhat sarcastically. 'Still the same old Evelyn.'

'No, I've changed,' she told him. 'Besides, it's not as you think. I've come to visit his grave.'

Asher apologised, telling her he was sorry, and if she wanted, as one friend to another, he would take her in the car to where the man was buried. She thanked him, then he asked who he was?

'An American,' she told him. 'We met while you were in France. But I never stopped thinking of you David – not for one moment.' They had been standing at the promenade rail whilst they had been talking, his hand upon the rail for support. And although he'd said nothing in reply, she must have sensed his doubt over her last statement. For the next moment he was aware of *her* hand, which had reached across to him, a hand which she had placed upon his own. And for all his inner pride, he had wanted to pull his hand away, but strangely he could not. And he let it lie there. For stranger still, he felt in some way *that* was where it belonged.

After he had collected Evelyn in the car, and after he had driven her out to a little churchyard where the American was buried, David Asher stood at a respectful distance while he watched Evelyn lay flowers on the man's grave: a Lieutenant-Colonel no less, one Raymond O'Brien. It had stopped raining by then, he noticed, and somewhere in a treetop he heard a bird start to sing. He lit a cigarette and stood there listening, watching Evelyn as she looked down at the American's gravestone, noticing a great sadness come into her eyes.

'He meant a lot to you, this man?' he asked, wandering over.

197

'Never more than you David,' she said, turning to him. 'But don't hate me for seeing him. I was lonely. Please don't hate me.'

'Hate you, Eve' he said, almost astonished. 'I don't think I could ever hate you.'

'And what about love, David? Do you think you could ever . . .?' He saw her look away. Then after a moment she said. 'Sorry. That was awful of me. Of course you couldn't. It's been too long, hasn't it – those two years. And you've your own life now – most probably another girl?'

'What makes you say that?'

'Oh just the way you are sometimes – the way you look, as if you're thinking of someone – someone special.'

He thought of Kathleen; (whenever did he not?) Then he said wistfully: 'As a matter of fact there was a girl.'

'*Was*, David?'

He nodded. 'It didn't work out. I mean . . . well . . . I thought I knew her, but – '

'But what, David? Didn't she make you happy?'

He smiled weakly, thinking back. 'Happy? Oh yes – she made me happy – more happy than I can say.' Then his smile began to fade. 'Not that it matters now.' He looked down at the gravestone, at the flowers upon the wet earth. 'And this man – he made you happy too?'

He saw Evelyn turn and smile gently down. 'We never really had our chance,' she said. 'You see he was killed in that dreadful air crash.'

Her words took him by surprise. For somehow he knew she was talking about the crash which had brought him to the island. But he was puzzled.

'What was an American soldier doing onboard a British bomber?' he asked.

'He was en-route to County Antrim – the American's have a base there. You see Raymond was a Liaison Officer for the allied forces and he was going back to Ireland. I was set to leave Guy and join him there. We were going to start a new life – get a piece of land.

Start a farm.'

'A farm, Eve? Somehow I can't imagine it. I mean you in Ireland on a farm!'

Evelyn smiled.

'Nor could I until I met Raymond. But just to hear him talk . . . well, he made it sound so wonderful. The O'Brien's were born to the land, that's what he used to say. Farming was in his blood. And Ireland too – he grew up there.' He saw Evelyn turn and look at him. She smiled again. 'Thank you for bringing me out here David. It was kind of you.'

He told her not to mention it. Then said: 'Oh, and it goes without saying not to mention it to Guy.'

He saw her flinch – flinch not so much at Guy's name, but with pain as she pulled her coat around her shoulders to protect her from the graveyard's chill.

'He's still hurting you?' he asked.

She shook her head. 'It's nothing.' Then she turned and looked at him – looked at the gash over his eye, his tired and weary face. She took her handkerchief and dabbed away some weeping blood. 'No, darling. It's you I'm worried for – you.'

He had already explained his accident. *'An argument with a kerbstone'* he had said to her, making light of the fact that he had blacked out, fallen like some helpless child, like the pathetic shadow of a person he had become.

'Oh I'll be all right,' he said with a kind of tired cheeriness. 'Don't worry about me. You see it's you I fear for most Eve – you with Risdale. You know you really must think about leaving him – leaving him for good.'

'Yes, but only for you,' she said. And then she went to kiss him, but he wouldn't have it, and he drew back. Rebuffed, she drew back too, tucking the blooded handkerchief away as she said quite seriously: 'Anyway, if I did leave Guy, what would I do for money – how would I live?'

'Why you silly fool, safe but poor,' he smiled. 'Safe but poor!'

Her expression changed and she laughed. What a pair they made, she told him – him with his cut – her with her bruises.

'I mean just look at us, David. Aren't we two of the sorriest creatures?' And he had to agree. 'Do you really think there's any hope for us?' she asked. 'Any hope for the two of us, together, a future?'

He shook his head. He had wanted to say it was impossible, but instead he just asked her something – something which had always puzzled and saddened him – that if she professed so much undying love towards him, why had she not waited those two years for him? Why had she married Risdale instead? And why had she not written, not once, nor even come to the hospital to visit him?

She had just looked at him, tearfully, unable to answer. Or so he had thought. For the next moment she just reached out to him, and he felt her soft hand upon his cheek, hearing her say: 'David. Don't you understand? Do you really not understand?'

And in that same moment, a horrible sickening feeling came over him as he saw the awful truth.

'My God!' he exclaimed. 'Risdale told you I was dead.'

5

She had not bargained for this. She had not planned it either. But even though she had sometimes wished it, especially on those nights when she had been younger, when her Da had come home drunk, the fact of the matter remained: he was dead. He was dead and there was nothing she could do.

And then again, as she stood there looking down at his lifeless body heaped at the foot of the stairs, it occurred to her that maybe there *was* something. For with Michael and Eamonn still absent, perhaps she could turn this to her gain, to elevate her standing and in doing so benefit the Cause. Yes, she saw her chance now. This was not so much a tragedy as an opportunity, a moment to grasp the mettle and effect the changes she so desired. And she knew exactly where to begin.

It did not take her long to find the old metal trunk where her father kept his things. It was upstairs, beneath his bed, the key in his pocket which she promptly retrieved from his body. Then dragging the trunk from its hiding place she pulled it into the middle of the room. She placed the key into the lock. *Snick*. The trunk fell open.

Her Da's papers were lying inside, and she began to sift through them. Some were written in her Da's hand, others typed by the women of the Cumann na mBann. There was a ledger too, a large black book. It was filled with figures – figures and names – names of the men who had been present at the meeting just hours before, those who'd been gathered around that dusty candlelit table beneath Cahill's Bar, including the owner, Brendan Cahill. Kathleen smiled as she read on. Yes, this was exactly what she needed, this one poorly guarded secret. This was her means to rise.

*

It was all perfectly clear to him now. It was all perfectly clear why Evelyn had never once visited him in hospital. She had believed him to be dead. Small wonder she had passed out upon seeing him that time at the Metropole.

He cursed himself that he did not realise it sooner, all too willing perhaps to lay the blame with Evelyn herself, forever the party girl, such was her reputation. But his mind had been muddled by illness, too confused to see Risdale's deceit. But what he *could* see was this: it was Evelyn who had been the victim in all of this. For quite obviously she had never received that Red Cross telegram informing her that he was still alive; it had been intercepted. And a muddled mind or not, he could easily guess by whom.

In fact, as he drove along the promenade road, his head all the better for the sea air, it was not too difficult to conjure up a mental picture of Risdale burning that Red Cross telegram on the marital fire, destroying the evidence, removing all trace of him from Evelyn's life should his sudden reappearance jeopardise their marriage. But what of the man's conscience, he wondered? Wasn't it enough that Risdale had removed him from Evelyn's life once already, telling her he'd seen him die in that foreign field? But what was he saying? Conscience? Why, the man did not possess one.

He drove on a while longer, then was snapped from his thoughts by a sudden splutter from the engine. The car was misfiring. It began to slow. He steered it to the side of the road and it stopped. Out of petrol? No, the fuel gauge said otherwise. It sounded more like engine trouble. Getting out, he went to take a look.

Lifting the bonnet he found the engine to be an oily mess, so he removed his jacket and rolled up his sleeves. Then he suddenly remembered seeing some overalls in the boot and he went and lifted the lid. Yes, there they were, lying neatly folded. Good old Rex! The man was always so fastidious!

Slipping into the overalls, he began tinkering with the engine, looking at the sparking plugs as he checked each one in turn, finding the last one to be loose. Yes, that was it – piece o' cake.

With the problem solved, he slammed the bonnet shut, then looked at his hands. They were filthy. Then searching Rex's overalls for a rag he found something else: a plain sealed envelope. Across the front was a single word: "*Joan.*"

Arriving back at the boarding house he found Joan in her room. She was sitting reading a book by an open window. The sound of cheerful holidaymakers filtered in from outside.

'I see it's stopped raining at last,' she smiled, looking out. 'I thought it would never clear. You know if it stays like this I might . . . . ' Finally she seemed to catch his expression. Her smile was quick to fade. 'Why David? Whatever's the matter?'

He stood there for a while, saying nothing. Then slowly he removed the letter from his coat.

'Look,' he said, sombrely. 'I found this. It's addressed to you.'

'Why that's Rex's writing,' Joan exclaimed looking at the envelope.

'I know. It was in the boot of the car – in the pocket of Rex's overalls – must have been there all the time. I mean since that night he – '

'You mean – ?'

David Asher nodded. He took out his cigarettes and lighting one he blew out smoke.

'Look, I'm afraid I took the liberty of reading it. It's not pleasant. But don't feel obliged . . . I mean – '

'No,' she said quickly. 'I want to read it,' she held out a hand. *'Please.'*

He passed her the envelope, then watched her take out the letter, recalling the words he had read as he watched her eyes flick across the page.

My dear darling Joan,
By the time you receive this letter I shall be dead and the suffering that I have endured since Leslie's death will finally be at an end. Please believe me, Joan, when I say that I have searched my soul for a reason to go on living when my own dear brother has been taken from us, but it would be hopeless of me to pretend, to justify my own life in the knowledge that I was responsible for his death.
On the night of the 26th of March, Guy Risdale requested that I fly a special mission, to prevent one of our own aircraft from reaching its

destination. The reason my darling I cannot say, only to tell you that
in Guy's own words that it was of great importance to national
security.

As you know, my darling, I have always carried out my orders
without question, never once shirking from my duty as a pilot officer
however ghastly those tasks have been, but when I found out that the
aircraft I had shot down was Leslie's you must believe me when I say
that something inside me died, something I could not rekindle,
something that would have made me a poor husband and you, my
darling, dreadfully unhappy, something that I would hate you to be. I
have always tried my best to live my life honourably, for my family,
my country and for you my dearest darling. Please find it in your
heart to forgive me as I know you will and be happy for me that in
atoning for my actions I have at last found the peace that my soul has
been searching for.

God bless you my darling
Rex.

Joan Handley sat with her head bowed, the letter crushed in her hand. From the open window David Asher heard a tinkle of ill timed laughter from the beach. Going over, he pulled the window shut.

'I don't understand,' said Joan, looking up at him, tearful and confused. 'Why would Rex be ordered to do such a thing?'

The truth was obvious, he thought. It had been there at the back of his mind, growing uglier ever since he had first laid eyes upon the American's grave. And now it was Joan herself who forced it from him. For in the long silence that passed between them he saw her gaze up at him, then heard her say quite perceptively:

'You know something, don't you, David? You *know* why Guy sent Rex out to shoot his brother's aircraft down, don't you?'

He took a good hard pull at his cigarette, then began to tell her. It did not make for pretty listening.

*

The next morning, around midday, David Asher made a second visit to the Mayeville to see his friend Captain Letherington again, or rather the person under his charge.

'Well by all means, old chap,' Letherington had said amiably, granting permission as he sat there in his "office" in the old dining room. 'But why all the interest?'

'Oh, let's just say I've twenty five thousand reasons,' he had replied.

Letherington had looked at him perplexed. But that same perplexity told Asher much – Letherington was unaware of his prisoner's boast.

Not that he believed in the existence of that money. Surely it wasn't true? Though if it were, he saw scant reason why a hard-line Nazi like Korten should get to keep it. For in times such as these – hard times, desperate times, post war times, he knew there were far more deserving souls around. One did not have to look far.

But as he left the Mayeville after seeing the man, he was of the opinion that the German was simply bluffing. And giving no more thought to it he reached into his coat for his cigarettes, flicking up his lighter – Rex's lighter.

As he did so he began to think of Rex himself, or more pertinently the man's suicide note. Poor Joan, he thought. She had not taken that discovery well, nor his explanation as to why Risdale had sent Rex to shoot down his brother's aircraft. She had just sat there confused, confounded at his allegations, until she had said:

'Evelyn? You're saying Evelyn is the cause of all this?'

'Yes, indirectly. You see she was about to leave Risdale for another man – an American called O'Brien. That is until Risdale decided to put a stop to it.'

'What do you mean?'

'I mean he found out that O'Brien was onboard Leslie's aircraft, then sent Rex on some false pretext to shoot it down.'

Joan Handley had looked up at him. There was more than a little doubt in her eyes.

'No, I can't believe it,' she had gasped. 'Not of Guy. He wouldn't. He wouldn't be capable . . . . would he?'

David Asher knew he damned well *would*. He knew firsthand

205

from the way he'd abandoned him in that foreign field.

'Capable? Oh, I'd stake my life upon it.'

'And what about the lives of all those poor souls onboard,' she asked him. 'The crew? Don't you think he might be plagued by guilt. Don't you think his conscience might bother him?'

'You have to *have* a conscience before you feel like that, Joan. And clearly he doesn't.'

Then a moment later, after seeing that Joan was struggling to take everything in, he said: 'Look. If it's any consolation, Rex can't have been aware of the true nature of what he was asked to do. You've only got to read his letter . . . "of importance to national security." Isn't that what he said? He was under the impression his mission was to preserve some greater good.'

'And it was all a lie?'

He nodded. 'It looks that way. Thank God Rex never found out the truth – he idolised Risdale.'

A moment passed before Joan looked up at him. She asked him what he was going to do about it. He replied naturally that he was going to the police. But she reached out and took his arm. 'No, David. Please! Not the police.'

He looked at her with surprise. 'But in heaven's name why not? We can't let Risdale get away with it . . . this is cold blooded murder . . . . someone's got to speak out.'

'I know, David. It's just . . . . well, you see I received word from the R.A.F. today. They've given permission for Rex's service to go ahead – to go ahead with full military honours on the hillside. And if news broke out . . . . well, the scandal would overshadow everything. And I think Rex deserves more, don't you?'

It took David Asher but a moment to agree. 'Yes', he said. He would hold back. He would hold back until the service was over. Then it would be a different matter.

6

The return of Michael and Eamonn O'Callaghan was a muted affair, the atmosphere in Cahill's bar that night more of a wake for their dead father than a homecoming for heroes.

Though as darkness fell and the beer and spirits flowed, the difference between commemoration and celebration began to blur. And by late evening, when the music had sloughed off its melancholic dirge, when it became obvious to Kathleen that all thoughts of their Da were swiftly evaporating, she could almost see the questioning look in Michael's intelligent brown eyes: who would take his place?

Yes, there was little doubt in Michael's mind, she thought. Michael had been unfathomable to her in the past, but now, ever since her eyes had been opened, cast wide by the airman's treachery, she felt like a changed woman. There was a fire in her belly, a confidence, a strange clarity which enabled her to read Michael like a book. Yes, it was abundantly clear what was going through *his* mind: as eldest son was it not his right to assume command? And who could stop him? Yes, Brendan Cahill had been a big man in his day – the days when he had fought shoulder to shoulder with the likes of Michael Collins and his men of the Republican Brotherhood, but what was he now? A worn out barman too fond of his own ale? And then there was Eamonn – no contender at all but for the fact he was Da's second son. A deadly foot soldier, but a fool. No, the man who'd fill their Da's shoes would be he himself – that's what Michael was thinking. But he would soon need to think again!

Though for the time being Kathleen held back, content to let them down their stout, their Jameson's, to tap their feet and dance their jigs and to allow Michael the freedom to drink and drink some more, to lull himself into a kind of unguarded stupor, ignorant of the surprise that awaited him. For it was all neatly in place now. All carried through in her brothers' absence, carried unanimously in fact,

207

settled the previous day when she had shown Cahill and the others some of the pages from the ledger she had found in Da's trunk, a record of the funds which each man had embezzled. Kathleen afforded herself a smile as she thought back. Her Da was many things. But a lazy bookkeeper he was not.

And then, before long, when she was tired of the whole charade, and when she felt the time had come, she went across to where her brothers were standing at the bar. She noted that Michael barely registered her presence, hardly raising his brown eyes from the foaming collar of yet another beer. In fact she knew he would have paid more attention to a dog if it had come into the room at that exact moment, but it did not matter. For she could already see Brendan Cahill behind the bar, flushed and nervous, knowing what was about to happen. He was serving Michael at the time, sliding his empty glass beneath his frothing tap, filling it to the brim again when Kathleen said:

'That's enough with the drink, boys. There's work to be done.'

Now she had Michael's attention! Her brother swung around, the expression on his handsome face one of surprise, and then yet mirth. He cracked a smile.

'Will yer listen to that!' he laughed. *'Work,* she says. **Work!'**

'I'm just telling you, Michael,' she persisted calmly, firmly. 'We're to go across the water again soon and I want you to have your wits about you.' She shot Cahill a glance. 'No thanks to some, we're short of funds.'

She saw the smile slide from Michael's face.

'And who are you to be giving me orders? Who do yer think you are?'

Kathleen looked at Michael, then at Cahill. Then she said even calmer still.

'Ask him.'

*

It was a poor tribute, these half dozen men, this guard of honour with their polished buttons and their pressed blue/grey uniforms. They could never do justice to a man like Rex, thought David Asher as he stood there on the breezy hillside, watching as they hoisted their rifles towards the clear blue sky, the men pausing in readiness before unleashing their rattling salvo.

They were all gathered some distance away from where the aircraft had actually come down, near to the cliffs and close to the sea, the crash site itself still strangely off limits. But even at that range there was still evidence of the crash to be seen. For he could not help but see the sparse patches of undergrowth where the gorse lay black and charred, burnt and withered by the fire. It set a pretty picture, one that he could not easily put from his mind. Why, he could almost smell the reek of aviation fuel, the stench of death, imagine all too easily those terrible last moments before it happened: the lumbering bomber on its evasive path; the panic in the cockpit; the feeling of betrayal as the crew watched in horror as the seemingly friendly fighter poured a hot stream of lead into their aircraft.

Asher bridled at the thought. Yes, Risdale had pulled some tricks in his time, but this! *This!* It was all he could do to hold himself back, to stop himself from speaking out, from shouting the truth across that very hillside.

But it was the lay preacher, Clifford Handley, who was doing all the talking now, beginning the service with his eulogy, standing before them with that pious look on his face and a prayer book in his hand, working the small gathering like a snake-oil salesman.

They had all been transported to the hillside courtesy of the R.A.F, taken in a battered three ton truck that had worked its way up a loose rocky track towards the top, whereupon it had disgorged all five of them: Victor, Clifford, Evelyn, Joan and himself. Guy had come by separate means, along with some dignitaries: three "brass hats" and the stout and fearsome looking Air Vice Marshall, Sir Arthur Mawsbury-Browne. They made for a motley choir as, after Joan had stepped forward, scattering the ashes, they had all joined in as one to sing: "Nearer my God to Thee."

'Nearer my God to thee . . . . Angels to beckon me . . . . . Nearer my God to thee . . . . Near to thee.'

And then they all bowed their heads in prayer for a moment,

Clifford Handley citing from the Book of Revelations as the seagulls wheeled and mewed, cackling overhead almost in mockery of his misquoted words: *'And a war broke out and an Angel fell from heaven, and the Angel called to Satan and said, you are the deceiver of the world, repent and see the glory of God, lift up thine eyes and you shall see his bounteous gifts before you'.*

And at that very moment, as if in subconscious obedience, David Asher *had* lifted up his eyes. And in doing so *had* seen those bounteous gifts. And it had been truly wonderful. Like an epiphany. Like an epiphany twenty five thousand times over.

*

Later that day, when the service was over, David Asher was sitting by his bedroom window back at the boarding house. Upstairs, Joan was packing, preparing to leave; she had no reason to stay, or so she had told him. Besides, she had made it clear she would rather be elsewhere when he broke the news over Risdale's involvement in the crash; it was all too much for her, she had said – the shock. She needed time.

Respectful of her wishes, he had promised to wait until that next morning before he spoke of it, when she was safely onboard the boat back to the mainland. And as such the rest of the day began to drag, Asher filling his time the best he could. A visit to the bank had passed an hour, then back at the guesthouse he had played a hand of bridge. Suppertime had eventually come and gone, though by late evening he was restless again, unsettled by the lengthening shadows, the going down of the sun. It was a time which always reminded him of the hospital. A time he had once embraced, when he had actually willed the night to come and with it Kathleen. But now? Now that time meant nothing to him, nothing but pain and to enforce the feeling that he was lost without her, just a lonely man upon a lonely isle, sitting at his window, staring aimlessly at the collapsing twilight.

He lit a cigarette and tried to lift his mood; self pity was not his game. Besides, he had good reason to count himself lucky. His health for one. It was improving. For almost imperceptibly he had noticed the signs, like in his walking, as if his legs were gaining strength. And then there was Evelyn too. He had no reason to doubt her now, yet every reason to believe that she cared.

'No, not just cared,' he remembered her saying that first night on the island. *'Loved.'*

And it made him feel good that she felt that way, that she *still* felt that way, as if perhaps he wasn't as alone as he'd imagined, and that there was still something decent in the world that had not been sullied by Risdale's lies, a kind of bond between them that had endured. He hesitated to call it anything else, nor dared to think that perhaps that bond might blossom into something resembling a future. For his heart was still fragile, raw like a wound, but secretly he lived in some kind of hope that, for the sake of Evelyn at least and all she had been through, that one day, they would have their champagne.

Yes, his life was not so bad. And certainly not as bad as some. Risdale for instance. What a heap of trouble that man would find himself in come the morning, the deaths of Les Handley and his crew to answer for, not to mention the American, O'Brien. Risdale must have been insane to have brought that aircraft down, or insanely jealous at least. But there was something about that crash, or in particular the crash site itself, to which he felt drawn. And, as such, as the light rapidly faded outside, he was minded to return there.

Ten minutes later, armed with a torch in his coat pocket, he was at the wheel of the M.G. as the headlights cut a yellow slash through the drenching moonlight. It was a rock he had seen upon that hillside – that was his epiphany, his promise of "bounteous gifts". And it was a huge rock at that, one that lay about a hundred yards from where Rex's service had taken place, the boulder notable for one particular reason – the way the forces of nature had fashioned it, giving it form – a human form: a face.

The moment he had lain eyes upon it, well, it had taken him back – back to something Korten had vaguely said about that twenty five thousand pounds. The German had told him that the money was hidden somewhere near to the crash site, in a bag – in a bag near the rock face, to which he had taken to mean somewhere along the cliffs perhaps, the rock face itself. But in view of his discovery, well, he began to think again.

As such, within less than half an hour, he found himself gunning the M.G. up the hillside, following the same rocky path as before, almost in the tyre tracks of the R.A.F. three tonner which earlier had taken them to the summit. But although the little car was game, its narrow wheels spinning like fury as it fought for grip, he could not persuade it all the way. And falling short, but only marginally so, he abandoned it, setting off on foot, his torch in hand.

Reeling like some hopeless drunkard after battling through thick and near impenetrable gorse, he found himself at the top, weak and dizzy and exhausted. Looking around he tried to get his bearings. Somehow it all seemed different now, strange in the moonlight, the landscape featureless and bereft of detail, melded into one shade of dirty silver. And then a stroke of luck. The moon slid from behind a cloud and suddenly it appeared. The "rock face"! He could see it! He could see it now!

Going over he wasted no time. He began to move the smaller rocks and shale away from the base with his bare hands, hunting like a dog frantic for a bone, though all he found was nothing much at all. And the next moment he was distracted, interrupted by a noise. He turned and flashed his torch into the pewter coloured gloom. A fox? No. He'd heard that there *were* no foxes on the island. The wind perhaps? Yes, the wind stirring the undergrowth.

Swinging back his torch beam, he continued his search, tossing aside the loose rocks once again. Then, lifting a stone, his hand struck something. He shone his torch. The beam picked out the bag. It was true!

Grabbing it he brushed off the dirt. He looked inside. He gasped. The money was there. But so too was that noise again. Louder this time. And then a gunshot, louder still.

7

In a small room at the local police station, David Asher sat patiently on a chair while a doctor tended his wound.

He had been shot – shot of all things!

He let the doctor finish his work, dressing his arm where the bullet had grazed him. Then, when he was done, the doctor closed his bag and made his way over to the door where a tight-lipped police constable was standing guard. The constable opened the door. And when the doctor had gone, Asher eased his coat back on and fumbled for his cigarettes. It was 3 a.m. There was still no word of an explanation.

Then, out by the front desk, he heard footsteps. Seconds later a man came into the room. It was Guy Risdale.

'Well. Quite a night for surprises,' said Asher, sarcastically. 'Shot at by the army. Arrested by the police. And now the R.A.F.' He looked up at the man. 'Perhaps now you're here maybe you wouldn't mind telling me what's going on.'

He saw Risdale nod to the immobile Constable who suddenly sprang to life, leaving the room and the two of them alone.

'All in good time, Asher,' he said, dropping into a chair opposite. 'But before that, perhaps *you* can tell *me* something – who the hell gave you permission to be on that hillside?'

'Why you of course.'

'Yes, just for the duration of the service . . . . so?'

'Well actually I left my hat up there. I went back to fetch it.'

'Don't try and be funny, Asher'

'I wasn't. It's a rather fine hat.'

He saw Risdale give him his standard look of contempt. 'Well, if you persist in playing games,' said Risdale, 'then we'll see how amusing you think this is when Mawsbury-Browne gets here.'

'The Air Vice Marshal? He's coming here? Good – that'll save me the job.'

'What the devil are talking about?'

'Oh, nothing. Just something I found that he might like to see, something that was in Rex's car – a letter he jotted down before he killed himself – proof I suppose you'd call it.'

'Proof of what?'

'Proof that this whole damn thing's been a cover up – a cover up of your own making.'

He saw a worried expression come into Risdale's eyes. Then a sudden look of realisation.

'So,' said Risdale sitting back. 'I take it you've found Rex's suicide note? Well, aren't you the clever one.' The man lit a cigarette and eyed him scornfully. 'I did wonder what brought you all this way to the island. I must admit, I thought you'd come to lay some sort of claim to Evelyn.'

'Yes, I rather thought you did. I suppose that's why you tried to turn me against her with that filthy lie of yours – that tale about her wanting rid of me.'

He saw Risdale shrug with indifference. 'Well, one has to do something Asher. I mean when you have a wife as beautiful as Evelyn, well, sometimes you just *have* to employ any means at your disposal.'

'Like you did with O'Brien, you mean?'

'O'Brien?'

'Look, it's no use pretending, Risdale. I told you. I found Rex's letter . . . . all that nonsense about getting Rex to bring down that aircraft for the "greater good", that was just an excuse, wasn't it – a convenient way of getting rid of O'Brien so he couldn't take Evelyn away from you.'

He saw Risdale draw on his cigarette. The man looked at him through the smoke.

'Well, I don't know what to say, Asher. Yes. All right. You've found me out, haven't you. Okay. I'll not deny it. Yes, I *did* send Rex out to get rid of O'Brien. I sent him out because I wanted that man dead.'

As he spoke, Asher became aware that someone else had entered

214

the room. It was Mawsbury-Browne himself.

'That's perfectly correct,' the Air Vice Marshall said gruffly. 'As did we all.'

*

At a meeting she had convened in the cellar of Cahill's bar, Kathleen was sitting around the long candlelit table with the others. She was looking at the papers in front of her, the so called fund raising mission which her Da had planned before his death. As far as she could tell, it was not so much a mission to raise funds than to recover them, to reclaim money which had been due to them, but owing to some kind of misfortune, had been lost en route to the Republic. It had not been a trifling amount either. No, she thought. There was certainly nothing trivial about the sum of twenty five thousand pounds.

She noticed that following that misfortune, the money now supposedly lay on a hillside across the water, the result of an air crash where debris had been strewn. Moreover, that same hillside was tantalisingly close, yes, across the water indeed, though not nearly as far as the mainland. Certainly it was tempting. But to try to recover it might tempt fate yet further still. For she realised the way her Da had come to learn of the money's whereabouts seemed all too suspicious, as if the information had been leaked on purpose – the purpose being to lure them into something.

'A trap?' asked Cahill, when she'd put that possibility before them.

'It's possible,' she nodded.

'Ah away wid yer,' said Michael, who still appeared aggrieved at her sudden rise within their ranks, seeming to misread her caution, perhaps believing it to be weakness instead. 'It's there for the taking. I say we go get it.'

'And if there's soldiers?' she asked.

'Then they'll get it too,' chipped in Eamonn. 'Fight fire with fire – that's what Da used to say.'

Kathleen looked down at the papers again. She sensed a dilemma: As much as she loathed her brothers, she did not want to lead them

215

into an ambush. Then again she could not let slip such a vast amount, one that was so badly needed. If only there was another way, she thought, one less reckless than her Da's approach, less likely to see them dead.

Then she heard Cahill pitch in again.

'No, perhaps Kathleen's right,' she heard him say. His voice seemed cautious, considered, as if the man had latched on to her thoughts, perhaps wondering if there was not a better way himself. 'Maybe we shouldn't go crashing in. Maybe we should wait.'

'Wait?' stormed Michael, his tone the opposite of Cahill's. 'Wait for what – for that money to float its way across the water to us all by itself? No, I say we go get it. And we go *now!*'

She saw Cahill pull on his glasses. The man looked at her.

'Supposing we have a show of hands?'

Kathleen nodded. They took their vote.

*

He was back at the boarding house, back in his room, lying on his bed as he stared at the ceiling. How had he managed to get things so utterly wrong?

It had been his readiness to blame Risdale which had blinded him – that was his downfall. He had been too keen to discredit the man, too swift to redress the balance over what had happened in France, and for coming between himself and Evelyn, for treating her so miserably. Yes, he could see it now. For it was the next morning, and even though he'd had the benefit of sleep, it was the benefit of hindsight which was proving of greater value. O'Brien, for instance – he'd had him pegged as an innocent man in all of this. That is until Mawsbury-Browne had enlightened him . . . .

'He was a Republican sympathiser, acting as a courier for the rebels.'

'Then the money I found?'

'O'Brien's – Irish/American donations from the U.S.A., bound for the Republic.'

'And you thought you'd stop it getting there? – thought you'd just blow that aircraft out of the sky?'

216

'Oh stop being so bloody sentimental, Asher,' Risdale told him. 'It was the only way – that money was O'Brien's by law – legitimately raised. We could hardly walk up to the man and politely ask him to hand it over, could we. We had no right.'

'And what about the rights of Handley and his crew?' Asher had asked. 'Don't they count for something?' He shook his head. 'Five men dead! Five men dead and for what – a few filthy pounds?'

'Better five dead than five hundred,' said a voice.

It had come from a man who had been standing in the background, a tough looking army officer who had suddenly stepped forward. But it did not take Asher long to see the man's point, realising, most probably, that the money would end up spent on guns and explosives and ammunition, all of which would be turned against them. As such the officer and his men had been dug-in on the hillside for weeks now, waiting for them to show themselves.

'A trap you mean?' said Asher.

'That was our intention, until tonight when it was unfortunately compromised.'

Asher apologised. He said he'd had no idea. Then he asked the officer if he thought that they would still show themselves in spite of it.

'Oh they'll come,' the officer replied, adding "and the sooner the better" for he could not keep his men on that hillside forever. 'Oh they'll come all right. And when they do . . . .'

It was only after the man had spoken, that Asher realised he'd seen the man's face before, recognising his scarred and pitted cheeks, recalling the time when the soldiers had come onto the ward at the hospital. And if those things were insufficient enough to jog his memory, then the moment he heard the officer's name, it brought it swiftly back: Armstrong.

*

Kathleen did not have long to wait before her decision to delay pursuit of the money was vindicated. It had been her casting vote in favour of caution which had settled it – settled after their show of hands had failed to do so, much to Michael's annoyance. He had

217

groaned audibly, thumping the table. But the next moment their chairs were being scraped back, the candles were being snuffed out, and the men had returned to their drinks upstairs in the bar. But it was only a few days later, in that same bar, when she spotted something in the newspaper.

It was just before the bar was due to open, and the noises of that morning were echoing softly in the background: the clink of empty bottles in their crates, a tuneless whistle as tables were cleared, the swish of a broom as damp sawdust was pushed over floorboards wet with beer. She had been browsing a copy of the Irish Times in her Da's old booth when she saw it, an article about an "accident" across the water, a shooting near the crash site of an R.A.F. bomber. There was even mention of money.

She showed it to Brendan Cahill.

'So that's the end of it,' he sighed.

Kathleen shook her head.

'Not one bit. In fact it's only the beginning.'

'What'd yer mean?'

'I mean it proves the money was there in the first place.'

'I never thought of it like that. You're right. But what good is that now, with no safe way of getting it?'

She told him: 'None at all, unless we can think of something.' Then she looked away, pondering the situation until she said. 'Tell me Brendan. What do you think will happen to that money now?

Cahill shrugged.

'I've no idea. I expect the British Government will lay claim to it. Then it will end up lining some gobshite Englishman's pockets. Who knows.'

Yes, who indeed, thought Kathleen. And then it came to her: Colm Boyle.

*

Later that day, Kathleen was walking down O'Connell Street heading towards Merchant's Quay. In the shadow of the Four Courts just across the river, she came to a once fine Georgian house, now let to rooms. Pushing open the door, she went inside.

The communal hallway was dingy and cold. She went up the stairs and reaching the top floor she tapped on a half open door. A frail voice answered.

'Yes?'

Colm Boyle was standing by an open window, watering some geraniums in a window box. He was dressed in black – an old black frock coat. And at his throat he wore an old fashioned winged collar. His spectacles were pushed high up onto his wrinkled brow. She guessed he was seventy now, if not more, a fine lawyer in his day and sympathetic to the Cause. But for a long while now he had fallen on hard times.

On seeing her, Boyle came over, weaving his way through heaps of dusty law books that lay scattered upon the floor. He greeted her with a smile.

'Kathleen me darling. How are yer? Take a seat, why don't yer.'

Boyle gestured her to a chair. A cat, one of many in the room, had taken up residence upon it and he scooped the creature up before producing a handkerchief. He flapped it over the upholstery. Kathleen sat down and watched Boyle pick his way back across the room to a gas ring that he proceeded to light, filling the kettle and placing it on the ring. As he began to lay out tea cups, she heard him say: 'May I offer me condolences on the death of yer dear father. He was a wonderful man.'

Kathleen said nothing, resisting the truth – no, he was not a wonderful man. He was about as far from wonderful as Ballycastle was from Skibbereen. And too fond of the whoring, the baccy and the beer.

'Thank you, Mr. Boyle,' she replied pleasantly, quickly moving on should the kind old man begin to regale her with any stories about her father that he might have. 'I expect you're wondering why I'm here?'

Boyle turned from the cups and she saw him give her a sly smile.

'I take it that it's something to do with the O'Brien money?'

Despite his years he was still a wily old fox, she thought.

Just then there came a pop and the gas went out. Boyle stood

219

back. 'Well will yer look at that now! No sooner have I lit the blessed thing than it's gone out.' He appeared a little lost for a moment as he looked at the gas meter, his hands placed over his coat pockets. Then she saw him turn to her with a soulful gaze and say: 'Would yer be having a sixpence about yer, Kathleen?'

She dug in her pocket and produced a coin. Boyle took it from her and went and fed the meter. He lit the ring again and finished making the tea.

Bringing Kathleen her cup, he offered to put some whiskey in it, but she declined, watching instead as the old man topped off his own with a gleeful smile. He went to a chair behind his desk and when he had settled, she said to him, 'I want to ask you, Mr. Boyle, what do you think will happen to that money now?'

Boyle sipped at his tea and nodded. 'That's a good question,' he said. 'You see there's most definitely an anomaly.

'In what way?'

'In a way that makes it difficult for the British Government to keep it. You see as far as I'm aware, they've no legitimate right to the money. It was raised freely by donation, so as far as I see the British Crown have no legal claim.'

'Then what do you think will come of it?'

As Kathleen spoke, Boyle was carefully tipping some of his tea into his saucer. He put it down on the floor beside him. He softy called: 'Puss, puss, puss?'

She saw a cat shoot across the room and began to lap thirstily at it. Boyle stared down and ran a hand across the cat's arching back.

'Mr. Boyle?'

Boyle looked up.

'What, me darlin'?'

'You were saying – about the money?'

'Oh yes, the money! Well the British have no right to it – it belongs to the Republic.'

'So you mean it will be returned?'

Boyle smiled. He shook his head.

'I'm afraid not, me darlin'. Having a right is one thing – proving it is another.' She heard the old man sigh. 'I'm sorry, Kathleen, but you'd better get used to it – you'll never see that money again. It's gone – gone.'

She thought for a moment, then said: 'That's as maybe, Mister Boyle. But could *something* not be done? – to force their hand? There's always *something*.'

The man gave her a doubtful look. She saw him shrug.

'Well, I suppose I could always try.'

'Then I'd like you to do so,' she said, getting up and putting her cup on the desk, then smoothing down her skirt. 'Oh, and something else if you'd be as kind – can you find out where they've taken it? Where the money is now?'

Boyle said he would, and she thanked him and went to leave. Before she did so she asked him what she owed.

'Ah, away wid yer,' he said pushing at the air with his hand. 'I'd be a poor soul if I couldn't do something in the name of yer poor dead father, wouldn't I now?'

She thanked him again. And instead, pausing by the door, she opened her purse and took out all the sixpences she had for the gas meter, her mind suddenly returning to the last time she had done so. She had come a long way since then. She still had far to go.

8

The excitement was over now. The excitement was at an end or so it seemed. Three weeks had passed with Armstrong and his men dug in on that hillside, and all without incident. And now David Asher had heard he was calling it a day. So that was it. They had not fallen for it; they were not coming, apparently much to the dogged Major's surprise. Yes, the excitement was well and truly over now.

Not that Asher craved such things; the war had cured him of that. In fact now he did not long for anything much at all, except perhaps for an end to the longing itself: his feelings of emptiness whenever he thought of *her*. It seemed unbearable of late – more so in Joan's absence. She had long since caught the boat to the mainland, but not before he had put it to Mawsbury-Browne that, of anyone, Joan was deserving of the truth surrounding the crash. Begrudgingly the Air Vice Marshal had agreed. Then, finally in possession of it, and sworn to uphold its secret, Joan had quietly taken her leave. Asher had already told her he did not want payment for anything he may have done to bring the truth to light, such as it was, though nevertheless, that next morning he'd found a note of thanks on his doormat together with the keys to Rex's car.

"For services rendered", it had said. A generous gift, he'd thought, though one he barely deserved.

After she had gone, like Joan, he had for a time considered the prospect of returning home himself. But he came to the conclusion that there was nothing left for him there, nothing but the temptation of going to see *her* again. So he chose to stay – stay and fill his time as best he could.

On one occasion, and for want of something better to do, he had gone to the cinema, sitting up in the balcony. He had entered just as the programme had begun, a newsreel first, a potted history of the war: the Battle of Britain to the fall of Berlin – five years of misery boiled down to ten short minutes. Then afterwards, when the lights had briefly come up, when he had casually looked around as he had lit a cigarette, he had noticed Evelyn. She was sitting just across from him, apparently on her own.

He'd waited a few minutes just to prove that that was so. Then, when the lights had gone down again, he'd made his way over.

'Slumming it aren't we Evelyn?' he had whispered, slipping into the seat beside her. 'The *cinema!*'

Evelyn turned. 'David? What are you doing here?'

'Oh just the same as you most probably – at a loose end.'

She told him her reason was anything but – she was using the place as a refuge.

'A port in a storm?' he asked. 'From Guy, you mean? Then he's still – ?'

'Oh a leopard doesn't change its spots, David. In fact he's been worse of late – if that's possible.'

He did not doubt that in the least. For even though he knew his accusations concerning Risdale and the crash had been wide of the mark, he also knew Risdale's temper must be at boiling point because of it.

'Actually, that's probably my fault,' he confessed.

'Your fault? How?'

'I may have stirred up some trouble for him over something – put him in bad with the top brass.'

'Well I suppose that explains it.'

'His temper, you mean?'

'No, his demotion – at least that's what he's calling it. He's got a posting to the Air Ministry in London. A desk job – penance for something, or so he says.'

'Then you've leaving the island – going back with him?'

'Maybe. That's unless –'

He saw her look across at him in the smoky blue/black darkness. Her eyes were feline, beautiful.

'Eve, nothing would please me more, but – '

'But what, David? I told you – you've simply to say the word and I'll stay.'

'I know. And bless you for that. It's just – '

'It's just what, David? Oh why won't you tell me? Isn't this our chance to be together like we always wanted?'

Just then someone "shushed" them from the back. 'Oh shush yourself' snapped Evelyn.

'Look, this is hopeless. I can't explain here,' he said. 'We'll have to arrange to meet somewhere. I'll call you at your hotel.'

'Soon, David?'

'Yes, soon,' he replied.

*

It was only a short time later when Kathleen saw Colm Boyle again. If fact the old man's visit could not have come quickly enough, such was her anger that the O'Brien money – *their* money, was in the hands of the British now, and all hope of its return was nigh impossible.

Moreover, if their unlawful possession of it had not served enough to provoke her ire, there was still that faint suspicion in her mind that they had tried to use it as bait with which to trap them. So when she saw Boyle that day she was eager to receive him, looking up as she sat in her Da's booth in Cahill's bar, seeing Boyle in the doorway, dressed in his old black frock coat and winged collar, his hair slicked down with a lick of tap water, his rheumy eyes on the whiskey on display, his dry lips smacking with anticipation. She told Brendan Cahill to pour him a large Jameson's, then she beckoned him over, sitting him down opposite.

'So? You've news for me, Mister Boyle?'

'Ah, I have that, me darlin'. News indeed.'

'About the money? You've found out what's going to happen to it?'

'Oh, Kathleen. You're still not deluding, yerself are yer? I told yer, the likelihood of getting that money returned is slim – slim to none. Did I not say?'

'So you did, Mister Boyle . . . . then?'

'Then what, me darlin'?'

'Your news? – news you said?'

'Oh, yes – yes, news. I forgot! I know where the money's been taken. It's gone to a bank for safe keeping.'

'On the island?'

'It is that.'

'And do you know the bank in question?'

Boyle said he *did*, and Kathleen thought for a moment. 'Then I want you to do something for me Mister Boyle,' she asked. 'I want you to draw up a document – an order of right of possession over that money – something I can present to the bank to make them give it back.'

'An order of – ?' The old man seemed slow to catch on, she thought. But the next moment she saw him crack a smile. 'Ah, I think I understand yer now, Kathleen – yer want to do things *right*. And will yer be taking the order to the island yerself?'

'Yes, Mister Boyle. I will, but I'll need someone to do the presenting, of course.'

'Ah, and have yer anyone in mind?'

She looked at the wily old lawyer in his old black frock coat. 'I have that,' she smiled. 'Just the man.'

*

In her hotel suite, Evelyn Risdale was packing. She had not long risen and was still in her silk dressing gown. Clothes lay everywhere. Her expensive dresses were draped over the bed. Guy's uniform lay over a chair. Just then the telephone rang. She reached over and picking it up she brushed back her dark tousled hair.

'Yes, hello?'

'Evelyn? It's me.'

Nervously she glanced over her shoulder. Guy was in the adjoining bathroom. The door was closed; she could hear the taps running. She cupped her hand around the receiver.

'David, where are you?'

'Just along the seafront. We were going to arrange to meet, remember?'

'Yes, yes.' She glanced over her shoulder again. 'Yes, my darling .... look, I'm just packing to leave. Just give me a few minutes, will you? I'll meet you on the promenade.'

At that moment the bathroom door came open and Evelyn turned. Guy was standing behind her in his bathrobe. On seeing him, Evelyn turned back to the telephone. 'Oh and coffee for two, please. Yes, room seven. Thank you so much. Bye'. She put the receiver back on its cradle and for a moment she felt Guy's eyes upon her, then she sighed with relief as she watched him slink back into the bathroom. He closed the door.

Ten minutes later, Evelyn had dressed and had slipped out of her room. Feeling like a fugitive she crept down the stairs, escaping into the bright sunlight outside the hotel. Crossing the seafront road she went onto the promenade, but David was nowhere to be seen. And so she waited, giving thought to what she might say to him when he arrived. For this, she realised, was her last chance to win him round.

Of course she knew why his feelings towards her had cooled. It wasn't so much the time they had spent apart, but a small matter of trust. In fact she supposed "distrust" was a better word for it. And, in a way, she knew also that it was all of her own making. For the way she had openly flirted with other men in the past, teasing some, throwing herself at others, and all in front of him, had only helped to put doubt in his mind. But that had been the "old" her, the young, reckless party-girl, the one who had wanted everything – that is until she had suddenly grown up that day when Guy had told her bluntly of his death. Then she had wanted nothing – nothing but him back again.

But there was someone else in David's life now. Or rather there *had* been. For she recalled him saying so that time they had stood in the churchyard when he had driven her out to Raymond O'Brien's grave.

'As a matter of fact there was a girl,' he had said.

'*Was*, David? . . . . what, didn't she make you happy?'

Then she remembered him smiling weakly, obviously thinking back.

'Happy? Oh yes.' His voice had been wistfully. 'She made me happy – more happy than I can say. Not that it matters now.'

226

But it *did* matter! Clearly it *did*! In fact that girl mattered more to him than anyone in the world. One only had to see his face, that sad far away expression that sometimes came into his eyes, a mix of longing and hurt. Yes, hurt – *that's* what it all boiled down to; she had hurt him in some way and he could not allow himself be hurt yet again. But *she* would never hurt him, never, not now – that was the "old" her. But how could she prove it?

She looked along the promenade once more, then looked at her wristwatch. She wondered if he might not come at all, but just as the thought crossed her mind she heard the sudden toot of a motor car and saw his red sports car. It was parked just along the seafront road, at the kerb, the car's hood folded down. And from it she could see him waving cheerily.

And so they drove off, venturing out along the coast. She lit him cigarettes along the way and they sat together and watched the countryside slip by in a companionable silence. Then, before long, they turned off the road towards the sea, going down a long narrow lane, before the lane itself petered out, revealing a quiet beach beyond.

Getting out they walked across the sand. She noticed that thoughtfully he had brought a rug which he produced from a wicker basket. But after he had laid it out for her, just as she was making herself comfortable upon it, she saw him go back to the car where he proceeded to take something from the boot. She could not see what it was, but she saw him take it to a rock pool nearby and place the object in the water. Then he stood up, looking out across the sea. He seemed to be staring at something far away, she thought, but all she could see was the froth and bubble of low clouds upon the horizon – the horizon towards the coast of Ireland, the faint outline of which she thought she could see, miles off in the distance, rising like a ghost through the mist.

Eventually he turned and she watched him walk back. He came and sat down beside her on the rug. The breeze ruffled his hair and he looked quite boyish, she thought, much healthier, far different to when he had first come to the island. The very sight of him then had

227

almost made her weep. The very prospect of never seeing him again made her feel like weeping more.

'So, you're leaving,' he said to her, sounding quite "matter of fact".

'Yes, this afternoon,' she replied, trying hard to sound equally so. She looked across at him. 'I don't suppose you'll miss me.'

'Please, Eve. *Don't*,' he told her, appearing to sense where her conversation was leading. 'Can't we just . . . I mean . . . . isn't this hard enough?'

'Then why make it harder still,' she said. 'You know how I feel about you. I've told you – you only have to ask and I'll stay. Isn't that what you want – what we *both* want – for us to be together again like we planned.'

'And for how long, Eve. How long would it last?'

'Before what, David?'

'Before you'd tire of me – go looking for someone else?'

There it was again! He had skewered her on her past, on her "old" self.

'Is that what you think David?' she asked, feeling helpless in her anger. 'Is that what you think after all I've said? After all I've told you? I've changed. I've changed since that day Guy lied about what happened to you. I became a different person.'

'Then what about O'Brien?'

'Raymond yes, I'll admit to that. But what did I say to you about him? – I said that while he and I were together I never stopped thinking of *you* – not for one moment.'

'Then what about Risdale? Who were you thinking of when you decided to marry him?'

'Oh that's unfair, David. He'd told me you were dead, for God's sake. What was I supposed to do? I was lonely. Haven't you ever been lonely? Weren't you ever lonely in that hospital – lying there, wondering why I wasn't at your side? Or were you too busy thinking about *her*.

'Her?'

'Don't pretend, David – that girl you told me about – that girl

228

you're always thinking of.'

'Yes. Yes but that was different.'

'Was it, David? How? So what are you trying to say? – that it was fine for you to fall in love with someone, but not for me?'

He was quiet for a long moment, she noticed. Then slowly a look of contrition came into his eyes.

'Yes. Yes, you're right, Eve,' he said quietly. 'I'm being hurtful to you. I'm being hurtful for no good reason. Forgive me?'

'Oh David, what's to forgive,' she sighed. 'You were only being hurtful because you've been hurt yourself. And you're still afraid it will happen again – that I'll betray your trust like that other girl. But I won't. *I won't.*'

She saw him look up. As if the word "betray" had hit some raw nerve, a tender wound. She put her hand to his face. She smiled weakly. 'Listen my darling. I'm going back with Guy, but only as far as the mainland. Then I'm going away. I'm going far away somewhere to wait for you – to wait until that day when your love for me comes back again – for as long as it takes – *forever* if that's what you need.'

She saw him smile at her, heard him say. 'Bless you Eve. Bless you Eve my darling.' Then she saw him get up and go to the rock pool, returning with something at his side. She could not make it out at first, but then she realised – it was a bottle of champagne – "their" champagne.

He opened it and poured some into glasses which he had taken from the basket. He handed her one and told her he was sure that that day would come very soon. And then, raising their glasses in hopeful prospect, she felt tears come into her eyes. She drank her champagne. Bittersweet.

*

With Kathleen's "Right of Possession" order drawn up to her satisfaction, presided over by Colm Boyle himself, the old man's frock coat and winged collar looked warm for that hot summers day as, after taking the boat to the island, the bank loomed large and almost intimidating before those tired but intelligent spectacled eyes.

Stopping at a public drinking fountain outside, he paused, cupping a little water into his dry mouth, patting a little more onto his hair, slicking it down and parting it either side neatly with his comb. As he did so he recalled Kathleen's instructions:

He was to present the document to the manager no less, not his chief clerk, nor his first cashier, nor any other employee come to that. Yes, it was to be delivered to the head man himself, and done so in the proper fashion, punctually at 2.30 p.m. in the manager's office, with all the forcefulness he could muster. For the bank had to know that she would not accept the outrageous retention of that money – *her* money. Why, it was tantamount to collaboration!

He found himself suddenly in the banking hall, sweating beneath the old fashioned winged collar, the vast building like some great temple before him, a shrine to commerce with its fine wood panelling, its opulent marble floor, its magnificent chandeliers which sparkled from its high vaulted ceilings.

He went to one of the cashiers at the long impressive counter. He asked for the manager.

'Yes, me darlin'. I've a document. It's terribly important – to be delivered by hand, in person.'

He saw the cashier go, then a moment later come back again. Then he was ushered over to the far side of the banking hall, towards a door and the manager's office beyond. By the banking hall clock he noted it was 2.27 p.m.

*

Ten minutes before and, at exactly 2.17 p.m. David Asher was saying goodbye to Evelyn after driving her back to her hotel, parked along the seafront a safe distance away should they both be seen. After they embraced, he spotted Risdale's Bentley just along the road, packed and ready to leave. Risdale himself was pacing up and down. After a moment he turned to Evelyn and said quietly that she ought to go. And Evelyn turned and smiled, kissing him one last time. As she did so an army truck came thundering by. He saw it was Armstrong's truck, guessing that the major and his men were leaving the island, on their way to the boat which had not long docked at the quayside.

As the lorry passed, a wolf whistle came out of the canvas cavern at the back. It threatened to cheapen their last moments together, but was rescued by Evelyn's three whispered words. They brought a lump to his throat and he watched Evelyn get out, turning with a wave, before slowly walking away.

He did not wait for her to get to Risdale's car. It was more than he could bear to see *that*. So feeling wretched, he started the car and drove away. For want of a distraction he headed for the bank.

It took him no more than five minutes to drive there, and parking in a side street he walked around to the entrance, just in time to see a slim blond woman walking up the bank steps. He only caught a glimpse of her, but she looked exactly like Joan, he thought. And he wondered if, for some reason, she had returned to the island. But as her back had been turned when she had entered, he thought little of it, and going up the steps, he went through the large double doors himself.

The banking hall was busy inside, filled mostly with tradesmen, eager to pay in their takings before the place closed, mid afternoon – the "shopkeeper's stampede", one of the cashiers had told him it was called, a friendly young woman by the name of Miss Teare whose window he usually went to. And that day being no exception, he began to join her line as he waited to be served, listening to the rhythm of the building: the ring of coin, the rustle of notes, the thump of a rubber stamp on a counterfoil.

As he did so he looked about him at the people. There was a pretty naval "wren", a butcher in a straw boater, a rather rotund army officer, amongst others. But where was the blond girl? Ah! He could see her now. She was over the other side of the banking hall, near the counter, filling in a form as far as he could see. Was it Joan? He still couldn't tell. All he knew was that from the way she stood, she looked strangely familiar.

*

In the manager's office, he was most cordially received. He was invited to sit down, asked if he would like to take off his frock coat, (which he declined). Then he was given a cup of tea by a secretary.

'Oh, thank yer me darlin'.'

When the secretary had gone, he presented the manager with the Right of Possession document. And, with his chief clerk standing at his side, the man began to read.

Though it was not long, perhaps less than a minute even, before the manager's eyes began to narrow with a kind of confusion. His forehead began to crease, seemingly with puzzlement. Eventually, with a shake of his head, he looked up.

'But this . . . . this is preposterous!' he said. 'You say we owe you twenty five thousand pounds? By whose authority?'

Michael rose and kicked back his chair.

'By the authority of the Irish Republican Army!' Drawing aside the frock coat he pulled out his revolver. 'Now get over there.'

The next moment, equally as quick and similarly armed, Kathleen was through the door in seconds. She closed it behind her.

'He's read it?' she asked.

'Yeah, he's read it,' said Michael.

'Good.' She looked at the terrified manager, the cowering chief clerk. She levelled her revolver. 'Then you'll know exactly why we're here.'

*

The clock in the banking hall had just struck the half hour, and when David Asher glanced down at his watch to confirm that it was so, when he looked up again he found that the slim blond girl had vanished. Strange, he thought, but he paid it no mind as the queue before him began to lessen, the customers beginning to dwindle as they were swiftly served by the quietly efficient Miss Teare. In fact he noted there was something akin to a smooth and diligent routine about the place that afternoon, like that of a well oiled machine. For already he saw an employee checking with his own watch against that of the banking hall clock, before moving across the marble floor towards the double doors at the entrance. There he proceeded to shut one of the doors, shooting the bolts top and bottom, all in readiness of closing time, all still several minutes away.

*

Their footsteps echoed in the labyrinth depths below the bank. Keys jangled in the locks of the huge strong room door. The thick steel issued a clank, a groan. They pushed it open.

'Well! Will yer take a look at that!' exclaimed Michael, pulling off Colm Boyle's spectacles which he still wore about his face, almost beaming as he saw the money before him, stacked in neatly banded bundles upon the dusty dimly lit shelves. Kathleen saw his expression. She told him not to get any "ideas".

'We're just here to take what we're owed,' she said, 'nothing more.'

'Sure,' he replied with a derisive snort.

'I mean it, Michael. You hear me?'

'Yeah. Yeah. I hear yer.' He gave the manager a swift jab in the ribs with the barrel of his revolver. He waved it at the chief clerk. 'You two – inside.'

They went into the musty strong room, finding a bag whereupon Kathleen gave it to Michael who crouched with it on the floor. Then she began clearing one of the shelves, throwing him the banded bundles, Michael tucking them away quickly with one hand, the other on his revolver which was trained on the two men who were over in the corner next to a telephone on the wall. The next moment Kathleen saw one of the men glance at the telephone, but Michael must have seen it too. For she saw him flick his gun barrel at the man and say: 'Get away from that thing! Or you'll be doing yer talking to this!' And the man backed away immediately, Michael then telling them to sit on the floor and to keep their hands where he could see them. Then with the bag filled, he and Kathleen went to the door, Michael only pausing to rip the telephone wires from the wall.

'You'll never get away with this,' Kathleen heard the manager say as they were about to heave the heavy door shut.

'Get away with what?' she said angrily, giving them one last look. 'You mean taking what's rightfully ours? Why, it's *you* who're the criminals – **you!**'

*

He was by now, nearing Miss Teare's window. And he looked about

233

him again. Most of the other people had been served, he noted. The pretty naval "wren" had gone. So too the butcher in the straw boater. The rotund army officer was still there, but so too was another person, a latecomer he presumed, a broad shouldered ox of a man who merely loitered, showing little inclination of wanting service, as if he was just waiting for someone. But then he heard Miss Teare call 'Next please!', and he was being served himself, passing the time of day with the young cashier as she dealt with his cheque.

It was only after it was cashed, as he turned, tucking his money away into his wallet, about to leave, that he heard the sudden click of heels upon the marble floor. And looking up he saw the slim blond girl once again. This time she wasn't alone. By her side was a figure in an old fashioned frock coat, and, joining them as they walked to the exit, was the ox of a man whom he'd seen earlier. He still could not see her face, but he knew it wasn't Joan; she was a little taller, he thought. And he paid her no mind as, with her companions, she walked across the banking hall, noting only that her pace was quite brisk, almost hurried, as she went with them towards the door.

But then he noticed something else: a scarf. It had fallen from the girl's coat pocket, or so he thought. And going over he bent down and picked it up. He called after her.

'Miss!'

But the girl kept on walking. So he called a second time, more insistently, but still she did not stop, nor even check her stride. So he began to stride after her, or at least as best he could, though within a few paces he had caught her, placing his hand gently on her arm. Then the girl stopped.

For a moment she stood quite still, he noted, neither turning but appearing to look straight ahead, staring perhaps at the oblong of daylight that was framed by the single open door; the view of the street, towards which her two companions continued to stride.

It was only then, that she finally turned.

An explosion! An explosion like a bomb going off in his head! It hit him squarely like nothing before, his sudden recognition like some huge shock wave which rocked him on his heels. He did not understand. He *could* not understand. And least of all the revolver which she had suddenly produced and was now holding inches away from him, ramrod straight.

He could not find the words, lest speak them. Though suddenly he was vaguely aware of a voice from somewhere else – 'Shoot,' it said, his senses telling him it came from the frock coated man who had turned from the door to bawl at her. '*Shoot!* What are you waiting for – **SHOOT HIM!'**

And for a moment, he saw the intention in her eyes – cold blooded intention as the revolver began to shake, her finger on the trigger as it took up the pistol's mechanism. Tighter. Tighter. Tighter.

Then . . . .

The noise was deafening as the gun went off, the echo of the shot, together with the screams of the few who still remained in the vast banking hall ringing around the building. David Asher staggered back, his hands to his face, covered with blood. He looked across at Kathleen and for a second they held each other's gaze. Then she crumpled to the floor.

Looking over he saw that the shot had come from the army officer. For he was standing with his service revolver drawn, the weapon emitting smoke. And then another shot – this time from the frock coated man as he fired over the heads of the prostrate crowd, striking the army officer in the chest, his khaki tunic staining crimson upon the bullet's impact, his revolver slipping from his hand as he sank to the floor.

'C'mon,' Asher heard the ox like man bellow, being nearest to the open door to the street. 'C'mon, Mikey. Let's get outta here.'

But the frock coated man just stood there, appearing to look back at Kathleen lying on the floor, Asher hearing him shout: 'No. I'm not leaving without – '

He did not catch the word, if one was uttered. For if indeed it was, it was lost in the man's footfalls as Asher saw him pound back across the banking hall floor, seemingly to help him tend to Kathleen wounds.

235

But when he got there, Asher just felt the *thud* of the man's boot upon his chest as he kicked him away, then saw the man attempt to retrieve something that was caught beneath the weight of Kathleen's body. It looked like some sort of bag, he thought, a sack like bag, but with a drawstring around its top which was entangled about Kathleen's wrist. The man pulled it this way and that. Then from the door his ox like accomplice bellowed across again. 'Mikey. Quick. Somethin's going on outside – soldiers!'

And indeed there was. For Asher could plainly hear the sound of a heavy vehicle pulling up, then the crash of an opening tailgate, then the scuffle and scrape of boots upon the road.

The frock coated man ran back to the door, peering out into the street. As he did so a bullet zinged in, splintering the wooden lintel above his head. They both ducked back, pushing the door quickly shut behind them, securing the bolts. Then, standing with their backs against it, their chests heaving, he saw them look at each other. He knew exactly what they were thinking – they were trapped!

9

They were Armstrong's men out there, outside the bank. Of that David Asher was sure; they'd been on their way to the quayside when they must have heard the shots. But that didn't matter now. Kathleen was injured, unconscious, bleeding. She needed help.

They had been ordered to stand against the wall, customers and staff alike, ordered by the man he knew as "Mikey". And upon his command they'd obediently filed across the room, all but Asher himself. He had stayed with Kathleen, kneeling at her side.

'You!' Mikey had barked at him. 'Are yer deaf? – the wall, I said!'

Asher had looked up. 'She's dying, damn you. Can't you see? She needs help.'

But the man did not seem interested. He simply flicked his gun with insistence. Then, with a look of disgust in his eyes, and struggling to pick her up, Asher carried her to where the others were standing, laying her down, looking to see what he could do.

There was a fleshy wound to her shoulder which was pumping blood. It oozed through her blouse which he tore open, the buttons scattering across the cold marble floor. He took out a handkerchief and fashioned it into a pad, compressing it to the wound.

The two men meanwhile were busy at the front windows, one having first gone to the dead army officer to relieve him of his gun. Now Asher could see them peering out, their eyes darting to the activity in the street.

He could not see out himself, though no doubt Armstrong would be deploying his men by now he thought, erecting a makeshift barricade, setting up a machine gun behind sand bags perhaps, training it on them from across the road. And indeed to some degree he was right. For he heard the ox like man say:

'Look! They've the whole stinking army out there. What are we gonna do?'

The other did not speak, but coming away from the window, Asher saw him point his revolver at one of the staff and say:

'You old man. Is there another way out of here?'

'Only a back door.'

'Is it locked?'

'Always.'

'Then where's the key?'

'In the manager's office.'

He waved his revolver again.

'Show me.'

He marched the man away at gun point, though when he had gone, Asher heard a voice at his side. It was the cashier, Miss Teare. 'No, there *is* another way out,' she whispered. Then nodded. 'Through that door and down to the basement air raid shelter. Then along the passageway and through a door and up into the street.'

'And is that street door locked too?'

'Yes, but there's a key. It's just above the lintel.'

He nodded his thanks, then whispered he would give it a try – they both should. But the cashier shook her head; she was too frightened to move. So with one man gone and the other still occupied at the window, Asher struggled Kathleen up into his arms and began to slowly edge away, going toward the basement door. Before he could get there, the ox like man turned.

The noise from the man's revolver resounded like thunder as he unleashed a shot towards him. But it was a poor shot at that; it fell short, ricocheting off the floor with a small cloud of dust and marble splinters. But before he could fire again, and with the door ajar, Asher was through it in seconds, disappearing from view.

He found himself at the bottom of some stairs. He had stumbled more than once coming down them, but had never let Kathleen slip from his arms. But now, in the subterranean warren below, he was tired, confused, faced with a choice in front of him: the passage to his left or to the right?

He chose left and found himself entering a tunnel. He went down it and came across the air raid shelter where he lay Kathleen down on

238

one of the benches, snatching up a blanket and drawing it over her. Looking up he saw a flight of steps and a door at the end. Going over he felt along the door's lintel and found the key. Turning it in the lock the door opened. He went back for Kathleen. He took her up into the street.

The sunlight was blinding as he staggered out, but blinking it away he was struck by a kind of familiarity. It was the same street in which he had parked the car. Yes, and he could see it there at the kerb, as he had left it, the hood folded down which allowed him to lower Kathleen gently into the passenger seat.

The car started at the first time of asking. The tyres spun. The car roared away.

*

It was dark when Kathleen woke. For a moment she neither had clear recollection of events, nor where she had been taken. All she knew was the sharp pain in her chest. All she remembered was *him.*

As the fog of unconsciousness began to dissolve, she lifted her head and looked around her. She was lying in what appeared to be an abandoned cottage. Weeds sprouted from the floor. Ferns grew from the walls. Through where the roof had been, smoke was being charmed into an inky black sky. Suddenly she was aware of someone's presence. She looked across.

He was tending a fire, kneeling in front of it, placing kindling under a cooking pot. She watched him stir it, bringing some steaming liquid to his mouth. Then the next moment, noticing she was awake, he came over.

'Here. See if you can drink some of this.'

She felt his hand beneath her head. He eased her up. She winced in pain as he brought her forwards. She sipped, swallowed, coughed. She felt him ease her down. The next thing she heard was the sudden snapping of twigs.

'Don't worry. It's only the fire,' he said. 'You'll be safe here.'

'Here?'

'Just a place I came across – up in the hills, off the road. I was going to take you to a hospital, but – '

239

She knew what he meant.

'No. I'm glad,' she said.

'Glad for what?' His voice sounded angry. 'Glad that you'll probably die of a gunshot wound instead of on the gallows? You do know you've been shot, don't you? I mean I've done all I can but I'm no doctor.' Then she saw him look down at her, almost hatefully, hearing him say: 'But then again, you're no nurse, are you – never have been.'

She saw him walk back over to the fire again and stare deeply into it. She sensed his realisation had not come suddenly. 'How long have you known?' she asked.

'About your dirty little secret? Long enough,' he said.

Suddenly it became clear.

'You knew, didn't you? – that morning in Cambridge when I asked you to go away with me. When I waited for you, but you didn't come.'

'And what did you expect? – that I would? – that I'd go away with you and pretend nothing had happened – live a lie?'

It became clearer still.

'Then when I saw you in that car, with that woman – ?'

'You think I had a choice? Why, it was all I could do to stop myself from telephoning the police.'

'You mean – ?' She recalled Armstrong's pursuit, how he'd chased her through the town. 'But I thought – '

'Well you thought wrong. I couldn't do it. I couldn't damn well do it!' She saw him kick at the fire. 'God! To think I even defended you that time at the hospital when the soldiers came – kept telling everyone what an *angel* you were. Christ, how you must have laughed.'

She told him it wasn't like that. It wasn't like that at all.

*

When she woke again it was to a wave of pain. It was still dark. She could see him leaning over her, his handsome face lit by the glow of the fire. But there was a look of concern in his eyes.

'What's wrong?' she asked

240

'Shh! Lie still.'

'No. Tell me.'

'It's your shoulder. I can't stop the bleeding.'

She could feel him pressing something to her aching wound. She heard him say something about needing bandages, about going for help. She saw him glance at his car parked in the darkness.

'No, not the hospital,' she begged. 'They'll come for me there. You know they will.'

'All right,' he said. 'But where?'

She closed her eyes. 'Here,' she sighed. 'Just let me die right here . . . . here in peace.'

'*Peace?*' She heard him say with a kind of confused anger. 'Why the hell should I? You wouldn't let me die, back in Cambridge, back on that ward. Oh, no, you wouldn't let me die, but by God, since . . . . sometimes I've prayed for it. *Peace?* You think I've had a moment of it without you? – thinking about you – thinking what might have become of you – what might have been?' She saw him get up and look down at her. 'No, you silly fool. You think I'm just going to let you die after that?'

She saw him walk away to the car. She called after him. 'David!' He turned and she saw him look back. 'I just want you to know . . . . back there at the bank – the gun . . . . I couldn't . . . I'd never . . . . I mean I just couldn't.'

She saw him smile, knowingly. She watched him drive away.

*

At the wheel of the car, he drove as quickly as he could down the rutted track that led off the hillside, the headlights cutting through the darkness as he turned out onto the road. He was a mile into his journey before he realised he had absolutely no idea where he was going. Then it appeared he wasn't going anywhere. For the car gave a splutter then suddenly died – he was out of petrol. *Hell and damnation!*

He sat there for a moment, then got out and began to walk, remembering a telephone box that he'd passed about a half a mile back. Reaching it he went inside and picked up the receiver. He

241

heard the operator: 'Number please?'

And for a moment he was lost again, thinking only of getting her to a hospital, knowing it might save her life, yet take it also. Then, just as he was about to speak, he suddenly changed his mind. Perhaps there was another way.

*

When the telephone rang in Evelyn Risdale's suite, she was fast asleep. She pulled herself up between the sheets and switched on the bedside light. Glancing at her watch she let out a sigh. Who could be calling her at two o'clock in the morning?

She reached for the telephone and briefly heard the voice of the switchboard operator before one that was more familiar.

'Evelyn? Is that you?'

'David?'

'Oh thank God you're there. I thought perhaps you'd left. You said you were leaving?'

'No darling. Guy was too busy up at the bank. There was hold up. Did you hear? He drove up there to see what all the fuss was about.'

'Is he with you now?'

'No, of course not. I'd hardly be talking like this. No, he's in the military hospital along the coast. He managed to get himself wounded. It was a frightful scene – two men and a girl. The girl and one of the men got away apparently, but the other – '

'Yes, I know Eve. Look. I've got myself into a bit of a fix. I need your help.'

'Anything, darling.'

'Then bless you Eve. Now here's what I want you to do . . . .'

A moment later, Evelyn had jotted everything down. Within minutes she had dressed, thrown her coat around her shoulders and had hurried down the stairs to the hotel foyer. It was an endorsement of her urgency that for the first time in years, she had left a bedroom without so much as a lick of makeup.

Going outside, she stood on the deserted seafront. Guy's green Bentley stood before her. Jumping in she slid behind the wheel. It had been an age since she had last driven, and never once his precious brute of a car, though bracing herself, she turned the ignition. She pressed the starter.

Immediately there came a whine and a mighty roar from under the bonnet. The pistons began to pound. With a grinding of gears, she put the car in first, the car lurching forwards, snorting as if with rage. She heaved round the steering wheel and moved the car out from the kerb, flapping at every conceivable switch to bring on the lights. Miraculously, a moment later, the car spat out two bright arcs across the darkened promenade. And after pulling out into the road, clipping the car parked in front as she did so, she stamped on the accelerator.

She headed off into the night, out on the coast road towards the military hospital.

*

Outside the same hospital, Major Armstrong was returning to his truck. Following the siege and subsequent taking of the bank, he had bad news – they were one man less. Nevertheless, the soldier's death had not been in vain. For although two had evaded capture, one man now lay in his charge. And not just any man at that. Interrogation revealed him to be part of the three strong Republican unit he'd trailed for years, ever since that night in London.

At the news he'd raged at the man.

'Did you kill him? Did you kill the *boy*?'

The big man had just grinned – grinned like a fool, admitting to killing the old man, then adding that his brother Mikey had done for the boy.

Armstrong sat in the truck and thought about this "Mikey". He thought about the girl too. He wagered that both were still somewhere on the island, the latter badly wounded, most probably needing help. In fact, according to witnesses at the bank, the girl had already acquired some, notably from the person who'd spirited her from the scene in a bright red sports car, a man of whom he'd already had the pleasure, if indeed shooting the poor fellow, then arresting him up at the site of the crashed aircraft could be described as such.

Whilst dwelling on the subject, his attention was drawn to a figure who was just leaving the hospital, emerging into the murky porch lighted entrance. Now what was *she* doing there? Yes, her fool of a husband was a patient, wounded in the raid. But even so, it was three o'clock in the morning. And what was that she was carrying? Field dressings? Bandages?

'Sergeant Morris!' he called, nudging awake the man next to him. The sergeant blinked the sleep from his eyes.

'Sir?'

'That girl getting into the Bentley – Mrs. Risdale. Do you remember where we saw her last?'

The sergeant peered through the windscreen.

'Yesterday, wasn't it sir? Down on the seafront with someone in a red sports car?'

Armstrong nodded. Yes. And he knew that "someone" very well indeed.

*

His return had taken an age – an age to find petrol for the car, to get it started again, to get him back along the road once more and up the rutted track to the ruined cottage where Kathleen lay. In his absence he saw that the fire had burned down. And he went and banked it up, raking the dying embers as he called over, telling her that everything would be all right now, help was on its away – help from someone he knew and could trust.

'Did you hear that, Kathy? I said – '

Looking over he saw that something was wrong. And moving quickly to her side he found her cold – cold and barely alive. Her wound had almost bled her out. He almost wept.

Pulling the blankets around her to preserve what warmth and life he could, she suddenly stirred.

'*David?*' he heard her whisper, seeing her eyes open, searching blindly for him.

'Yes, my darling. I'm here.'

He squeezed her hand and he felt her weak reply, helpless, dying right in front of him.

'Is it still dark, David?'

'Yes,' he said. 'It's quite dark.'

'And can you see the stars?'

'Clearly,' he whispered. 'They're very bright.'

'And can you see our stars, David?'

'Yes, my darling, they're both there.'

'And are they close?'

'Yes, he choked. 'Side by side.'

He saw her smile, closing her eyes as he noticed that the heavens seemed to be lit with a strange light, the air filled with a sound like thunder, like the coming of a storm. And then he suddenly realised it was nothing of the sort. It was the coming of a motorcar.

It was Evelyn – Evelyn in Risdale's Bentley. She was coming up the hillside track towards him, the car's headlights raking the sky. It slew to a halt. He saw Evelyn step out.

'Thank God,' he cried. 'You've brought what I asked?'

'Yes,' she replied, breathlessly. 'Am I in time?'

He did not answer; for he was already tearing open the dressing and bandages she had given him, quickly attending to Kathleen's wounds.

When he had done so he stood up.

'What now, David?' Evelyn asked, looking down.

He shook his head. 'I'm not sure.'

'You mean – ?'

'I don't know . . . . yes I do – I should never have listened to her. I should have taken her straight to the hospital.'

'No, I should have come here sooner. If only I'd – '

'No, don't blame yourself Eve. You've done enough. I couldn't have asked for more.'

Suddenly a voice came out of the darkness.

'Nor I, Mrs Risdale. Thank you for showing us the way.'

He looked and saw Armstrong. He looked at Evelyn and saw betrayal.

10

It was his friend Peter Letherington who came to his aid, standing him bail some three days later after Armstrong had seen fit to have him placed in jail. But the major had warned him – he hadn't heard the last of it; he would be facing charges. David Asher told him he could not have cared less. It was Kathleen who mattered – the very girl who Armstrong had unwittingly saved, arriving just in time to get her help.

Armstrong said he could not make him out.

'What do you mean?' he asked.

'A man like you – someone with an exemplary war record – France – everything – risking your life against the enemy, just to help one of them now.' He saw the major look at him with a cynical glare. 'I just don't understand.'

Asher had complimented him on his "homework". But then he said: 'I wouldn't expect you to, major. You've probably been fighting the war too long to understand a thing like love.'

Armstrong had snorted.

'Love? You're telling me you're in love with that girl?'

Asher felt confused. 'Once . . . . now? I don't know. Maybe.' He tried to shrug off his confusion by turning on Armstrong instead. 'Anyway, what the hell would you know? I'll lay you ten to one you've never loved anyone in your life.'

Armstrong shook his head

'No, perhaps not "love" in the way you speak of it. Not in the shallow, superficial sense. But I had a son once – William. A fine boy. That is until that girl and those other two cowards shot him in the back.'

Asher suddenly fell silent. He'd had no idea – no idea at all.

'Yes, there's plenty you don't know about that girl,' said Armstrong. 'Plenty.'

Asher reluctantly agreed. But conversely, he said there was plenty that the major did not know about the girl either, namely that he owed her for his life.

'Then I expect you'll be interested to know what's to become of her,' Armstrong said, sounding uncommonly sympathetic, he thought, explaining that upon recovery from her wounds she would be taken from the hospital to a holding billet, before being transferred to the mainland to stand trial.

'And then what?' he asked.

'And then she'll be hanged, of course.'

*

After speaking with Armstrong he took his car and drove to see Kathleen. She was being cared for in a room at the local cottage hospital, and although still weak, she seemed to be recovering well – well enough in fact, he had noticed, for two of the major's men to be standing guard outside her door.

He recognised one from his arrest – a burly sergeant who had led him quite forcefully away from that abandoned cottage and into their truck.

'No hard feelings, sir,' the sergeant had said to him, sounding genuine enough when the man had spotted him leaving Kathleen's room. 'For the strong arm tactics, I mean? No offence meant, sir.'

Asher had smiled.

'None taken, sergeant,' he'd replied, accepting both his apology and the cigarette which the man had kindly offered him.

Asher snapped up his lighter. And as he did so, the sergeant stepped closer and said. 'You know for what it's worth, sir, Mrs. Risdale didn't actually tell us that you and the girl were hiding up at that old place.'

He looked up with surprise. 'Is that correct?'

'Yes, sir. We just followed her from the military hospital – a hunch – you know how it is.' The sergeant shrugged. 'Just thought it worth a mention.'

He thanked the man gratefully, then went out to his car. There he sat quietly, thinking of Evelyn. And as he did so he felt ashamed – ashamed over his cruel misjudgement. For he realised finally that she *had* changed. And *he* had changed too, his feelings for her growing stronger as they had done before. And he promised himself that he would not doubt her again.

And what of Kathleen, he thought? What could he promise her now, in view of Armstrong's prediction:

'And then she'll be hanged, of course.'

And then it came to him. For what was sweeter than love if not life itself – to help her cheat that hangman's rope. And he knew where he would find the means.

*

Within half an hour of driving away, he was back, of all places, at the abandoned cottage where he had taken Kathleen after the robbery. It looked different now, he thought, in the daylight, the unease and apprehension of that uncertain night removed, lessened by the fact that Kathleen was, at least for the moment, safely in hospital receiving the care she needed. But that was not to say that the tumbledown wreck of a place was benign. For like all such ruins, it had its secrets. Why, the biggest secret of all had been placed there by his own hand!

By God it was warm, he thought as he walked about the place, going amongst the weeds, roaming through what had been a garden, coming to an old vegetable patch in which, in his desperation, he had unearthed some old potatoes in order to make Kathleen soup, pausing at an old well, from which he had collected water for her to drink.

He rested at the well for a while and loosened his tie. Yes, by God it was hot. And slipping off his jacket, he rolled up his sleeves, squaring up to the well's handle that spanned the gaping stone mouth. He began to haul away, winding up the bucket which clonked its way to the top. And as it arrived, he smiled. For in all the commotion, excitement and turmoil of Kathleen's arrest, and in all the major's haste to get her straight to hospital, to make her well again, just to make sure she would be fit enough to hang, there was one thing which they had missed, one thing in the whole wide world which might be used to set her free.

Part Four

<u>1</u>

He spent the next few weeks wondering how? – how in the world he could do it? In fact was it possible at all? – could he actually help her escape? Yes, he had the means now, but not the plan. And alone?

As such he had turned again to Evelyn. He had gone to see her soon after Letherington had stood him bail, going to her hotel, assuming that Risdale would still be absent. Luckily that was the case. And he knew it the moment Evelyn opened the door to him. For seeing his look of slight apprehension she had beamed at him, saying:

'Oh don't worry darling. He's still in hospital. Isn't it wonderful!'

He'd had to smile. But swiftly his smile had faded; he had his apology to make. And he did so, telling her how sorry he was for ever thinking she'd intentionally led Armstrong to that ruined hideout.

'Forgive me?' he pleaded.

'Oh shush,' she replied, pressing her finger to his lips. 'What's to forgive?' Then she handed him a whiskey, saying he looked in need of it.

He told her she was right – he *did* need a drink, especially in view of all the trouble he'd landed himself in with Armstrong.

'And you?' he asked. 'Did he make trouble for you as well, for trying to help me?'

'Oh, a mere rap across the knuckles. Nothing I couldn't handle.'

'Well bless you for that,' he said. 'It was a bloody marvellous thing you did. ' He tipped his glass at her in way of a salute, then drank, then sighed. 'The pity is, it seems all our good work will go to waste.'

'What do you mean? She's going to be all right, isn't she?'

'Oh yes, for the time being, until she's well enough to stand trial.' He looked across at her. 'And you know what will happen to her once that's over, don't you?'

Evelyn looked back at him. He knew she understood. 'You think it will come to that?' she asked.

He nodded grimly. 'Armstrong seems to think so. Then again he's got good reason to want to see her hanged – those two insane brothers of hers – they killed his son.'

Evelyn said she had no idea, but it explained why the major appeared so driven.

'And what about you, David? I suppose you think she shouldn't be hanged just because of the way you feel.'

He shook his head. He said. 'It's not a case of *feelings*, Eve. It's just – '

'It's just what, David?'

He walked over to the window and gazed out, thinking back. 'It's just that Kathy was the one who looked after me in hospital. She was incredible. She never gave up on me, even when things were bad.' He turned and looked at her. 'That's why I can't give up on her now – why I feel like I should do something.'

'Yes, I know my darling, but you've got to be realistic. What *can* you do?'

He threw the remains of the whiskey to the back of his throat. 'We can help her escape,' he said. 'That's what we can do.'

'We?'

He saw Evelyn give him an "old fashioned" look. Her almond eyes widened with a kind of exasperation.

'I swear, David. You'll push me too far one day.'

'Then? . . . . are you saying no?'

'Of course not. It's just . . . . well, you realise we'll get more than a simple rap across the knuckles this time if things go wrong, don't you?'

'Yes, naturally. That's why you and I might need an escape plan

250

ourselves. You favoured Ireland once, didn't you?'

'Ireland? Oh, maybe once, David. But if you're offering to whisk me away – the French Riviera's very nice this time of year.'

'The Riviera!'

'I was joking darling. No – anywhere to escape from Guy!' He saw her expression become serious. 'But you think it might come to that – the need to go away?'

He shrugged. 'Maybe. But maybe not if we go the right way about it.'

'And how would "the right way" be exactly?'

He told her he had not figured that out yet, though he believed brute force to be unwise, favouring something along the lines of "good old fashioned bribery". And then to illustrate his point he said: 'You know what they say, Eve – every man has his price.'

'Oh not Major Armstrong,' she countered with a firm shake of her head. 'The man's absolutely incorruptible – more so if what you say is true – that the girl's got blood on her hands over his boy's death. And even not, well, can you really lay your hands on that amount of money to bribe someone?'

He gave her a knowing smile, thinking of the well at the ruined hideout, the bag which he had placed there and had subsequently taken, the one which had been tethered to Kathleen's hand when he had carried her from the bank.

Yes,' he said. 'As a matter of fact, I can.'

*

Yes, he had the means now but not the plan. But then, those few weeks later, that too suddenly fell into place. In fact it came to him with such a monumental rush as to make him dizzy, the sheer simplicity of it taking him aback as to make him wonder why it had not occurred to him before. Or maybe it just appeared simple, in theory at least.

He had just come from the Mayeville when it happened. For in better health, and in the absence of Heinrich Korten who'd already been taken to the mainland to stand trial, they had moved Kathleen into the same top floor room, pending a date for her own prosecution.

251

And, it was while he was walking away, after visiting her, crossing the road to the promenade that he happened to turn and look back, noticing that the balcony of the top floor room in which she was being held, was directly adjacent to that of the one at the imperious looking Grand Hotel next door. And who was behind that hotel's balcony rail? Why, he could plainly see it was Victor Handley, the "businessman".

Duly he went up to the man's suite. And duly business was conducted.

*

The next day he rose early. He rose early to go once again to the Mayeville, but this time not to visit Kathleen. It was to see his friend Peter Letherington, to pay back the money he owed him for settling his bail, and perhaps, if he was willing, to add to that payment a little "interest".

He hoped to catch Letherington on his own. For Letherington had been joined by Armstrong's men now who had been billeted on him, mainly to guard and oversee Kathleen's transportation to the mainland, as and when it came.

'What's the matter, Peter. Don't they trust you or something?' he had joked upon entering the man's office, finding him alone, Armstrong's men in another room upstairs. But his friend had looked somewhat vexed at his comment.

'Not funny, David,' he'd replied sourly. 'Not funny at all.'

'Oh, come on old chap. I was only pulling your leg.'

But it was clear that Letherington was not in the mood for "leg-pulling". And then he began to tell him why.

'I'm in trouble, David. Big trouble. Have you heard?'

'Heard about what?'

Letherington was sitting behind his desk, his eyes full of despair. 'Well, you may as well know – take a look at this.' The man passed a letter across. It was a summons for Letherington's court martial, over the death of a prisoner.

'Korten? Korten's dead? But how?'

'The damn fool jumped ship on me at Fleetwood when I was

taking him to the mainland – made off through the dockyards. I had no choice, David. I had no choice – '

'You mean – '

'Yes, but I only meant to wound him, honestly, but . . . . well, you know how it is?'

'Yes. Yes, of course old chap. Don't go getting yourself all worked up. I understand. Here, have a cigarette.' Asher reached into his pocket. He still felt surprised. 'So, Korten eh?' He shook his head. 'I had no idea. So he never got to face trial?'

'No, but they'll make damn sure that I will.' Letherington rose sharply from his chair. He began to pace the floorboards, lamenting his situation. 'You know they'll throw the ruddy book at me for all this. I can see it now. I'll be cashiered, *that's* what'll happen – dishonourably discharged.' Asher saw his sorrowful doom laden eyes flick across at him. 'And you know what that will all mean, don't you? Forfeit of pension. Loss of pay. I'll be finished. Finished!'

He tried again to calm his friend down. 'Now hold on Peter. Hold on a minute. You don't know that for certain, do you? I mean Korten? Korten of all people! You know some might consider you've done the whole world a favour.'

He heard Letherington give a short despairing laugh.

'Ha! That's easy for you to say. You're not the one facing ruin. You know I've a wife back on the mainland, don't you. A very expensive one as a matter of fact!'

He sat the man back down and gave him the cigarette. And taking out a box of matches in lieu of his gold Ronson lighter which had inexplicably gone missing, he lit one for his friend and one for himself. Then he said. 'Listen, Peter. Don't let's have any more talk about you being ruined. It's not going to come to that. Besides, I've brought that money I owe you. *And* more.'

Asher took a great bundle from his pocket and threw it on the table.

'Great Scott!' he heard Letherington gasp. 'Great Scott!'

Asher drew calmly on his cigarette. 'Just a friendly gesture, Peter. And that's just the beginning.'

It was to a telephone box he went next. For Kathleen had given him the number of a contact she knew in Ireland – a "good man", or so she had said. And, in turn, Asher had told her that he would try and ring the person as a matter of courtesy, to let someone back home know that she was still alive but captive, so too her brother, her eldest having disappeared into the ether.

Yes, it was just to give them the news of her. At least that's what he led her to believe.

The contact was a man by the name of Brendan Cahill, a bar owner in Dublin apparently. But when he tried telephoning him he was told by the operator that all lines to southern Ireland were unavailable. And he came out of the telephone box dejected and walked to a café nearby on the seafront, buying tea which he took to a seat by the window.

As he sat there gazing out, with the waves crashing against the shore, it set him thinking about what would happen if he could not get in contact with the man. For although he himself had helped a score of airmen escape from occupied France over the treacherous mountains of the Pyrenees, he knew all would be lost if he could not get this one man to send a boat just fifty miles across an ocean. Success seemed to hang in the balance. And failure was unthinkable.

He left the café feeling dejected once again, and went to a tobacconist's kiosk along the promenade and bought a box of matches in lieu of his missing lighter, together with a map of the island. Then he sat on a bench and studied the map, looking at the western coastline which ran parallel with that of the eastern coast of Ireland. He was looking for an inlet or cove, a suitable rendezvous point should a boat be arranged. The place needed to be accessible by motorcar too, he thought, though not overtly public. After a few moments of deliberation his finger came to rest at a spot which caught his eye. He folded up the map and slipped it into his pocket, then walked off to complete the next stage of his plan – the last man in his jigsaw.

*

It took him longer than anticipated to find Clifford Handley, Victor's evangelical brother. For he'd had little to go on aside from Victor's assurance that the man was "still somewhere on the island", and the fact that occasionally he was in the habit of conducting, ad hoc, open air prayer meetings upon the beach, after which the hat would be passed. And after which, most usually, he would be found drinking the contents of that hat into a blind oblivion.

Though eventually, after a day of exhaustive door stepping, he found the man at a rundown boarding house in one of the back streets, a cheap establishment which clearly proved, that if the wages of sin were death, then the profitability of Godliness did not pay a great deal more.

After the front door had opened to a waft of boiled fish and cabbage, Asher found himself confronted by the landlady, he presumed, a woman in her mid fifties who had a cigarette wedged in the corner of her red lipstick painted mouth and carpet slippers on her feet. He'd followed in the tracks of them as the woman had showed him up a dingy stairway to a room.

Clifford Handley was sitting on his bed inside. Beneath the centre parted hair, his face looked chubbier than he remembered, his suit a little tighter. The man bade him welcome and Asher sat down. Though before their conversation had hardly begun, the same woman came back in with tea, pouring it before leaving again.

'She's such a treasure,' Clifford sighed, when she had gone. 'lost her husband in the Great War – treats me like a son.'

Asher looked across. As well as a lipstick stained cigarette stub in the ash tray next to the bed, he noticed there were creased indentations within the two pillows. *Not quite like a son*, he imagined.

'Evidently,' Asher remarked. 'Then I take it you've no plans to leave the island?'

'Ah, alas I must. You see I've received the calling.'

'You don't say.'

'Yes. Africa, as a matter of fact. On a mission from God, you understand.'

255

Asher said he understood perfectly. For he was on something of a mission himself, one that he gauged to be close to the man's heart.

'Oh?' said Clifford. 'And what might that be?'

Asher pulled out his cigarettes. He pulled out his money

'The saving of souls.'

*

That evening, he heard news which hastened his plans: Kathleen was to be taken to the mainland that next day. He had twenty four hours. He could not waste time.

He went straight to find Armstrong, eventually tracking him down to the billiard room at Risdale's hotel. Risdale was there himself, out of military hospital, none the worse for his injuries apparently, and mashing chalk into the button of his billiard cue. The man looked up from the smoke-enshrouded table as he came in.

'What the devil . . . . you've a damn nerve coming in here.'

'Just stay out of this, Risdale. And get on with your game.' He nodded at Armstrong. 'It's the major I've come to see.'

Armstrong looked exhausted, he thought, supposing that the man had been up on the hills all day with his unit, looking for Kathleen's brother. He asked Armstrong if they could speak in private and the major took him through to a bar in the next room. There they sat down and Armstrong said: 'All right. What do you want?'

'The girl,' he said. 'I hear you're taking her across to the mainland tomorrow.'

'You heard correctly. So? You want to say your goodbyes?'

'More than that,' he said. 'I want to marry her.'

Armstrong looked at him hard.

'You what?'

'Yes,' he said. 'And I'm not asking you to understand.'

Armstrong gave a snort.

'Good, because I don't – never will. Apart from the fact you seem to think you owe her something.'

'Only for my life.'

'Yes, after she took my son's.'

'Then perhaps that's all you need to understand,' he said, in way of explanation. 'She took a life and saved a life. And now she's going to pay with her own. Isn't that enough for you?'

He saw Armstrong give a kind of noncommittal shrug.

'Maybe. I don't know. Perhaps I'll find out how I feel once she's dead.'

He told the major that that was where the man had the advantage over him; he did not have that same luxury of time. 'And that's why I have to do this now,' he said, 'marry the girl – before it's too late.' You understand that much, don't you?'

Reluctantly, Armstrong said he *did* understand, then asked if he had a chaplain. Asher replied that he'd already notified one.

'Then bring him to the Mayeville tomorrow,' he said. 'And get it done.'

*

When he stepped outside after meeting Armstrong, David Asher found the darkness closing in around him. He lit a cigarette and noticed that his hand trembled as he held the match; his fears had begun to descend.

He allayed them in the knowledge that he'd done all he could, even finally making contact with Kathleen's man Cahill, informing him of his intentions and his plan, the Irishman saying he would do what he could to play his part. But still his doubts prevailed, the dark clouds gathering ominously above his head, seeming as if to follow him as he walked back along the seafront to his car, the rain beginning to fall upon the brim of his hat.

Slipping behind the wheel, he sat for a moment wondering – wondering if he'd really thought of everything. No matter. The stage was already set. The players assembled. Too late now, he thought. Too late. The show was about to begin.

Oh Kathy. Oh Kathy. Oh Kathy. What have you done?

On the morning of that last day, Kathleen woke to her thoughts. She woke to her thoughts of regret in the stinking billet on the top floor of the Mayeville. She knew not the time; there were no clocks, nor much else – a table, a chair, a slop bucket, a bed. Climbing from it she went over to the balcony doors. Locked – locked as always. Why did she even try!

She came back to her bed and sat down. Somewhere she thought she heard a clock strike, perhaps down on the seafront, but the chimes were lost in the atrocious weather outside. Eight? Did she count eight? She did not know. All she knew was that sometime, in the not too distant future, at a time like this, she would be sitting waiting for the ring of footsteps in a corridor, the solemn march of men: Chaplain, Warder, Executioner. *Oh Kathy. Oh Kathy. Oh Kathy. What have you done?*

She found herself lost in her tortured thoughts again and she began thinking of *him*. Yes, she had lost him too. For he was with Evelyn now, or that's where his love lay. Not that she could deny him *that*. She herself had had her chance. He had loved her once and she had loved him. It was just the war which had got in their way. It was as simple as that. But now? Why, even on those occasions when he'd come to visit, which had been few and far between, he'd seemed distant, distracted, his mind elsewhere. Did he even know that they were taking her to the mainland that very day? She doubted that very much. And she sank back with the realisation of the cold and desolate truth – he wasn't even coming to say goodbye.

*

When David Asher woke that same morning it was to an evaporation of all his fears. He rose from his bed, washed, shaved, dressed and set about the task in front of him. With a kind of mechanical detachment he collected his belongings and cleared out his wardrobe.

He left a month's rent under a clock on the mantelpiece. At precisely 9 a.m. he walked out. He had a feeling he would not be back.

The first thing he noticed outside was the weather. It had changed – changed overnight – changed for the worse. There was a kind of storm blowing. And along the seafront road in the front gardens of the guesthouses, he could hear the end of season death rattle as the vacancy signs swung back and forth upon their little wooden gallows. And along the promenade, he could see the line of flanking palms, bent in the wind like a procession of hunched old men. The light was dismal too. Grey. No, darker still. Just like night.

He began to walk to the Mayeville, the roar of the sea in his ears, his head bowed, his hand to the brim of his hat. He glanced out to the darkened bay. The waves were thrashing madly, smashing themselves into the sea wall. He felt a roll of spray spatter against his coat and he grabbed at his collar and pinched it up around his neck. He thought of Cahill and he pictured his small boat dipping and pitching somewhere out in the ocean. He tried to shake the image from his mind and direct his attention to his task. It was less than ten minutes away now.

But first he went to a telephone box. He called Evelyn. Though the unnaturalness in her voice told him it was awkward – Risdale was there. Of course! – back out of hospital. Would that make things more awkward still? He was relying on her.

'The car?' he said. 'Can you still get the car, Eve? Can you still bring it to the place we arranged?'

He heard her say she'd try.

Try? But he *needed* that brute of a machine: Risdale's Bentley – big and fast. And he needed Evelyn too.

He tried not to panic as he came out of the telephone box and into the squall. Looking across the seafront road he saw the Mayeville. On the ground floor in Letherington's office, through the diamond taped windows, he spotted the silhouettes of two men, picked out by the narrow spread of Letherington's desk lamp.

In contrast, the adjoining Grand Hotel was ablaze with light. And looking up at Victor Handley's suite he saw the man already at the balcony window. Then, directly above, a white flag pole with a red Manx flag which rippled stiffly with pride. Damn this storm, he thought. It would ruin everything.

But then he spotted the raincoated figure of Clifford Handley upon the pavement, making his way along, a bible in one hand, the fingers of the other pressing firmly down on the crown of his hat. Then, looking up again, peering through a curtain of drizzling rain at the Mayeville's top floor balcony window, he could see a dim light of occupancy. Good. Letherington was playing his part too.

Now it was *his* turn.

*

In their hotel suite, Evelyn was looking at Guy's tunic jacket which hung over the back of a chair, thinking about the keys to his car which she knew to be in one of the pockets. It was nearly 10 a.m. and the two of them had not long risen. Oh, why did he have to come back now for heaven's sake!

Employing a distraction she went into the bathroom and turned on the taps. She began to lay out his robe.

'I'm running a bath for you, darling,' she called. 'All right?'

She heard his grunt of disapproval from the bedroom. He was busy reading the newspaper, he told her. 'Besides, I'll have my breakfast first,' he called back, sounding testy. 'Don't bother.'

'Oh it's no bother darling,' she protested. 'I've drawn the water now. Your robe's here.'

She waited a moment then heard the sound of the newspaper crumpling as it was laid down, the mumble of something before Guy came walking in, yawning, unshaven. He began to take off his pyjama jacket. As he did so, Evelyn walked out of the bathroom, closing the door behind her.

She wasted no time in getting the car keys, slipping into her clothes and making straight for the door. Though no sooner had she got there than Guy suddenly reappeared again, standing there in his robe, an angry look upon his face.

'Going somewhere?' he asked

Her reply came like a reflex.

'Yes, for a walk, darling. I've got the filthiest headache.'

'Really. A walk? – you've seen the weather?'

She told him she *had*. But it didn't matter; she had her raincoat. 'Besides. I'm not going far. Just for some air.'

'Liar!' he said back. **'Liar***!*' he thundered again. Then reaching out he grabbed her arm. 'I know where you're going. You're going to see David Asher. You've been seeing him, haven't you – seeing him behind my back, all while I've been in hospital.'

She tried to act amazed. In fact she *was* amazed; how did he know? A guess? She looked up at him with feigned perplexity.

'David? No. You're being ridiculous, Guy. Why I haven't seen him at all.'

Suddenly she saw Guy bring something out from the pocket of his robe.

'No? Then perhaps you wouldn't mind explaining this!'

It was David's gold Ronson lighter. And she was speechless.

The next moment she saw Guy begin to move towards her. And like an animal sensing danger she began to back away. Suddenly she found her voice again.

'No, Guy . . . . no Guy, please! *Please*. I'm sorry! I'm sorry!'

He told her it was too late to be sorry. And that was no lie. For suddenly, from somewhere she saw he had his Luger pistol in his hand. And then that hand had whipped the pistol across her face, her head snapping sideways as she felt the blow, finding herself falling back onto the bed.

Guy was quick to straddle her. And as he did so she felt him hit her twice more. But upon the third strike she caught his hand, the two of them struggling, before, in the last throes of exhaustion, her other hand came in contact with something solid on the bedside table. Curling her fingers around it she swung it blindly, hearing the resulting thud, and a grunt from Guy as he fell to the floor.

Evelyn rolled off the bed, breathless, panting. She looked down. Guy was lying unconscious amid the broken bedside lamp. Picking up the Luger from the carpet, she slipped it into her raincoat pocket. Stepping over him she went to the door.

261

They searched them both, naturally – both Clifford Handley and himself, the preacher voicing his disapproval as one of Armstrong's men ran his hands over him, the soldier even thinking to look in his bible, which prompted more of the same.

'Why, this is an outrage! I'm a man of God!

It seemed to cut no ice with Armstrong. He was sitting behind Letherington's desk, clearly there, thought Asher, to personally oversee Kathleen's transfer to the mainland, the man telling Handley that he did not even care if he was the Lord God himself! – he would be subject to the same treatment as everyone else. And when it was done to his satisfaction, Asher saw the pock faced major turn and say:

'All right, Letherington. Get your man to take them up now, will you.'

Letherington's sergeant went across the room. He removed some keys from a hook. Then he turned to the hallway to lead them up. Before he could do so, Letherington suddenly stepped forward.

'That's ok, sergeant. I'll deal with this.'

Well done, Peter. Good man.

They went up the stairs.

*

In her room on the top floor, Kathleen was immediately alerted by footsteps on the creaking treads. She was sitting on her bed, the rain drumming at the balcony windows, a candle lit and flickering alongside of her to ward off the gloom. Then she heard something else – the shuffle of feet on the landing, the brief jangling of keys. She turned towards the door, though as it swung open, what she saw then set her mind racing.

At the periphery of her candlelight stood three men: a chaplain in ecclesiastical collar, a tall army captain and a third man whose face was obscured by the shadows. As the captain walked in he threw a hand down to his holster. He began to remove his pistol.

Her thoughts moved at speed. *Holy Mary* – was this to be some kind of summary execution? For the next thing she heard was the locking of the door, then the reciting of words from the chaplain at her side. But then, at the same moment, she saw that the third man was David.

'Come on, Kathy,' she heard him say. 'We're getting you out of here.'

It all began to happen fast after that. She saw him take some keys off the tall captain and move to the balcony doors. Swiftly he unlocked them. He beckoned her out and she was immediately hit by the squally blast, the rain in her eyes as she looked over. On the adjacent balcony she saw a length of timber lying across – a flag pole. It was spanning the yawning gap to the balustrade. He bade her to cross it. She couldn't.

'No, David. I can't.'

'You've got to, Kathy – **TRY!**'

But she was too frightened. And appearing to sense her fear, he told her to wait. And she saw him go back inside, watching through the glass as the tall captain handed him the pistol, saying something like "you'd better make this look good, David," though the man had hardly uttered those words when she saw David land a blow, the man crumpling to the floor. After he had done so she watched as David turned to the chaplain next, tying him with the captain's leather Sam Browne webbing belt, gagging him with his tie. He came back onto the balcony and told her he would cross first.

'Look. There's nothing to it. Watch.'

She did just *that*, seeing the pole bend alarmingly as he crawled out, sure that it would break. But it did not. And with that reassurance, she began to crawl out too, looking down at the pavement, glistening wet and hard, the iron railings below gleaming like spears should she fall. But that did not happen either. And a moment later she was across, falling only into David's arms as he took hold of her, the two of them taking off through the hotel room and away.

*

On the ground floor of the Mayeville, Major Armstrong was still at Peter Letherington's desk. His head was cocked to one side, listening.

It was not the noise from the upstairs room which had begun to arouse his suspicions, but rather its absence; all had gone quiet. Drawing himself up, he walked slowly into the hall.

At the foot of the stairs, he paused. He leaned forward towards the stairwell and listened again. Nothing still. Not a murmur. Lifting his foot onto the first tread, he began to climb.

Once upon the upstairs landing it did not take him long to realise that something was wrong; the door was locked and his calls to the other side were returned by an incoherent mumble. He stepped back. And taking two paces, he kicked with his boot. The door shuddered and splinted. It burst open.

On seeing the two men on the floor, he dashed past them straight out onto the balcony. He looked up and down the street.

He bellowed long and hard to his sergeant.

*

Next door at the rear of the Grand Hotel, they were descending a zigzag stairway, their feet clanking noisily upon the iron treads of an exterior fire escape as they found themselves in a backyard below, and in turn, at a gate at the end. There he fumbled with the latch, pushing it up. They both stumbled through into a wide alleyway beyond.

There David Asher stood gasping. He looked up and down, expecting the car, expecting Evelyn – no sign of either.

'What is it David?' he heard Kathleen say breathlessly at his side. But he was too breathless to answer himself, to wearied from exertion – so too Kathleen, he presumed, still weak from hospitalisation. Besides, he was too busy looking out for the car. And then. And then he saw lights – two headlights from one end of the wide alleyway coming towards him.

'It's her!' he said, stepping out into the middle and frantically waving. 'It's Eve. I knew she'd come.'

But as the lights drew nearer, it was clear it wasn't Evelyn at all. And with the running out of them both, they just stood there, beaten as the army truck came towards them out of the driving rain, before it ground to a halt, before they saw Armstrong getting out, his revolver drawn and ready.

The man came towards them, his face grim but with a hint of satisfaction. Though the next moment his expression changed as there came the squeal of tyres from the other end of the alleyway, then the roar of a car being driven at speed, then the sound of scattering dustbins, the splashing of wheels through the puddles as the Bentley hurtled towards them. It skidded just short of the major and for a moment the man seemed stunned. Making use of it, Asher made a lunge for the rear door. He bundled Kathleen and himself inside.

The Bentley was reversing back down the alley almost as quickly as it had arrived. And, within a few moments more, with a grinding of gears, it was skidding out into the street and speeding along seafront road. From the back seat, he caught Evelyn's eye in the rear view mirror.

'Cutting it a little fine there, weren't you, Eve?'

'Just keeping you on your toes, David.'

'Well put your toe on that accelerator and let's get some speed out of this thing.'

'Yes, if you can tell me where we're going?'

'To catch a boat, of course,' he said. 'Ireland.'

*

At the wheel of the army truck, Armstrong was swinging the vehicle out onto the seafront. There the engine promptly died.

As he tried to restart it, his sergeant appeared.

'It must be the damp, sir. I'll take a look.'

Armstrong slammed his fist against the wheel; he hadn't time for this! And after climbing out he slammed the door as well, hearing as he did so the sound of a man running towards him. It was Guy Risdale. He was holding a blood soaked handkerchief to the side of his head. His breath rasped like a file.

'C'mon. I've just seen them . . . . if we're quick – '

'No, the truck's had it,' shouted Armstrong, seeing him run to it.

'Then over there,' Risdale called, spotting a car.

It was a passing grey Austin and Risdale flagged it down. Pulling out the driver, Armstrong slipped in behind the wheel. Risdale jumped in alongside him. The car sped off along the seafront.

*

Out of town the Bentley gathered speed. The wipers lashed away the rain. The water hissed beneath its wheels. The countryside flashed past, the trees bent to the storm.

'You think your man Cahill will be as good as his word,' he asked.

'The boat?' said Kathleen. 'Yes, it'll be there.'

'In this weather?'

'Like I said, David – he's a good man.'

'We'll soon find out.'

But then he suddenly felt the brakes come on. The car skidded to a halt.

'No we won't,' said Evelyn, pointing at something. 'Look!'

They were on a narrow track at the top of some cliffs, and in their way he could see a tree lying across, blocking their path.

'Ok. We'll just have to walk from here. It's not far,' he said. 'Eve? Is there a torch in that glove box?' He saw her reach in and take one out. 'Good. We may have need of it. 'C'mon.'

They climbed out the car, clambering over the fallen tree, setting off down a steep hill that cut through the cliffs towards the sound of crashing waves. And then, suddenly the bay was there before them, the sea rising in it like some terrifying beast, mauling at the foreshore as it pounded in, thrashing then falling with the rush and roar of rocks and pebbles thrown up in its wake. David Asher looked out. He could see no boat, nor any chance of one.

In a vain hope he took the torch. And through the mist and gloom he flashed a sequence of pulses. He waited – no reply. He tried again. He shook his head.

'It's no good,' he said. 'If there *is* a boat out there, it'll never see us in this.'

Then he heard Evelyn say that she had an idea. And she turned, leaving him without a clue as to what she was going to do.

*

Rushing up the beach, Evelyn soon found herself climbing back up the track, a torrent of rainwater gushing back down, the flood almost ankle deep by the time she came to the car. Pulling the car door open, she leaned across. Flicking at one of the switches the headlights came on, the beams slicing through the gloom as they cleaved a path straight out across the sea. Slamming the door shut she went to make her way back, though as she did so she heard the sound of a vehicle. Squinting through the rain she saw it quickly draw towards her. A figure jumped out.

On seeing Guy she turned on her heels, scrambling up a bank and into a sodden field, heading towards the cliff path to divert him from the beach. Stumbling in the cloying mud, she soon found it was hopeless; he was nearly upon her. Then she remembered his Luger pistol in her pocket.

Turning, she drew it, gripping it in both hands as Guy came towards her. He stopped abruptly. She thrust it out before her. She dripped in her raincoat. Guy's voice dripped with contempt.

'Ok Eve. You've had your fun. Now give me that damn pistol. Or I'll – '

'Or you'll what, Guy? You'll beat me? Punch me? Slap me? No, you're never going to treat me like that again, ever.'

But she was too hesitant in pulling the trigger, too unsure that she could do so. And in that moment of indecision she felt him grab the pistol. He turned it on her instead.

*

A shot – that's what he heard next from where he stood on the beach. A shot from somewhere upon the cliffs. David Asher looked up. He saw nothing – nothing but the strong and strident beams of the Bentley's headlights, the shafts of which, not ten minutes earlier, had picked out a small fishing boat which had entered the bay. And now, across the storm tossed ocean, a rowboat from that vessel was coming through the waves.

It came in fast, scooting in on the curl of a breaker, one crewman on the oars, another with a revolver. He saw Kathleen wade out to meet them, catching a rope which was thrown, pulling the rowboat to the beach as she tried her best to hold it steady in the battering waves. He went to help. Though as he did so, he saw a man come onto the beach behind him, emerging through the mist and rain.

'It's Armstrong,' he shouted. 'Quick – get aboard.'

Kathleen did as she was bade and Asher waded out to the rowboat himself. But he did not climb in. Pausing only long enough to snatch the revolver from the crewman's hand, he returned with it to the beach.

'David. What are you doing? Come on.'

'No, not without Eve – go.'

'But David!'

'Go I say!'

The crewman was waiting on his oars, the other in the surf, holding the rowboat steady. After a long hesitation, she gave a nod.

On a wave the rowboat rose up. It began to recede, moving out into the storm tossed ocean.

'God bless you, David,' he heard her call to him. 'God bless you.'

But the next moment, Armstrong appeared. The man levelled his revolver in the rowboat's direction. Asher blocked his line of fire.

'Stand aside, Lieutenant Asher.'

'Sorry, major. I can't let you do this.'

'Stand aside I say!'

He would not do so. Then raising the revolver he'd taken from the crewman, Asher fired instead.

From where he stood it took him five rounds to do the damage. And when it was done, he saw Armstrong turn, looking towards the cliffs where he'd fired the shots, seeing the car upon it with its headlights shattered from the gun's reports. The bay was now plunged back into its gloom, the rowboat all but invisible upon the unlit waves.

'I'll make you sorry you did that,' said Armstrong.

'What? Now the girl's gone, you want to kill me instead?'

'Don't think I won't. Now – the pistol if you please.'

Asher went to hand it over. Though, in that same moment, he quickly pushed Armstrong to the ground. Then he fired. It was the pistol's last round, but his aim was true; he shot the man dead.

And in the pistol's fading echo, he could see that Armstrong was confused; he had swivelled around, clearly perplexed by the bearded, dishevelled gunman who had come up behind him through the mist and was now lying slumped upon the sand. It took the major a moment to realise. 'My God. It's *him!*' Then Armstrong turned his gaze to the cliffs where the man had obviously been hiding. 'The boat must have drawn him down – the sight of the boat and the chance of freedom.'

'More like the sight of you, major,' said Asher, 'and the chance of putting a bullet in you before he left.'

Armstrong nodded. 'Yes, a bullet in the back, just like he did to William.'

Asher knew he meant his boy. 'Then this is the man?' he asked. 'He's the one who – ?'

The major nodded again forlornly. 'Yes, the filthy swine.'

Michael O'Callaghan was still dressed in the black frock coat that Asher remembered from the bank, muddied now, tattered and torn. Eventually Asher looked across at Armstrong and said with a weary sigh: 'Well, he's a dead swine now, major. You can rest easy.'

To his consternation, Asher saw Armstrong shake his head.

'Rest? You think I can rest while one of them still has their freedom?'

Asher was confounded – confounded at Armstrong's insane persistence.

'For God's sake man. The girl?' he said with exasperation. 'You've got the one responsible. What more do you want?' Asher lifted his eyes to the churning waves. 'Besides, in a storm like this, in that small rowboat? Why, more likely as not she's lost her life as well.'

'Is that what you'd like me to think?'

'Well it's better than what you believe – that when your boy was killed she as good as had her finger on the trigger.'

'Well didn't she?'

Asher sighed wearily again. He felt done in. 'I don't know,

major,' he said, spent almost beyond words. 'I just don't know anything anymore. But don't spend the rest of your life chasing shadows. For pity's sake. Can't you ever stop? What do I have to do to convince you?'

Armstrong fell silent for a long moment, as if in sad contemplation. Then, after a while the man gave Asher that same forlorn look again. 'I don't know either, Lieutenant,' he said back, his voice sounding desolate. 'Maybe I need to convince myself.'

'What? That she's dead?'

'Just something.'

As they spoke a body washed up on the beach before them.

Asher looked across. 'Is that enough for you?' he asked, nodding over. 'Are you satisfied now?'

But before the major could speak, Armstrong's sergeant appeared. The man went to check on the body of Michael O'Callaghan, then to the other lying in the surf. 'They've both had it, sir – you all right?'

Armstrong said nothing. He just had a look of quiet resolution about his face thought Asher. Then, holding his gaze for a short while, the major simply nodded at him, perhaps in thanks, he did not know, then turned to leave.

As he did so his sergeant looked confused.

'But what about the girl, sir?'

Asher saw the major stop and turn one last time. The man gazed back to the ocean for a moment, looking first to the oarsman's body amid the smashed rowboat, then to the lashing waves. 'Why, she's out there if you want her,' he said. 'At the bottom of the sea.'

*

When Armstrong and his sergeant had left the beach, Asher remained there alone, watching, waiting, looking out through the grim grey curtain of rain to the waves for any sign of life. But there was nothing to be seen, and he felt crushed, broken like the battered rowboat which lay in pieces at his feet. And yet he waited longer. Then longer still. Then, giving up all hope, he turned.

But as he did so he thought he saw something. And quickly he turned back and focused his gaze. Was that a distant light he'd briefly seen? A distant flashing light perhaps from that small fishing boat which had come to collect her? Or was that light half imagined, he wondered, conjured up in his mind to satisfy his longing that she was safely onboard? In honesty he did not know. But he knew Morse. And he knew he'd seen something resembling it. And like a drowning man himself, he clung to that belief.

And so he left the beach, weary but hopeful that it was all finally at an end. And he set about trying to find Evelyn. And he began looking for her everywhere, searching until the rain had stopped, until the storm had passed, until that pewter gloom of that dreadful day had collapsed into a beautiful starlit night. It was only then, when high upon the cliffs, that he found the body.

He had discovered it by the fading beam of his torch. And he'd looked down at it, lying there in the long wet grass, cold and still, a gunshot wound to the back. And he did not need to ask himself who had done such a thing. Instead he simply reached down, saying, almost in a whisper:

'There there, Eve. It's over now. It's over.'

Then he lifted her up, taking her back along the cliffs, away from her husband's body in the grass.

And as they walked away together, it struck him that Risdale's fate had been sealed by his uniform – his *British* uniform, his death at the hands of Michael O'Callaghan in that place something of an irony. For he remembered that Risdale had once left him in a field far from home, but that did not seem to matter now; it was all in the past.

Besides, he had a future now: his life with Evelyn, perhaps as destiny had always intended. For she had always meant the world to him. And Kathleen would always mean the stars.

End

About the Author

P.J. Peacock is the acclaimed author of four novels. His first, Towers of London, was shortlisted for the prestigious CWA Orion Debut Dagger award for crime fiction. His work has also received both short and longlistings for the Hodder and Stoughton sponsored Harry Bowling prize, together with numerous awards for non-fiction and short story writing.

www.pjpeacock.co.uk

CPSIA information can be obtained
at www.ICGtesting.com
Printed in the USA
LVOW11s1731160717
541568LV00001B/9/P